Torey Hayden

Overheard in a Dream

A novel

HARPER

HARPER

An Imprint of HarperCollins*Publishers*
77–85 Fulham Palace Road,
Hammersmith, London W6 8JB

www.harpercollins.co.uk

Previously published in other
languages as *The Mechanical Cat*
First published in English as *Overheard in a Dream*
by HarperCollins 2008

2

© Torey Hayden 2008

Torey Hayden asserts the moral right to be
identified as the author of this work

A catalogue record of this book is
available from the British Library

ISBN-13 978-0-00-726093-5
ISBN-10 0-00-726093-8

Printed and bound in Great Britain by
Clays Ltd, St Ives plc

Mixed Sources
Product group from well-managed
forests and other controlled sources
www.fsc.org Cert no. SW-COC-1806
FSC © 1996 Forest Stewardship Council

Overheard in a Dream

A novel

Also by Torey Hayden

One Child
The Tiger's Child
Twilight Children
Ghost Girl
Just Another Kid
Beautiful Child
Somebody Else's Kids
Silent Boy

Chapter One

The boy was so pale you would have thought he was a ghost. A wraith. Something insubstantial that would vanish into nothing at all. He was small for nine, slender and fine-boned. His hair was pale as moonlight, very fine, very straight. His skin was milky-white with a dull translucence to it, like wax. Such fair colouring meant that at a distance, he appeared to have no eyebrows or eyelashes at all, and this incompleteness only emphasized his ephemeral appearance.

"Meow?" said the boy.

"Hello, Conor," James replied. "Won't you come in?"

"Meow?"

Around his waist he wore numerous coils of string with bits of aluminium foil wrapped around them. Four of these trailed down behind him and onto the floor. He gripped a small toy cat by its hind legs. Extending the cat out in front of him, as if it were a scanning device, he rotated it slowly, pointing it at every corner of the room. Then he began to make an oddly mechanical noise, a sort of ratcheting "ehhh-ehhh-ehhh-ehhh" that sounded like a sluggish machine gun. Then a new sound started, a soft whirring sound. "Whirrrr. Whirrrrr. Whirrrrrrrr." He stepped into the room just far enough to allow Dulcie to push the trailing strings forward with her foot and close the door.

The child avoided looking at James. His eyes darted nervously here and there. A hand came up alongside his face and he flapped it frantically. "Whirrrrrrrr," he went again.

James rose from his chair in order to encourage the boy into the room, but the child reacted with panic, pointing the stuffed cat at James like a gun. "The cat knows!" he said loudly.

James stopped. "You don't like me coming towards you."

"Ehhh-ehhh-ehhh-ehhh. Whirrrrrrr. Whirrrrrrr."

"You would like me to sit down again."

"Whirrrr."

"That's all right," James said quietly and returned to the small chair beside the playroom table to sit down. "In here you can decide how things will be."

Conor remained rooted just inside the door. He looked James over carefully, or at least that's how James interpreted his behaviour, because Conor's eyes never met his. Instead, the boy flicked his eyes back and forth repetitively, as if he had nystagmus, but James sensed it was simply a method of gaining visual information without eye contact. Then he extended the toy cat again and took a step further into the room. Still gripping the cat tightly by its hind legs, he raised and lowered it as if scanning James's body. "The cat knows," he whispered.

The play therapy room was spacious and painted pale yellow, a colour James had chosen because it made him think of sunshine. Not that this was really necessary, as there was usually a surplus of the real stuff pouring through the large east-facing windows and in the heat of summer, the room had a downright Saharan feel. Nonetheless, the colour pleased him.

As did the room itself. All the toys and other items in the room James had chosen with care. He knew exactly what he intended to create in the playroom: a place where nothing would constrain a child, where nothing looked too fragile nor too fancy to be touched, where everything invited playing with. When he'd first described to Sandy how he wanted to create a playroom, she had remarked that he'd never grown up himself, that it was his own childhood he was equipping. No doubt there was some truth in this, as the boy does make the man, but what she'd failed to appreciate was that these were also the tools of his trade and he'd quite simply wanted the best.

Very cautiously Conor began to move around the perimeter of the room. Holding the toy cat out in front of him like a divining rod, he went in a clockwise direction, keeping very close to the walls. The cat's nose was touched to the furniture, the shelving, the various playthings along the way. "Meow? Meow?" he murmured as he went. It was all he said.

Having circumnavigated the room once, Conor immediately started on a second round. There was a low bookcase on the right-hand side where James kept many of the smaller toys. On top of the bookcase were wire baskets full of construction paper, glue, string, stickers, stamps, yarn, sequins, and other odds and ends for making pictures.

"Whirrrr. Whirrrr. Whirrrr. Meow?"

"If you want, you may take any of the things out of the baskets," James said. "Everything in this room is to play with. All things are for touching. In this room, you decide."

"Meow?" the boy replied.

The direction Conor was moving meant that he approached James from behind. The first time he had skirted widely around James as he sat at the small table. This time Conor slowed down as he drew near.

"Whirrrr. Whirrrr. Ehhh-ehhh-ehhh-ehhh."

James sat motionless so as not to frighten the boy.

"Whirrrr," came the whisper behind him.

The child's breathing was fast and shallow, giving a hollowness to the sound like a rheumy dog panting. Then came the very soft touch of the toy cat against the back of James's neck. With staccato quickness it touched him and then was gone. The boy whirred. The nose of the cat came again, so lightly that it just tipped the hairs on James's skin.

"Meow?"

James turned his head and there was the briefest moment of eye contact between them. James smiled.

"The cat knows," the boy whispered.

Thinking that someone as well known as Laura Deighton wouldn't want to sit out in the waiting room with Dr Sorenson's clients, Dulcie had allowed her to go into James's office to wait for him there. James hadn't expected this. A flicker of alarm went through him when Dulcie told him, because, of course, Laura Deighton would notice that he had her books on the shelf and, quite understandably, she would then assume that he had read them.

James wasn't a Laura Deighton fan. He knew her books only by what he'd read about them in *The New York Times* Book Review, that they were "complex", "profound", and worse, "literary", which, James knew, were all euphemisms for pretentious and/or unreadable. However, Laura Deighton was native to this corner of South Dakota, and since James was a newcomer and hence an outsider, he was acutely aware of the need to show respect for local icons. Consequently, he had bought the books – in hardback, even – and had set them up prominently on the bookshelf in his office to show his local loyalty. He did intend to read them at some point. He'd just never quite got around to it.

When he entered the office, he found Laura Deighton's attention was not on books, however. She was standing beside the window, her interest absorbed in something outside. She didn't turn immediately.

"Dulcie will keep Conor busy for a moment so that we can talk," James said. Going to his desk, he set down the folders and his notepad. He adjusted his suit jacket and straightened his tie. Only then did Laura Deighton finally drag her attention away from the window.

She was an unremarkable-looking woman. In early middle age with the mousy-coloured hair that is the aftermath of a blonde childhood and eyes that weren't really any particular colour at all, neither brown nor green, she could have been mistaken for any ordinary woman down at the supermarket, any one of those of a certain age who go a little soft around the waist, a little saggy here and there, who don't stand out for any reason.

Her clothes, James noticed, weren't really appropriate to the situation. It wasn't simply that they lacked style. They were too casual for a first meeting of this kind, even by South Dakota's relaxed standards. Jeans … okay, maybe it was possible to pull off jeans if you were twenty-seven and leggy, or if they were a fashionable brand and dressed up, but Laura Deighton's jeans were a cheap brand that the local ranchers favoured. The white shirt was nondescript and the tweed jacket fitted her carelessly. She wore no jewellery and little makeup. Depression? James wondered. Or maybe this was how creative genius dressed.

James felt vague disappointment on seeing her. He thought there'd be some aura of glamour around her, some presence that would make it impossible to mistake this literary giant, risen from the cornfields of the Midwest. In fact, there was nothing.

"Do sit down," he said. He gestured broadly towards the sofa and chairs.

Laura ignored them. She came over, extended her hand to shake his and then sat down in the chair beside his desk. "I appreciate your seeing Conor at such short notice."

Silence followed. James preferred to let the client set the tone of the interview, so he never started off by asking questions. This didn't appear to unnerve her the way it did some parents, but she was obviously anticipating questions. She looked at him expectantly.

When he didn't speak, she said once more, "Thank you for seeing Conor at such short notice. Conor's paediatrician – Dr Wilson, over at the clinic – recommended we bring Conor in to you. He said you'd come here from Manhattan, that you'd been in a practice there."

"Yes," James said.

"He spoke very highly of you. Said it's a renowned practice in New York, that to have been a partner there, you'd be a real high flyer." She chuckled. "And I can tell you, that's serious praise coming from Dr Wilson."

"Thanks to him for that recommendation," James replied, "but I'm sure there are also many good professionals out here too."

Silence then. Again she looked expectantly at James. When he didn't say anything further, she said, "Until now we've had Conor at the Avery School. In Denver. Have you heard of it?".

"I don't know it well," James replied. "I've only been out here since February, but Dr Sorenson has mentioned it."

"They work on a very structured behavioural program. Called 'repatterning'. The school has an excellent reputation for success at socializing severely autistic children."

A pause.

"Although," she said with faint sarcasm, "maybe that's simply because they do to the failures what they've just done to us. We received a letter right out of the blue saying they didn't want Conor back this autumn. That they felt Avery wasn't 'helpful to his needs'. It was worded wonderfully. Like it was their fault things didn't work out, when you knew they meant just the opposite. That they think we've got a funky kid. So here we are with absolutely no place to send him. Completely stuck."

James looked at Laura closely. He was finding her difficult to read. On the face of it, she appeared straight-talking, but her words and body language gave off none of the usual subtle subtext. She sat absolutely still in a relatively neutral pose that was neither open nor closed. She made good, although not outstanding, eye contact. Her tone of voice was even but not very nuanced.

His inability to glean more intuitive information from her surprised James. He'd been prepared for other challenges in meeting Laura Deighton. Would her fame unnerve him, for instance? Or more likely, would he take an instant dislike to her? The literary people he'd known in Manhattan were, to a person, pompous and self-absorbed, and he hated these traits. When he'd discovered she was coming in, he caught himself feeling a certain gratification at the fact he'd never actually read any of her books. But her blankness was unexpected. There was just no discernible subtext. That was where James was accustomed to doing all his "reading", where he got so much information about clients, there in that intuitive space beneath words and gestures. With Laura Deighton, it was as if this space did not exist.

"Has Conor always been in a residential program?" he asked finally. "Have you not found suitable programs locally?"

"It needs to be residential. Our ranch is out beyond Hill City. Realistically, we just couldn't be driving him a long distance every day."

"Was Dr Wilson clear with you about what kind of therapy I do?" James replied. "Because if I took Conor on, I would expect to see him three times a week."

Her eyebrows lifted slightly, although perhaps not so much so that it could be interpreted as surprise.

"I'm a child psychiatrist," James continued. "What I prefer to do with the children I see is traditional play therapy, which means having them in on a very regular basis."

She was silent a long moment. "No. I hadn't quite realized that's what you did. So perhaps it's not appropriate. Conor's autistic. I know in the old days it was common to send autistic kids to psychiatrists, but, of course, we understand now it's not a psychiatric condition. It's neurological. Consequently we've always had Conor in behaviour-based treatment because that's the proven way of teaching life skills to children like him."

"Did Dr Wilson give you any reasons why he thought it might be helpful for Conor to come here?" James asked.

"No, he just suggested it." She paused. Her silence was at first expectant, but grew longer and more indistinct.

Then without warning, the mask slipped. Her shoulders dropped in a gesture of despair. "Probably just because I'm so desperate. I know I'm driving Dr Wilson demented with my calls. It's just that Conor's so difficult. Home for a month and he's destroying us."

Sympathy washed over James. He leaned towards her, his folded arms on the desk, and smiled reassuringly. "Yes, I can understand. Children like Conor can be very demanding," he said softly. "Don't worry."

The muscles along her jaw tightened. She wasn't teary but James knew she was in that moment just before tears.

"Why don't you tell me a little bit about how Conor is at home?" he said. "That'll give us a better idea of whether or not coming here would be appropriate."

Laura became teary.

He smiled gently and leaned forward to nudge the box of tissues towards the edge of the desk. "Don't worry. This is a very hard moment. Most parents feel pretty upset."

"It's just … just *such* a nightmare. Like one of those night-mares where you keep doing the same thing over and over and it never works out, it never achieves anything."

She took a tissue. The tears hadn't really materialized, so she just clamped it tightly in her fist. James had a strong sense that she was feeling deeply conflicted in that moment, that self-control was a huge issue but that at the same time the burden of this boy was so overwhelming that she was desperate for help.

"Is Conor your only child?"

"No. We have a daughter too, who's six."

"When did Conor's problems first start?" James asked.

Laura let out a slow, elongated sigh. "When he was about two. He seemed all right when he was a baby, although it's hard to know with your first child. There were things I had always been concerned about. He was very jumpy, for instance. If you came up behind him or there was a loud noise, he'd always startle badly. Dr Wilson said it was just a temperament thing, that it simply indicated he was a sensitive boy, and not to worry about it. Otherwise, he was a good baby. He slept well. He didn't have colic or anything."

"Did he seem to develop normally to you?"

"Yes." Her voice had a plaintive, almost querulous note of bewilderment to it and James wondered how often she'd had to give these details. Or was stopped from giving them. In this era of insurance and accountability, there often was little time spent on collecting psychosocial histories beyond what was needed to prescribe the appropriate drug. James had found listening carefully to the parents' initial version of events was one of the most valuable thing to do, not only for the concrete information it provided in building up a picture of a child's problems, but also as a way of cementing that crucial relationship with the parents, because they often felt so desperate and unheard.

"Conor was always timid," Laura said. "He cried easily. He worried about things. Even as a little, little boy. But he was very bright and interested in things. He talked early. Even by a year old, he could use several words."

"So you say the difficulties starting showing up after he turned two?"

Twisting the tissue between her fingers, Laura nodded. "It started with his becoming very clingy. He'd always been inclined to be clingy but suddenly it got much worse. He never wanted me out of his sight. I couldn't even go to the bathroom without him. He began having these terrible temper tantrums. Dr Wilson was still telling us not to worry. Kids have tantrums at that age, he kept saying, but I don't think he realized how bad they were. Conor would just go frantic and do things like literally rip the wallpaper off the wall with his fingernails. To complicate things, that's when I got pregnant with Morgana and it was a challenging pregnancy. I had some serious medical problems. And we were having some financial difficulties, which meant the pregnancy wasn't very well timed – it hadn't been planned – so a whole lot was going on."

"Can you describe Conor's behaviour in a little more detail?" James asked.

"He got really hyper, really agitated. He wouldn't sleep. He could go days without sleeping. Which, with a new baby …" She let out a defeated sigh. "And the screaming started. He'd be sitting, playing normally with his toys and then suddenly he'd get all panicky, and start screaming and screaming. He had been in a nursery program two days a week, but we had to take him out because his behaviour upset the other children so much. The school wouldn't keep him." She put a hand over her eyes for a moment in a gesture of desperation and then rubbed her face. "It just got so distressing to live with. Finally Dr Wilson arranged for him to go into the children's unit at the university hospital in Sioux Falls to be assessed. That's when autism was diagnosed."

James nodded thoughtfully.

"And now …" Laura said. She sighed again. "It's getting just like that all over again. 'Difficult' doesn't half describe living with Conor. For example, everything has got to be just so. His room, his toys, his food. Everything must be in a special place and in a special order. I can't do anything for him if it isn't exactly the same way I did it before. Like at breakfast, I can't put the eggs on the table if the juice hasn't been poured first. All these little rituals have to be followed precisely. Like those wires. Did you see those? Those bits of string around his waist? There must four of them. Exactly six feet long. Each with twelve bits of foil. Then there's that frigging cat. That cat rules everything in the house. It goes everywhere he goes, does everything he does, investigates every molecule that comes in contact with Conor.

"This all makes even the smallest, most ordinary task a trial. Try giving a bath to a kid who must have string, foil and a stuffed cat on his person at all times. Or putting him to bed. It's like putting Frankenstein's monster to bed. All those wires have to be attached to the bedpost and crisscrossed over the bed just so. If they're not just so, he'll sit there 'adjusting'. He can be up for hours 'adjusting', scanning the cat over them, 'adjusting' some more and all the while he is making noises – buzzing and whirring, or worse, meowing. This then wakes Morgana. She goes in to see what's going on. She means no harm. She's just being your typical, nosey six-year-old. But if she tries to help him or she touches his cat, he freaks. So then I yell at her for upsetting him and she cries. Then he cries. Like as not, I end up crying too."

James smiled sympathetically. "That must be very difficult. What about your husband, Alan? Does he help much with Conor?"

Laura leaned back in the chair and expelled a long, heavy breath. "Well, there's another issue …

"It's not so good between Al and me at the moment," she said softly, and James could hear emotion tightening her words. "That's a whole other story. A long one and I don't want to go into it right now. But the short answer is: yes, he helps when he can. It's just I don't know how long that's going to last, because we're splitting up." She looked over tearfully. "So, see, this is why I can't cope with Conor at home. Even I have to admit I need help."

Chapter Two

"Laura Deighton, huh?" Lars said, leaning over the appointment book that was lying open on Dulcie's desk. "So is the boy coming in then?"

James nodded. "I couldn't get her to agree to three times a week, but we're going to do Tuesdays and Thursdays."

"What's she like?"

"Seems okay," James replied.

"Not all …?" Lars wiggled his hand in a gesture that James took to mean "above herself".

"No, not really. Just trying to cope with some big challenges, like all parents of autistic children."

Lars rolled his eyes teasingly. "But then you'll be used to celebrities, won't you? The high-falutin' crowd. City Boy." He grinned.

City Boy, indeed. Culture shock was too mild a word for what James had experienced in moving from Manhattan to Rapid City. South Dakota might as well have been the dark side of the moon. James did manage to do what he'd

dreamed of – set up his own private practice in family therapy – but it hadn't turned out to be exactly like his fantasies.
Even at South Dakota prices, James had discovered he
couldn't afford to go it alone. Consequently, he'd ended up
in partnership with a local psychiatrist, Lars Sorenson. If
James had wanted freedom from the strict Freudian theory
that had ruled his life in New York, he couldn't have done
better than Lars, whose ideas of psychiatry had more to do
with football scores or gilt hog prices than Freud. James's
former colleagues would have frozen stiff at Lars and his
homely country doctor approach. Indeed, James himself had
taken so much thawing out when he first came that he'd probably left puddles behind him, but if Lars had noticed, he'd
never let it bother him. In the end, James was grateful for the
partnership. Lars was never in such a hurry that he wouldn't
stop and listen or answer one more stupid question about "real
life", as he liked to call living and working in Rapid City. And
while there was a lot of good-natured teasing, he had never
once laughed outright at James's city-bred ideas.

"Ehhh-ehhh-ehhh-ehhh," Conor murmured. "Ehhh-ehhh-
ehhh-ehhh, ehhh-ehhh-ehhh-ehhh." As before, he stood only
just inside the playroom door.

James listened carefully to the noise. It had a distinctive
mechanical sound, like a car ignition turning over on a cold
morning. Turning, turning, turning but never catching.

"Ehhh-ehhh-ehhh-ehhh. Ehhh-ehhh-ehhh-ehhh, ehhh-
ehhh-ehhh-ehhh."

Conor had the stuffed cat clutched tightly against his chest.
Slowly he lifted it up until it was pressed under his chin, then
higher still until the head of the cat lay against his lips. He

stopped the ignition sound. Taking one hand off the cat, he flapped it frantically. "Meow?" he said.

Was he making the noise on behalf of the toy? James wondered. Was he trying to make it ask something that Conor dared not voice himself? Or was it the other way around? Was the cat putting its words in Conor's mouth?

"Meow?"

"When you're ready, Conor, you can come all the way into the room and we'll shut the door," James said. "But if you wish to stand there, that's all right too. In here you can choose what you want to do."

The boy remained immobile in the doorway, the toy cat pressed against the lower half of his face. His eyes flickered here and there but never to meet James's gaze.

An expectancy seemed to form around them and James didn't want this. He didn't want Conor to feel there were any expectations of what he should or shouldn't be doing, so James attempted to diffuse it by lifting up his spiral notebook. "This is where I take my notes. I am going to write in it while I sit here. I will write notes of what we are doing together so that I don't forget." He picked up his pen.

For a full five or six minutes Conor stood without moving, then very cautiously he began to inch inward. As with the first session, he stayed near to the perimeter of the room and kept well away from James, sitting at the small table. Once, twice, Conor circumnavigated the room and pressed the cat's nose lightly against things as he went.

He was saying something under his breath. James couldn't hear at first, but as Conor passed the third time, he could make out words. House. Car. Doll. Conor was naming the items he saw, as he passed them. This was a good sign, James thought.

He understood the meaning of words. He knew things had names. He had at least some contact with reality.

So it was when Conor came again on Thursday. And again the next week. Fifty minutes were spent quietly circling the room, touching things lightly with the nose of the stuffed cat, naming them. James didn't intrude on this activity. He wanted the boy to set his own pace, to construct his own sense of security within the room, to understand that James had meant what he'd said: that Conor alone would decide what he wanted to do in here. That was how trust was built, James believed. That was how you made a child feel safe enough to reveal all that was hidden. Not by schedules. Not by reward and punishment. But by giving time. There were no short-cuts. Even when it meant session after session of naming.

Three weeks passed. During the sixth session Conor circled the room upon entering and again touched everything he could easily reach with the toy cat's nose, still murmured the names, but this time it was different. He elaborated. Red house, he whispered. Brown chair. Blue pony.

For the first time, James answered Conor's murmuring.

"Yes," James said, "that's a blue pony."

Conor's head jerked up abruptly. "Ehhh-ehhh-ehhh-ehhh." He stared straight ahead. The hand not holding the cat came up and fluttered frantically in front of his eyes. "Ehhh-ehhh-ehhh-ehhh."

James sat very still.

Moments passed.

Slowly Conor exhaled. Extending the cat away from his body, he touched its nose to the edge of the shelf. "Wood," he murmured very softly.

"Yes, that's made of wood," James said.

The cat was retracted instantly.

James watched the boy, who kept his head averted to avoid eye contact.

"Ehhh-ehhh-ehhh-ehhh." There was a long pause, then Conor whispered, "Brown wood."

"Yes, the wood is brown."

Conor turned his head. Not to look at James. His eyes never left the far distant point they were fixed on, but his head inclined a little in James's direction. That was all that happened.

"Bob and I were thinking of going over to the Big Horns to squeeze in a couple of days of elk hunting," Lars said and sank down in the beige-cushioned softness of James's office. "You want to come?"

"That's a very kind invitation, Lars, but I don't know one end of a rifle from the other."

"You can borrow one of Davy's guns," Lars replied. "Davy killed his first buck when he was just twelve. Did I tell you about it? A six-pointer."

"Yes, you mentioned it."

"So come with us. Time you got blooded, Jim. How else we gonna make a South Dakota man out of you?" Lars laughed heartily. "It'll just be Bob and me. We'll take some beers and some grub and have a great time."

"When?"

"Next weekend."

Relief flooded through James. "Well, damn! Wouldn't you know it? I've got the kids coming out next weekend. Remember? Because I'm taking Monday and Tuesday off the following week."

"Oh Jesus, yeah."

"Darn. I'm sorry to miss it. Maybe next time."

Stretching his arms up behind his head, Lars settled back into the chair. "So how's it been going between you and Sandy? Is she getting any more reasonable about the kids?"

"Not really. They can come out at Easter but she says no way over Christmas," James replied, but he couldn't quite keep the disappointment from his voice.

"Why not? I thought you got to alternate Christmases," Lars said.

"The court says yes. But Sandy keeps on about how disruptive it is for them at their ages."

"Yeah, but they're your kids too. You've got the right to spend time with them."

"I know, but all this fighting over them isn't good for them either. I don't want them to grow up seeing Sandy and me at each other's throats the whole time. And she's probably got a point. It *is* disruptive for them at Christmastime. Sandy always goes to her folks in Connecticut. They have one of those big old Cape Cod houses and do Christmas with this enormous ten-foot tree and all the trimmings. The kids have their grandparents there, their cousins, their aunts and uncles, their friends. Christmas is supposed to be a happy time. Desperately as I want Mikey and Becky with me, I want what's best for them more."

"You're a pushover, Jim," Lars said, shaking his head. "You need to learn how to stand up to her. To say: 'This is important to me and I'm going to fight for it.'"

"I already have, Lars. That's how I've ended up here."

"Well, once in a lifetime isn't enough. You need to keep at it."

James nodded morosely. "Yes, I know."

The day was one of those in autumn of pure lapis lazuli sky and crystal air. From the large playroom window, James could see out over the city to the open plains beyond. Below in the street the dappled tints of gold and orange flickered restlessly in the sunlight, but the sky stretched ever onward, a clear, almost luminescent blue.

Gentle joy always filled James when he stood at this window. Clichéd as the vision was, he knew there was a metaphorical eagle somewhere inside him that would one day spread its wings and soar in response to this infinite landscape. His heart still felt depressingly sparrow-sized most of the time, but seeing such immensity always gave him hope of greater things.

Not that his sparrow's heart hadn't had its own share of struggling to get free. The most horrible moment had come two years ago when, after ten years of training, James suddenly realized that he couldn't bear the thought of spending another day in the sheltered prison of psychoanalytic theory. That moment still relived itself with soul-shattering clarity. He'd been fighting his way through heavy traffic on FDR Drive in Upper Manhattan when the insight mushroomed up with all the subtlety of an H-bomb going off. His hands went rigid on the steering wheel; sweat ran down the sides of his face and his heartbeat roared up so loudly into his ears that it drowned out whatever the hell was playing on that jazz station he always listened to but didn't really like. He realized then that things had to change. He had to get out of the life he was living ...

God, what that moment of insight did to Sandy. She'd been beyond furious when he told her. The rows they had.

And some of her anger was justified. She'd supported him all those years. She'd put her own career on hold while he'd finished medical school, then the training, the internship, the residency and his own analysis to emerge as a fully qualified psychiatrist. Sandy had stuck through it all for the chance of a brownstone on the Upper West Side and private school for the kids. Those were her goals in life and she'd worked just as hard to achieve them as he'd worked for his.

"Theory?" she'd screamed when he'd tried to give voice to his confusion. "What the hell's this sudden thing with *theory*? How can you wreck our entire lives over something like that? It isn't even *real*. So what if you don't believe it? You're not a priest, for fuck's sake. Believe in something else."

How did he explain it, his inarticulate longing for something beyond the narrow corridors of analysis, the domineering views of his colleagues and the shadowy brick-and-mortar ravines of Manhattan? A panic attack in the middle of rush-hour traffic hadn't been very subtle, but it got the message over.

James began to dream ceaselessly of escaping to a world where everything was simpler. He was, however, still dreaming of civilization. A small practice out in Queens perhaps. South Dakota had never entered his head. Then, in the fated ways some things happen, he had run into an old friend who had another friend who had known Lars from medical school and knew too that he was looking to expand his practice in Rapid City. James had gone home that night and looked South Dakota up on the internet, and the first picture to fill up the screen was of a lone pronghorn antelope standing on the flattest, emptiest land James had ever seen. The sheer otherworldliness of it felt like the answer to everything.

Except for Sandy, of course. The idea of moving to South Dakota quickly reduced the whole matter to a simple choice for her: staying with him or staying in the city. New York won, hands down. The gut-wrencher was that she got custody of the kids.

What kind of impostor filled a room with toys for strangers' children and then hardly ever saw his own? He had access, of course, but now two thousand miles separated him from their routine of splashy bath times and "dinosaur kisses." His greatest fear was that he'd become a stranger to Mikey and Becky. A very nice stranger, to be sure, but a stranger nonetheless.

When Conor arrived, James began reflecting his words immediately. If Conor said "doll's house", then James said, "Yes, that's a doll's house." If Conor elaborated and said, "big doll's house", then James mirrored that back in a sentence, "Yes, that's a big doll's house." James felt quite secure in interpreting Conor's extensive naming of items in the playroom as an embryonic effort at interaction. It was conversation at a most rudimentary level, like an infant's speech, but James recognized it as conversation.

Conor was increasingly attracted to the low shelves and their baskets of small toys. He didn't take the baskets from the shelf, didn't even touch them, but more and more often he would stand in front of them and press the cat's nose against their mesh. "Meow? Meow? Basket. Wire basket. Silver wire basket."

"Yes, silver wire baskets. Baskets full of toys. Toys you can play with, if you want. In here, you decide."

Conor lifted the cat up and continued on his journey around the room. Coming to the expanse of windows, he paused. He didn't go near them enough to look down on the vast view visible from the playroom, but he reached the cat out and pressed its nose to the glass. "Window. Meow?"

"Yes, those are the windows. We can see out," James said. Conor moved on.

In the far corner was what James called his "road sheet". Made of heavy-gauge white plastic sheeting, it was about four by four feet in size and printed with an elaborate layout of roads just the right size for toy cars and little buildings made of Lego bricks. It had been folded up on the shelf when Conor had been in the playroom previously, but now it was lying flat on the floor.

Coming up to it, Conor stood stone still. Not a muscle quivered. A full minute passed, feeling an eternity long. "Meow?" he whispered.

"That's the road sheet," James said. "Toy cars can drive there."

The muscles tensed along Conor's jaw as he stared at the plastic square on the floor. Raising one hand, he flapped it frantically in front of his face for a few moments.

"Man on the moon," he said with very precise clarity. "July 20, 1969. Neil Armstrong accompanied Buzz Aldrin. Apollo Project. Put the first man on the moon. July 20, 1969."

Surprised by this sudden burst of speech, James studied the boy. Exact regurgitation of overheard conversations was common with autistic children, but it was the first time in the three weeks Conor had been coming that James heard him do it. Did Conor have any understanding of the words he had just said or was it simply autistic echolalia?

"Something has made you think of the men who went to the moon," James said carefully.

"One small step for man, one giant leap for mankind."

James probed further to discover if there was any glimmer of meaning. "Yes, that is what Neil Armstrong said when he stepped on the moon, isn't it?"

Conor raised his head. "The cat knows."

Chapter Three

In an ideal world, all child therapy was *family* therapy. As a child's problems virtually never arose in isolation, James considered it as vital to see the mother, the father and the siblings as it was to see the child him- or herself.

Everyone in the business knew this, of course, but things seldom worked out that way nowadays. Philosophies had changed. The business model had taken over psychiatry just as it had everything else. "The bottom line" and "accountability" had replaced "self-discovery" and "insight". Insurance companies often refused to pay for more than twelve sessions of therapy. Behavioural contracts and token economies provided a swifter intervention than play therapy. Drugs provided an even swifter one. Both mothers and fathers worked and were generally unavailable for therapy during office hours. And everyone was in a hurry. Impatience had become the motif of modern life. As a consequence, the main function of many psychiatrists was simply to prescribe drugs. James often felt like a dinosaur for trying to turn the clock back to a slower, more humanistic model.

South Dakota hadn't been a good place to choose for a renaissance of traditional therapeutic values. They were a self-reliant people, not used to talking to strangers about their personal problems, so it was hard enough to get them through the door at all. And with agriculture still the main industry, they understood "bottom lines" acutely well. Many parents of his young patients had refused outright to come in for therapy sessions themselves because of the additional cost. In the end, James had had to go "commercial" to create a genuine family therapy setting by coming up with the concept of a "package deal" – that he would see each member of the immediate family for three sessions for one set price. Truth was, he was quite proud of that idea and thought it would work, but no. Too often he still had to charm them in.

Laura Deighton was going to be one such, James could tell. It became apparent almost instantly that from her perspective, Conor had sole ownership of his problem. When James raised the issue of family therapy, of seeing her, her husband and their daughter as well as Conor, Laura had actually stood up. She literally started to leave and James had no doubt she would have done so, if he hadn't pulled back immediately. This reaction fascinated him, because, of course, it said so much more to him about how unwilling she was to look at the problem than words could have done.

Conor's father, Alan McLachlan, however, was just the opposite. When James explained how Conor's therapy would work, Alan agreed straightaway. "Yes, of course," he said. He'd be happy to come in.

With the same care that James had put into designing the playroom, he had laid out his office for use in interviews and adult therapy sessions. Beyond the desk, he'd created a rectangular-shaped "conversation centre" with soft, comfortable chairs and a sofa. The coffee table, the end tables and the plants had all been chosen with care to give a pleasant, airy, relaxed atmosphere. He'd purposely picked real wood and natural materials to help mitigate the artificiality of the situation and used a pale beige upholstery to give the room an open, positive feeling. Lars kidded him about such attention to detail, but James was pleased with the effect. He felt it worked.

Laura Deighton had shown little interest in his conversation centre and seated herself beside his desk before he'd had the chance to encourage her elsewhere. When Alan came in, however, he had moved naturally to the sofa. Sinking into the beige-cushioned softness, he settled down comfortably. So comfortably, in fact, that he soon was resting one scuffed and, as James noticed, rather dirty cowboy boot on the edge of the coffee table.

Alan wasn't a tall man. James was six foot, so not a giant by any means, but he must have had three or four inches over him. Alan's hair, thick and rumpled by the removal of a red-and-white duckbilled hat, was the uneven grey of galvanized metal. His eyes were the same misty Celtic blue as Conor's. He looked older than his fifty years. His face was ruddy and lined, his skin long since gone to leather from a lifetime spent outdoors, but he still had about him a worn-out handsomeness.

James had been a little nervous about Alan. He'd never come face to face before with that iconic stereotype of the West – a cowboy – a man who rode horses as part of his daily working life, who gathered cattle, branded them, calved them and, when necessary, wrestled them to the ground and cut off their balls. It all spoke to James of the kind of mythic masculinity that existed only in movies, and he worried about finding common ground. Alan didn't help James's confidence at all with the way he'd so casually put his boot onto the coffee table. It was like territorial marking. Subtler than peeing, perhaps, but James felt like it meant pretty much the same thing.

"Thank you very much for coming in," James said.

"Nope, my pleasure."

There was a pause then while James waited for him to set the tone of the session. In the brief silence James found himself wondering about Alan and Laura as a couple. What had attracted her to this country man? How did he cope with having a world-famous wife?

Alan didn't give James much time to think, however, as he almost immediately asked, "So how's Conor doing?"

"We're still establishing trust," James replied. "He seems very uncertain in the new situation."

"Yeah, he doesn't deal with new situations well. Autistic kids are like that." A pause. "So what do you actually do with him in here?" Alan asked. "Because I wasn't quite clear what this was all about from the way Laura explained it."

"And how was that?" James enquired.

"Well, it's her version, so who knows. To be honest, I'm pleased you've asked me in yourself, because this way I actually stand a chance of understanding what's going on."

"You feel you haven't been consulted as much on Conor's treatment in the past as you'd like?"

Alan let out a long, heavy breath. "I don't think it's not being consulted so much as that I've long ago lost track of what led to what led to what."

A pause.

James waited calmly. He was getting the sense of a man who thought quite deeply but wasn't quick with words, who took time to organize his thoughts and get them out. How had someone like that ended up with a woman whose life was made of words?

"I never wanted Conor in that Colorado school," Alan finally said. "That's the first thing I want to make clear. I mean, who sends their young child seven hundred miles away? We shouldn't ever have done that. Autism happens. A lot of people have autistic children. They cope with it. They don't put the kid away."

"So how did the decision come to be made?" James asked.

"Laura. This, here," he said with a broad sweep of his hand. "It's about the fact that Laura needs treatment."

James was not quite certain what Alan meant. "You're saying that coping with Conor is causing problems for Laura? Or coping with Laura is causing problems for Conor?"

"Both, really. I don't think they're two different things," Alan replied. "But the biggest problem up to now has just been getting Laura to take responsibility for it. When she said this was a family therapy thing, that we couldn't get Conor in here unless we were involved too, I thought 'Thank *God*. She's *finally* taking me seriously.' She's always pooh-poohed the idea of therapy and been so quick to blame it all on Conor, make it all Conor's problem. But it's also been about Laura not being able to cope with him. That's how I got railroaded into sending him to Avery."

"Can you tell me how you saw Conor's problems starting?" James asked.

"We had a couple of absolute shit years. It was about the time Conor was two or three. Everything just happened at once. I was having some serious money problems with the ranch. People assume because Laura's work is well known that we must be wealthy, but there is a big difference between literary and commercial. The truth is, both ranching and book-writing are very uncertain ways to earn a living.

"So we were having major financial problems. Right in the middle of it, Laura got pregnant. It was unplanned and quite complicated. We thought Laura had actually lost the baby, because she miscarried, but apparently it was a twin pregnancy and she'd lost only one. Anyway, cue for lots of medical problems and bills just at a time when we desperately needed her earnings. Poor Conor. His little life just got turned on its head. I was gone all the time because I was hiring out to other ranches to earn some extra money and Laura felt so unwell. Conor's always been a sensitive kid, and this just made it worse. He got fearful of just about everything. I didn't think much of it at the time. I thought he'd settle down once things were more stable, once I was able to be around more and the baby was born. What I didn't appreciate was that during all this time I was away, Laura was falling apart too.

"I felt bad – feel bad even now – because I know I left Laura to cope on her own too much of that time, even when I did see signs of trouble. But, Christ, it's hard to know what's right. I was working all the hours God sends to save the ranch and I just couldn't be in two places at once.

"The turning point came when the preschool told us they couldn't keep Conor any longer. After that, he was home all the time. Laura just was not handling it. So that's when she started looking into residential placements for Conor ... I felt I had to let Laura have a chance to recover, because otherwise

… Well, to be honest I was afraid if I didn't, I was going to end up on my own with two young kids."

Alan fell silent.

James sat back in his chair. "So did placing Conor in the residential school help Laura recover?" he asked.

"Things settled down." Alan lifted his shoulders in a faint shrug. "But I guess 'recovery' implies they got better. That didn't happen. It just got buried, because that's Laura's way of handling things. And I've about had my fill of it."

"Horse?" Conor said in a sing-songy tone that was halfway between a statement and a question.

"Yes, that's a horse," James replied.

"Whirrrr, whirrrr." Conor stood the small plastic animal up on the table. He reached into the basket and drew out another animal. "Elephant?"

"Yes, that's an elephant."

"Whirrrr, whirrrr. Pig?" he said, taking out the next animal.

Conor didn't look over as he did this. He didn't encourage the slightest amount of eye contact. James was interpreting Conor's behaviour as an attempt to interact, but it may not have been. If James wasn't fast enough responding, Conor would quickly move on to the next animal. It could be simply the self-referencing play so typical of autistic children.

The next animal out of the basket was one that James himself wasn't all that sure about. A wildebeest or something else equally odd to be in a child's play set. Conor looked at it and perplexity pinched his features. "Cow?" he asked and his high-pitched tone betrayed a genuine question.

"You've found a cow," James replied, reflecting back Conor's words to indicate he was listening. Whatever the creature was, it was undeniably cow-like so James was comfortable with calling it a cow.

"Ehhh," the boy muttered under his breath. "Ehhh-ehhh-ehhh-ehhh!" Then his fingers abruptly splayed wide and the plastic animal clattered to the table top as if it had become too hot to hold. Snatching up the stuffed cat, Conor clutched it tightly. "Ehhh-ehhh-ehhh-ehhh! Ehhh-ehhh-ehhh-ehhh!"

James could see the boy was becoming agitated. "Ehhh-ehhh-ehhh-ehhh," he kept repeating, like an engine that refused to catch. He started to tremble. His pale skin and colourless hair gave him a naked vulnerability that made James think of newly hatched birds, owlets and eaglets, almost grotesque in their nakedness.

"You didn't like it when I said that," James ventured. "Are you worried that it may not be a cow?"

"Ehhh-ehhh-ehhh-ehhh."

"You want to know precisely what that animal is. You don't like not knowing," he interpreted.

"Ehhh-ehhh-ehhh-ehhh! Ehhh-ehhh-ehhh-ehhh!" Conor sputtered frantically. Bringing up the stuffed cat, he pressed it over his eyes. "Meow? Meow?"

James picked up the plastic animal and examined it. "Perhaps it's a wildebeest. Or a yak. No, I don't think it's a yak. They have lots of hair. Perhaps it's an auroch. That's a kind of wild cow."

Without warning Conor took the cat by its hind leg and swung it like a weapon in a broad arc that cleared the table entirely. All the plastic animals went flying, as did James's notebook. Making a shrill, piercing noise that caused the inner parts of James's ears to vibrate, Connor screamed. His complexion went from white to red to a deep blotched colour like clotted blood in milk. He slid off the chair onto the floor and pressed the cat over his eyes.

Emotional upset was an expected part of play therapy and as long as the child was not hurting himself in any way, James found the best response was to remain in his chair, calm and composed, to show things were still in control and then endeavour to put words to the child's inarticulate distress.

"You're feeling very frightened," he said quietly as Conor lay on the floor and howled. "You feel so scared you want to scream and cry."

His words seemed to upset Conor more, because the boy began to shriek even louder.

"In here, it's all right to scream, if that's what you need to do," James said. "No one will be angry. No one will be upset. It's safe to cry in here. Nothing bad will happen."

Minutes ticked by. Still Conor thrashed and shrieked. Temper? James wondered. He didn't think so. There hadn't been any precipitating event that he could discern. Panic? Just plain terror at a world full of things the boy didn't know? Or frustration, perhaps, at his wordlessness?

Conor grew hoarse. Pulling himself into a foetal position, knees up, head down, arms around his legs, the stuffed cat tucked in against his heart, Conor at last fell into hiccupping silence.

Several more minutes passed with James still sitting quietly at the table and the boy curled up on the floor. Then finally Conor struggled slowly to his feet. Carefully he checked the status of his four strings and adjusted them at his waist, then he looked over at James, staring him straight in the eye. Tears were still wet over his cheeks and snot ran onto his upper lip.

In an unexpectedly normal, boy-like gesture, Conor raised his free arm and wiped his nose on his sleeve.

"Here," James said, getting a box of tissues. "Would you like one of these?"

Suspiciously, Conor regarded the box.

James pulled out a tissue and lay it on the table near where Conor was standing.

For a long moment Conor simply regarded it, his brow furrowing as if it were a mysterious object. Then he reached out for it. With great care he began to smooth the tissue out flat on the tabletop, a difficult task given that he was still clutching the stuffed cat against him with the other hand.

"York?" Conor said unexpectedly. Reaching down on the floor, he picked up the small plastic cow-like animal. He examined it carefully. "Yes," he whispered. "Yes, the cat says yes." He nodded. "York."

"You mean 'auroch'?" James ventured.

"Yeah," the boy responded in his typical high-pitched sing-song voice. He didn't lift his head to acknowledge James had spoken. "York. Ee-york."

"Aur-och," James murmured.

"Oar-ock. Auroch. Yes. The cat says yes. An auroch. A wild cow." The words were spoken very deliberately, as if they took effort. He set the plastic animal on the table. "The cat knows."

James felt excited. They had communicated. In his mind's eye he saw himself as one of those scientists who operated the big satellite dishes that listened for signs of alien life in outer space, that were alert for the slightest variant crackle that might indicate conscious intelligence. You heard it and that was enough to go on, to keep up the belief it existed. The slightest crackle, the smallest sign.

Chapter Four

From the moment James saw Mikey emerging from the skyway wearing only his underpants, he knew things weren't getting off on the right foot. Becky came mincing along behind in that way she had when she found her brother totally disgusting. Then she saw James and virtually bowled Mikey over in her excitement to reach him. "Daddy!" she cried and threw herself into his arms.

James scooped his eight-year-old daughter up into a bear hug.

"Guess what?" she said gleefully. "Mikey threw up. That's how come he's got no clothes on. Look. He got throw-up on my dress."

"Hey, Michael, buddy, what happened to you? Too many yummy airplane meals?" James endeavoured to lift both children at once which made them squeal.

"He had too many M&Ms," Becky replied. "Because Mum bought the bag for both of us, but then I went to the bathroom and Mikey pigged down practically all of them while I was gone. So it's his own fault. I don't feel sorry for him."

"You should, you little monster," James said playfully and smooched her on the nose. "He's your brother, no matter what." Then he whisked Mikey up in his arms again. "I bet you threw up polka dots, huh, if it was M&Ms?" Mikey giggled. "Your mum should know better than to give you a whole bag of candy."

"I've got a surprise for you," James said, as he collected their bags and headed for the car.

"What is it?" Becky asked as they left the terminal building.

"Just wait and see. Out here. In the car park."

"A pony?" Becky asked hopefully.

James laughed and ruffled her hair. "No, silly, I wouldn't come to pick you up riding a pony, would I?"

"Uncle Joey says everybody rides horses out here."

"No, look at Daddy's cool car!" James pointed to the copper-coloured '71 Ford Mustang convertible. "Isn't that beautiful?"

Sandy had kept the Range Rover because it was a safe car for the kids. James drove out to South Dakota in a clapped-out Ford Taurus his brother Jack had picked up off eBay. Buying the convertible with its over-sized, futuristic bonnet and powerful Boss 429 engine was James's first acknowledgement that his old life was over.

Becky wasn't quite so impressed. "It's just a *car*," she said with disappointment.

"It's a *classic* car."

"It's an old car," she replied disdainfully.

"It's a cool car. For cool people. Like us, huh, Mike? What do you think? Does your dad drive a cool car or what?"

"Yeah, I like it," he said and ran his hand along the fender.

Becky peered through the window as James put the suit-case in the boot. "The back seat's really little. I don't see how you get in. There's no back doors."

"Here. You open the front door, then press the lever down on the back of the front seat and tip it forward, like this."

"It's kind of stinky in here. Like somebody smoked."

"That was a long time ago, so don't worry about it. Just get in. You too, Mike. And fasten your seat belts."

"Where's your other car?" she asked. "The real one."

"If you mean the Jeep, that one isn't actually mine. It belongs to Uncle Lars. Usually when you visit, we trade. He takes this car, because yes, you're right, there isn't really lots of room for getting in and out. But Uncle Lars is hunting elk this weekend, so he needed to use the Jeep himself because it has four-wheel drive. Anyway, this car's way nicer. You'll see. If the weather stays nice, I'll put the top down. You'll love it then."

"Daddy?" Mikey asked. "Is Uncle Lars our real uncle?"

"He's not an uncle by blood. Uncle Lars is my partner in the practice. But he and Aunt Betty are Daddy's good friends and they always remember you in nice ways, so we make them honorary members of the family."

"Yeah, we got another uncle like that," Mikey replied. "His name's Uncle Joey."

"Yes, the guy who thinks we all ride horses out here. So who's he?"

"Well, basically he's Mum's boyfriend," Becky replied.

"Then he's *not* your uncle," James muttered irritably.

"Mum said we should call him that. Probably just 'cause like with you and Uncle Lars, he's her good friend," Becky said.

"Uncle Jack's your uncle back there. He's your real uncle. And I'm your real dad."

"Yeah, I know."

"Yes, well, be sure to remember it."

James missed the kids so much that it had become easy to want the visits to be perfect, to cram in all the treats and fun he missed sharing with them on a day-to-day basis. Anyway, a little spoiling never hurt.

Their new family tradition had become a trip to Toys 'R' Us for a shopping spree on the day Mikey and Becky arrived. It always started with James playfully exclaiming that because they were not with him all the time, he "didn't have enough toys at his house" and they needed to "get something to play with" while they were there. This always generated squeals of excitement and a pleasurable orgy of toy shopping.

Before going to Toys 'R' Us, James first stopped off at the house to take the suitcase inside. It was at that point Mikey vomited all over the kitchen floor.

"I wonder if he's got stomach flu," Becky said.

"Let's hope not," James replied as he filled a bucket with water and disinfectant.

"Let's hope *I* don't get it," Becky said. It sounded like a threat.

Mikey wasn't well at all. Clutching a plastic dishpan, he lay down on the couch in front of the TV.

Becky, tired from the long journey and miserably disappointed at this turn of events, started to moan. She didn't like what Mikey was watching on TV. She didn't want to be around him because he was sick. There weren't any good DVDs to watch. The clothes in her suitcase were all wrinkled.

She'd forgotten to pack her hairbrush. Most of all, however, she moaned about not going to Toys 'R' Us. She wanted to go. Now! Desperately. *Please* couldn't they go? Why couldn't Mikey just walk around for a little while?

James gently explained that Mikey was too sick at the moment to be taken out.

Becky wasn't in the mood to be understanding, wailing what was the point of coming all this way when there was no trip to Toys 'R' Us?

"I hope there are other reasons for coming besides toys," James said, feeling a bit hurt.

"This is the worst visit in the world," she exclaimed, adding "I wish I was home" as she stomped off.

Things went from bad to worse overnight. Mikey continued to vomit, and James was up and down all night comforting him. He came out bleary-eyed into the kitchen to find Becky spooning sugar into her Coco Pops.

"Hey, not the whole bowl," he said

"I wish you had a parrot, Dad," Becky replied brightly.

"A *parrot*?"

"Uncle Joey's got a parrot. His name is Harry and he can say 23 words. I wish you had one, so I could talk to it."

"I don't have one because parrots really shouldn't be kept in captivity. They're too intelligent. They need lots of stimulation. It's cruel to keep them as pets."

"Guess what else Uncle Joey has?" she said. "A house out on Long Island right on the beach. He's going to take me and Mikey and Mum out there on the weekends when it's summer."

"Lucky you," James replied.

"Know what he got me? That Barbie horse that I've been wanting so bad."

"Becky, I got you the Barbie horse."

"No, not *that* one. That's the old kind. Uncle Joey got me the one that has legs you can bend so that you can pose it like it's really walking. And guess what else? He got me the carriage that goes with it too and I didn't even ask for it."

"What's Joey do to afford all this loot? Rob banks?"

Becky laughed. "No, silly. He's a lawyer."

"Pretty much the same thing."

Mid-afternoon and Mikey was still vomiting, so James packed up Becky, Mikey and the dishpan into the Mustang and headed for the walk-in clinic.

During the interminable wait to see a doctor, Mikey staged a sufficient recovery to want a Coke out of the vending machine. It took two hours, a blood test and most of James's patience to learn that Mikey had "just one of those things kids get". Mikey sipped the rest of his Coke and looked generally pleased with himself.

"If Mikey's feeling better, can we go to Toys 'R' Us now?" Becky asked.

"That's clear on the other side of town and it's practically dinnertime. I think what we really need is a decent meal."

"I want to go to McDonald's. They have a playground."

"No, we need something healthy. What about that Italian deli that does take-out? We could pick up some of their lasagna and take it home. You loved that last time, remember? You can help me pick out a salad."

* * *

By the time they got to the deli, Mikey wasn't feeling so hot any more. He didn't want to go in and smell food.

"Okay, look, here's what we do," James said. "I'm going to park here by the window where I can see you the whole time. Becks and I are going to pop in and get our food, and we'll be right back. You lock the door while we're gone. We'll be just in there."

The deli was unexpectedly busy. James wasn't focusing on anything other than getting through the mob of people to place his order, so he jumped at the tap on his shoulder and someone saying hello. He turned.

There in the other queue stood Laura Deighton.

"Mummy, look at this," a small voice called. "Can we get some of these?"

"Bring it here so I can see it, Morgana," Laura said.

James looked over. Morgana? Conor's sister? He gaped in astonishment. She was everything Conor was not: a sturdy, athletic child with enormous brown eyes and a tangle of loose, dark curls bouncing down over her shoulders. When she caught James staring, she met him with a bold gaze and broke into a cherubic smile. Yin and yang. That was the first thought to cross James's mind.

"Is this your daughter?" Laura asked, looking down at Becky. "What a pretty little girl."

"Yes. Yes, this is Becky. My son's out in the car. He's not feeling very well."

"Sorry to hear that," Laura said.

"We've just popped in to get some decent food so he doesn't have to smell us cooking," James said wryly.

"We've come in for goodies," Laura replied. "Alan has Conor tonight, so we're having a girls' night out."

James looked down again at Morgana, who was clutching a bag of amaretti biscuits. She was an astonishingly beautiful child with her vibrant eyes, curly hair and little bow mouth, like one of those idealized children painted on heirloom plates to commemorate a golden era that had never really existed. Beside her, Conor would appear as pale and insubstantial as a ghost.

Becky, ever the social butterfly, was delighted by this unexpected opportunity to make friends. With smiley openness she said hello to Morgana, asked how old she was and within moments the girls had wandered off together to look at displays of cookies on the adjacent shelves while James and Laura waited in the queues.

"It's great to see you. How are you doing?" Laura said brightly, as though they were old friends.

This took James by surprise because over the weeks he had been seeing Conor, Laura had made herself remarkably scarce. So scarce, in fact, that James had had the distinct feeling she was avoiding him. And while she had agreed to the family therapy format which meant she would have at least three individual sessions herself with James as part of Conor's treatment, Laura had made no arrangements to follow through on this. As a consequence, James built up an image of her as reclusive, anxious and, most likely, tongue-tied. Now, however, he found her quite the contrary: friendly, relaxed and genuinely interested in the children. She commiserated with James about Mikey's sickness and his experiences at the walk-in clinic.

James glanced around to see where the two girls had gone.

"They seem to be enjoying each other," Laura said.

James smiled. "It'll be the highlight of Becky's day. She always misses her friends terribly when she's here." He craned to see over the low shelves. "Oh good heavens. Hold on a second. They've gone out to my car."

James started for the door but at just that moment the two girls burst back in. "Hey, Daddy!" Becky cried. "Guess what! Mikey's thrown up everywhere!"

"Shush, shush, not such a loud voice," James said, catching her by the shoulder.

"He missed the dishpan! It's all over your car."

"Oh geez," James said. "Listen, go tell the man at the counter we can't wait for the lasagna. Tell him sorry."

Laura materialized beside him. "Let me help you." She pulled napkins out of the holder on one of the small tables. "Morgana, you and Becky go in the restroom and bring us some paper towels."

Becky hadn't been exaggerating. Mikey had vomited over his clothes, across the console, the gear shift and onto the adjacent seat.

"Hey, fella, you okay?" James asked, reaching in to ruffle his son's hair, which was just about the only part of him free from vomit.

"Sorry, Daddy," Mikey whimpered.

"Accidents happen. As long as you're okay." Standing in the brisk October dusk, James felt bleak at the prospect of trying to clean up Mikey and the car with a handful of deli napkins.

Laura put a hand on his arm. "Why don't we just mop things up enough for you to take Mikey home? Becky can come in my car and I'll follow you. That would be easiest."

* * *

James knew it was a bad idea. As he drove home, he tried to reassure himself that letting Laura do this was not breaking the rules. It was so important that he not make any mistakes this time around. Good boundaries with clients did not include any kind of personal relationships with them. But then he was in a genuinely bad situation. She was simply helping him, like any decent person would. Besides … if he was honest with himself, James had to admit she intrigued him. She wore her fame, her accomplishments so lightly they were almost illusory, as if they were nothing more than stories themselves, and yet there was something also illusory about Laura, the way she could be so friendly, so concerned and willing to help with Mikey and yet eluded James's efforts to get her in to talk about her own son.

Chapter Five

When they arrived at the apartment, the two girls bounded off together, Becky chattering excitedly about a toy horse she wanted to show Morgana. Laura lifted Mikey out of the car and took him inside while James went in search of cleaning supplies and a rag out of the box at the back of the garage. By the time he came into the apartment, Laura had run a bath and was washing Mikey, as if it were the most natural thing to enter a strange house and bathe a child she'd never met before.

James took over from there. With Mikey finally clean and tucked into bed, he came back into the living room to find Laura, hands sunk deep into the pockets of her jeans, scanning the bookshelves. Embarrassment shot through him. While he owned most of her books, they were all in his office, because the only point of buying them had been so people at work could see he owned them. The novels on these shelves were the sort he actually read – Terry Pratchett, Tom Clancy, Stephen King – relaxing, unpretentious storytelling that you could leave on the back of the toilet or risk dropping in the bath.

"That's my fun reading," he said sheepishly.

She smiled enigmatically.

"I do *have* yours," he added quickly. "But they're at the office at the moment. I'm always switching back and forth."

Her smile eased into a grin and she glanced over. "So does that mean you've actually read any of them?"

James felt his cheeks redden. There was an uncomfortable pause and then he admitted, "I wish I could say yes. I *intend* to. It's just been very busy since moving out here."

"At least you're honest."

Desperate to move the conversation away from his embarrassing lack of intellectual reading, James said, "Would you like a cup of coffee? Then we can try to pull the girls apart."

Laura followed him into the kitchen. Hands still deep in her pockets she strolled around the room, studying the kitchen with the same care as she had his bookshelf. The way she circled the room, inspecting everything, reminded James of Conor.

That brought to mind the fact that Laura had not yet mentioned her son. Normally parents he met outside the office pounced on him, anxious to ask how things were going, to tell of their child's progress or get some free advice. James was grateful, of course, that she hadn't done any of these things, since it would have been inappropriate to discuss a case outside the privacy of the office, but it was still curious that she never mentioned Conor at all, even casually.

Taking the coffee to the table, James sat down. "I've been hoping to see you in the office," he said.

Laura ignored his comment. She lifted the coffee and sipped it. "Mmmm. Good coffee. Tastes like New York coffee."

"Can I get Dulcie to give you a call this week and make an appointment?" James asked.

Laura's brow drew down as she looked into the mug of steaming liquid. A silence developed and several moments slipped by with no response. "I've got to admit, I'm not really into that concept," she said at last.

"Which concept is this?"

"Therapy."

"Why?" James asked.

Setting the mug down on the table, Laura leaned forward on her forearms and stared into it as if some answer were in there. Finally she smiled at him. "Because everyone's reality is different."

That was an unexpected answer. James cocked an eyebrow.

"Therapy, the way I see it, trades on the assumption that 'normal' exists and that my perceptions, whatever they might be, should be brought into line with it," she said. "Whereas I think there *is* no 'real world' out there. No absolute reality. Everything is subjective. So why should I accept what you tell me is reality?"

"That's an interesting take," James said. "I get the impression you're worried your perspective will be overridden or judged as not as good or acceptable as other perspectives. Perhaps you think that a therapist might get in there and try to change perceptions you don't feel are wrong." He smiled at her. "But that's not quite what therapy is. It's simply about fixing things that don't work. Just as if your car stopped working. You'd take it to a garage and let a mechanic repair it. You wouldn't expect him to do stuff you hadn't wanted done or to customize the car to his liking and not give it back to you. You'd expect him simply to find out what's wrong and repair it so that you can enjoy your car again. Same here, except that I work with people, not cars. Your relationship with Conor has stopped working. So you've brought Conor to see if I can fix that. And because relationships always involve more than one person, I need to see everyone involved to do my job properly. I'm not going to make anyone think or do anything they don't want to. I'm just going to try and fix what's broken."

Her cheeks flushed. She ducked her head and James saw tears come to the corners of her eyes. He sat back in a casual manner to lessen the intensity of the moment, because this wasn't the time or the place. Indeed, he was deeply relieved that the girls had remained occupied playing in Becky's room.

"Sorry," Laura murmured. "I hadn't meant it to get this far."

"Not to worry."

"I think it was the 'relationships stopped working' comment." She was tearful again. "Sorry."

"Not to worry."

"It's just … well … 'relationships not working' is a bit of an understatement," she said wearily. "Because it's not just Conor …"

James knew he ought to stop her right there. The appropriate place for this conversation was the office. Here at his own kitchen table, with the girls chattering in the next room and apt to burst in at any moment, was most definitely not the place to encourage the conversation in the direction it was going. But James sensed a rare chink in Laura's armour, and if he had learned anything from that whole tragedy in New York, it was to recognize that sometimes you had to break the rules. So he said, "What's happened?"

"Alan left me."

"I'm sorry to hear that."

"It's given me such a shock," she said and tears thickened her voice.

"So how did this come about?" James asked.

"We had the stupidest argument. Over a lawnmower, would you believe?"

James smiled sympathetically. "That must have been upsetting."

"It was so stupid. Al had been in town and found this lawnmower on sale. It was a good price, but it was this huge, heavy thing and wasn't self-propelled. I'm the one who cares for the yard, so any lawnmower we get, I'm the one who'll be using it. I wouldn't even be able to push that beast. So I said he needed to take it back.

"Al flatly refused. We've got this weird relationship regarding money. We always have. And that's what this was about. He'd paid for it, so he wasn't going to take it back, because then it was as if I'd said he made a bad choice with his money. It escalated from there, because I didn't want to get stuck with this crap machine and he didn't want to take it back. So in the end I just said, okay, *I'm* going to take it back. I went out and got in the pickup, because the lawnmower was still in the back of it and I took off for town.

"This isn't like me," she said and looked over. "I'm normally not at all confrontational. Before I even got into town, I was regretting I'd made a big deal out of it. I almost turned around then ..." Her voice caught. "But I didn't. I'd gone all that way, so I thought I might as well make use of it. So I went to the grocery store. When I got back to the ranch, he was gone. And, of course, he'd taken the kids."

Laura's shoulders dropped. She let out a long, slow breath. "That was the very worst moment I've ever had." The tears glistened yet again. "Coming into the house, finding it empty, realizing they were gone."

"When did this happen?" James asked.

"Last Friday. Alan's come back since. He was only gone over the weekend. Took the kids to his mum's. But it made me realize I've got to do something. We're in serious trouble." She paused and looked over at James. "I'm thinking, okay, maybe I'll do this with you. Maybe I'll come in."

"Lawnmower?" Alan said in disbelief. "Laura thinks this was all about a lawnmower? She thinks I moved out of my house because I was upset over a fucking *lawnmower*?" Leaning back into the sofa, he shook his head. "Well, there's a beautiful example of just why we're going to hell: Laura lives in another world. She completely misses what's happening in this one."

"You're saying Laura commonly misinterprets things?" James asked, curious. Surely a good writer would be skilled at insight and interpretation.

"Not 'misinterprets'. Laura's not misinterpreting. It's more that she's got her own version of the world. Things aren't true and untrue to Laura. Not the way they are for most of us." Alan paused and lowered his head, thinking. "How exactly do I explain it? I don't want it to come off sounding like I think she's a pathological liar or something, because it's not that clear cut. Lying means there must be a truth somewhere and you know you're not saying it. With Laura, it's all much more fluid than that. Almost as if no truth exists and so you create it as you go along."

Like a storyteller does, James thought.

"In the early years that's why I loved her so," Alan said. "I mean, you're around Laura for a while and you realize she isn't quite like other people. She's got this weird, wonderful way of thinking, not the sort of thing you can get at with just intellect. There's a passion about creative people, don't you think? Growing up in a family of bankers and accountants, I admired that. Maybe even identified with it a little, because I think what gave me trouble as a kid was that I was just that bit more free-thinking. Nothing like Laura, of course, but enough to know there was something better to be had than just making money. And I got off on the idea that *she* wanted to be with *me*. In a way, that's what attracted her in reverse. She wanted ordinary. That's actually what she told me once. That I was 'real' to her. I was her anchor ...

"But this fey quality, it isn't special anymore. It's just frigging hard work. These days I feel like one of those game show contestants who has to guess what's behind the curtain. You know? Guess between this one and that one and you win the prize. But when the curtain opens, there's another curtain behind it. Or a box to be opened. And inside is another box. Nothing is like it looks. Everything just hides something else. I've never found the real Laura. To the point that I'm not sure she even exists.

"I'm fed up with it. With all the lies and evasions. You ask her something and she'll tell you whatever story is in her head at that moment. And she's so good at it. You never know if it's the truth or not."

Finally Alan looked over at James. "You want to know the real reason I left. It had nothing to do with lawnmowers whatsoever. Shall I tell you what happened?"

"Yes, of course," James said.

"Our daughter, Morgana, is six. She was supposed to go to this kid's birthday party right after school last Friday. She was so excited about it, because she doesn't get invited to a lot of birthday parties. Morgana seems to get on with kids okay, but she plays by herself a lot. Mostly just because we live so far out. Anyway, so this was special. Morgana kept chattering on about what she wanted to wear and what she wanted to get this little girl for a present and all that. It's all she talked about.

"The day of the party happened to be the same day Laura threw her tantrum over the lawnmower. I was pretty fed up and didn't want to be around when she came back. Since we'd already arranged that I was going to pick Morgana up from the party, I decided to go into town early. I popped Conor in the car and thought I'd take him to the car wash with me. He likes that.

"Anyway, there were roadworks on the main street, so I took a different way that goes down around the park. As I'm driving by the park, who should I see there but Morgana, playing there all on her own.

"I thought, what the *hell*? I jammed on the brakes and leaped out and grabbed hold of her. I said, 'What are you doing here?' She started crying right away – bawling – and I just felt such relief that chance had taken me down that road.

"Morgana was so upset I couldn't really get an explanation out of her as to what had happened. All I could reckon was that whoever was in charge of this little girl's birthday party had taken the children to the park and then hadn't done a very good head count when they left. This got me fuming, so I stormed over to their house.

"I was rattling the door and saying 'What the hell is wrong with you, leaving a six-year-old alone in the park?' and this girl's mother looked at me like I was a madman. She says, 'Caitlin isn't having a birthday party today. Her birthday's in August.'"

Alan's shoulders dropped in a defeated way. "Anyhow, so then the story came out." He looked over at James. "Turns out Morgana had made the whole thing up. She was desperate to be able to play in the park on her own, because that's what the town kids did. She'd wanted to wear that new outfit to school but Laura had told her she couldn't, that it was for special occasions like birthday parties. And the damned set of marking pens we'd bought for this girl's birthday present was something Morgana had been wanting for herself. So she cooked up this whole birthday scenario and *carried it off*. This is a goddamned first-grader we're talking about.

"Something inside me just snapped when Morgana told me that. I thought, here she is, at six, doing just what her mother does. Showing that same devil-may-care attitude towards the truth. Acting like you can just make it up as you go along and it's the same as if it were real. I thought, hell, this is the fucking future. Morgana is going to become another Laura. So since Conor was already in the car with me, I just took off. I thought, I'm *not* going to let this happen. I'm not going to let Laura fuck both these kids up. So, I didn't go home. I took the kids and went to my mother's house in Gillette."

Alan drew in a deep breath and let it out slowly. "The problem is, it was just a gesture. I can't leave the ranch. Not really. It's *my* ranch. I've got too many responsibilities there to be able to just walk out altogether. Besides, walking out would hurt the kids too much. Laura and I have to sort this out like adults. But it was a gesture that needed to be made, because it finally got the point across to her that I'm fucking serious. Things have got to change or else I *will* take Conor and Morgana away from her."

Chapter Six

Clad in jeans and running shoes, her hands sunk deep into the pockets of an oversized grey sweatshirt jacket, Laura looked to have just come from the gym the day she arrived for the first session.

"Won't you come in?" James said, pleased that she'd kept her promise to show up.

As before, Laura eschewed the carefully laid-out conversation centre in preference to the chair beside his desk. Sitting down in it, she kept her hands in the pockets of the open sweatshirt jacket, crossing them over in front of her to closely wrap it around to her as if the room were chilly. Such a contrast, James thought, to the confident woman he'd met at the deli.

"How are your kids?" she asked. "Did Mikey get better in time to enjoy some of his visit?"

"Yes, they're both fine, thank you. It was just a twenty-four-hour thing. He was his normal tornado self the next day," James said and smiled.

"Did they get back to New York okay? That's a long way for little ones to travel?"

"They're a couple of little adventurers. They enjoy the excitement of going on their own and all the fuss the airlines staff make of them."

Laura wrapped the sweatshirt jacket even more tightly around herself. "I'm feeling very nervous," she said at last and smiled apologetically.

"Why is that?" he asked gently.

She shrugged slightly. "I dunno. I guess because I know Alan's already been in. You've already heard his version of everything. I worry I'm disadvantaged."

"I'm not here to take sides," James replied. "Remember the other week at my place? When I was saying that what this is all about is simply getting things working again? That's the truth. I'm not here to judge either of you. That wouldn't be helpful. I'm only here so you and Alan and Conor can untangle things."

"Yeah," she said, sounding unconvinced.

A moment passed in silence. Laura glanced around the room. Finally she gave him a brief moment of eye contact. "What do you want me to talk about then? Conor? Alan?"

"In here you decide. You're in control of the session."

"If I were actually in control, I'd control it by not being here," she said and grinned.

"You have that choice as well. If you need to leave, you can. In here you *do* decide. That's what it's all about."

James could tell from her expression that it had not occurred to her that she actually did have the freedom to get up and walk out. Now she seemed even more unnerved.

"You really are feeling uncomfortable," he said to give her a way into talking to him.

"Yes."

A couple of moments of silence passed.

"I wish it were more natural, this. Like the night at your place. I mean, I *can* talk." She laughed self-consciously. "It's just when I get in a situation like this, I lose it."

"That's okay," he said gently. "Don't worry about it."

The room grew quiet. She was looking down at her hands as they rested one on top of the other on her lower abdomen. They were still inside the pockets of the sweatshirt jacket, so she stared at the grey material.

"What's making this hard …" she started tentatively, "… is … that before we discuss Conor or Alan, I want to tell you about something else. Because it's informed my whole life … you need to know, if you're going to understand what's happening. But I don't know how to start telling you."

"That's all right," James said. "Take your time. The pace is yours. There's no hurry."

"It's just, well, more that I've never really told anybody about it." She frowned. "No, that's wrong. I have. I've told quite a lot of people, actually. But never in a context like this. Never in a way that acknowledges its legitimate place in my life. Never truthfully, from beginning to end." She shrugged apologetically. "That's what's actually kept me so long from coming in. I just can't figure out how to start this without making everything sound crazy. Yet, at the same time I know I've got to. Because what if I really did lose Alan? Or Morgana? Or Conor? That can't happen. So I've got to start with telling you about this one thing, because otherwise, nothing else will make sense."

James nodded.

There was total silence, so complete that the subtle noises of the outer office and waiting room flowed into the room like an incoming tide.

Laura finally took a very deep breath and let it out with measured slowness. "It starts the summer I was seven. In my home town, which is west of here in the Black Hills. In June. Early evening, maybe about 7 pm. I was walking alone along this little dirt path that ran from the end of our street, which is called Kenally Street, through an empty lot that bordered the lake and then out to meet the next street over, which is Arnott Street. It was just a kids' path through a vacant lot that belonged to an old man named Mr Adler. You know the kind. We used the path as a shortcut to school and as a quick way to get down to the pier at the end of Arnott Street.

"Anyway, that particular evening we'd had thundery showers in the late afternoon. When the clouds finally parted, the sun was left hanging just above this low, humpbacked mountain that everyone calls the Sugarloaf. I was walking directly into the sunlight and I recall looking up at it and wondering why it was that you could look directly at the sun when it is that low in the sky and it doesn't hurt your eyes.

"Then just to my right, I caught motion in my peripheral vision, stopped, turned my head and found myself still sun-blind. I couldn't see clearly for a moment or two, but when I could, there was this woman standing there."

Laura paused and drew in a deep breath.

"She was like no one I'd ever seen before. Not even in my dreams. She was in her twenties, tall, with broad, bold features and dusty-coloured skin. Her hair was a soft black colour like charcoal, thick and very, very straight. It hung loose just past her shoulders. This caught my attention straightaway, because this was in the early 60s, before the Flower Power generation, so women wore short Doris Day 'dos or Jackie Kennedy bouffants. If their hair was longer, it was done up in a chignon or French roll. I'd never seen a grown woman who had her hair loose and unstyled.

"The other really noticeable thing was her muscles. She was quite thin but she had these taut, prominent muscles. I remember thinking that if I reached out and touched her, her flesh would feel hard like my brother's, not soft and mushy like Ma's.

"More than anything else, though, the feature that defined her most was her eyes. They were deep-set, beneath dark, ungroomed eyebrows, and they were the most extraordinary colour. A light, light grey that towards the edges of the iris was vaguely yellowed, like the eyes of a wolf.

"All her clothes were creamy white. The top was loose and blousy and had an elaborate design embroidered down the front and on the cuffs, but the embroidery was white on white, so you couldn't actually tell what it was without looking closely. Her pants were like these baggy shorts boys wear now that end just below the knees, but they were made of the same white woven material as her top. On her feet she was wearing Roman-style sandals, the kind that lace up over the ankles.

"I remember staring at her because she looked so strange. And also because she looked really very beautiful in a wild sort of way. She stared right back at me. Not discreetly, the way adults usually look at people they'd interested in. She *stared*. The way young kids stare at each other. She had this bewildered expression on her face, as if she were as startled to see me there trotting along the path through Adler's vacant lot as I was to see her.

"That moment of staring felt like forever to me. We just stood, locked in one another's gaze. I wasn't frightened of her at all. If anything, I felt a wary excitement.

"Finally she turned away and started moving towards the corner of the lot. There wasn't a way out onto the street there. Just an old, untended lilac hedge. The lilacs were tall and scraggly but even so, you still couldn't get through them. I never bothered to wonder why she was going that way. All I knew was that she was getting away and I couldn't let that happen. I had to follow her. So I did."

Laura stopped.

James raised his eyebrows. "And?"

"My next memory was of getting hit by crab apples that my foster brother was throwing. When I looked around, I was standing in the alley at the other end of the path. Over by the gate into our backyard. This was more than half a block away from where I'd seen the woman.

"I remember looking down and seeing the knee-deep weeds in the alley, seeing their colour. They were that pale yellow everything goes when it is baked dry in the summer heat, and there was hard, rutted soil beneath them. For a moment I wondered if this woman had magicked me there because it was quite a way away from the path through the empty lot. I was seven and still hopeful about things like fairies and magic. But I wasn't a naïve kid. I think I already knew by then those things didn't really exist. I was also experienced enough with my imagination to know that *it* did. This wouldn't have been the first time I'd become so engrossed in playing an imaginary game that I'd lost track of where I was and ended up somewhere else."

"So you recognized seeing this woman as an imaginary experience?" James asked.

"Oh yes. Definitely yes. I'm not talking about aliens or the paranormal or anything like that. I imagined her. Real as she looked to me in Adler's lot, I knew even then that if I'd reached my hand out, I could never have touched her. I knew she had come from inside me."

"So what do you think happened to you during that period between seeing her and your ending up at the gate into your backyard?" James asked.

"Simple. I'd followed her. I walked into another world that evening," Laura said quietly. "A world inside my head. Nowhere else and I knew it was nowhere else. But it was another world, nonetheless, and no less real for being in there instead of out here. I experienced it with immense clarity. As vividly, as vibrantly as I can see this room around us right now."

She looked directly at James. "Does that sound crazy?"

James smiled gently. "No, not crazy. Many children are gifted with astonishing imaginations and can create some very detailed fantasies."

"It was astonishing all right. But it proved to be much more than a child's fantasy because it didn't end there with my childhood. That's why it's so hard to talk about. Because there *is* a type of craziness about it and I do know that." She studied her fingers a moment. "But I also need to tell you about it. Because that night on the path through Adler's lot has influenced everything that's ever happened to me since."

This had not been what James had been expecting at all. Fascinated, he leaned forward towards her. "Fantasy tends to be a reflection of our lives, of needs that aren't being fulfilled, of desires we have," he said. "I'd be very interested to hear what your childhood was like at that point."

Laura grew thoughtful for a moment. "Most people stereotype my childhood straightaway when they hear that I was a foster child," she said at last. "They assume it must have been unsettled and full of traumatic events. The truth is, for the most part, it was actually quite a good childhood. I was happy.

"I only ever lived with one family. I had been with them since I was only a few weeks old, so it always did feel like *my* family. My foster parents had four sons of their own, all older than me, so I was the daughter they'd never had and I felt very cherished. Mecks was their name. I called them Ma and Pa and they always treated me as if I were their own child. I was well loved and knew it."

"How did you come to be in foster care?" James asked.

"My mother developed an embolism and died only two days after I was born. I was a bit of an accident anyway, as my two brothers are eight and ten years older than I am. This was not an era when men were very domestic. My father felt he could cope with two school-aged boys but not with a tiny baby. So, I went to the Meckses very early on."

Laura grew pensive. "In many ways it was an idyllic life for an imaginative child. I was essentially a last-born child, which meant I was spoilt a bit, given my way, left largely free of expectations. And it was an amazing environment to grow up in. The Meckses had this huge, old, turn-of-the-century house with a big staircase in the front hall and a banister you could slide down, just like kids do in the movies. Everybody in town called it 'the lake house' because it was built right at the very end of Kenally Street and so backed onto Spearfish Lake. We even had our own bit of shoreline. Thinking back on it now, I suspect the house wasn't as grand as I remember it. In fact, it was probably downright shabby by adult standards, because there was a lot of peeling paint, stained wallpaper and squeaky floor-boards by that point. But it was a kid's paradise.

"Pa had converted part of the attic into a bedroom for me when I was five. It was gigantic – this huge, dark, draughty space that baked in summer and froze in winter, I couldn't stand upright in three-quarters of it because of the slope of the roof – and I thought it was heaven on earth. I was one of those kids who was always making things, always had a 'project' going. And always collecting things. I was big into collecting. Rocks, leaves, horses – you know, those plastic Breyer horses that were so popular in those days – all sorts of things. Pa built me shelves under the eaves for everything and made a desk out of an old door." She grinned charmingly at James. "It was wonderful."

"And into all this came your imagination," he said.

"Oh god, yes. That was my favourite thing of all – pretending. At seven I was in my horsy stage. I desperately wanted a real one, but there was, of course, just no way to have one. So I spent about two years pretending to be one myself. 'Butterfly the Trick Pony'." She smiled. "I used to wear this towel over my shoulders for a horse blanket.

"In the attic I'd also 'built' myself a horse by attaching a cardboard head and a yarn tail to the stepladder. I'd straddle the top of the ladder and pretend I was Dale Evans's very best friend, and she and I would ride out to meet Roy on the range or we'd round up wild horses and shoot bad guys.

"In fact, that's why Torgon stood out so much. While I wasn't at all surprised that a strange lady had popped up in Adlers lot, what *was* remarkable was that she wasn't a horse!" Laura laughed heartily.

"Torgon?"

"Yes, that's what I called her. Right from the beginning, because I knew that was her name. I thought her arrival was very auspicious. It happened right at the point where I was always pretending to be Butterfly the Trick Pony. One of the horsy things I liked to do was eat raw porridge oats and Ma was convinced eating so much roughage would give me appendicitis. I overheard her tell Pa how much she was looking forward to my outgrowing my horsy stage. So I have this wonderful memory of sitting in the bath that night I'd first seen Torgon. I was sluicing water up and down my arms with a washcloth and thinking about what had happened, and I remember feeling such an incredible sense of pride in myself because I had seen Torgon and not simply another horse. I just knew it meant I was growing up!" She laughed so infectiously it was hard not to join in.

"What about your natural family?" James asked. "Did you have contact with them?"

"Oh yes. My dad was living here in Rapid City at the time. He drove up to see me every third Sunday like clockwork. My brothers Russell and Grant always came with him, so despite the fact I didn't live with them, we were still all quite close.

"Dad would pick me up at the Meckses and we'd always go out on the highway to this diner called the Wayside and have their Sunday special, which was a roast beef dinner with apple pie for dessert. Then afterwards, if it was at all nice, we'd go for a drive through the Black Hills. If the weather was bad, we went bowling." Laura grinned. "As a consequence, I'm a devilish good bowler, even today!

"I lived for those Sundays. My dad was very good at knowing how to make a kid feel special. He always arrived really enthusiastic to see me, always full of news he thought I'd like to hear, and without fail he brought a present. A *good* present, you know? Not just a couple of pencils or socks or something. Mostly it was a new Breyer horse statue for my collection. This meant so much to me. I absolutely coveted these horses. They cost quite a bit of money, so most kids didn't have many of them, but because my dad gave me one almost every month, I had the biggest collection of anybody else in my class. I didn't have a lot of status otherwise, but in this one way, I was best.

"Of course, what I wanted most was to actually live with my father and my brothers. Content as I was at the lake house with the Meckses, it was different from what other kids had, and different is awful when you're little. I hated always having to explain why my last name wasn't the same as theirs, how I came to live with them, why I didn't live with my own family. So I dreamed relentlessly of the day when I'd be reunited with my birth family. Dad liked this game too, this idea that I was at the Meckses only temporarily. One of the happiest rituals of those Sunday visits revolved around his telling me how he was always just on the verge of taking me back to him, and then we'd plan how it was all going to be when he did. He was always telling me this was going to happen in about six months. Once he got a new job or bought a house with a yard, *then* he would come for me. Or his favourite reason: when he got a new mum for me. He loved talking about this. Every visit he would regale me with tantalizing stories about all the current prospects and whether I'd approve or disapprove. Then we'd make lots of exciting plans about what we and this new mum were going to do once we were all together again.

"I was incredibly gullible," Laura said lightly. "I *never* doubted him. Not once. Month after month, year after year my dad would tell me these stories about what he was doing to get me back with him and I always believed him. I must have been at least nine before I even fully realized 'in another six months' was an actual measure of time and not just a synonym for 'someday'."

"Did you feel resentful when you did figure that out?" James asked.

"No, not at the time. He was so reliable in other ways, like the way he always came every third Sunday, always brought me a present, always took me out to do fun things. Even when I did realize that a lot of actual six-month periods had gone by, I still believed he was trying his hardest to reunite us."

"And throughout this time did you have this imaginary companion? This Torgon character you were telling me about?" James asked.

Laura nodded. "Oh yes. Torgon and I were only just getting started."

Chapter Seven

"Hi Becks!"

"Daddy! Hi ya! Guess what? When the phone rang, I *said* it was going to be you! I told Mum. She and Uncle Joey were going to take us ice skating tonight, but I told her I wanted to stay in because I thought you might phone. And you did! I got psychic powers, don't you think?"

"Yeah, probably so, Becks," James said and chuckled. He didn't remind her he phoned most Friday evenings.

"Thanks for sending me that Ramona Quimby book, Daddy. I didn't have that one. And it's really good! I'm almost clear through it already and I only started it last night. I was so happy when I opened up your package and saw that's what it was."

"Well, thank *you* for your nice long newsy letter," James said. "I got it on Monday. What a nice surprise in my mail box."

"It was so long, it was practically like a Ramona Quimby book too, wasn't it?" Becky replied gleefully. "My teacher says I'm probably going to be a writer when I grow up, because I'm so good with details."

"Yes, you certainly are. I like your details. And I'm glad to hear you're enjoying gymnastics so much."

James's words were interrupted by noises of a muffled struggle on the other end of the line. "Get off!" Becky was muttering. "I'm still talking!"

"Daddy! Daddy!" Mikey's voice broke through.

"Hi, Mike, how's it going?"

"Becky won't let me have the phone and it's my turn."

More muffled struggling and the sound of Becky muttering, "Pushy little pig. You give it back to me afterwards."

"Did you get the postcard I sent, Daddy?" Mikey asked. "It's got a lighthouse on it."

"Yes, I did. Thank you very much."

"I did all the writing on it myself. I even wrote your address."

"And a Superman job you did too," James said. "It was very easy to read. The mailman got it right to my door with no trouble at all."

"Dad?"

"Yes, Mike?"

"When can *we* come to your door again? I miss you. I want to see you."

"Yes, I miss you too, Mikey. Big lots. And that's one of the reasons I'm phoning. To make arrangements with Mum for you two to come out over Thanksgiving."

"I don't want to wait that long. I miss you now."

"Yeah, I know. Me too," James said. "Every night I say, 'Goodnight, Mikey. Goodnight, Becky' to that picture beside my bed."

"Yeah, every night I say 'Goodnight, Daddy', to *your* picture," Mikey replied. "But I wish it was really you."

"So why don't you put your mum on the phone so we can make some plans."

"Okay, Daddy. Kiss you," he smacked into the phone. "Love you forever."

"Love you forever too, Mikey."

A moment's pause as Mikey dropped the phone noisily on the table. Then Sandy's voice, deep for a woman's voice but soft and darkly fluid, like molasses over gravel.

"Well, yes, I got your email," she said. "And I want to know exactly what you're playing at."

"It should have been quite plain, Sandy. I'm not paying the kind of mortgage I'm shelling out on that place to have Joey living there and I know he is, because the kids have told me. Let Joey pay the damned mortgage."

"The mortgage was part of the settlement, James."

"Not if he's living there."

"The mortgage was part of the settlement," she repeated in short, clipped words that emphasized their meaning. "Because *our* kids are living in this house. That's still happening. So why are you even bothering with this shit?"

"Because I'm earning a South Dakota wage and paying for a West Side brownstone. Joey's a fucking corporate lawyer. In Manhattan, for Christ's sake. He can afford to pay his own way."

"Well, if you think you can have the kids any time you want and then turn around and say you aren't going to pay the mortgage …"

"This has nothing to do with when I get the kids. We agreed those dates in mediation, Sandy."

"Yeah, well, we agreed the mortgage in mediation too."

"*Sandy*."

She slammed the phone down.

"You got to ignore her, Jim," Lars said. "It's like in playing football. If you want to complete a good pass, well, then you just got to think of nothing but that pass. You got to totally ignore the other team because they're doing nothing but trying to put you off your concentration. Same with Sandy. She doesn't want you to complete any passes, whether it's getting the kids out here at Thanksgiving or telling the shifty lawyer guy to move the hell out of your house."

"I know it," James said in frustration and sank back into the chair. "It's just when she starts in with that patronizing tone …"

"It's interference, Jim. Nothing else. She's just running interference. You got to take your mind off her and put it on the positive. On what you want to accomplish."

"She so knows how to twist the knife," James muttered. "She knows she can hurt me through the kids."

"Jim, don't let her get to you."

"She makes me feel pathetic. That's what I hate. She acts like in coming out here, I've run away when in fact, I've done just the opposite. I've faced up to myself, to where I went wrong. I made some bad choices and took some wrong turnings but when I realized that, I took action to create a better life. It just wasn't the one she thought she was signing up for."

Very slowly, Conor began to talk more. It was difficult to tell if it was meaningful speech or simply echolalia because it was made up largely of phrases James himself had used first, but it became increasingly clear that Conor wanted to interact.

One morning when he arrived, Conor said, "In here, you decide," at the doorway of the playroom, almost as if it were a greeting.

"Good morning, Conor. Won't you come in?" James replied.

"Ehhh-ehhh-ehhh-ehhh."

For a long moment Conor remained in the doorway. He pressed the cat against his face, over his eyes, then lowered it and pointed it around the room.

"In here, you decide," he said again. "In here, you go around the room." He began his usual counter-clockwise perambulation. Once, twice, three times he went around the room.

"Where's the boy's auroch?" he said suddenly. "In here, you decide."

"Yes," James said. "In this room you can decide for yourself if you want to play with the toy animals."

"Where's the boy's auroch? You decide."

"Would you like me to help you find the basket?" James asked.

"Find the basket with the animals," Conor replied, although James couldn't discern if it was a genuine response or simply an incomplete echo.

Rising from his chair, James crossed over to the shelves. "Here are the animals," he said, and lifted the red wire basket out. "Shall I take it to the table for you?"

"In here, you decide."

"That's right. You decide if you want me to take it to the table."

"Take it to the table."

Conor followed. Lifting the cat up, he scanned the basket, then reached in and lifted an animal out. "Here is a dog," he said and set it on the table. This seemed to please him. There was almost the hint of a smile on his lips. "Here is a duck." He set that up too.

James watched him as he progressed through the basket of animals. While the boy's actions were slow and obsessive, they were not quite the same as the rote repetitions of an autistic child. They were nuanced in a way that made James quite certain they had meaning, although he couldn't even speculate at this point what it might be.

"*Here* is the boy's auroch," Conor said with emphasis. "The auroch will stand with the others." He surveyed them. "There are many animals. How many? How many is many?" Then he started to count them. This was new. James hadn't heard him count before. "Forty-six. Forty-six is many. Forty-six in all," Conor said.

"You like seeing many animals," James said. "I hear a pleased voice counting."

"There is no cat."

"No, there's no cat among them."

"Many animals. Forty-six animals. But no cat," Conor said.

"No. All of those animals, but none of them is a cat," James reflected back to indicate he was listening carefully.

"Now they will die," Conor said matter-of-factly. "The dog will die." He pushed the dog on its side. "The duck will die. The elephant will die." One by one he went through the plastic animals, pushing them over on to their sides. There was no distress in his voice. The animals all died with the same equanimity as they had lined up.

"Died. Many animals have died," Conor said. "No more in-and-out. No more steam." He pulled his toy cat out from under his arm where it had been stashed. He scanned it over

the fallen animals, pushing the cat's nose up against each individually. "The cat knows."

The cat knows? James thought. The cat knows what? Or
perhaps he had been misunderstanding all this time. Perhaps
it was "the cat nose". Perhaps Conor believed the cat was capable of scenting something.

"Where's the rug?" Conor said suddenly and looked at
James.

James looked up blankly.

Conor turned his head and glanced around the room.
Abruptly his face lit up and he crossed over behind James to
get the box of tissues.

Coming back to the table, Conor pulled tissues out of the
box and laid them one by one over the plastic animals. This
took up most of the space on the table. And most of the tissues
too.

When he was finished, Conor surveyed his work. "Where
is the dog?" he asked. Then he lifted one tissue. "The dog is
here. Where is the duck? The duck is here." Repetitively he
went through all the animals, asking where an animal was
and then lifting the tissue to say that here it was. There was a
repetitive, sing-song quality to his questions and answers.
This reminded James of a baby's game of peek-a-boo.
However, there was also a stuck-record quality to it, as though
once started he couldn't stop himself.

"You are concerned that the dog won't be there, that the
dog might not be under the tissue, if you can't see him," James
ventured to interpret. "You want to look again and again to
make sure."

For a brief moment, Conor looked up, looked directly at
James, his eyes a cloudy, indistinct blue. He had registered

James's comment and by his reaction James guessed his interpretation must have been correct.

"You are worried about what you will find under the tissue, so you must look," James reiterated.

"The dog is dead," Conor replied.

"You think the dog is dead and so that's why you've put a tissue over it."

"A rug."

"So you've put a rug over it."

"The cat knows."

"The cat knows the dog is dead?" James asked.

"Ehhh-ehhh-ehhh-ehhh."

"You are making your worried sound," James said.

"The dog is dead," Conor said very softly. "The duck is dead. The auroch is dead." He looked down at the toy cat in his hands. "Someday the cat will die too." And as he stood, a single tear fell, wending a wet path down over his cheek.

Chapter Eight

"So what exactly happened to you that night you first saw Torgon?" James asked, once Laura was settled for her next session. "When you experienced this intense imaginative episode?"

Laura sat in silence for a few minutes. "Well, as I followed Torgon towards the lilac hedge, I was in her world. One moment I was on the path through Adler's vacant lot and the next moment I was on this high promontory of chalky white stone. The soil itself was white. Not crumbly like in the Badlands, but actual rock that was pushed up in great, distinct ribs to form the cliff, as if a giant had slammed together a handful of blackboard chalk. Below us was this massive broadleaved forest that stretched off in all directions. Sort of what I'd expect the Amazon Basin to look like, if you viewed it from high up. I remember the trees undulating restlessly in the breeze, almost like waves in an ocean. That's how it got its name. From that point on, I always called it the Forest because of that view from the cliff."

Laura paused pensively. "When I say 'I went there' or 'I went with her', that's not quite right. It's hard to describe what really happened, because I was aware 'I' myself wasn't there. This was one thing that was different about the Forest from my other fantasies. In all of those, I was always at the centre of the action, imagining myself as the star, doing things with the characters I created. The Forest was completely different. It was more like seeing a movie.

"At first I couldn't figure out what Torgon's role was. It was immediately obvious that she was a leader of some kind. You could tell that straightaway from the way people treated her. I assumed at first that she was a queen, but came to realize that she was, in fact, a kind of holy person. Not a priestess exactly, but of that type. The word in the Forest people's language for her role was *benna*."

"So they had their own language?" James asked.

"Yes. Although the only time I was aware of it was with words like *benna* that didn't have an equivalent in English. I'd 'hear' those words."

James listened with fascination. He had always found children's imaginary companions intriguing, partly because he'd had no similar companions himself so it was hard to conceptualize the experience. Becky, however, had gone through a phase at three when an invisible tiger named Ticky had accompanied her everywhere, so that had given him a valuable second-hand experience. He knew that imaginary companions, outlandish though they could seem, were a normal, healthy part of childhood and usually indicated a child of above-average intelligence. It was unusual that Laura's imaginary world had come into being so late, as the more usual age for this sort of thing was between three and six, but it wasn't unheard of, especially in highly creative children

James looked at Laura. As she talked about the Forest, she relaxed. The anxiety of the previous session had entirely gone and she sat back in an open, comfortable position. Her eye contact was excellent, her smile ready.

"Torgon didn't live in the village where the others lived she said," because she was considered divine by her people, an embodiment of their god, Dwr. So she lived in a walled compound in the forest, a sort of monastery. There was another high-status holy person living there as well. His name was Valdor, but he was always called the Seer because he had divine visions. This was actually his role, sort of like an oracle. He wore long, heavy white robes with gold embroidery on the edges and he was very old when I first saw him – in his mid-seventies, perhaps. There were some women also living in the compound. Like nuns. And children. Lots and lots of children of all ages. They came from the village, from wealthy families mostly, to get an education at the compound. They were called acolytes, even though they didn't do anything very religious.

"That first night I went …" Laura gave a small quirky smile. "I was actually a bit disappointed to find out all this. Up until then my life had been all about comic books and TV shows. I was passionate about Roy Rogers and Dale Evans, and I can remember thinking, why couldn't it have been Dale Evans who popped up in Adler's lot? But it took no time at all for me to fall in love with Torgon. She was this amazing person. Very charismatic. And intelligent. Really savvy, you know? In a streetwise sort of way. But she was also very emotional. Her moods could change with breathtaking suddenness and she was never the least bit inclined to rein them in. Yet she could still be so appealing, so charming, even in the midst of the most unreasonable behaviour. I loved that about her, that complicated wildness."

"Who knew about Torgon? Did you tell anyone? Your father, for instance?"

"Kind of," she replied and became thoughtful for a moment.

"I'm hearing something more in your voice," James said. "Did your father not approve?"

"It's not so much that he disapproved. Just that he didn't get it, so there wasn't much point in telling him. I spoke to him about it, but he didn't 'hear' me, if you know what I mean."

"Can you clarify that a bit?"

She considered James's request, then nodded. "Like, for example, I remember once when I was eight. I was on my annual visit to his house here in Rapid City. I came every August to stay a week with him and my brothers. It was the highlight of my life in those days. Not Christmas, not my birthday, but that last week in August when my dad took his vacation and I got to come and stay with him.

"I slept on this rollaway bed that he put in the corner of his bedroom. For a long time, it had become my practice to go to the Forest during that period between getting in bed and falling asleep. I liked to do it then as it was a nice relaxing time and I didn't get interrupted. At the Meckses no one ever even noticed because I was up in the attic, so I'd never paid much attention to whether I was talking out loud or not. But, of course, in Dad's small apartment, he heard me and came in to see what I was doing. I remember him silhouetted in the doorway, asking, 'Are you talking to one of us?' I said no, that I was just playing.

"He came on into the room then and sat down on the edge
of the bed and said, 'You seem to be having an awfully good
time in here by yourself. What are you playing?'

"Torgon had been coming to me for about a year by then
and I was really into all the details of her life. For example, she
was the elder of two daughters and had this sister four years
younger who was named Mogri, and I knew all about the
kinds of things they had done together growing up. I knew
tons of other stuff too. The Forest society had an incredibly
rigid hierarchy of castes and which caste you were born into
counted for everything there. It determined who you were,
what work you could do, which other members of society you
could associate with. The highest caste was a religious ruling
class that consisted of the Seer, the *benna* and their offspring.
They were almost like a royal family, because they had
absolute rule. The next highest caste was the elders, who made
laws and arbitrated on civil matters. Then it was the warrior
caste, and then the merchant caste and the traders, and so on
and so forth. The very lowest caste was composed of the workers, the people who did manual labour. They weren't even
allowed to live in the same part of the village as those of the
higher castes. They were actually walled off and kept out of
the main village, except to do their work. Torgon and her
family belonged to this lowest class. Her mother was a weaver,
and her father built and repaired carts. Because she was low-
born, it had come as a huge shock to everyone – including
Torgon herself – when she was identified at nineteen as the
next *benna*. So suddenly here she was, thrown from the lowest
class to the highest. She was twenty-three at the point she had
appeared to me in Adler's vacant lot, and even then, she was
still finding it hard to adjust in her work."

"Goodness, that *is* all complex," James said, thinking these were most extraordinary thoughts for an eight-year-old to be having. Trying to envisage Becky saying things like this to him, he could easily imagine how disconcerted he would feel as a once-a-month father to find out Becky spent most of her time playing pretend games about holy people and caste systems, and worrying over an imaginary twenty-three-year-old's vocational problems.

"The thing is," Laura replied, "I did know that. By the time I was eight, I had already realized other kids didn't think about these kinds of things, or if they did, then not in this kind of detail. I didn't know why I did. I didn't know why it was in my head and no one else's, but it was. When my dad asked me what I was doing that night, it was like he had come in part-way through a movie. I was following the storyline and every-thing made sense to me, but how did I catch him up on that when he didn't know all the stuff that went before?

"And I remember that sense of confusion. I lay there, studying his face in the gloom and not saying anything because I didn't know what to say. I could tell by his expres-sion he was hurt. He thought I was keeping things back from him on purpose, that I was probably sharing these stories with the MecKses because they were my everyday folks but not with him, because he wasn't around enough. Which wasn't true at all, because I didn't share it with anyone, but I could tell he was thinking that. So I told him I was playing make-believe because I wasn't sleepy yet, and was filling time until I was.

"My dad gave me this special smile he always saved for whenever he was going to do something he thought would really please me, and he said, 'You know what? I've got a good idea. I think you deserve a later bedtime. From now on, you can stay up an extra half-hour each night. You'd like that, wouldn't you? To stay up later?'

"I said yes because I could tell he wanted me to be really happy about it, although the truth was, I didn't want a later bedtime. I preferred going to bed when I did because I wanted to be with Torgon.

"He smiled warmly. 'And one of these days, you'll grow up, Laurie. When you're little, pretending is lots of fun, but as you get older, you don't need to pretend anymore because you have real things to think about and real things are always much nicer.'"

Laura leaned back in the chair. "I remember my father kissing me then and pulling up the covers. Tucking me in, and leaving. Torgon was gone for the moment and I was there alone, lying in the darkness.

"I'd always known, of course, that people outgrew their imaginary games. By eight most of my friends already had. I'd convinced myself, however, that I was going to be an exception to this and it would never happen to me. I'd hold on to Torgon and the Forest forever. That night, however, was the first time it dawned on me that I might be wrong. Maybe I wouldn't be different, and someday Torgon would be gone.

"This huge, aching loneliness washed over me in that moment and I started to cry. I was thinking, if losing all this is growing up, then I don't want to do it. But what if I had no choice? What if the time came when I could no longer see the Forest? What if my mind stopped being able to fill up with its sights and sounds and scents? What if I was no longer privy to the complexities of Torgon's life? I remember thinking that I'd have too much mind for my head if Torgon wasn't in it.

She was different than my pretend games like Butterfly the Pony. Torgon was organic. She was not so much something I'd created as something I'd discovered. She was my other half, the part of me I needed in order to be whole. She was the union of me and not-me."

Laura's session stayed with James in a way that didn't usually happen. Part of it was undoubtedly the strangeness of this imaginary companion. People motivated to come into therapy because of the breakdown of a marriage usually talked about relationships. James had already noticed that Laura wasn't going to be drawn into conversations about Conor. He could accept that perhaps that relationship had broken down so far that there was going to have to be some new groundwork laid before Laura could be coaxed back into a bond with her son. However, as the breakdown in her relationship with Alan had been the reason she herself had given for agreeing to therapy, James had assumed that was where they'd start. That she'd chosen instead to talk about her relationship in childhood with an imaginary person was curious but also gripping.

Part of the session's staying power was also the manner in which Laura spoke. While living in New York James had made the acquaintance of several writers, mainly because Sandy thought they made impressive guests at dinner parties. He had often been less than impressed. Most had seemed joyless and unpleasantly pretentious, forever fretting about the demands of their "gift" and, in equal measure, the world's lack of appreciation thereof. Laura's dissimilarity to those former dinner guests was starkly apparent straightaway. Here was such a natural storyteller that while James didn't have trouble maintaining the appropriate professional objectivity with Laura herself, he was struggling to keep his distance from her story, to remember to stop the narrative occasionally to ask questions or analyse what was said instead of getting caught up in it.

Going over to the bookshelves in his office, James took down one of Laura's novels. He looked at the cover, which was unusually plain. The top four-fifths was pale blue and the bottom fifth was off-white. Spare as the design was, James still got a sense of the South Dakota plains from it. Too much sky against a flat, pale earth. Laura's name was in a large plain font across the top. The title, *The Wind Dreamer,* was written small in comparison and in a handwriting font at an angle that slashed downwards through the blue into the minimalist earth like a spent arrow.

Turning the book over, James looked at Laura's photograph. She was smiling. Looking directly at the camera, she had a very appealing expression. Very open. James was struck by this openness because it had not yet been an expression he'd seen in real life. What crossed his mind was that perhaps it was here, in her books, that Laura truly was most herself.

Sitting down in his office chair, he opened it.

"Hey, you!" The door to James's office pushed open and Lars popped his head in. "I'm off," he said. He paused. "What are you reading?"

James lifted the book.

Lars raised an eyebrow in amusement. "Becoming a fan?"

"Nah. Just doing homework."

"What's she actually like?" Lars asked with curiosity.

"Interesting," James replied. "Complex."

"Well, yeah, I could guess that." Lars paused. "My cousin knows her brother quite well. According to him, it was a very ordinary family. Clever. They all did extremely well at school. But no literary background, nothing especially creative. Her brother's an insurance salesman. But that's what he said too. 'She's complex'."

James nodded.

"Extraordinary talent fascinates me. Especially when it comes out of nowhere," Lars said. "I always wonder how it happens."

"Yes."

A pause.

Lars shrugged. "Listen, what I actually came in to say was: when you come over tonight, would you bring that fishing reel you bought? That one you said you couldn't get set up right? I got the rest of my ice fishing gear out last night and if we can't get that reel sorted, I found another one you can use."

James grinned. "You're determined to get me out there killing some innocent creature, aren't you?"

"Yeah, well, more just still trying to get the city stink off you," Lars said and laughed. "Anyway the game on TV starts at eight, so the rest of the guys will be coming in about a quarter to. If you want to come over with the reel a little earlier, I can have a look at it."

"Okay, see you later," James replied.

When Lars had gone, James took the book over to the conversation centre. Settling back on the couch, he put his feet up on the coffee table and started reading.

It was the story of a young Sioux named Billy, who was haunted by his native culture. Born into a family who had left the reservation for the amenities of the city, given a white man's name at birth and a white man's education, Billy was a model of "modern integration" when he assumed his post as a teacher in a community college. However, his heritage, increasingly symbolized in the storyline by the South Dakota Badlands, overarched his contemporary urban lifestyle. He began to hear the voices of "the others", of the sky and the land and the spirits of his ancestors.

The book opened with Billy's poignant efforts at fourteen to give himself a native name. Having no real connection to the spiritual tradition of his heritage, the only native naming ceremony he had witnessed was on an episode of "Star Trek". Thus it was First Officer Chakotay who guided him as he "received" his name from the only natural thing he encountered in his city apartment at that moment – the wind.

What was clever in Laura's writing – beyond the simple fact that she had a compelling narrative style that quickly drew the reader in and didn't let go – was that she was capable of creating a very substantial reality from Billy's thoughts. Initially James couldn't tell if these "others" Billy experienced were literal and Billy was having a paranormal experience, or if they were metaphorical and Billy was simply personifying his conflicts of identity.

This uncertainty bothered James at first. Gripping as the style of writing was, he was irritated at not being able to tell if he was reading a realistic exploration of the human mind or just a fantasy. Indeed, it bothered him so much that he got up and did a quick search on the internet for reviews to see how others had resolved the issue.

The reviews made much of Billy's Native American ancestry and the tendency in these shamanistic cultures to incorporate visions and visitations into their religious beliefs, often brought on by drug use, sleep deprivation or fasting. None of the reviews labelled the book as fantasy or "magical realism", so James took this to mean the spirits were all in Billy's head and reading the remainder of the book would make this clear.

James knew what the reviewers didn't, however, and that was about Torgon. Laura's vivid description of her childhood encounter loomed over Billy's experiences of "hearing" the sky or "seeing" his ancestors flying before the thunderclouds on the plains. Had the novel been an acceptable way for Laura to explore her own experiences with Torgon?

Drawn back into the story, he read on.

When James next looked up, it was 9:45. He stared at the clock in astonishment. *How* had it reached that time? The long-planned evening of beer and football with Lars's buddies would be almost over by now, to say nothing of how worried Lars would be that he hadn't shown up and that he wasn't at home or, indeed, reachable on his mobile phone, since he always left it turned off at work.

Had the phone in the front office rung at any point? He hadn't heard it, if it had. Closing the book, James stared at its deceptively plain cover.

This scared him, this unexpected enthrallment. He found it deeply unsettling that Laura Deighton's imagination had so successfully managed to overpower his real world.

Chapter Nine

"Close the door," Conor said abruptly. He was just inside the playroom. Dulcie had already shut the door and gone.

"Today you want the door shut," James said.

"Today you want the door shut," Conor echoed. There was a pause. His eyes flicked over James's face and moved on. "Shut the door," he said.

James caught the slight grammatical change and it intrigued him. Conor wasn't always echoing. He often manipulated sentences, changing their structure subtly. It was easy to mistakenly believe they were just echoes, because normally one paid conscious attention only to the meaning of conversation, not the grammar unless it jarred. Increasingly, however, James noticed that Conor was doing this.

Changing the grammatical construction indicated Conor understood the meaning of the words. But then why echo so much? Was it for safety reasons? The echoed phrase was safe because someone else had said it first. Conor knew he wasn't risking anything by echoing. Following the echo up with a subtle re-phrasing made the sentence his own.

James decided to pursue this possibility. "That's right," he said. "Shut the door. You know how to use words, don't you?"

"You know how to use words, don't you?" Conor echoed.

"Sometimes it's scary to say things that are different."

"Ehhh-ehhh-ehh-ehh-ehh," Conor replied.

"Don't worry. In here you decide. If you want to use your own words, you can. But if you prefer to use my words, that's all right too. It's your choice."

"Ehhh-ehhh-ehh-ehh-ehh."

James opened his notebook to write.

"Shut the door," Conor said tentatively.

There was a pause.

"Close the door," Conor said.

"Shut the door. Close the door. Yes, that's right," James said. "Two different words can do the same job. You're smart about words, aren't you?"

"Yes, that's right," Conor replied and James suspected it wasn't an echo.

"What's so depressing to me," Alan said at the start of his session, "is that I've already fucked up one marriage. I've been through all the shit of fighting with an ex, of losing kids, of not getting to see them grow up. Been there, done that. So I can't see how, for the life of me, I've ended up here again. I so thought I had it right this time."

"What about your life before Laura?" James asked.

"I come from a family of high flyers who've been out in Wyoming since early pioneer days. My great-granddad founded the first bank in Gillette. When he retired, his son – my granddad – became the bank president. Then when the time came, it passed to my dad, who was *his* son. So, of course, it was just assumed that I'd go into banking too.

"I did try. I went to college and got the necessary business degree. I found my trophy wife in Fran. We got married in June the year I graduated and she was pregnant with our first daughter by July. I was in the bank by August. I did everything I should. But I hated my life. The world of banking just seemed so hideously dull and dusty to me. I was crap at it because I just didn't care.

"It was through the bank, though, that I got into dealing cattle. Started out by giving loans. That's part of why I was so bad at it, because I kept lending money to these dirt poor ranchers who wanted to do something stupid like go buy some fancy continental bull like a Charolais that was completely inappropriate for Wyoming conditions. Pretty soon I was going out to see the cattle. Just checking out our investment in the beginning, but I liked going. I liked getting out of the bank. Before I knew it, I'd bought a few myself. And then I bought a small ranch to keep them on. That's what did it. Up until that point I could keep up the pretence that I was really a banker. But I was *good* at cattle. I could do with cattle what my dad could do with numbers, and I loved it. That was a new feeling for me – doing something I loved – and I loved everything about it. The sounds, the smells, being outdoors. Being successful.

"When my father found out about the ranch, he went cold as the North Pole towards me. To him it was all about the legacy, about who was going to take over the bank after him, who was going to keep the McLachlan name on the office door and I was letting him down. I wasn't living up to my obligations. I hadn't even managed to produce a son, just three daughters.

"To Fran, the ranch was an insult. It was blue-collar work in her eyes. She kept saying 'But I married a *banker*,' as if by buying the ranch, I had reneged on some deal we had. She absolutely refused to move out to the country, which was, of course, all I wanted to do. And what I needed to do, if I was going to make a decent business of it.

"I stood my ground. I was almost thirty by then. Old enough to understand you can only go so far in fulfilling other people's dreams, no matter how much you want to make them happy. But I lost a lot while learning that lesson. My relationship with my dad never did recover. And Fran and I only lasted about a year more. Then she met someone else and that was that. Which gutted me, because I had three gorgeous little girls and I hardly got to see them after that.

"So it was a lot different this time around. I went into this marriage with my eyes open and have really tried to avoid making the mistakes I made the first time out."

"How did you meet Laura?" James asked.

Unexpectedly, Alan laughed. "I ran over her foot at the gas station!" And he laughed again, a deep, full-throated guffaw. "Really. I did. I'd stopped at this place out on the Pine Ridge reservation for gas. She was already there, but she'd driven up on the wrong side of the pump. So she was trying to pull the hose around to her gas tank. I was thinking, 'Stupid woman driver', because she'd blocked the way to the other pump. I tried to squeeze my truck by and I ran over her damned foot."

James's eyes widened.

"Broke it too," he said cheerfully. "So it only seemed gentlemanly to ask her out to dinner."

"It's surprising she went after you did that!"

He laughed again. "Yeah, I thought so too. But she did. Whatever else you might say about her, she's a good sport, is Laura."

A small, wistful silence drifted in. "I can still remember our first date, that night I took her out to dinner. We went to this place called the Mill. She had the cast on her foot, so we couldn't dance or anything. We just had a meal and talked, but it was really noisy in there, so I said, 'Let's go somewhere else.' I was thinking of the Bear Butte Lounge over on the highway, because that's a nice quiet spot, but when we got in the car, Laura says, 'Let's go out to the Badlands.' That sounded a pretty strange idea to me, but I thought, 'What the hell? Why not?' It was a nice spring night. All starry. So, we went out past Wall and we parked at one of the overlooks and just sat in the car and talked.

"We talked and talked." His smile grew inward. "And you want to know what happened? We actually talked all night long. About the Black Hills mostly. I remember telling her about the ranch and my cattle, and she started telling me all these stories about how the land where the ranch was had been sacred ground to the Sioux. She was working out on the reservation at the time, so she was really well-informed on all this Indian stuff. And Laura can be such a fantastic storyteller, if you get her going."

He laughed. "I was bowled over. All I could think of was that here was somebody who thought about the land just like I did, who *loved* this country, you know, right into her soul. So we talked and talked and never did anything else. Never even kissed that night. Not once, which makes us sound like a couple of real squares, but it was so good to talk like that with someone.

"Anyway, next thing I knew, it was five thirty in the morning and we were still sitting at the overlook in Badlands, and I thought, 'Oh my god, what the hell am I going to say to Patsy?' Patsy's my middle daughter, and she was home from college for the Easter break and staying at the ranch with me. I just knew she was going to go back and tell my ex-wife I was staying out all night with women! I didn't get home until after eight, because the Badlands are a good ninety minutes away from the ranch, and there's Patsy in the kitchen when I came in. 'Good date?' she asks. And I said, 'It's all right, Pats, it's not what it looks like.' And she laughs. I could tell she didn't believe a word I said. She says, 'Don't worry, Dad. I understand.' But I knew she didn't.

"I felt protective of Laura. I didn't want Patsy to think Laura was the kind of woman you'd just take out and get it off with on the first date. So, I said, 'Pats, if you're going to tell your mother about all this, you might as well know I'm going to marry her. You can tell your mother that too.'" Alan laughed heartily. "So, that's the point when I decided I was going to make Laura my wife, although it was almost two more years before I informed Laura of it!"

"It sounds as if your attraction was pretty instantaneous," James said.

"It was. I just knew it was the right thing. Straight off." Alan looked over at James. "So now I keep asking myself: how did it all go so wrong?"

Chapter Ten

Conor's strange relationship with speech made James think of Laura, as he watched the boy moving around the room. *Wind Dreamer*'s eerie world still haunted James, hanging like cobwebs in the quiet corners of his mind to catch his thoughts at unexpected moments, pulling them back into the ghostly realm of the Badlands and the young man's quest experiences. Interesting, James thought, how she could create something so powerful with words alone. Interesting, likewise, that Conor seemed to find words so dangerous that he confined himself to naming things, describing their obvious physical characteristics or repeating things that others had already said.

While doing his usual circumnavigation of the playroom, Conor had stopped at a large basket of Lego on the floor. He paused and pushed the cat's nose into it. Reaching in, he then picked up a little Lego person. He studied it carefully. "Here is a man. With black hair and yellow shirt." Putting the man into the same hand as the stuffed cat, he bent down and looked into the box again.

"Garden things!" he cried with unexpectedly delighted surprise. He lifted up some Lego flowers.

"You sound happy that you have found some flowers," James said.

Conor bent back over the box. "*And* trees. Flowers and trees. Things for a garden." He rooted energetically through the basket.

Astonished by Conor's sudden animation, James leaned forward to watch.

"Many trees. See?" Conor said. He didn't make eye contact but he was definitely interacting with James. As he took them from the basket, he set them up on the edge of the bookshelf.

"Yes, there are lots of trees in there and you are finding them."

"There are trees on the moon," Conor replied.

This was said with equanimity, slipped in quickly as if it were nothing more than another descriptor. "Three trees on the moon."

As the toy trees ran out, Conor's cheerfulness waned. He pawed through the Lego, just in case one had been missed but said nothing more.

Finally he straightened up and began arranging the ones he'd found in a very straight line along the bookshelf. He counted them, not aloud, but with his finger.

"What's this?" he asked. It was the plastic road sheet, folded up on the shelf where he was lining up his trees.

"That's the plastic sheet with roads drawn on it," James said. "Remember? We've looked at it before. When it's laying out on the floor, children often like to drive toy cars along the roads or make houses from Lego and create neighbourhoods."

Clutching the cat to himself with one hand, Conor used the other to gingerly pull the sheet off the shelf and let it fall to the floor. It was heavy-gauge plastic, so it fell open easily, but it fell upside down. This seemed to mesmerize him. He bent and straightened the upside-down sheet out.

"The roads are on the other side," James commented.

Conor rocked back on his heels and looked at it. "I think it's the moon."

James recalled Conor's previous encounter with the plastic sheet and his odd echolalic comments regarding the moon landing. It had seemed a bizarre response. James could see no connection between the white sheet or, indeed, the plastic Lego trees and the moon.

Taking the Lego man from his other hand, Conor attempted to stand him up on the sheet. The plastic wasn't quite flat, so the toy fell over. He tried again. Again it fell over. Frustrated, he shoved the little man under the sheet until it disappeared completely from view.

This pleased him. Conor pulled it out and then put it under again in a way that reminded James of his earlier fascination in covering up toy animals with tissues. However, as with so many other things Conor had done in the playroom, an intensity then began to overtake his actions and he repeated the behaviour several times obsessively.

Obsessive and compulsive behaviour is normally associated with anxiety and James noticed the way the boy's muscles were beginning to stiffen with anxiety as he moved the figures. Conor brought a hand up and flapped his fingers frantically.

"Ehhh-ehhh-ehh-ehh-ehh. Ehhh-ehhh-ehh-ehh-ehh. Ehhh-ehhh-ehh-ehh-ehh," he cried.

"I hear your worried noise. You feel frightened when you think of the moon," James ventured.

The boy began to rock back and forth. Bringing his hand up, he waggled his fingers in front of his face.

"Conor?"

"The cat knows," the boy murmured.

James watched him. *Knows what? What does that damned cat know?*

When clarifying his therapeutic philosophy, James had come up with his mantra "in here you decide". In his experience, people only made substantial and lasting changes in their lives when they themselves actively decided to do it, but even more importantly, if they felt they were in control of doing it. So many of the difficult issues people had with life were about control.

This was the cornerstone of his approach with children, who were by default powerless, but he found it equally important to apply this principle to his adult clients. Consequently, he tried to say nothing to Laura or Alan that might make them feel he was pushing them in one direction or another.

When Laura came in for her next session, James decided not to mention that he had read *The Wind Dreamer* in case it made her feel on show as a writer.

"I'm curious about this imagination of yours," he said instead. "From what you said the other day, it's clear you spent a lot of time with Torgon and her world. How did this work out in relation to other children? Kids at school, for example. Did you have many friends when you were that age?"

"All this stuff going on in my head probably makes me sound like I must have been a lonely, friendless kid but it wasn't really that way," Laura said. "I didn't have a lot of friends, but I didn't want that. I loved my own company. With my kind of imagination, I always had something fun and exciting to do.

"I did have one really good friend and I think this was because she loved pretending as much I did. Her name was Dena. I met her in first grade and we were absolute best friends from that moment.

"We were an odd couple in some ways. While I didn't live in a conventional family setup, the Meckses were solidly middle class and everyone had solidly middle-class expectations of me. For instance, both my brothers were honours students all the way through school, so my dad expected to see straight A's on my report card too. It was all so different for Dena. She was the middle child of seven and came from this brawling, beer-drinking cowboy family who were all packed into a dinky house on the alley behind Arnott Street. Every Friday night all her aunties and uncles and cousins would come in from the country and they'd spill out into the yard, playing cowboy music on their guitars and getting drunk. Dena was a dead loss at school. She could never understand math and was always in the lowest reading group, and yet she was perfectly happy. No one in her family ever cared what she got on her report card. Often as not she forged her mother's name on it and they never even saw it. And they didn't seem to notice.

"What Dena and I did have in common were our imaginations. When Torgon came, I told Dena about it straightaway. I knew she'd understand. And she did. She thought it was wonderful. Almost immediately we made up our own game based on Torgon. We played it in this enormous cottonwood tree on the alley beside Dena's house. Shimmying up to great heights, we fought off hostile natives and tigers and bears and all the other fierce things we could think of, even though these things didn't really seem to exist in Torgon's world. Horses didn't exist there either, but even so, in our game I gave Torgon the most beautiful grey horse to ride that was just the colour of her eyes."

Laura smiled. "None of this was the real Torgon, of course. It was just our play version. Like pretending to be Dale Evans didn't resemble the real Dale Evans's life. It's hard to express that – how the game we were playing was different to the real Torgon and her world, even though both of them were inside my head. But Dena always understood the distinction."

James nodded. "She sounds like she was a very good friend."

"Yes, she was. I lost touch with her when I moved away at twelve. I've always regretted that."

The poignancy of other times, other roads not taken intruded. The small silence grew thoughtful as it lengthened.

"I suppose I did want more friends," Laura said. "In a way. I mean, I don't recall consciously wanting it, but then maybe it was just because I knew deep down it wouldn't happen."

Laura readjusted her position in the chair and sat back quietly for a moment. "I remember this one girl in particular. Her name was Pamela. She was one of those 'perfect' kids. You know the kind. They do everything right. Everyone loves them or at least longs to be like them.

"I fantasized quite a bit about being friends with Pamela. She was in the fast group in math like me, so I was sure if I showed her my science projects in the attic, she'd think they were cool. She read a lot, so I dreamed of us making plays together of stories we'd read. And I just knew she'd understand about Torgon, about the real Torgon, who was so much more than a game of make-believe in a cottonwood tree.

"My chance came in the spring of fourth grade. When I was out playing, I found a duck sitting on a clutch of eggs in the underbrush by the lake; so during Show-and-Tell, I told everyone in the classroom about how, if the duck sat on them long enough, the eggs would hatch and we'd have ducklings in 28 days' time. I must have talked quite eloquently, because afterward the teacher allowed me to stay up in front of the class and answer questions from the other kids. I was Celebrity-for-a-Day because of it.

"At recess, Dena and I were playing hopscotch when Pamela strolled over. I remember her standing beside the hopscotch diagram and watching us, her hands stuffed into her coat pockets.

"'You wanna play?' Dena asked.

"'No,' she said in a bored sort of way. When it was Dena's turn, Pamela beckoned me over beside her. 'Come here. I want to ask you something.'

"I readily abandoned Dena."

"'Can I come over to your house after school tonight?' Pamela asked. 'I'll ask my mum at lunchtime if I can come, but she'll probably let me. I want to see the duck. So can I?'

"Of course I said yes. Indeed, I was delirious with joy. I shot out of the school at lunchtime and ran all the way home to tell Ma the news. Pamela, who had never so much as talked to me in the playground, wanted to come to *my* house to play! I could hardly eat a thing for lunch, because I had so much to get ready. I rushed up to my bedroom to straighten up my things and make my bed. Maybe Pamela would want to see my horse collection or my rocks or my pressed leaves. Maybe Pamela would like to see how I could turn blue water clear, like magic, with my foster brother's old chemistry set. Maybe Pamela would feel like drawing. Just in case, I clambered up to reach the top shelf where I kept the box containing drawing paper. Then I asked Ma if she would bake some of her special peanut butter cookies that were shaped like cats' faces.

"Pamela did come. She walked home with me. She came into my house, looked at my room and had a glass of milk and cookies at my table. She wouldn't eat any of the peanut butter cats, because she said she didn't like peanut butter cookies; so Ma opened a package of Oreos for her. Then Pamela said, 'Can I see the duck now?'

"I took her down by the lake. We crawled on hands and knees into the willowy darkness and Pamela muttered about the awful smell of duck poo. The duck, sitting on her nest, hissed at us.

"'I want to see the eggs,' Pamela said. I fended off the duck and got one for her. Pamela examined it carefully. 'Can I have it?' she asked. I didn't think to say no or even wonder what she wanted it for, since she didn't have any way to hatch it. I just gave it to her. Then we crawled out of the underbrush again.

"Pamela put the egg into the pocket of her jacket. 'Okay,' she said casually, 'see you at school tomorrow.' She turned around and started walking off.

"'Hey,' I cried. 'Wait a minute! Don't you want to play?'

"She shook her head. 'No, I got to be home by 4:15. I need to practise my piano. I promised my mother I wouldn't be late.'

"'But ... but, we haven't done anything yet,' I said.

"'I only came over to see your duck eggs, Laurie. Now I've seen them, so I got to go.'

"'But don't you want to do something together?'

"'I said, I need to practise my piano.'

"'Do you want to come another time? My horse collection usually looks nicer. I polish them with hand lotion and it makes them really shiny. Do you want to come see them after I've polished them? I'd let you play with Stormfire. He's the one that's white and bucking up on his back legs. He's my best horse. When Dena and me play, I always save him for myself and she never gets to play with him, but I'd let you.'

"'No.'

"'Ma doesn't always make peanut butter cookies. Lots of times she makes chocolate chip. Do you like them better?'

"Pamela said, 'Laurie, didn't you hear me? I only wanted to see your duck eggs. I've seen them, so now I want to go.'

"I stared at her blankly."

"'Why do you think I'd play with you?" she said 'You're crazy. Everybody at school knows you're crazy.'

"'That's not true!'

"'Yes, sir,' Pamela replied. 'You talk to yourself and that means you're crazy. That's why nobody wants to play with you.'

"'I'm not crazy,' I retorted indignantly. 'And lots of people want to play with me.'

"'Just Dena. And you know what her dad does? He works at the water treatment plant. He stands in people's poo all day.' She pinched her nose. 'That's why *she* plays with you, because she's too stinky to play with anybody else.'

"'She is not stinky,' I said. 'Besides, she's not my only friend. I have lots of friends. Friends you don't even know about. Friends who wouldn't even like you.'

"'Yeah, sure, Laurie, I bet. Like who, for instance?' she asked.

"'You don't know them.'

"'Yeah, because probably you just made them up.'

"'No, sir, *real* friends.'

"'Crazy people think everything's real. They don't know any better. That's why they're crazy,' Pamela said and gave me a haughty little smile. Then she turned, let herself out through our gate and walked on down the street."

Laura paused. She leaned back into the softness of the sofa and sat for several moments in deep silence.

"The thing was, I *wasn't* lying," she said. "This is what people always kept accusing me of. That what I experienced wasn't real, and therefore it had to be lies. Black and white to them. Real or unreal. Truth or lies. But it wasn't like that. I *wasn't* making it up. It wasn't false. There *was* another world there. Like ours, but different. I could see it but, for whatever reason, they couldn't. I don't know why. But that didn't make it unreal."

There was a long, reflective pause.

"I remember learning about bees when I was in fifth grade," she said softly, "about how bees can see beyond the visible colour spectrum. Humans look at a white Sweet William flower, they see it as plain white. To us that's true. But if a bee looks at the same flower, it sees intricately patterned petals. That's because bees can see on the infrared spectrum beyond what human eyes can. The pattern is there for them, but it's invisible to our eyes. And when I read that, I remember thinking, 'That's *just* like it is with the Forest.' Simply because we can't see the pattern on the flower, that doesn't mean the bee is lying. Because I can see the Forest and other people can't, that doesn't mean I'm lying."

Laura stopped speaking and looked at James. Again the silence, spinning out around them like thread.

"I've been trying to figure out how to share this whole thing about Torgon with you in a way that shows the vibrancy of it all; how something can be real and unreal at the same time and so beautiful. Because if you can't get a sense of that, then it does quickly reduce what I'm saying to nothing substantial …"

Her breath caught and James sensed a sudden upsurge in emotion. He didn't speak. He let her rest in her feelings without pressure.

Finally, Laura leaned forward and lifted her handbag off the floor. "I did a lot of writing when I was younger. Recording Torgon's world. That's how I learned to write, trying to capture all that. So I was thinking … perhaps if I gave you some of the stories …" She lifted a small sheaf of typewritten pages from her bag. "I thought maybe this would give her world more immediacy for you than my third-person account of what was going on … it would make it easier to understand what I was saying …"

James reached his hand out. "Yes, that's a good idea. I'd like that."

"They aren't all that well-written. I was a teenager when I did most of them."

"I'm sure they'll be fine."

"They're just stories. Events that happened in Torgon's world. I'd see it and then I'd write about it as a way of understanding it better. That's what I always used writing for. To make sense of things."

Chapter Eleven

It wasn't until that evening when James was home that he had time to look at the material Laura had given him. It was old. James recognized the uneven pressure of a manual typewriter in forming the words, and that the edges of the pages themselves were yellowing and gently foxed, as if turned many times.

Pouring a glass of wine, adding another log onto the fire against an unexpectedly stormy autumn evening, James sat down and began to read.

There was a knock at the door, but without waiting for an answer the acolyte pushed it open.

"It's dark in here," she said with sudden surprise. This was Loki. She was only eight and had just been sent to the compound to start her life as an acolyte. She hadn't mastered the rules yet.

"Usually one waits outside the benna's quarters until given the command to enter," Torgon said and then added, "and when an acolyte does enter, the first act is obeisance."

Loki flapped her hands in frustration. "Oh, I am sorry. I always do it wrong. What do you wish I should do now? Go out and come in again?"

"No, just remember it for next time."

Loki glanced around inquiringly. "It is very dark in here, holy benna. Did you not notice? My mother says one shouldn't work in darkness for it offends the eyes."

"Aye, your mother's right," Torgon said and threw back the coverlet to rise.

Loki's eyes went wide, "Holy benna! You have no trousers and no boots!"

"I returned during the heavy snow. My trousers became wet, so I've removed them to let them dry more easily."

"I didn't know you would have legs like everybody else," Loki said, astonished. "Or feet. For feet are very ugly, don't you think?"

Torgon laughed. "I am all over just as any other woman, Loki, ugly feet and all."

The girl blushed. "Oh, I did not mean offence to your feet!"

"My feet are not offended. Nor am I, not by your words nor by my feet. Before Dwr chose me as his benna, I was a worker's daughter and had much need of my feet for standing on, when toiling in the fields."

"You were a worker's daughter? Truly?"

"Aye. So this is why one must always tend one's tasks with pride, for Dwr takes as much pleasure in good work as in good breeding."

Loki nodded.

"Anyway," Torgon said, "it is in my mind you must have come here on a task, Loki, for I did not bid you come."

"I was sent to say the evening meal is ready."

"Ah, well. Say to the Seer that I shall take no food tonight."

"*Why? Is something wrong with you?*"

Torgon grinned. "*You are* very *new among us, aren't you*"?

The girl ducked her head. "*I'm sorry. Am I not supposed to ask you questions?*"

"*Well, perhaps not quite so many.*"

Within moments of Loki's departure, the Seer entered. "*You are unwell? What overtakes you?*"

"*No real illness, Just a minor grumbling, but my stomach wants a rest from eating.*"

The Seer came over and leaned down very close to Torgon to scrutinize her face. She looked back at him, studying his watery old man's eyes, as it would be unseemly not to meet them. Clasping her head firmly between his hands, he probed her jawline with his fingers. "*We shall burn the cleansing oils tonight,*" *he said.* "*I can feel evil building in your bones.*"

'*I'm all right, truly,*" *she managed to say, as he kept his grip on her face.*

"*Then you'll come into the dining room as usual. The soup is thin so will sit easily enough in your stomach.*"

Torgon said, "*I have no hunger and fear feeling worse, if I should eat. Send an acolyte with a bowl of soup here to my cell and if I am well enough, I shall eat it.*"

"*You* will *eat it,*" *he declared.*

"*If I feel well enough.*"

"*You will* eat *it. You have gone too thin since you've come here and I fear you're full of worms. So it is of no matter if you bring the soup back up. Better if you do, in fact, for then I shall have the chance to see which worm infests you.*"

*   *   *

It was Loki who came. She unlatched the door and then backed into the room, carefully carrying the wooden bowl, trying not to let the thin broth spill.

"You have forgotten yet again to knock," Torgon said gently.

"Oh!" the girl cried in despair. "I beg your pardon." Her shoulders sagged. "It's just there are so many rules here and I am not yet used to them. Shall I go back out and knock?"

"No,"' Torgon said. "But, yet again, please try harder to remember. You'll get a nasty cuff about the ears if a holy woman catches you not waiting for permission."

"Why do you not cuff me?"

Torgon managed a smile. "Perhaps I shall when I am feeling better."

The girl smiled back. "I think not. I think you care not for cuffing, for I've never seen you do it."

Nausea swept over Torgon again, and she took a deep breath to quell it.

"You look most unwell, holy benna," Loki said and set the bowl of soup down on the small table near the window. "I had the retching illness once," she added cheerfully. "I brought up my stomach twelve times in just one night. And then each of my brothers took it. I have four brothers."

"You have a large family. Your parents are much blessed."

"My father is a mighty warrior of the benita *band and pleased to have so many sons."*

"He'll be pleased to have you too, for it is the nature of fathers to love their daughters well. And your mother will be grateful for your help in caring for so many men."

Loki smiled.

"You must miss your family now that you are here," Torgon said.

"Yes, a little," she said, then glanced up nervously. "Is that wrong of me to say?"

"No. It is natural, because you love them. I missed my family too when I first came to the compound. Indeed, it often made me cry at night."

"It did?" Loki said, shocked. "Didn't your mother teach you not to? Did she not say it would shame your father if you cried?"

"My father is a worker. He does not shame that easily."

"Truth be said, holy benna, I do find a little water in my own eyes sometimes. I didn't say for fear you would be angry with me." A pause. "Truth be said, holy benna, you are much different than I thought you'd be."

"For one thing, you thought I'd have no legs!"

Loki laughed. "It's just I thought you'd be even more frightening than the Seer is, since you are holier than he. I thought you'd have no wish to speak with little children."

"Not so. Indeed, I find your talk makes me feel rather better."

"Truly?" Loki asked with a surprised smile. Then her small face brightened. "You know what you should do? Ask holy Dwr to make it so you won't fall ill. That would be good, not so?"

"Except I couldn't," Torgon replied.

"Why not? You're godly. And to my mind it isn't a very godly thing to bring your stomach up."

Torgon smiled. "But I am not a god."

"The laws say you are 'god-made-flesh'. That's why we must do obeisance to you."

"Aye, but god-made-flesh means I am the same as any other person."

Loki's brow furrowed. "How can that be so?"

"What point is there in being flesh, if a god does not experience all of what being flesh entails? That includes falling ill. And *bringing up one's supper. So, you see, it wouldn't be right to ask Dwr to spare me this, for this is how Dwr wants me."*

Unconvinced, Loki pondered.

"Besides, illness isn't Dwr's domain. Dwr governs the realm of consciousness, of choice and good and evil. All else is in Nature's great realm and even holy Dwr can not change the laws that Nature's given."

"But is not illness a kind of evil?" Loki asked, "for otherwise why do we call in the wise woman to frighten off bad spirits? Are they not evil? Would that then not make it part of Dwr's domain? And therefore should we not fight against it and try to change it to make the world a better place?"

Torgon raised an eyebrow. "Be careful with your speech, little one."

Loki ducked her head. "I'm sorry," she said quickly. "Have I said something wrong again? It is a fault of mine. There is so much to learn here. So very many rules. I'm not good at it. I fear that I must not be very clever."

"It is not that you are not clever, child. Your real problem is that you are."

"How old were you when you wrote that story?" James asked at the start of Laura's next session.

"I can't remember now exactly," Laura said. "I didn't start putting the stories down on paper until in my mid-teens, but I remember very clearly how old I was when I first experienced it. Eleven. I even remember the day. It was a Saturday morning in the fall and that afternoon Dena and I got together to go to the park. I remember us perched right up at the very top of the monkey bars, sitting there like a couple of sailors in a crows' nest, just talking. Adolescence was very much on

Dena's mind by that point. She was telling me how she had been counting her pubic hairs and then asking me if I had any starting to grow. As Dena was talking, I remember gazing off across the park at the trees flickering gold in the sunshine. Torgon wasn't with me at that moment, but for no particular reason the glinting sun on the coloured leaves made me think of her.

"I said, 'I feel like I'm going to explode sometimes.'

"'How come? What's the matter?' she asked.

"'Torgon and stuff. The way Torgon's world sort of lays down over everything I see. It's like a transparency. So that everything here has a kind of layer of that world over it.'

"'You're *still* playing that?' Dena asked, surprised. Because she didn't realize. The winds of change had long since blown through our relationship. By the time she was about nine, Dena was no longer interested in pretending, so, slowly it stopped being part of what we did together. I had to explain that yeah, I did still have it all in my head.

"I said, 'It's never gone away. I still hear them all the time, talking to each other. I hear everything Torgon says. Even what she thinks and doesn't say aloud. I hear her thoughts. I feel what she feels.'

"'Weird,' Dena said. 'How do you do it?'

"I shrugged. 'I dunno. It just happens.'

"'Know what?' she said brightly, 'I got this picture of your mind like one of them big radar dishes that they track satellites and alien spaceships and stuff with, kind of turning back and forth, picking up these weird voices.'

"'No, it's more ordinary than that,' I said. 'More like I'm just in the next room and can hear them talking through the walls, and then I can go in their room, if I want.'

"'Okay, so do it now,' Dena said. She wasn't challenging me. She was just curious. She said, 'Go where Torgon is now and let me see you do it.'

"Immediately I was in Forest. I didn't even have to do anything. It just appeared before me. Torgon was in the altar room with the Seer. It was later on the same evening that she'd been talking to Loki but now she was busy with some part of the holy rituals. I looked back at Dena and said, 'There.'

"She said, 'Oh give over, Laurie. You didn't do anything.'

"I said, 'I did. You asked me if I could go where she was and I have.'

"'Oh, give *over*, Laurie.'

"I was annoyed because I knew she thought I was just making it up. I said, 'OK, so I'll tell you the whole story about what was going on right from this morning. About how Torgon was in her room when this little girl named Loki came in and Torgon wasn't feeling good. She felt sick to her stomach. And you know what, Dena? When she felt like that, it sort of made me feel sick to my stomach too. I could feel what she felt.'

"'Did she puke?' Dena asked. 'Did you see her puke?'

"'Dena, stop it. I'm trying to tell you something serious.'

"'Yeah, well, so did she puke? That's what *I* want to know.'

"'In the end, yeah, but so what?'

"Dena's eyes got wide. 'Wow. *Weird*. You got somebody puking in your brain.' She paused a moment, shaking her head. Then she looked over at me. ' I got to tell you something,' she said.

"'What's that?'

"'Well, I don't think you ought to go around talking to a lot of people about this. It's okay with me. I understand you because I'm your best friend.'

"'I don't go around talking to a lot of people,' I said. 'Just you.'

"'Yeah, well, the reason I'm saying this is that … I hate to say it, Laurie, but you *do* sound sort of nuts when you talk about this.'

"'But I'm not. You know that.'

"'Well, yeah, I know,' she said, 'but sometimes when you're talking to me, I got to remind myself of it.'

"Then without even a pause Dena said, 'Know what Keith Miller did in Miss MacKay's class yesterday? He came up behind Sally and ran his hand right down her back to see if she was wearing a bra.'

"As Dena spoke, I remember watching the light through the leaves again, autumn gold against autumn green, fleeting, flickering colours, and wondering, *what is real*? What determines if something exists? And I remember I could still feel that faint, sickish feeling."

Chapter Twelve

At the end of his next session, Alan said "I want talk about the possibility of your seeing Morgana too. That was part of the package, wasn't it? Part of how it works in here?"

James nodded.

"Good. Because like I said in that first session, Morgana is already starting to do stuff I don't want her to get in the habit of."

Alan paused. "Shit, isn't it awful to hear me say that?" He grimaced. "To even consider the possibility that we've fucked up two beautiful, innocent kids? That's not saying much for us as parents, is it?"

"Don't think about it that way," James replied. "It's important not to focus on problems in terms of ownership. I know that's a very popular attitude these days, but it's narrow-sighted, because nothing happens in a vacuum. The family is a milieu and Morgana is part of the family. So it's natural she's both affecting and affected by what's happening."

"Okay."

"This is the reason I find it so important to include parents and siblings in therapy when I work with a child."

Alan said, "It's also because I can see what you are doing is helping Conor and I want that for Morgana too." He smiled. "I *am* beginning to notice changes. Just little things, but they're there. Sometimes, for example, I can tell Conor's listening to me. He's not quite as much in a world of his own."

"Conor's doing well in here," James said. "We're moving slowly, but it's steady. He's definitely starting to be more responsive."

"That is so great to hear," Alan said with feeling. "It would just be the best moment of my life, if we can turn Conor around."

At the start of the next session Conor went straight to the shelves and pulled the plastic road sheet out. He scanned it with the cat and then laid it on the floor upside down so that its plain white surface was uppermost. He ran his hand over it, smoothing it out flat. "Eh-eh-eh. Whirrrr. Brr-brr-brr."

Pushing his hand underneath the sheet, Conor left it like that for several moments. Then he began to move it here and there, like a kitten under a blanket.

"Terria," he murmured and lifted his hand out.

"Pardon?" James asked.

"The Taurus-Littrow landing," he replied and smoothed the sheet out with his hand. "There is no grave here. Where's the man?"

James wasn't able to follow the boy's train of thought at all. He jotted down "Taurus-Littrow" and a phonetic spelling of the word "terria" in his notebook.

Conor looked up, looked right at James. "Here is terria." There was a certainty to his speech that James hadn't heard before and with it a slight urgency, as if he could perceive that James didn't understand what the word meant and that this worried him. It also gave Conor's words a definite sense of communication.

"Here is terria," Conor said again. He patted the upside-down road sheet. "*Terria*. Yes, that's terria. Where's the man?"

"Do you mean the toy man? That you were playing with last time?" James asked. "He will be in with the other Lego toys. There. In the basket."

Conor's shoulders sagged in such a clear gesture of defeat that James knew he hadn't made the right guess. He felt a bit defeated himself because despite Conor's so obviously wanting to tell him something, he just couldn't get it.

Giving up, Conor rose and left the white plastic mat on the floor. The cat clutched to his chest, he wandered towards the large windows. Until this point, he'd always ignored them. Now he stopped and looked out. Several moments elapsed in silence.

"Where's the man in the moon?" Conor asked.

"We can't see him at the moment, because the moon hasn't risen yet."

Alarm spread over Conor's features. He lifted the stuffed cat up and pressed it against his face. "Eh-eh-eh-eh-eh-eh."

"I hear your worried noise," James said. "You don't like not being able to see the moon?"

"Where is the moon man gone?"

"You mean the men who landed on the moon? They're not there anymore. They landed on the moon a long time ago, but now they are back home on earth."

"The man in the moon can see us, but we can't see him. He can see us. Eh-eh-eh-eh-eh."

"Do you feel afraid of the man in the moon?" James said gently. "He isn't real, Conor. There isn't a real man there. It's just patterns on the surface of the moon and when we look at them from earth, it looks like a person's face to us. But there isn't really a man in the moon."

"The Taurus-Littrow landing site. 1971," Conor cried out.

"It's confusing, isn't it?" James said in an effort to interpret Conor's fear. "We say 'man in the moon' to talk about how the moon looks to us from earth, but that isn't talking about a real man. It's just an expression. But then there have also been astronauts who have walked on the moon and they are real men. But they didn't stay on the moon. It's too barren. No one could live there. So now they've all come back home to earth."

The boy started to cry. "No! Don't want the man in the moon to come home!" Pressing the stuffed cat over his face, he crumpled, sobbing, to the ground.

Unlike the boisterous, self-assured child James had seen chasing Becky through his apartment, Morgana stood in the waiting room, clutching her father's hand tightly and regarding James with a suspicious gaze.

"Hello," James said. "How nice to see you again."

She pressed herself against Alan's leg.

James offered his hand. "The playroom is this way. Why don't you come with me and I'll show you."

Reluctantly Morgana kissed her father goodbye and took James's hand. He walked with her down the short hallway from the waiting room and opened the door to the playroom.

She hung back a moment and peered in, then stepped cautiously through the door. No matter how much he coaxed her, James couldn't talk her into coming further. Closing the door gently, he crossed to the small table and sat down.

"I've never seen a doctor's office that looks like this," Morgana said dubiously as she surveyed the playroom. "Dr Wilson's is lots different."

"Dr Wilson and I are different kinds of doctors. He's the kind who helps us keep our bodies well. I'm the kind who helps us keep our feelings well."

She glanced over. "Does your kind of doctor give shots?"

"No, not usually."

A look of enormous relief crossed her face. "Oh *good*."

"Were you worried that I might give you a shot?" James asked.

Nodding fervently, she said, "*Yeah*, 'cause I thought *all* doctors gave shots." She smiled sheepishly. "So I didn't like coming in here by myself. If I was going to have a shot, I wanted my daddy here too."

She looked around the room with more confidence. "There's sure lots of toys here. Do all these belong to Becky and Mikey?"

"No. Their toys are at my house. The toys in this room are for the boys and girls who come here to see me."

"Like my brother, huh?"

"Yes," said James, "and today, like you too. So, while you're here, you can play with anything that interests you. It's up to you. In here, children choose what they want to do."

"*That* sounds nice." She gave him a cheerful grin. "What's that?"

"My notebook. I like to write notes to help me remember what we've been talking about."

"How come?"

"Because perhaps we've been working on solving a problem and I wouldn't want to forget anything important a child has told me," James said.

Placing her hands flat on the table, Morgana leaned forward on them and looked at James closely. Her eyes twinkled. "Know what my brother does?" Her tone was conspiratorial. "He piddles in the garbage can in the kitchen because he thinks it's a toilet." She laughed heartily. "But that's a secret. Don't say to my mum I told you."

"Why not?"

"Because my mum would say it isn't nice to tell you." She laughed again.

James laughed too.

"I told Becky. She said Mikey piddled in the bath once. She said he even did a Number Two once and it floated."

"Yes, I'm afraid she's right."

"Boys can be *really* disgusting."

James nodded.

"How come Becky doesn't live with you all the time?"

"Because Becky's mum and I are divorced. Mostly Becky lives in New York with her mum, because that's where her school is and her grandma and grandpa and her cousins. But even though things didn't work out between Becky's mum and me, I still love Becky – and Mikey too – just as much as always, so we want to spend time together too. That's why she and Mikey come out here."

Morgana's smile had faded. "My folks are doing that too. Getting divorced, I mean."

"How do you feel about that?" James asked.

"I don't want them to."

"Can you tell me more about it?"

"At school I know this girl named Kayla, and when we were in kindergarten, her folks got divorced. Now she only gets to see her dad two days a month and sometimes he forgets. I don't want that to happen to me. I really love my daddy a lot."

"Of course," James said.

"You don't ever forget Becky, do you?"

"No. Dads never forget their children, even if they can't always see them."

"There's something else too about why I don't want them to get divorced," Morgana said.

"What's that?"

"Our ranch. 'Cause I love our ranch. I really, really, really love our ranch and I want to live there forever. Even when I'm grown up. I'm going to be a rancher like my dad. But my mum says when she and Daddy are divorced, then me and Conor can't live at the ranch anymore because we'll live somewhere else. But I don't want to. But then I want to be with my mum too."

"You have some big worries."

"Yeah," Morgana replied, her brow wrinkling, "I do."

She watched James's pen as he wrote. "Except, know what?" she said. "Kayla says she's gets two Christmases now. First she gets one with her mum and then she gets another with her dad and his girlfriend. And know what else? Santa Claus comes to *both* places!" Morgana gave an impish smile. "I wouldn't mind *that* part."

James smiled back.

Turning from the table, Morgana looked around the room. "You sure got a lot of toys in here. It's like a toy store, practically." She wandered away to see what she could find.

After exploring the variety of toys and materials in the room, Morgana settled on nothing more exotic than a piece of paper and a box of crayons. These she brought over to the table and then sat down opposite James. Selecting a blue crayon, she painstakingly wrote her name in large, rounded letters.

"There. I've done that well, haven't I?" she said in a pleased tone and showed it to James. Then she selected a green crayon. She appeared about to draw but then instead went around the letters of her name again with the second colour.

"Guess what?" she said. "I can read."

"That's very good."

"I'm in the best reading group at school. Even though I'm just in first grade, I get to read real books. Not the baby books they teach you with."

"Yes, real books are more interesting, aren't they?"

"I knew how to read when I was only three."

"Obviously, reading is a strength for you," James said.

"Know something else though?" Morgana said brightly. "My best friend doesn't know how to read at all."

"When you're six and just beginning, sometimes reading can be very hard," James said.

"Oh, he isn't six. He's eight."

"Some children find reading much harder than others."

Morgana selected a third colour and went around the letters of her name again. "No, it's not 'cause he finds it hard. It's 'cause him and his cousin are homeschooled but they don't get taught reading. He says no one at his house knows how to read."

"That's very unusual," James remarked.

"Well, I thought so too. I didn't believe him at first. 'Cause I thought, there aren't any grown-ups who don't know how to read. But he's right. He really doesn't know how to read. He doesn't even know the alphabet. So guess what?"

"What's that?" James asked.

"I said I'd teach him. I'm going to bring him one of the books from school."

"You're a very thoughtful friend."

"It's 'cause him and me are best friends. We play together all the time. Every day almost."

"What kinds of things do you like to play together?" James asked.

"Kings and queens, mostly. That's our favorite game." She burst into unexpected laughter. "He's *so* silly. Know what he says? He says when he grows up, for his job, he's going to be a king. For real. He really thinks that! I told him he couldn't be, because there aren't any for-real kings anymore, 'cause they only happen in fairy stories. But he said I'm wrong. And you know what? I asked my mum and she said that's true. There *are* for-real kings still, although she said she didn't think anybody in South Dakota could get to be a king." Morgana laughed merrily. "So now I tease him. I call him the Lion King."

"Why do you call him that?"

"'Cause I just told you. 'Cause he wants to be a king when he grows up."

"I mean the 'lion' part," James said.

"Well, two reasons. One reason: because he's got long hair like a lion's got. His hair comes clear down to his shoulders like this." She demonstrated. "Really, it looks just like girl's hair, but I don't want to make him feel bad, so I call it lion hair. And reason two: because he's always being a cat."

"A cat?" James said, intrigued. "How does he do that?"

"Well, *pretending*, of course," she said with a laugh. "We always meet down by the creek. That's where we play. If he gets there first, then he hides in the rocks and jumps out at me and tries to scare me. He goes 'Rowrrr! Beware of me! I'm the Great Cat!' He means a mountain lion. But I don't get scared. I just chase him around!" She laughed again merrily and gestured with her hands.

A pause followed. Morgana looked down at her paper. Throughout her conversation, she'd continued to embellish her name with different colours. "Look. I made it like a rainbow." She lifted the paper up to show James. "See, I know the colours of the rainbow. I know the colours in the right order. Want me to say them? Red, orange, yellow, green, blue, indigo and violet."

"That's very clever of you," James replied.

"Yeah, I'm smart. I can tell you my IQ. It's 146. I know, 'cause my folks got it tested." She pursed her lips. "I'm not supposed to tell people though, 'cause my mum says it makes my head swell up. But you're a doctor, so I thought you might be interested."

James smiled at her. "Do you know what an IQ is?"

Morgana sucked her lips in between her teeth and rolled her eyes around, then a shrug and a grin. "Not really." Then her brow furrowed in a pensive expression. "But I do know you got to have one if you're smart. And that it's what makes you do good at school."

"Yes, I suppose you could say that," James replied.

A small pause.

"So can I ask you something?" Morgana tipped her head questioningly.

"Yes, of course," James said.

"I don't know what Conor's IQ is, but I know he's got one too, 'cause you know what? He knew how to read even younger than me. He was only *two*. My dad told me."

"That's pretty amazing," James said.

"But this boy who rides the school bus with me says Conor's retarded."

"How does that make you feel?"

"I don't care that he says that, 'cause it isn't true. 'Cause Conor could read when he was two. So it can't be true and you can't make something true just by saying it."

"Yes, you're right."

"But what I want to know is then how come Conor doesn't go to school like I do and get good grades? If he's got an IQ, how come he's like he is?" she asked.

"That's a hard question to answer," James replied. "We're made up of lots of different things and our IQ is just one of them. So sometimes even if our IQ is good, something else needs help."

"I wish he could be more like a real brother," Morgana said wistfully.

"You would like a real brother," James reflected.

She nodded. "I wish he'd take care of me. He's nine. That's three whole years older than me, but you know what? Most of the time *I* take care of *him*."

"I can see why that would be hard," James said.

"And he scares me."

"How does he do that?"

"At night in his bedroom. He talks to himself and I can hear him through the wall."

"And that frightens you?" James asked.

She nodded. "Yes, because he always talks about the ghost man. That's how come Conor's got to adjust his wires all the time, because his cat sees the ghost man coming. So Conor stays up all the time. Talking and adjusting. Sometimes I go in and try to get him to go back to sleep, but then he wants me to sit inside his wires with him. He says if we sit in the wires, his cat will save us from the ghost man."

"It sounds like you and Conor talk quite a bit," James said.

Morgana nodded. "That's 'cause I listen."

"And does Conor say who this ghost man is?" James asked.

"It's the man who lives under the rug."

"I see. And have you noticed anyone living under any of the rugs at your house?"

"No," Morgana said. "They're just ordinary rugs."

"Yes, I think that's right. Conor gets confused about things," James said gently. "It's probably best not to pay too much attention."

"Yeah. That's what my dad tells me too. He says that these are just Conor's words for his feelings in his head. But still it makes me scared. I'm little and he's big and so, really, he should be brave to me, but instead I got to be brave to him. And it doesn't matter what I tell him. Conor keeps waking up in the night, worrying. He keeps saying the cat's seen the ghost man in the hallway and if we aren't careful the man will come and get us."

Chapter Thirteen

"Everything changed the year I was twelve," Laura said at the beginning of the next session. "I started junior high. The new school was in the opposite direction from the primary school, so when Dena and I walked home together, we reached her house first and I had to go the last two blocks alone.

"My foster brother Steven started to lay in wait for me in the alley between Kenally and Arnott Street. We'd always had problems getting on. He was a year older than me and the only one of my foster brothers I had any trouble with, but he could be really mean. My dad said I should just ignore it, that it was probably just jealousy, since he was the fourth of four boys and then I came along and stole all the attention; but fact was, Steven had problems with a lot of people. He was always getting into trouble at school.

"When I was younger things between Steven and me were tolerable, mainly because I was as strong as he was and a lot more coordinated, so I could give as well as I got, if I had to. But by junior high he had beefed up to where he had a real size advantage.

"Anyway, he started ambushing me those last two blocks home from school. If other boys were with him, they usually didn't do much more than push me down and then run away. Once this one kid, Bruce, kicked my lunch box and broke my thermos, but mostly it was just scrapes and bruises.

"If Steven was on his own though, it was worse. All he could think of was sex. So if he pushed me down, then he'd sit on me and try to pull my panties off. I could usually escape by wiggling out of them, but then he'd run after me, waving them and throwing them down wherever he wanted.

"One afternoon, I saw Steven waiting with these two other boys named Jimmy Hill and Loring Bardon. I knew they meant trouble, so I tried to evade them by going down by the lake. I was a really fast runner in those days, lots faster than Steven, and I knew way more shortcuts, so I was normally pretty successful at getting home safely. I thought I was going to manage it this time, because I'd used a secret path along the lake that hardly anyone knew about. Then just as I was coming up to our fence by the back alley, I heard Steven shout 'Charge of the Light Brigade!' I threw down my school books and ran back down the slope towards the lake, which was a big mistake, because I tripped in the long grass and fell.

"They were immediately all over me. Loring held down my arms and Steven climbed on top of me. Jimmy was standing up above us, laughing and kicking dirt at my face. Then Steven said, '*Let's do it.*'

"Jimmy said no right away, but Steven was already starting to unbuckle his belt.

"I began to cry. Steven was a big boy by then. He was thirteen already and built like a Mack truck, so there was no way I could push him off. Besides, there were three of them. But

Jimmy held out. He said, 'I don't think we ought to do this, Steve.'

"Steven said, 'What's the matter with you? Can't get a hard-on?' And he wasted no time. He had my panties down and his dick out and he did do it to the best of his ability.

"I screamed when he tried. This scared Loring into letting go of my arms, but it didn't make any difference to Steven. He put a hand over my mouth and came down really close and said, 'You're not going to tell anybody, are you?' and the way he said it, it was a threat. He smiled at me then, just a little bit, and said, "Cause you're Nobody. And nothing's happened, if it happened to nobody."'

"How awful for you," James said sympathetically. "It must have been very frightening. Did you tell anyone?"

"Two Sundays later my dad came for his usual visit. He was alone, like he usually was by then. My brother Russell had already graduated from college and was working in Sioux Falls. Grant was a junior at Stanford. So I hardly ever saw them anymore. It was just Dad and me. But nothing had changed. Dad still took me down to the same diner for the same roast beef dinner. On that Sunday I can remember us sitting across from each other in one of the green vinyl booths. The expanse of Formica tabletop between us felt enormous to me.

"'You seem very quiet today,' Dad said after we'd ordered our meal. I didn't reply, so he asked if I was feeling all right. I just sat there. All during the previous two weeks I'd been planning to tell him about what Steven had done that day. I'd played the scene over and over again in my head, figuring out just what I was going to say, just how and when, but once Dad was actually there, I didn't know how to start.

"Finally, I said, 'Dad? Am I ever really going to get to come and live with you?'

"He said, 'Yeah, sure. Of course, Laurie. I'm working on it right now.'

'When?'

"'Well, where I'm at now isn't really very big. You're used to this nice house and this enormous amount of ground to play in and the lake ...'

"I said, 'I don't really care about that. I'd be okay in something smaller.'

"'Plus, we need to get a nice mum for you,' he added.

"'I'm old enough to not need a mum to look after me anymore,' I replied. 'Grant and Russell were my age when they lived with you and they did okay without a mum. I wouldn't be a lot of trouble, Dad, I promise. Please, can I come live with you now?'

"'Why? I thought you were happy here with the Meckses.'

"'I hate Steven,' I said. 'Steven Mecks. I call him Steven Sex.'

"My dad didn't ask why.

"The waitress came then with our roast beef dinners. Dad put ketchup on his meat and started eating. I wasn't hungry. I thought maybe I had a bug, because all of a sudden I felt like I was going to throw up. But I didn't. I just sat, staring at the food.

"My dad suddenly smiled and leaned across the table. In a very conspiratorial tone of voice, he said, 'Well, I do have special news. There *is* someone I'm close to, Laurie. Her name is Marilyn and I know you're going to like her. She has nice black hair and is very pretty.'

"At the mention of black hair, I saw Torgon instantly. The thought of Torgon coming to rescue me felt good. It cheered me up. My dad said, 'But you've got to give me a little more time, Laurie. Another six months. Maybe then you can come.'

"Less than two weeks after that Sunday with my dad, I was upstairs in my bedroom. It was a Friday night and quite late. I'd been reading in bed and then I turned off the light to go to sleep. That was still my best time for going to the Forest, that period between lights out and falling asleep, because I was relaxed and would often drift off from Torgon's world right into dreams.

"Then ever so softly, my door creaked open. Steven's form appeared indistinctly out of the darkness. I sat up and told him outright he couldn't come up into my bedroom. That was my private space and I had the right to tell him to get out. He ignored me completely and crawled onto my bed.

"I said I was going to scream for Ma and Pa. He reached out and grabbed my hair with one hand and put the other over my mouth. He said, 'You yell and you're going to be in big trouble.'

"I broke free and tried to leap out of the bed but he caught hold of my pajama top. 'Listen, Laurie,' he said, 'you do as I say. If you don't, I'll kill Felix. I mean it. If you don't do as I say, you'll find his bloody little body right here on your bed waiting for you tomorrow night.'

"Felix was my kitten. He was the runt of the litter, a little black-and-white ball of fur I'd lavished hours and hours on over the summer, nursing him back to health. I absolutely worshipped him. He was so sweet-natured. And so trusting. He would never realize he shouldn't let Steven pick him up.

"So, when Steven pushed me down on the bed that night, I let him because of Felix. He pulled down his pajama bottoms. His dick stuck out from his body like a coat hook. A dinky coat hook. It'd hardly grown yet. He was this great big boy and he had this dinky little dick. But he didn't care and certainly the size didn't matter to me. It was just as awful, being small.

"When he'd finished, he left and I just lay there in the darkness. The worst part for me actually wasn't that Steven had raped me, because he'd already done that to me before. It was that he had threatened Felix. Felix would never be safe again. Nor would I. I was now trapped into doing whatever Steven wanted. In that one stark moment I realized things on Kenally Street had changed forever. I knew then I could no longer stay.

"I waited breathless in the darkness until I heard absolutely no sounds in the house below. Then I ventured out and tiptoed downstairs. It was almost two o'clock in the morning by that time. Going into the kitchen, I took the telephone receiver down from the hook. I dialled my dad's number.

"A woman's sleepy voice answered.

"Thinking I'd made a mistake, I hung up right away and dialed the number more carefully. Again the same woman answered, her voice still sleepy but now also annoyed-sounding. 'What do you want?' she asked. I said, 'Is my dad there?' She said, 'You've got the wrong number. Please don't phone here again,' and hung up.

"I put the kitchen light on to see what I was doing and then dialled again, very carefully.

"And again she answered. So before she could hang up, I said, 'My dad's name is Ronald Deighton. Is he there?'

"There was a pause. I could hear the woman saying, 'Ron? Ron? Wake up. It's for you.'

"Then 'Hello?' and it was my dad's voice. I started to cry with relief. I said, 'Dad, you've got to come get me. Right away.'

"All hell broke loose when I told my dad what had happened. I'd phoned him at 2:15 in the morning and by eight a.m. he was at the Meckses' front door. This absolutely horrible scene followed with Ma crying and my dad shouting at Pa about getting the police. Steven was sitting on a chair at the kitchen table and looking so scared that I actually felt sort of sorry for him.

"'Get your things, Laura. You're coming with me,' my dad said at the end of it.

"How I'd *longed* to hear him say those words. *You're coming with me*." She shook her head sadly. "I dashed upstairs with a suitcase and started pitching clothes in. I put in some of my plastic horses. Not many of them would fit, but I wasn't very concerned. No matter. We'd get them later.

"The importance of what was happening only started to register when I went to take down a mobile that was hanging over the little gable-end window. I saw the lake through the window, the sun skittering over the ripples near the shore. Suddenly I wondered what it was going to be like not living on the lake anymore. A terrible sense of loss washed over me in that instant. Then Dad shouted up the stairs and the feeling passed. I was soon lugging my suitcase to the car.

"My dad said to hurry up, that he had to be back in Rapid City by lunchtime, so I put my suitcase in the car. Then I said, 'Wait a minute. I've got to get Felix.'

"My dad said, 'Who's Felix?'

"'My kitten. You know. I told you about him in the summer,' I said. 'Just a minute. I'll get a box for him.'

"My dad shook his head. 'You can't take a cat with you, Laura. We live in an apartment building. They don't allow any pets.'

"I started to cry then. It was Felix I'd done all this for. He was the only reason I'd told anybody about what Steven had done. How could I now leave him behind? But I had to. There was no choice.

"The Meckses didn't come out to say good-bye when it was time to leave. They remained in the house. As I got into Dad's car, however, I could see them gathered around the window in the living room, all of them, even Steven. They didn't wave; they just watched. On the front porch Felix sat with his ears pricked forward, watching too.

"I remember pausing at the gate, looking at the house, at the Meckses in the window, at Felix on the step, and I knew at that moment that whatever else might happen to me, that however happy I might be again in the future, I would never be happy in quite the same way as I had been there. Leaving Kenally Street was childhood's end for me. Even at twelve I recognized it as that."

"'There's something I need to tell you,' my dad said to me as we left the Black Hills behind and sped down the interstate towards Rapid City. 'Remember how I mentioned Marilyn to you the other week?'

"'Yeah,' I said.

"'Well, Marilyn and I decided to get married.'

"'That's great! When?'

"'Well, actually,' he said, 'we've already done it.'

"'*When*?' I asked, stunned.

"'I meant to tell you. There just hasn't been a good chance.'

"'How could you *not* tell me something like that, Dad?'

"'I meant to.'

"I spent the remainder of the journey bewildered. Trying to reconcile this unknown Marilyn into my long-held fantasies of living with my father was impossible because I knew absolutely nothing about her except that she had black hair.

"As it turned out, this was probably just as well, because nothing could have adequately prepared me for the person who greeted us at the other end. When we pulled into the carport at my dad's apartment building, out came this *girl*. She was only five years older than my brother Russell, tall and slim and pretty in an insubstantial way. She had this little puff of black hair on top of her head, done in a bouffant like Jackie Kennedy's, and her eyes were very round and filled with a dazed sort of happiness, like the expression on a Tiny Tears doll.

"When she saw me, she cried a little too enthusiastically, 'Welcome! Oh, welcome, welcome! So, you're little Laurie! And oh, and aren't you pretty? Look at your nice hair!'

"I stared at her in disbelief. She was probably the only person in the universe to ever say I had nice hair, because basically it was a long, greasy straggle the colour of dog sick.

"My dad had told me I could have my brothers' room, since both of them were away from home by then. He took my suitcase in and put it on one of the two twin beds, telling me I could choose which one I wanted. The room was smaller than our bathroom on Kenally Street and crammed full of Grant's and Russell's things. The window looked out onto the brick wall of the apartment building next door. I remember sitting down on the bed and looking around me and thinking that somehow this wasn't how it was supposed to be.

"I never went back to the house on Kenally Street. Ever. The Meckses packed up the rest of my things, and my brother Grant stopped by and picked them up for me. I didn't go with him. I never saw Ma or Pa or Steven or Felix ever again.

"Once I was settled at Dad's, I had to go through my belongings and get rid of lots because my new bedroom was just too small. There was no space for my collections or my projects. For a while, I set some of my horses up on the dresser beside Grant's model planes, but I always felt funny when I looked at them. One night when Dad and Marilyn were out, I collected the horses all together and threw them one by one down the wall incinerator in the apartment building. I don't know why. Maybe I just outgrew them. I don't know for sure. All I do know is that I had this overwhelming urge to get rid of them, so I did, and I've never really liked horses since."

Chapter Fourteen

A shriek of pure panic rent the darkness. Sudden and electric, a lightning bolt of sound shook James from a deep, dreamless sleep and sent him hurtling for the doorway well before he was awake enough to know what was happening. Frantically, he groped for the light switch in the hallway.

"Becky? Becks? Wake up, honey. You're having a bad dream." James said as he came into the spare bedroom where she was sleeping with Mikey.

Mikey was already sitting up in his bed. "It's not a dream, Daddy," he said through the darkness. "She's having a terror."

"Becks?" Sitting down on the edge of the bed, James drew his young daughter close. "Daddy's here."

"I'm gonna put the light on," Mikey said and climbed out of his bed. "That's what Mum always does."

Becky clawed at James, clutching his pajama top so fiercely that the hairs on his chest were caught in her grip. The overhead light came on. Becky's eyes were wide open, but she didn't look at James. She didn't respond to his voice. Instead, she screamed and thrashed against him.

"Shh-shh-shhh," James whispered. "I'm here. Daddy's here."

Mikey stood beside the bed, his face puckered with worry. "I wish she wouldn't do that," he murmured.

"She's all right. She'll go back to sleep in a moment and she won't even remember it."

"How come she never remembers?"

"Because that's how it works," James said. "Know how I know? Because when I was a little boy, sometimes I had night terrors too."

"How come it happens?" Mikey asked.

"Well, it usually happened to me because I got way too tired, and that might be what's happened to Becky too. You two had a long journey today and we stayed up pretty late."

"Oh."

"But sometimes it happened to me," James said, "because I was feeling upset about something and didn't know how to say it. Has anything been upsetting Becky lately?"

Mikey drew his shoulders up in an exaggerated shrug. "I dunno."

Slowly Becky's distress quieted. She blinked vacantly and James could tell she still wasn't awake. "Shh-shh-shhh," he whispered and smoothed back the hair from her face. "Close your eyes, sweetheart. It's time to sleep."

At last her eyes drifted shut and she fell silent. Very gently, James lay her back on the bed and pulled the covers up around her.

Rising, he turned to look at Mikey. "You too, cowboy. Come on. Under your covers." He tucked his young son in, pulling the blanket right up to his nose.

"Will you leave the light on?"

"Let's turn this overhead one off because it's too bright. I'll leave the hallway light on instead. How's that?"

"Okay."

James laughed. "You look like a Furby, lying there. All I can see is sticky-up hair and two great big eyes looking over the edge of the covers." He leaned down and kissed Mikey's forehead.

Mikey didn't smile back. "I'm looking like I'm a Furby 'cause I'm scared."

"And what makes Furbies scared, huh?" James asked gently.

"I don't like it when Becky does that. It's got me all woke up now and I'm scared to be here by myself."

"Well, you're not by yourself, cowboy, because Becky is right there. And I'm just down the hall. Really close." He smoothed Mikey's hair. "But I'll tell you what. You scoot over and I'll lie down with you until you're not feeling scared as a Furby anymore, how's that?"

"Will you stay 'til I go to sleep?" Mikey asked.

"Yes, 'til you're safe and sound asleep again."

James lay down in the twin bed and pulled the blankets up. Mikey snuggled in close. Cheek pressed against Mikey's head, James's nose was filled with his little-boy scent, a faintly saline mixture of baby shampoo and something warmer, like the smell of sunshine on an old wooden floor.

They lay in cuddly silence for several minutes. In fact, Mikey remained still for so long that James assumed he'd fallen back asleep. He shifted in preparation to go back to his own bed.

"Daddy, don't go," came Mikey's small voice.

"Are you still awake?"

"Yes. I can't sleep."

"Why's that?"

"I'm scared."

"With your daddy right here?" James asked and drew his small son in closer against him. "There's nothing to be scared of."

"Daddy?" Mikey asked after several quiet moments.

"Yes, Mikey."

"I wish we lived here."

James hugged him tight. "Yes, I wish you did too. With all my heart. You're my best boy and girl in the whole world."

"Why can't we?"

"Well, because you've got everything back East. Mum's there and your school and all your friends."

"We could go to school here," Mikey said.

"But you'd miss Grandma and Grandpa. And all the cousins. And going to the beach."

"I don't like Uncle Joey," Mikey said.

"Why's that?"

Mikey sighed. "I don't know."

"Does he do anything to make you not like him?" James asked.

"No. I just don't. I like him all right in the daytime, because he buys us stuff. But not in the nighttime. That's when I want you."

"Yes, that's when I want you too," James said. "And in the daytime as well. It's hard, isn't it, when Mum and I don't live together. When I live out here and we don't get to see each other very much. I feel bad about those things."

"Yeah," Mikey said. "Me too."

* * *

Long after Mikey finally fell asleep, James remained in the small bed with him. It was he, now, who was wide awake.

He had instantly recognized Becky's night terror for what it was, not only because it was quite a common phenomenon among the children he worked with; but because, indeed, as he'd said to Mikey, he had suffered them himself for a while when young. He didn't remember anything about them other than vague, formless sensations of fear. His parents' distress when talking about his night terrors had always been much more upsetting to him than the experience itself.

But when had Becky started having them? How was it that Sandy had never felt it significant enough to mention to him? It made him feel isolated and impotent.

And certainly the little conversation with Mikey afterwards hadn't helped any. What was he doing out here, so far away from his own children? How could he spend his days helping other people's children and so completely ignore the distress of his own? How did he balance his own needs and his kids' needs against the needs of others? That was the real question.

James finally slipped silently from Mikey's bed. He spent a moment looking at the two sleeping children. Smoothing out Becky's bedding, he bent and kissed her. She turned away in the darkness. He then kissed Mikey, who never stirred.

He went out into the kitchen to make a hot drink. While the milk was warming, he noticed the folder of stories Laura had given him sitting on the kitchen table. James picked it up and riffled through the typewritten pages. He couldn't sleep. This seemed as good time as any to take a break from reality.

So taking his cup of cocoa into the living room, he sat down in the recliner and began to read.

The year Torgon was nineteen, she and Meilor celebrated their betrothal at the midwinter feast. Then came the month of snow and with it the coughing illness known as Old Man's Chest. Word spread among the workers that it flourished in the holy household and the benna herself had fallen ill with it. And so it happened that in the last month of winter the holy benna died.

All the acolytes were sent home to observe the official mourning period with their families and await the selection of the new benna. When Mogri returned to her home among the workers' huts, she was dismayed to find her mother at the loom, making, of all things, the feasting robe for Torgon's wedding.

"Mam, it is not seemly that you should work. It is the benna's mourning period."

"Dwr loves busy hands as much as he loves bennas," Mam said off-handedly and continued weaving. When there was no answer, she turned. Seeing Mogri's worried face, she stretched out a welcoming arm. "Do not heed everything they teach you there. What happens in these next days is only meant for higher born. It will have little consequence for us."

What Mogri's mother meant, of course, was that the holy choosing would have very little to do with workers. They'd be allowed to watch the ceremony from the palisades and, if luck was with them, at night the sector gates would open and the workers could go in among the feasting tables to clear up what the higher castes had left. But that was all.

Then the unthinkable had happened.

Mogri and Torgon had been sleeping in the back room midst bales of wool for Mam's weaving stacked high around their pallet to keep the winter draughts away. The midnight knock, when it came, had terrified them. Certain that it would be drunken warriors come to take their pleasure among the worker girls, the sisters had clung together, pulling the hides up over their heads in hopes that if their father could not keep the bar across the door, no one would find them there.

Neither of them expected to see the light of holy candles fall across the mud-packed floor, nor glimpse the holy Seer, clad in flowing robes, the golden circlet on his head, looking like a god himself as he came in the room. But there he was. Da pulled back the hides to show him where they lay and the Seer's sacred dagger glinted in the light. He reached down and wrapped his fingers through Torgon's hair. Seared into Mogri's memory of that night was the look on Torgon's face as the Seer pulled her to the ground to cut her hair: a look of desolate bewilderment, a look hares have when they are trapped and know that certain death awaits.

It had felt most peculiar to Mogri when returning to the compound to know that Torgon resided now within the holy cells as the divine benna. Theirs was a close family and she and Torgon had been inseparable. They'd played together and shared their food, fought and argued and suffered all the petty jealousies that any sisters do. Mogri had thought many things about Torgon during their growing years together, but holy had not been one of them.

Three months passed and in that time Mogri did not see her sister once. The Seer explained that the new benna communed with Dwr. and awaited the coming of the Power. This unsettled Mogri. The new benna sounded strange and austere, as if she were someone Mogri had never known.

Then one night while Mogri was on her pallet in the acolytes' sleeping area, she heard a noise in the washroom, an odd, uneven rasping sound that did not filter clearly through the thick stone walls. Mogri rose up on one elbow to listen better.

On the adjacent pallet, Linnet moved. "What're you doing?" she whispered through the darkness.

"I'm listening to that sound in the washing room."

"Aye, I know. It's disturbing me too."

Then Minsi on the other side asked sleepily. "Why are you talking?"

"Someone's being noisy in the washing room," Linnet said.

"Ignore it."

"I've tried. I can't. And it's woken Mogri too. Whoever's in there should be cuffed."

"Don't be stupid," Minsi replied. "It'll be the divine benna or the Seer and you can't cuff them."

"I've cuffed the divine benna plenty in my day," Mogri offered.

"Aye, as a sister. But she's not your sister now. So go back to sleep. Both of you. And stop your talking or it's we who'll be cuffed." Then Minsi rolled over on her other side and pulled her cover up.

What was the noise? Mogri could not ignore it. It came now as a more syncopated sound, but remained too muffled through the walls for Mogri to make out.

Perhaps the Power had come over Torgon, Mogri thought. She had no idea what the Power really was, only that holy bennas had it. So who knows how it might show itself? Perhaps it would cause Torgon to fall down and writhe the way Mogri had seen a man do once within the marketplace.

Or perhaps it was not the Power. Perhaps Torgon had fallen ill and these were the sounds of her emptying her stomach.

If Torgon had fallen ill, Mam would be so upset. She'd always fretted over Torgon so. At the slightest sneeze she'd burn the *cleansing oils until the house and everybody's clothes would reek and once she'd even brought in the wise woman for Torgon's chest. It had cost Da more eggs than he could find in a full turning of the moon. Mogri still remembered going with him to the cliffs to pilfer from the nests of the high-flying hawks.*

If there was something wrong, Mogri knew she should try to help. Mam would expect that of her.

Did she dare? They were forbidden to leave the sleeping quarters without permission.

Cautiously she rose and tiptoed noiselessly through the rows of sleeping acolytes and out the door. Silent as a shadow she moved past the rooms where holy women slept, past the Seer's cells.

Light was seeping from beneath the door of the holy benna's cells. Mogri paused, then without knocking she simply lifted up the latch and entered.

Torgon was in the inner cell. When she saw Mogri, she jumped in surprise and gave a small, startled cry. Mogri jumped herself because at first glimpse she didn't recognize her sister.

"Is that you?*" she queried, squinting hard against the light.*

Torgon had grown gaunt and pale, and her hair, completely shorn the night the Seer had come into their family's hut, was barely more than stubble now, giving Torgon a boyish look. Only by her eyes, still pale as the winter sky, did Mogri know for certain it was her sister, and on seeing them, she knew too what caused the noise. Torgon had been crying.

"Whatever are you doing here?" Torgon hissed. "You must go. Immediately. This is my private cell. No one's allowed in here but me."

"But I'm your sister, Torgon." No. No, she wasn't. Not any longer. Dwr had stripped Torgon of all human ties when he had made a god of her.

"You shouldn't use my name," Torgon said, her voice grown softer. *"You must get used to that or the Seer will take his stick to you."* She brought a hand up and wiped her eyes. *"And you must go. Or he'll take his stick to me."*

"I heard you in the washing room and feared that you were ill. I only came because I worried."

Lowering her head, Torgon said wearily *"Thanks for your concern, but I am well. Go now, quickly, before someone notes that you are gone."*

"You look not well to me. Truth is, you look most unhappy to my eyes. Here. Take the comfort of my arms."

"Mogri, I'm not playing at some game. I am the holy benna now. You must not touch me."

"No one is here to see. What would it matter between the two of us?"

"Things are different now."

"Do you want them different, Torgon?"

"No," she said piteously and began to weep again. *"But if the Seer comes at me just one more time, I know I'll break."*

Crossing the room, Mogri sat down on the bed and gently put an arm around Torgon's shoulder. *"You're worker kind and made of tougher stuff than he."* She leaned near to kiss her sister's cheek. *"And you are still my sister too, no matter what the teachings say. Da's blood runs yet in both our veins, and even Dwr can not change that. I will not give up the right to call you by your name. I love you much too well for that."*

Torgon didn't answer. She only sat, her head still down.

Mogri glanced sideways at the fine, embroidered cloth of the benna shirt. She looked then at Torgon's stubbly hair and tentatively brought a finger up to touch it. *"Does it itch, when it's growing out like that?"* she asked.

In spite of herself Torgon turned her head and smiled. "Silly question, Mogri. Only you would think to ask it at a time like this."

"Well, so? Does it? It looks as if it would. And I must admit, I don't like it much. Such a style doesn't suit your face."

"Do you forget I didn't have a choice?"

A small silence came then. Torgon snuffled noisily and gave her eyes a final dab, examining the tears on her fingertips before wiping them on her shirt.

"What's it like?" Mogri asked. "Being the divine benna, I mean. Being holy. Do you now feel very different than when you lived with us?"

"No."

"'No? So did you *always feel holy?*" she asked in surprise. "Because if you did, you kept it very well disguised."

Torgon grinned. "No. Hardly, Mogri. I never felt that I was holy. Truth be said, I don't feel holy now."

"It's a most astonishing thing. You must admit. Mam still can't believe it's happened. But Da, he's quite adjusted, and he's so proud of you."

"Don't talk of this. You'll make me cry again." She lowered her head and brought a hand up over her eyes. "Do you know what night this should have been? My wedding night. This very moment I should be wearing that beautiful robe Mam had on the loom and dancing with Meilor at our marriage feast. Look me instead, sitting here, not knowing what to do, not knowing who I am. Not even fit," she said, gesturing to her shorn head, "to be called a woman."

"Doesn't the Power tell you what to do?" Mogri asked. "For I'd rather assumed it would."

"Power? What *Power? What is the Power anyway?*" Torgon asked. "I don't know. I wasn't taught that in the fields. nor when working at the loom."

Mogri sat in bewildered silence.

"*You know what my life is like?" Torgon asked. "If it is daylight I am not allowed to leave this room. If it is night I am not allowed to sleep. I may not even approach the window, if it's not the Seer's wish. The only soul I see is him. The only human flesh I feel is his when under guise of holy rites he relieves his lust with me. Otherwise, I sit. Alone. Each day, all day, and every day. 'Communing with Dwr', the Seer calls it. But what is that? I wish I knew. For my part I'm only sitting. And when I'm not sitting, I am with him. And if I don't do things exactly as he says, he takes his staff to me, as if I were naught but a stupid cow in need of breaking to the yoke.*"

"*And Dwr allows this? Because the divine benna is holier than the Seer.*"

"*I don't know what Dwr allows. I don't know anything except that I am suffering. Why has this happened to me, Mogri? I never aspired to anything more than being my mother's daughter, who knew happiness in work. How is it that I am now on this other path?*"

Chapter Fifteen

"Look at the marbles!" Morgana said, holding up a jar.

James grinned and nodded.

"You got such good stuff in this room." She brought the container over to the table. "There's a million colours. Aren't they pretty?" Taking the lid off, she put her hand in to swish the marbles around with her fingers. "I got some like these, but they're not so nice. I put mine in the fish tank."

Morgana lifted the container up to eye level and peered through them. "Know what? If you look through them like this, they make everything look wavy and green and pink and blue. You want to try?" She held the jar out to James. "Here. See the way they make everything look."

James obliged.

Tipping her head, Morgana watched him. "Can you tell me something?" she asked.

"What's that?"

"What exactly are you supposed to do with marbles?" she asked.

"There used to be a game of marbles. I don't know if children play it anymore, but I played it a lot when I was your age," James replied.

"Oh, I like games!" Morgana said enthusiastically. "Will you show me how?"

Leaving his chair, James beckoned her down on the carpet. He took a handful of marbles and felt unexpected pleasure at the sensation of the small spheres rolling around in his hand. Marbles had been hard currency on the playground of his youth and he'd been good at the game. He could still remember the gratification of winning steelies off the other boys, of their clicky weight in his pocket.

Morgana wasn't so impressed. At six she didn't have the coordination necessary for good control and her efforts at shooting resulted in their rolling off her finger unpredictably. After a few moments of playing, she said with strained politeness, "It's an okay game."

James rose and dusted off the knees of his trousers.

"I can tell you who *would* think these were neat, though," she said, stirring the jar of marbles again with her hand. "The Lion King. He just loves to play games like this. There's this game he plays at home with his cousin and he showed me how. It doesn't need anything you buy. We were down at the creek, so he showed me how we could play it using stones and drawing the game board design in the dirt. So I bet you he'd just love these marbles."

Putting the lid back on the jar, Morgana returned it to the shelf.

"Guess what?" she said as she came back to the table.

"What's that?"

"Me and the Lion King had a bad argument. I got mad at him."

"Why was that?" James asked.

"'Cause he can be really stubborn sometimes." Pulling out a chair at the table, Morgana sat down. "If you don't agree with him, he won't listen."

"That sounds annoying."

"It is. I was going to do this really nice thing for him. We got this book about tigers and how they're getting endangered and stuff, and it's got lots of really good pictures, so I knew he'd like to see it. I was supposed to put the book back, 'cause Mum said I wasn't to take it outside, but I didn't. I snuck it under my sweater like this," she said, demonstrating with her hands. She laughed conspiratorially. "Then I went really fast out the door and down to the creek to meet the Lion King.

"So, when he got there, I said, 'I brung you this book,' and I told him I wasn't supposed to, but I'd done it anyway because I knew he'd want to see. And know what he said? He said, 'You shouldn't have stoled it.' I said, 'I *didn't* steal it. It belongs to my family and I'm part of my family, so it isn't stealing.' He says, 'You still shouldn't have tooken it.' He says, 'You shouldn't never get knowledge by stealing it.' So I got really mad at him."

"You took a risk to bring him something nice and it felt like he didn't appreciate it," James said.

"Yeah."

"How do you feel about it now?" James asked.

"I'm still mad at him because he doesn't understand. He likes to see pictures of lions and tigers and things and these were really good. But he wrecked it. He wouldn't even look at the pictures. We just fought with each other."

"You must have felt disappointed too, as well as mad," James said.

She nodded. "He's always telling me off. He says when you're born you got a plan that makes you part of things and you're supposed to follow it. You can choose *not* to follow it and that's called free will. But really, you're supposed to use your free will to choose *to* follow it because that's the right thing to do."

"*How* old did you say the Lion King was?"

"He's eight."

"He sounds like a very unusual boy."

"That's just the kind of stuff him and his cousin learn. A man comes to their house to teach them, but all he seems to teach them is about being good and bad. The Lion King says he's got to learn it to make him a good king when he grows up."

"And yet this man doesn't teach him how to read?" James asked.

"No. The man doesn't know how to read." Suddenly Morgana's face brightened. "But guess what? The Lion King knows all his letters already. I taught him the alphabet song."

"Does his cousin come to play with you too?"

"No, she stays at home. We don't want her anyway. It's a secret, him and me playing together."

"Why is that?" James asked.

"We don't want anyone to know we see each other. So don't tell, okay? I've only told you because you said I could tell you secrets."

"Your parents don't know about this little boy?"

"No."

Concerned, James said, "I'm not sure that's a good idea, keeping a secret like that from your parents"

"My dad wouldn't like him."

"Why's that?"

"He's got long hair," Morgana replied. "Daddy says boys with long hair are hippies and he doesn't like hippies 'cause they camp on our land without asking. So he'd tell me not to play with him. Then he'd say, 'How come are you playing with a boy anyway?' He'd want to know why he doesn't have any friends his own age to play with. It takes too much 'splaining to tell my dad stuff."

"What about telling your mum?"

"My mum's got too much else to think about. Besides, I like having secrets."

"Some secrets are not good to keep," James said. "I'm thinking your parents may feel very worried if they find out you have friends they didn't know about. I think they should know."

"No, I don't think so. I never go where I'm not suppose to. I'm just down by the creek. I'm allowed there 'cause it isn't very deep, and I always tell them when I go out to play. And the Lion King would never, ever hurt me."

"Here is paint," Conor said. "Coleman School Supplies," he read on the side of the jar. "Blue. Blue finger-paint. Coleman School Supplies."

"You read well," James said.

"You read well," Conor echoed.

"Perhaps today you would like to finger-paint. Have you ever done it?" James asked.

Conor looked up briefly. "Blue and red and green makes brown."

"Yes, I suppose they would."

Conor picked up a jar of red finger-paint and unscrewed the lid. He sniffed it. Very gingerly, he touched the surface of the paint with one finger. "Jelly."

"Because it's finger-paint, it's very thick," James explained.

"The boy will paint," Conor said decisively.

"Shall I get you some paper?" James asked. "Or would you like to get it yourself? The paper for finger-painting is kept right there. Then we need to put some water on it first so the paint will work."

"A brush!" Conor replied abruptly. "The boy won't use messy paints."

"Today you don't want to finger-paint. You prefer to paint with a brush."

"Yeah." He set the jar of red finger-paint down on the shelf.

"The brush paints are over there in the tray of the easel," James said, pointing.

Whirring softly, Conor went to the easel. Picking up a brush from the yellow paint, he made a broad smear across the paper.

"Here is what isn't," he said and added another broad stroke of colour.

James didn't quite understand, so he didn't comment.

Conor turned slightly towards him. He seemed to be aware of James's confusion because he said, "Here is what *isn't*. Now is. Now is colour. Now isn't 'isn't.'"

"You are telling me that there wasn't anything there before?" James asked. "But now you have made something. You have created something that wasn't there before."

"Yeah. It isn't 'isn't.'"

There was a very faintly detectable note of pleasure in Conor's voice at the word repetition. A glimmer of a sense of humour? Conscious word play? This was sophisticated thinking.

Conor stepped back to regard his painting and said, "Where is 'isn't' gone?"

When James didn't answer, Conor turned around. His eyes rested briefly on James's face. "Isn't there," he said. "'Isn't isn't' isn't there." And smiled.

When he came to pick Conor up after the boy's session, Alan asked, "Can I have a word? Do you have time?"

James nodded. "Yes, come on back to my office. Dulcie? Could you mind Conor for a few moments?"

Alan said, "I've got something really great to tell you. Over the weekend I was out in the corrals by the house, fixing one of the water troughs. Conor was just hanging out with me, and all of a sudden this dead leaf was blown into the water in the trough. I didn't notice it right away but then Conor says, 'There's a maple leaf.' Clear as day. Just plain as anything. That's how he said it. Then he got a stick and fished it out.

"I haven't heard him speak like that – you know, in a *conversational* way – in years. Actually, not since he was a toddler. And he just said it so normally – 'There's a maple leaf.'"

"That's excellent news," James said warmly. "That's a real breakthrough."

Alan smiled self-consciously. "I mean, I suppose it's not much. My nine-year-old kid manages a complete sentence. Hardly like he's ready for Harvard. But ... you can't imagine how amazing it is to hear him say something normal."

"I don't want to sound over-optimistic here," James said, "but I have begun to seriously question the diagnosis of autism. It's understandable how it came about, given his rigid behaviour and echoing. But the truth is, the longer I work with Conor, the more convinced I am that we need to start thinking outside the box."

Alan's eyes widened.

"While he does show some distinctly autistic-like behaviour, overall he's a more flexible and imaginative thinker than youngsters on the autism spectrum typically manage. I'm seeing moments of abstract thinking that would be quite extraordinary even in a normal nine-year-old. I've certainly never seen it in an autistic child."

"Are you saying what I think you're saying?" Alan asked, his voice going soft with hope. "That he could get better?"

"Perhaps it's wiser just to say that I am feeling more positive every time I see Conor."

"*Wow*. That *is* fantastic news. It really is," Alan replied.

"I could really do with a chance to pick your brain, though," James added. "This morning I was re-reading Conor's file and looked through some of those reports from the in-patient unit that diagnosed him with autism. But I feel I'm missing a really clear picture of what was going on for Conor at that point. Not so much his behaviour as what was happening in the world around him then. You gave me an idea during our first meeting, but I'd find it very helpful if we could talk about it in more detail."

"Sure," said Alan and he crossed over to sit down in the conversation centre. After a pensive moment, he said, "It was Hell. For me it was the ranch. It started with an unusually cold spring, so I'd already lost calves and had huge feed bills. Then in June, I had a bad outbreak of TB among my cattle and the ranch ended up being quarantined. I had to slaughter almost a quarter of my herd and I wasn't allowed to sell any of the rest until there was an all-clear. As you can imagine, I got in the red very quickly. Seriously in the red.

"Up to that point, Laura and I had always pretty much kept our finances separate. We'd just kind of fallen into that pattern and it worked well for me, because I never wanted people thinking I'd married her for her fame or her money. Not that Laura was ever that wealthy, but you know how people think. Anyway, that year it got to the point where I had to admit how bad things were to her, because I was going to go bankrupt otherwise. I had to borrow money from Laura to keep things afloat until the quarantine was lifted, which made me feel like crap.

"Conor hadn't really been a problem before this. He was a sensitive kid. And a bit of a mama's boy maybe. Laura adored him so she fussed over him a lot. I decided to start taking him out on the ranch with me some, just to give him a little time in a man's world. I'd sit him up in front of me in the saddle and we'd ride together."

"How old was Conor then?" James asked.

"I dunno. Hardly been walking. Eighteen months, maybe? But he loved that. He was just the most enthusiastic little guy then. And smart. I'm not just saying this because I'm his dad. He really was quick to learn things, and he'd remember everything you taught him. Like, for instance, he loved the wild birds, and so I'd tell him their names. He'd sit in the saddle and say, 'Bluebird, Daddy! Meadowlark!' and he was always right. He was a little sponge."

Alan's expression darkened. "Then everything started to change …

"It was strange how the change happened," he said. "The first thing I noticed was that Conor started getting clingy. Not all at once, but a bit more and a bit more until it got serious. Until he got to the point where it wasn't Laura hanging onto him all the time, but instead him hanging onto Laura."

Alan ran a hand over his face and let out a long breath. "Laura and I had been married about three years by then and the honeymoon was very definitely over. I'm not saying our marriage was on the rocks or anything. We were doing okay. But I'd realized by that point that the woman who'd sat there talking to me all night in the Badlands wasn't really the woman I married."

"How do you mean that?" James asked.

"What I'd loved about her that night was how easy and open she was. But once the first glow of love wore off, I realized that like an iceberg, nine-tenths of Laura is below the surface, that most of her is just never going to be visible to me."

"So in saying nine-tenths is not visible, are you saying you feel that Laura was shutting you out of large parts of her life?"

"Well, I don't know if it's purposeful. That's the trouble. I don't think she does it to hurt. It's just that everything's a story to her. Real and unreal blend together so seamlessly in her mind that you never know which is which. You never know if what she is saying is authentic or simply her version of things and has no substance. It's like a mirror image. Like a reflection of what's real.

"When we first married, I didn't even appreciate it was happening, but after a while I started catching her out. And they are often the silliest little matters, but she just seems to want to keep this labyrinthine maze around herself for the sake of doing it. You ask her something and if she's in the mood, she'll tell you the truth; if she's not, she'll tell you whatever story's in her head. After a while it just felt evasive to me.

It gives me the feeling that she doesn't *want* me to know what's really happening to her."

"Can you give me an example of this lying behaviour?" James asked.

"I can give you a very good one. It was during this time when I had all this stuff going on with the ranch and my financial problems and Conor was starting to go downhill. I discovered something pretty strange. I answered the phone one day and this policeman was on the other end of the line. They wanted to talk to Laura about an injunction she'd just taken out. I'm, like, *what*?!" Alan stared at James. "It turns out, Laura was being threatened by some demented fan. He was actually stalking her. But she never told me a *single* thing about it. Never mentioned it once. Can you imagine that? Doesn't that seem weird?"

"Do you suppose that with Conor and your financial problems and everything, she was simply trying to protect you?" James asked.

"This guy was threatening her *life*. And I'm her *husband*, for Christ's sake. She was being so supportive of me during this financial crisis on the ranch. She never criticized me or made me feel like I was failing her, so I thought we were really close. I mean, doesn't it seem bizarre to you that someone who lives with you, who ostensibly loves you, wouldn't share this kind of thing with you? That's bringing self-reliance to new heights. And it made me feel like shit when I found out. I was already feeling half a man, and now she wouldn't even let me give a hand in protecting her."

Silence followed.

"I think this added to Conor's problems," Alan said. "He's such a sensitive kid. I'm sure he must have picked up on

Laura's anxiety about this guy. Maybe this was why he started getting so clingy at that time, because he sensed she was threatened and her fear made him afraid.

"Anyway, once I knew about the stalker, I didn't mess about. I got hold of the police myself and told them they better make sure that injunction worked, because my deer-hunting rifle was right there in the cabinet beside the phone and I had absolutely no qualms about defending my family. That worked, because this guy buggered off after that and we never heard from him again."

Alan leaned back into the soft cushions of the sofa. "So you get the picture of what I'm dealing with."

James nodded. "Yes, it does sound like Laura's behaviour is challenging. And like that was a very stressful period in all your lives."

Alan sighed. "And then right in the middle of everything, Laura got pregnant with Morgana. It was the last thing in the world we needed right then. We were so desperate for Laura's income. Plus, we'd already made the decision not to have more kids. I'd actually wanted Conor to have a brother or sister, but one was enough for Laura. She wanted to go back to her writing. That's her real world. And since I already had three girls from my first marriage and now a little boy, I caved in. I agreed to get a vasectomy and I did.

"Anyway, I guess you're supposed to keep on using protection for about three months after the snip. It takes a while for all the sperm to die off apparently. We didn't figure out what had happened initially. She was four months along before the possibility of pregnancy even crossed our minds.

"But wow. Laura was *so* upset when the test came out positive. She was absolutely adamant she was going to have an abortion. I kept telling her we'd manage. No, it wasn't a good time at all to be bringing another child into the family, but to be honest, when I found out she was pregnant I was thrilled. Then everything got taken out of our hands, or so we thought, because before she could arrange the abortion, she miscarried."

Alan shook his head in faint astonishment. "Just goes to show you how some things are meant to be. The fact is, Laura *did* miscarry. She had a horrible experience. Lots of pain, lots of blood loss. She was really unwell for about six weeks afterwards, so it was a shock to find out after all this she was still pregnant. The doctor told us it had been fraternal twins and she only miscarried the one, which is something we'd never realized could happen. But Morgana hung in there. Laura carried her to term and she was a strong, healthy baby. And despite all our struggles beforehand, we fell in love with Morgana immediately. Both of us. And, of course now we are so grateful we have her. Morgana is just such a gift."

James smiled. "Yes, she's a little character, isn't she? I'm thoroughly enjoying my time with Morgana in here."

"I'm glad we've decided to bring her in," Alan replied. "I know things haven't been easy for her either. She's so worried about the divorce. And I know that sometimes Conor takes so much of our attention that Morgana misses out."

"Yes, I got the impression she plays on her own quite a lot," James said.

Alan nodded. "Yeah. But saying that, I don't think she's lonely. Morgana has a fair share of Laura's temperament. She likes her own company. We're always asking if she wants friends over but Morgana usually prefers playing on her own."

"Who's the little boy she often plays with?" James asked.

A look of surprise crossed Alan's features. "Little boy? What boy is that?"

"An eight-year-old. I'm assuming it's a neighbour's child," James replied.

"We don't really have much in the way of neighbours out where we live. Certainly no one within walking distance. Did she say where he was coming from?"

"I didn't ask. But I got the impression they didn't live far away. They sounded rather 'alternative' in their lifestyle."

"Oh *fuck*," Alan muttered. "'Alternative'? God-damned New Age squatters again. I'm always having problems with them. We had a bunch in a teepee last summer and it took me about eight weeks to evict them." He paused and considered. "Or maybe it's Bob Mason's people. His land runs against mine on the north. He sold twenty acres last year to some folks from back East who want to play mountain men. Anti-every-thing, you know? No plumbing, no electricity. I told him he was being stupid for doing it, that they'd be nothing but trou-ble. But they had money and no local person would have paid that price for 20 acres."

Alan paused. His brow drew down. "You know, I'm really not at all happy with the idea of someone coming close enough to the house that they're meeting up with Morgana when she's on her own. Did she tell you where this was happening?"

"She mentioned being down by a creek where she's allowed to play."

"Creek? The only creek Morgana's allowed to play around is Willow Creek. That runs just below the house. We can see her the whole time she's down there, so nobody could approach her there without our knowing about it."

"Strange," James said with concern.

Suddenly an expression of understanding spread over Alan's features. He broke into a smile. "You know what it is, I bet? She's pretending." He laughed warmly. "Believe me, Morgana has a full working version of her mother's imagination. You've never seen a kid play make-believe like she does. So I'll bet that's what it is. I'll bet you good money this boy isn't even a real person. He's just an imaginary companion."

Chapter Sixteen

"I was no work of art at thirteen," Laura said. "My hair was lank and greasy. My face was full of zits. My boobs were non-existent. I was half a head taller than any boy in my class and clothes hung on me with the same elegance as a coat hanger. But to Marilyn I was just one, big, irresistible possibility.

"Within a month of my going to live with my father, I'd been taken to the hairdresser, signed up for a make-up course at the department store and enrolled in ballet lessons to make me graceful. If I dared complain about any of this, Marilyn always answered that while I might not like it now, I'd be terribly grateful in the future that she'd made me do these things." Laura looked sidelong at James and laughed mockingly.

"My social life was her next concern. 'Why don't you ask your friends over, Laurie? There's a football game on Friday night. What about asking everybody over for a little pre-game party?'

"I'd only just moved there. I didn't have any friends, but I knew better than to admit that. I tried to deflect her by explaining it was a high school football game and, as we were only seventh graders, no one I knew would be going anyway. So there wasn't much point to a party.

"'*Laurie*,' she cried in this tone that implied a particularly serious deficit of grey matter in my head, '*Fun*! A get-together to have *fun*! Teenage fun! These are the best years of your life. You need to take advantage of them!'

"Worse was the sock hop. In a misguided effort to socialize us, the junior high school held a sock hop in the gymnasium every other Friday after school. I would have preferred demonstrating toothbrushes to lions to attending one of these dances but when Marilyn found out about them, there was no peace.

"'You *must* go, Laurie! It's just for two hours. No, don't worry if no one dances with you. No one ever dances in junior high. The point is to *go!* Be seen. Show your face. It's the only way to be popular.'

"But the very worst was yet to come. One afternoon Marilyn picked up a copy of my school newspaper, which she'd found lying with my books. In it she saw an announcement for cheerleading try-outs. She had been a cheerleader in high school herself and she couldn't imagine anything nicer. 'Oh, *cheer*leading! Oh Laurie, how *exciting*!' She said this as if she'd just read about the Second Coming. 'I bet if we look through my things, we can find my old pompoms. Then I can teach you some cheers and you can knock 'em dead!'"

Laura looked over with a sardonic smile. "The trouble was, Marilyn never understood that I had no desire to knock anyone dead. The idea of being a cheerleader mortified me. The thought of doing such a vacuous thing in public was enough to raise the hair on the back of my neck. No, I wasn't glamorous. I wasn't exciting. And I certainly wasn't popular. But I didn't give a damn.

"All I really wanted was to be left alone and that was the one thing that didn't happen. Marilyn pestered me constantly. I was powerless to stop it," Laura said and shrugged in a way that indicated futility but not remorse. "It became intolerable. How I ended up handling it was wrong. I knew that even then at the time, but I was young and desperately unhappy. So I did the only thing I could think of. I lied to her.

"To get Marilyn off my back I fabricated this whole clique of friends to provide me with all the teenage fun she expected me to want. I created them from among real kids at school, kids who lived too far away from us to run into, but kids I knew well enough that I could talk to if we did chance across them downtown or something and they wouldn't think I was a complete weirdo. I made sure they were good-looking, well-liked kids, but not the school stars, because I knew that might be pushing my luck. Then I started saying I was going out with them after school to dances or over to their houses on Saturday mornings. I'd dress the part and then change back into my jeans in the restroom at the gas station before going off to spend time on my own."

"So you were away from the house?" James asked.

"Yeah."

"So what did you do? You were still quite young, weren't you? Thirteen?"

Laura nodded. "Yeah. And I didn't really do anything. Go downtown mostly and just walk around. Or to the park. But an awful thing came from it – I discovered that I *liked* lying. I could open my mouth and out flowed the most preposterous stuff, but Marilyn always believed me. This, in a way, egged me on. I developed a real eye for the kind of details that would make the lies substantial. Notes in fake-friend Cathy's handwriting would be left on the table with my school books so that Marilyn and I could have a girlish giggle over them when she brought my books to me and 'accidentally' happened to look at the note. I'd show her the necklace I'd borrowed from fake-friend Sally, which I then allowed Marilyn to fasten for me as I got ready for the school dance I wasn't going to attend.

"Marilyn's gullibility actually became a source of self-esteem for me. She wasn't stupid; therefore I knew I had to be pretty good. Moreover, it worked. Marilyn was content that I was now 'popular' and she left me alone.

"About a year later, Marilyn got pregnant," Laura said. "The news galvanized my dad. After years of hazy promises and no action, he finally decided we needed a proper house instead of an apartment. We ended up in this boxy little place in the suburbs with a chain-link fence going around the perimeter of a perfectly square yard and a single pine tree growing in one corner. The house had only two bedrooms, but there was an unfinished basement and Dad said I could have that for my room if I wanted, because they wanted the baby close to them in the other bedroom. The basement had hardly any natural light, was nothing but concrete walls and plumbing pipes, and I would have to share it with the washer and dryer, but I leapt at the chance. Like my attic on Kenally Street, it was enough out of the way to give me my much-longed-for privacy. So I didn't care what condition it was in."

A pause crept in. "Because, of course, what privacy meant was that at last I could be with Torgon. I could spend my free time in the Forest." Laura was pensive a moment. "Torgon had become a bit of an obsession by that point. Hard to describe. Some of it, I think, was just being fourteen. You know how some girls that age are infatuated with singers in boy bands or movie stars? For me, it was Torgon. I thought about her all the time. I dreamed about her. I idolized her. I couldn't get her out of my mind ... It was an odd sensation, the way I felt about her in those years. Like an awareness of not being in her world, but of not quite being in my own world either, of being in neither one place nor the other. That aura permeated my teens, that sense of being stranded between here and a place no one else could see.

"I suppose I turned to Torgon for comfort. I was incredibly unhappy in those first couple of years with my father and Marilyn. I don't think they were ever aware of just how unhappy. As a consequence I began desperately wanting Torgon and the Forest to be real. Tangibly real. The reason was simple. I wanted to go there to the Forest myself, which I couldn't do if it wasn't a real place. I wanted to leave Rapid City and my family behind and live there.

"I couldn't figure out how to do this, of course, but I did hit on the idea of making a catalogue of all my knowledge about the Forest, as if that might somehow peg it down as a real place. I started with mapping the countryside. I drew a diagram of the compound where Torgon and the Seer lived. I made pedigree charts for various families in the village. I even tried to make a dictionary of Torgon's language, although this was much harder than I thought, so I didn't get far. I spent hours and hours and hours doing this, and kept everything very carefully together in this loose-leaf binder in my bedroom. It quickly became the most treasured thing I owned.

"What I longed for most, however, was a picture of Torgon. I wanted to see her with my eyes, not just my mind. Unfortunately, I'm a rotten artist, so try as I might, I couldn't draw her. Besides, I wanted photographic quality. So I started combing through magazines, looking for pictures of people who looked like her.

"Then I happened upon a picture of Brigitte Bardot from the film *And God Created Woman*. The odd thing is, Torgon didn't actually look like Brigitte Bardot at all – she wasn't blonde or drop-dead gorgeous nor did she have that come-hither sensuality that Bardot was so famous for. But in this picture Bardot was standing in a field of crops, the wind pulling at her hair, which was rumpled and unbound, and her expression was pure Torgon – intense, knowing, very guarded. When I saw it, Bardot's physical differences just vanished for me. I was looking right into Torgon's face.

"I cut the picture out and stuck it on the wall of my room, so that I could look at it all the time."

"In October my stepsister was born. They named her Tiffany Amber, which is just the sort of trendy, girlie-pink name you'd expect Marilyn to choose. Tiffie was the best thing, though. I adored her from the moment she popped out, in spite of her stupid name.

"Then came summer again. And my fifteenth birthday in June. Two nights before, Marilyn came down to my room in the basement and sat down on my bed. I was at my desk.

"'Laurie, I've had something very strange happen to me today,' she said. I could tell by her tone of voice that whatever it was, I wasn't going to want to hear it.

"'Your father and I thought we'd do something special for your birthday. We thought a little party at the Bear Butte Inn might be nice,' she said and looked pointedly at me. 'A little *surprise* party.'

"She gave me credit for smarts I didn't have, because I still couldn't figure out what this was about. The atmosphere, however, was definitely growing overripe. Something awful was going to drop.

"'I phoned your *friends*, Laurie, to see if they might like to come to the party. And do you realize,' Marilyn said pointedly, ' that none of your friends *knows* you?'

"*Arrrggghhhh*! I wanted to drop off my chair in sheer mortification. Having to face Marilyn and my dad over this was nothing compared with what it was going to be like at school after Marilyn had phoned up all these kids I'd been using in my fake-friends scenarios. Most of them didn't know me enough to even speak to me, much less want to come to my birthday party.

"She wasn't going to leave it at that, of course. So when I didn't give her an answer, she shouted for my dad. There was no point trying to lie my way out of it; so, I owned up to what I'd done and made a desperate effort to get my parents to understand just how cornered I'd felt by Marilyn's demands. No one paid the least bit of attention to my explanation. Marilyn just wanted to know what I'd been doing with myself all those hours I was supposedly with friends. When I told her nothing, that I'd just been on my own, she turned to my dad and said, 'The way this girl acts is *not* normal, Ron.' That was the first time anyone had voiced it, although I suspect Marilyn, at least, had been thinking it for some time.

"I got grounded for two full months. Since it was summer, this meant I was stuck hopelessly at home all day with Marilyn and the baby. There was nothing I could do to escape her. All I did was play with Tiffie for hours on end, but there's only so much you can do with an eight-month-old baby.

"In the end, I was so restless it began to bother Marilyn as much as it did me. Finally, one afternoon, I asked if I could go to the library to get something to read. She said I could. She drove me downtown, told me to stay right there at the library while she did the shopping and then she'd come back to pick me up. Still chastened, I did exactly as I was told. Marilyn was happy with that. She was pleased to see me so obedient, and I'm sure she appreciated the break from me as much as I did from her. So a few days later when I asked to go again, again she said I could. Even though I was still grounded, the library became an acceptable compromise. She liked it because it was wholesome and supervised; I liked it because it was away from her.

"For the first week or two, I happily engrossed myself in the books and magazines. Then the novelty began to wear off and I grew horribly restless.

"In the reference room, there was this enormous oak table about fifteen feet long, maybe five feet wide, and a warm honey colour that had become glossy at the edges by years of shifting readers. I went in there and sat down. The room was virtually empty. It was a hot July day, the perfect sort for picnics or swimming, so most people were outside. This was back before most places had air conditioning, and inside the library the heat was stifling. The sun was streaming down through these high, old-fashioned windows and I remember sitting there, watching the dust motes drifting through the sunbeams. The room smelled of dust. Dust and wax polish and that strange acidic odor of aging books.

"As I sat, I grew aware of my body calming down. It was a soft, peaceful sensation, almost a sinking, as if all the tension was oozing downwards to my feet and running out across the floor. I sat for several minutes just feeling it.

"There were these small containers of stubby little pencils dotted down the centre of the table and next to them, piles of scratch paper so that people could make reference notes. I reached over and took one of the pencils and half a dozen small sheets of paper and I began to write …"

Laura paused. The room became very quiet.

"I began to write Torgon's name over and over again on the little pieces of paper. And then … I just started to write. It was the first time …

"As I wrote, the walls of the library vanished, the table dissolved, the barrier between us disappeared. I wasn't me anymore. I was able to be in her world, to see it, to hear it, to feel it in a way that was as immediate and awesome as that first experience I'd had of her in childhood. And just as that first moment on the path through the vacant lot when I was seven had changed everything, so too now, my picking up that pencil in the library, again changed everything."

Chapter Seventeen

"I've brought in the story I started that day in the library," Laura said. "I thought maybe you'd like to read it. 'In context', I suppose you could say."

"Yes, I'm appreciating these stories," James replied. "They add an extra dimension to what you've been telling me."

"This was a turning point, starting to write," Laura said. "Not just in regards to what was to become my future career but … the whole experience went to another level in a way that I didn't appreciate at the time. I'm not sure I still quite understand it, but that was the point at which things started to change."

As Torgon approached the hut, she saw the Seer standing in the doorway. He wore his long, formal gown, so she knew he'd come to perform the usual rites for a newborn child. The father, Donar, too, was there. It would have been his first glimpse of his newborn daughter after his wife Anil's three-day lying in. When Torgon reached him, Donar went fully down to prostrate himself in the dust at Torgon's feet, as a worker should.

"Rise."

There were tears in his eyes as he came to his knees. "Forgive Anil," he pleaded. "She has wanted a child for so long."

They went into the hut, dark already with afternoon shadows. There was no lamp burning, only the fusty gloom of unaired rooms. Torgon could scent blood from the birthing.

The baby clutched to her, Anil sat huddled amid the birthing straw. The baby was alive. That'd been Torgon's initial fear, that Anil was keeping a stillborn infant to her breast.

Tears ran over Anil's cheeks. From her position she could not prostrate herself in obeisance, but she bent her head.

Torgon knelt beside her. "Here, let me see," she said gently and held out her hands for the child.

Slowly, sadly, Anil unwound the garments binding the child to her and put it into Torgon's waiting hands.

The baby's lip was cleaved right up to the nose, leaving a spreading gap. "Ah," Torgon said, rising with the child in her arms. "It has had a moon kiss." Gently inserting her finger into the infant's mouth, Torgon examined it. The parting went back into the soft palate of the mouth.

"Please do not take her," Anil whimpered. "She has survived to her three-day feeding. She is strong."

"No," Torgon said gently. "It cannot be."

"Please? I will feed her myself. With a small spoon and the milk from my breast," Anil pleaded, the tears rolling down over her cheeks. "I will care for her. She will be no burden."

"No," Torgon said. "A moon-kissed baby never thrives." And with that, she took the infant and left.

* * *

Gently binding it close to her body, Torgon began the climb up the steep path to the high holy place. The path broke through the trees and Torgon could see the summit of the cliff, dazzlingly white in the setting sun. Steadying the baby against her, Torgon went down on one knee to show deference to Dwr and The One in this holy place. Then rising, she continued on up onto the precipice.

When she reached the top, Torgon sat down cross-legged in the grass. The baby cried from hunger, a weak, ribbony sound. It made water as she undressed it, the urine hot across Torgon's thigh. She smiled at it, feeling the softness of its skin with her fingertips. Then she unstrapped the small ceremonial dagger at her wrist.

Lifting the child over her head, holding it face upward to the sky, she spoke the holy words before lowering it again into her lap. Bending forward, Torgon kissed the child on its mouth to acknowledge that she knew only its body was defective, and so, in honouring the soul with a holy kiss, its soul would be allowed to return freely to The One. Finally unsheathing the ornate dagger, she slit its throat and let the blood flow out over her hands and onto the soft white fabric of her clothes.

The lake shimmered darkly in the starlight. Standing at the water's edge, the Seer in his long white robes looked almost incandescent. Beyond him the shadowy water lapped restlessly at the shore. He knelt before Torgon, going down in full obeisance, his withered old body prostrate on the ground. Then soundlessly he rose and began to unfasten the front of her bloodied clothing. He undressed her entirely, laying each piece on a small wooden raft that rested on the shoreline, until at last she stood naked in the autumn darkness. Without hesitation, Torgon then walked into the icy water until she was neck-deep and remained there. The Seer set light to the small raft containing the blood-stained clothing and pushed it out into the lake. Then he poured sacred oils into the water and they spread out under the flames in iridescent ripples. Like a fallen star, the raft burned brilliantly in the forest darkness.

Torgon emerged wet and shivering to stand on the shoreline while the Seer clothed her in new vestments. These weren't the benna's clothes but the long, loose, coarsely-woven garments of the dead. He pulled them on roughly, as if he were dressing an inanimate object.

Then he turned and began to walk through the forest. Torgon followed. No shoes were allowed her until she was reborn, nor any light, even in this darkest hour. She couldn't re-enter the compound while she was still unclean, so he took her to the isolation hut. Once she was inside, he barred the small door, anointed the handle with holy oils and strewed the doorstep with the scented herbs used in preparation of the dead body. Then he began a high keening to mourn her death. Then silence. With inaudible footsteps, the Seer had slipped away into the forest.

As Torgon's eyes adjusted to the dark, she was able to pick out the small rectangular window on the eastern wall that would provide the only light in the small hut during daylight hours. It was too high to see out of, but while in isolation, one was not meant to be seeing out; and this late at night, so deep in the forest, that made little difference anyway. The window was only a small patch of lesser darkness.

Miserably cold, Torgon clutched the robe tightly around her in a desperate effort to get warm again. Why was this the way things are? *That thought came to her with unexpected brightness, like sunlight through the golden autumn leaves. She'd wondered this on other occasions, of course, but then only for herself. So many of the rites and rituals meant suffering that it*

*was hard not to question them, especially in the beginning when
she was first learning to discipline her mind and body in the way
of a benna.*

*Now, however, it was the moon-kissed child's face she saw and
when this question came to her, it was with the flickering brilliance
of insight.*

The Power?

*Why should she feel the Power now? It was Dwr's will that
malformed babies should die. Why would Dwr's holy Power make
her question it?*

It was *the Power, bright and shining in the infrangible darkness
of the hut. Resplendent luminosity suffused her mind.* Why are
things as they are? *the Power whispered.* Why did she accept
them?

Torgon sat back. Why should the Power ask this of her?

*When Torgon awoke, it was Mogri's face bent close. Taking a soft
cloth, Mogri wiped away the perspiration from Torgon's temples.*

*Torgon turned her head to see the familiar white walls of her
cell in the compound. "What are you doing here?" she whispered.*

*"Shhh," Mogri said. Leaning down, she dipped the cloth in
warm water and brought it up again. With it came the green,
piquant smell of water herbs.*

"You shouldn't be here," Torgon said.

*"I'm here because the acolytes won't wash you like I will, and
you need washing. You've gone very sweaty. Now, shhh. You needn't
talk."*

*It felt good, the confidence of Mogri's hands, the familiar smell
of water herbs. The Seer never used water herbs, but then he
wouldn't have taken the liberty of washing her either. Her head
was still heavy with the aftereffects of the death oils the Seer had*

given in order that she might escort the child's soul to safety. Torgon
allowed herself to drowse.

"It was so strange this time, Mogri," she murmured.

"What are you talking of?"

"In isolation. The Power came over me."

"It was probably less the Power, Torgon, and more the death
oils. You did not have your soul when they brought you down from
the isolation hut and I feared greatly that you would not get it back
this time. You must have walked great distances among the dead
to find this child's spirit – too far, we feared – and there were many
who thought the dead had barred your way and wouldn't let you
back again."

Mogri paused. "It is perhaps not fitting that I should say this but
I feared less the dead were to blame than that the old man had
poisoned you with the death oils. He is very old, Torgon. I do not
believe he always thinks straight."

"It wasn't the death oils that caused the visions. It was the
Power. They came before I was given the death oils."

Mogri's expression grew serious. She quickly made the gesture
of deference with her fingers. "This is for you to talk with the
Seer about, Torgon, not me. I have no holy calling. You know
that."

"I cannot talk with him. He will say they were unholy things
which came to me. He will say I lost my way among the dead and
was seduced into darkness, but this is not so. It … the Power …
shone with great light. And in the light I saw other ways of doing
things. Ways that seemed not like Dwr's at all … At one point, I
saw Anil's baby, but she was well grown. She was five or six
summers maybe, with fair hair like her brother's, but curly, like
her father's, and the moon kiss was gone … No, not gone exactly,
but where it had been there was naught but a scar line. A crooked

line, as is with Bertil's mouth, you know? Where he caught it on the spear and it has healed."

Mogri shook her head. "Except a moon kiss never heals, Torgon. The child would just waste and die."

"I know that. But in the visions the Power brought me, it was different. The child thrived. Her soul was happy to be in such a body and would have found no blessing in her death."

Torgon sighed. "Why would Dwr send such visions to me, when they question holy laws? What am I supposed to make of them? They came so strongly and took me from the darkness into another place."

"Here, give me your hand," Mogri said gently and reached over. Taking Torgon's hand between both of hers, she pressed it to her breast. "What you need is the feel of living flesh. You've been too long among the spirit kind. Hold on to me a good moment. This is what you need most."

"Perhaps she was right, because the quicksilver brilliance of the Power faded from Torgon's mind with the warmth of Mogri's hand. Weary and wordless, Torgon let go of the feeling and lay back in her bed."

Chapter Eighteen

"I don't know where that came from," Laura said, looking at the yellowed sheets of school notebook paper covered in adolescent handwriting that James was holding. "It hadn't been in my mind at all, but that's what came as I sat there in the library. I was *horrified*. She killed that baby! Torgon *killed* it. Just like that."

"Do you suppose it could have been an expression of the turmoil you were feeling at that time?" James asked.

Laura sat back. "This is what I want you to avoid doing," she said quietly. "Pre-judging all this. Confining it to a box."

"No, I'm trying not to," James replied. "I'm simply remarking that you had many powerful negative feelings at this point in your life. Our minds are capable of some quite remarkable transformations."

"If anything, I think perhaps it was the other way around," she replied. "Because I was experiencing such powerful negative feelings in my own life, I was more open to what was happening in Torgon's. This was in the sixties. In those days, there was very little graphic violence around. There wasn't the gratuitous violence, the casual autopsy porn that you see everywhere these days on TV and in the movies. So I was genuinely repulsed that Torgon would do something like this. It was just so foreign to my way of life.

"I'd immediately recognized what was wrong with the baby – it had a cleft palate. One of my cousins had a baby like that, so even at fifteen, I knew quite a lot about it. I certainly knew it could be fixed and a child could grow up completely normally. But Torgon didn't even give the baby a chance. She killed it outright.

"That just sat with me in such a dark, secret way. I kept reading back through what I'd written, re-experiencing it each time. Asking *why*? It was the action, not the violence that upset me. I never thought: where did this terrible story come from or how could I write something so graphic about murdering children? To be truthful, it didn't even occur to me to consider my own role in it. All I was thinking was: how could such a sensitive, intelligent person as Torgon accept that killing the baby was the right thing to do? The mother had offered to care for the little girl herself. Why didn't Torgon fight for that? Just because she'd been taught that's what their god wanted, why didn't she stop and think for herself?

"But it compelled me as well. I had this faint ache – not an anxiety really – just a kind of pressure building up, that made me long to write the rest of it. My imagination had finally found form. Picking up that pencil in the library literally changed my life. From that moment on, writing overtook me like a physical force. It became all I wanted to do."

"What did your family think about this?" James asked.

"Marilyn showed a passing interest at first. She talked about how I might get famous if I kept it up and maybe even get a book made into a movie in Hollywood, because that happened to some writers. But then she kept wanting to read what I was writing and I could hardly share it, could I? Marilyn was expecting romantic stuff or at least something recognizable as a teenage girl's life. Not child murders.

"My dad said nothing about it at all. I don't know when it happened, but sometime during my teens, we'd become strangers. Or perhaps we'd always been. My father loved me. I was always certain of that, but I'd long since realized we lived in parallel universes.

"Unfortunately, Marilyn's tolerance didn't last long. My reluctance to show her any of my writing made her suspicious. She started to question just what precisely I was 'doing down there in the basement' in a tone of voice that implied it might be sex trafficking or something. When I complained, she said that no one who spent her adolescence shut away in her room was going to grow into a well-rounded individual.

"I felt really angry with Marilyn at that point. I was a straight A student; I helped out a lot with Tiffany; I did all my chores around the house without being reminded; I didn't drink; I didn't smoke; I didn't do drugs or go to wild parties. I wasn't aimlessly walking the streets any longer, and for more than a year I'd been completely honest about which friends I had and which I didn't. Why was she never satisfied with me?

"In the end, what saved me was Marilyn's getting pregnant again. It was a little boy this time and they named him Cody. Tiffie was two and between her and the baby, Marilyn finally seemed to have enough on her plate that she didn't need to worry about me. Or maybe it was just that the two of them offered a lot more scope for improvement than I did. Whatever, I was finally left more or less to my own devices."

A pause. Laura's expression grew a bit uncomfortable. She smiled awkwardly. "Actually I *had* been honest about my friends, but I was still finding it hard to stay completely within the confines of this world that everyone else seems to find so real. A more creative kind of fabrication had started happening at school. I had no evil intentions in doing it. I wasn't even doing it for attention. I just had such an enormous creative brew bubbling away in my head that it boiled over occasionally into what was going on around me.

"Guileless as I was at the time, it never occurred to me to think that what I was doing might be construed as taking advantage of people. It didn't even feel like lying to me. I was simply sharing all this bounty I experienced in my head that others didn't. I invented characters and storylines, added, took away, fleshed each one out until they were rich, multi-faceted personalities. I never cared if they were real people or not.

"In the end I was too successful at making them believable. One Saturday while I was out, my French teacher stopped by the house with a box of postcards. I arrived home to find Marilyn and my dad sitting grimly at the kitchen table. Panic flooded me. Even without knowing what had happened, I knew I was guilty of something.

"'Suppose you tell us what this is all about?' Dad said, shoving the box of postcards across the table.

"I looked blankly at them and shrugged. 'I've never seen them before,' I said.

"'No, I suppose not. Because Mrs. Patton has just brought them around for Sarah. Feel like telling us who Sarah is?' he asked.

"I swallowed hard.

"Meanwhile, Marilyn's eyes had gone cold and lustreless as a lizard's. 'Can you imagine how your father and I felt to have this teacher of yours come to our door all enthusiastic about having this box of postcards to give your little Sarah? What could we say to her? That there was no such person as Sarah and there never has been, that you just made her up?'

"A terrible fight followed. My parents were furious. Marilyn pointed out how I had hardly any friends, never dated, never attended school functions and virtually never invited anyone to the house. She said all I did was lock myself away in the basement and live in a fantasy world. 'There's something very, very wrong with this girl, Ron,' she kept telling my father. 'She's turning into a pathological liar. There's something sick about her.'

"I felt devastated. I wanted so much for Dad and Marilyn to understand what was going on for me, and that I didn't mean to hurt anyone. Torgon and the Forest had always made me feel so good, but I was beginning to realize maybe there *was* something wrong with it. I cried and cried.

"That night I managed to gather enough courage to try and explain my side of things to my father. 'We're done being mad at you, Laurie,' he said in this very gentle voice when we were finally alone in his study. 'I know some things got said this afternoon which shouldn't have, but people are like that in the heat of the moment and it doesn't really mean anything. You know we love you very, very much, don't you, and want only the best for you.'

"'I'm sorry about making Sarah up. I didn't mean it to get away from me … But, Dad, I've got to explain something to you. I see people inside my head, Dad. I see their faces as clearly as I see yours right now. I hear them when they talk. I know how they feel and what they think about.'

"'I know it sounds crazy,' I said. 'You're probably thinking Marilyn's right and I've gone nuts or something, but that's not what's happening. I *know* they're in my head and I never have any trouble telling what's out here in this world and what's inside me.'

"His brow furrowed. 'Oh, Laurie …' he murmured.

"'But the thing is, Dad, they *are* in there. Lots of them. Whole families. Aunts and uncles and cousins and grandparents. There's a world. A political system. Laws. Religion. Animals. *Everything* … and they're all in here.' I touched my temple.

"There was this long pause. Then I said, 'There's got to be a reason that all this is in my head, Dad. I feel that. Why would there be so much detail, so much happening, if it wasn't anything more than messed-up chemicals in my brain or whatever being nuts is?'

"He searched my face, his eyes going over it slowly, as if over foreign terrain. I became worried, because he didn't speak. Finally, I said, 'Do *you* think there's something wrong with me that makes me see all these things?'

"He smiled gently then, shook his head and said, 'No, I think you're just a little childish for your age, that's all. Most kids have outgrown these things by the time they're teenagers, but with the kind of life you've had … the things that happened. You got a bad start to life, Laurie. I'm really sorry for that. It's understandable that you're still a bit immature.'

"I frowned. 'I don't think what's happening to me is about being immature, Dad. I think it's about being different. I don't actually want to lose what's going on in my head. I just don't want to be so difficult for everyone.'

"'We'd all like to live in fantasy worlds, Laurie, but it's not the grown-up way of doing things. There's nothing wrong with you that a few more years won't cure. You've been very silly, but we've all been that at one time or another. All you need to do is stop the silliness and move on.'

"Leaving my father's study that night, I felt isolated in a way I never had before. He'd been warm and, in his own way, supportive, but he didn't have the slightest insight into my dilemma. I don't think he was even able to perceive there was a dilemma."

Chapter Nineteen

"You *told!*" Morgana cried angrily. The door had hardly been closed to the playroom before she rounded on James. "You said in here I could tell you secret things! You said in here I could do just what I want. You *said!* And then you *told!*"

"Here. Here, why don't you come over here and sit down and we'll talk about it," James replied.

"That was *my* secret, about me and the Lion King. I told you that. I said it was secret. But you *told.*"

"You feel I shouldn't have done that."

"I'm not ever going to tell you anything again, that's for sure. Not *ever.*" She folded her arms across her chest, pushed out her lower lip and glared blackly into the space between them.

"I'm sorry," James said. "I can see you're very angry with me."

"You lied *bad*," she muttered.

"I think you heard something slightly different from what I said," James replied gently. "I said in here it was all right to tell secrets. But I didn't promise that I would never tell anyone else. I keep secrets when I can, but you see, sometimes when children talk to me, I have to make hard decisions about what I hear. Because I'm older and I've learned more things, sometimes I realize something they are doing might be dangerous. When that happens, I have to decide whether or not it would be best to tell other people. I'm really sorry if I gave you the impression that in here I would always keep your secrets. I think what I actually said was that in here you could decide what you would tell me. But I'm sorry there was a misunderstanding. I'm sorry too that I hadn't realized until now how important keeping this private was to you. If I'd understood that, we could have talked first about my telling."

"I'm never going to tell you anything."

"I was concerned, Morgana," James said, "because the things you've told me about the Lion King make him sound like an unusual little boy. You're still little and so it's your mum and dad's job to take care of you and keep you safe. It's important for them to know what you're doing when you're out playing. I didn't 'tell' on you. I simply asked them if they knew the Lion King's family, because I was concerned for you. I wanted to make sure that you were safe."

"But they don't understand."

"Yes, I can see you feel strongly about that."

"Now they don't want me to see him. My dad says I have to stay home in the yard. He won't let me go play at the creek. I haven't been able to go since last Thursday and I haven't seen the Lion King in all that time and he won't know why I haven't come," Morgana said. She was close to tears. "He's the only friend I got."

"What about friends at school?" James asked gently.

"Not anybody like the Lion King. And I was teaching him to read. I brung home two books for him last week and now my dad won't let me go down to the creek with them."

"Why don't you invite the Lion King to come to your house instead?" James asked.

"He wouldn't come." The tears began to roll over her round cheeks. Lifting a hand, she pushed them back. "So why did you have to tell? The Lion King wouldn't ever hurt me. He wouldn't never have done nothing to me in a million years because he's my best friend."

"I really am very, very sorry, Morgana. I can see how upset you are."

A moment or two passed in silence as Morgana stanched her tears. Finally she looked up. "The only way I can go out to play with him again is to tell my folks he's just pretend. And that's what I'm going to do." A defiant tone crept in her voice. "And from now on I'm going to tell you that too. The Lion King isn't real. I just made him up."

"Painting" wasn't quite the right term for what Conor had started doing during his sessions. At the easel, he would load the brush with paint and then push it against the paper to watch the excess run down. This seemed to give him enormous pleasure. His body would go rigid with excitement and he would then slap the brush against the paper with increasing fervour.

On that morning Conor had started off with particular enthusiasm and the first sheet was soon sodden. James rose and helped him change to the next. Then the next. Then the next after that. Conor filled half a dozen sheets with slashes of dripping yellow paint.

All his concentration was focused on the act of painting. As always, he kept the toy cat tucked tight under his armpit to free both his hands, so he held a paintbrush in each and splashed first streaks of yellow, then ran a broad stroke of blue across the top of the paper. "Green," he murmured, more to himself than James. Using both brushes, he smeared the two colours together to turn them into a proper, if murky green.

"There is green," he said and turned, actually looking at James. "Yellow and blue make green."

"Yes, you're right. You've made green there."

Conor filled the brush again with blue paint and ran a broad stroke across the paper. He watched it run. Then he took the brush out of the red paint holder with his other hand and painted a heavy slash over the top. The red ran down through the other colours. He turned, his expression a mixture of excitement and fear. "Look. Blood."

"Yes, it does look like blood, doesn't it?"

Quickly, Conor added streak after streak of red across the paper until it was so wet it ran off the easel onto the floor. James noticed him becoming agitated, anxiety taking over from excitement. Slap, slap, slap went the brush.

"You are beginning to feel worried," James interpreted. "At first painting was exciting but now it's starting to feel frightening."

"Ehhh-ehhh-ehh-ehh-ehh! Ehhh-ehhh-ehh-ehh-ehh!" Conor cried. He let the red paint brush drop back into the paint container as if it had suddenly become too hot to hold. Snatching his toy cat out from under his armpit, Conor pressed it over his eyes. "Meow! Meow!"

James rose and quickly crossed over to him. Kneeling down, he put an arm around the boy's shoulders. "You're feeling very frightened," he murmured softly. "But we're safe here. The playroom is safe."

"Plug it in!" Conor cried. "Plug it in! Plug it in!"

Plug what in? James wondered.

"Ehhh-ehhh-ehh-ehh-ehh. *Ehhh-ehhh-ehh-ehh-ehh*." Conor grappled with his cat, clutching it tighter to his face, as if trying to block everything out.

James reached over and pulled one of the small chairs out from the table. "Here. I'm going to sit down. I'll sit near you until you feel more comfortable. The playroom's safe. I'll show you by sitting near."

Very cautiously, Conor lowered the cat. He looked at James, made genuine eye contact and took a slow, deep breath. Then he bent down and lifted up one of his trailing, foil-decorated strings. Stepping over to the nearby wall, he knelt and pressed the end to the baseboard. It didn't stick, of course, because it was just ordinary string but he laid it very straight and pressed it to the baseboard a second time, as if it might.

"I understand now," James said. "You're plugging your wires in."

Conor straightened out the other trailing strings and pressed them to the baseboard too. He made louder mechanical noises as he did so, sounding like rusty cogs turning, grinding.

"You're all plugged in now," James observed. "All four wires are against the wall."

"Whirrr. Whirrr."

"Ah. Have you turned yourself into a machine? I hear it now. I hear your motor running smoothly," James said.

"Zap-zap," Conor said. "Electricity, zap-zap. Strong. Kill you dead."

"You feel like you've become a mechanical boy, is that right? Mechanical Boy has electricity going through him," James interpreted. "Mechanical Boy is stronger than Conor. Conor is just a flesh-and-blood boy, but Mechanical Boy is made of wires."

"And metal. Strong metal. Galvanized metal. Metal alloy."

"Mechanical Boy is made of wires and strong metal," James reflected. "And I can see he is no longer frightened."

"Yeah. Red paint like blood. Blood dripping down the wall. Mechanical Boy can laugh. Ha-ha. Ha-ha, you can die, red paint like blood. Mechanical Boy is a strong machine made of metal alloy. Machines don't die."

The next session was taken up with finger-paints. Lifting a big dollop of red out of the jar, Conor smoothed it over the paper, pushing it around and around with the flat of his hand. He added more, squishing it up between his fingers. Throughout the activity, he said nothing. He whirred and buzzed and ratcheted, a robot boy with turning cogs and fizzing circuitry, but he used no words.

What was going on? James wondered. Why did he feel he needed the protection of turning into a machine before he could allow himself the freedom to use the paint?

And what about that cat? As ever, the stuffed toy never left Conor's person. It was now tucked up under his left armpit, which hindered the movement of his left hand somewhat, but he was so accustomed to moving with the cat stuck there that he was remarkably adept. What purpose did the cat serve?

Cats, blood, ghosts, death. Symbolism for what? James tried to imagine Conor's life at the time he began to create this scary view of the world? He was two. He attended daycare two days a week. His father was overwhelmed by financial problems. His mother was beset by fame and an unwanted pregnancy. What was happening to Conor? Something abusive at day care that he was too young to reveal? A response to his father's distress? A reaction to his mother's anxiety over a stalker? A result of developmental stresses? Separation anxiety brought on because his mother was continually preoccupied with imaginary people? A consequence of being a bright, perceptive child in a family upset over a baby they didn't want? Or was it Morgana's birth, taking Mum and Dad even further away from Conor? Did his preoccupation with death symbolize this separation?

But then who was the man under the rug? Had Conor perhaps ventured in on Alan and Laura making love and this was the "man under the rug"? "Dead" perhaps in the exhausted aftermath of orgasm? Or "dead" perhaps as symbolism for "weak", for Alan's letting Laura emotionally abandon Conor? Was the cat there to protect Conor from the ghosts of memories of an infancy when she was all his? Or from the "dead man" who was his father?

James looked at the boy. It had been much simpler to consider him autistic.

Conor, intent on his painting, did not want interaction. Whatever psychological issues the boy was working out with the paints, it was for himself alone at that point, an internal process being made external, and he wasn't ready to communicate it with James. James's only role was to sit quietly and observe.

As so often happened when there were quiet moments in the playroom, James's mind wandered back to Adam. Adam playing. Adam painting. Adam chattering in his soft, lispy voice. Adam dead.

My own ghost, James thought, as he watched Conor. *I'm just as haunted as he is.*

It *had* been James's fault that Adam had died. The tribunal was right about that. They all were, and the worst of it was that James knew that. If he had spent less time theorizing and more time observing Adam, if he had acted on what Adam said instead of simply watching and "interpreting", Adam might well be alive today. If *he* hadn't been negligent. The psychiatrist. The one who should have noticed the signs of brutal abuse and recognized them for the real symptoms they were, not some therapeutic displacement crap.

But he had noticed. That's what James had found so hard to tell the tribunal. He *had* seen the marks and noticed the weight loss. But abuse – *torture*, really, to give it its honest name – hadn't crossed James's mind when working with Adam. He was a five-year-old boy. Of course, he would be struggling with the Oedipal stage. Fantasies of fighting with his step-father for his mother's love were part and parcel of the expected symbolism of Freudian psychiatry. And theirs was such a respectable family, well off and well educated. Intelligent, articulate and likable. The parents had been the ones themselves to bring in Adam for help. Who was James to question that things weren't just as they had said, that Adam had inflicted those injuries on himself during his incomprehensible rages?

James never found the words to defend himself, not then, not even now. Despite the perfect clarity everyone had in hindsight, at the time things really had looked uncertain and inconclusive. It *hadn't* been blatantly obvious what the horrible conclusion was going to be. But, of course, the hard truth was that even when James had begun to suspect things weren't as they seemed, it only made him question his own judgement. He never was brave enough to accuse the parents. Because what if he were wrong? What if it were all just part of Adam's psychopathology? James's psychiatric training had covered self-inflicted injury far more thoroughly than child abuse. He was so worried he would lose his credibility by causing a big fuss over nothing. He hadn't meant to be blind or stupid. He was just an ordinary guy who'd got caught up in a truly horrific situation. His only real mistake had been trying to play safe.

So deep in thought was James that he missed the accident when it happened. Conor had leaned far across the table to pick up a new sheet of paper when the stuffed cat slipped out of its niche under his arm and fell with a slurpy splat onto the painting Conor had been working on. There was so much finger-paint on the paper that it splashed up as the cat landed.

A look of pure horror crossed Conor's face. He screamed with terror.

James jumped up quickly and lifted the toy out of the paint, but even that wasn't fast enough. Conor was instantly hysterical. He began to shriek and flap his hands wildly, red paint splattering in all directions.

"Here. Come here. We'll wash Kitty off," James said, trying to calm him. He placed a guiding hand on Conor's back to encourage him in the direction of the sink.

"Blood on the walls! Blood on the walls! No! No! No!" He flung himself about violently.

Tossing the paint-soaked cat over into the sink, James moved to restrain the boy.

"No! No! No!" Conor screamed. "Blood! Blood on the cat! The cat's dead!"

"No, it isn't blood, Conor. It's only paint." He grabbed the boy and pulled him in tightly, wet paint and all. Conor struggled, powerful in his utter terror. Pushing against James, he slapped James's face and kicked his shins. The two of them tumbled to the floor before James managed to secure the grip he was trying for. He lay half under the table, the boy clutched to him.

Conor continued to scream and struggle. James pulled the two of them into a sitting position and held on.

A minute passed.

Two minutes.

Three.

Conor was drawing in air in big, shuddery gasps, his voice gone hoarse from screaming. At long last he collapsed against James, his face pressed into the fabric of James's suit.

James looked down at the boy, at his milky skin, blotched and tear-stained. He waited for complete silence.

"Shall we wash Kitty off?" James asked when Conor was finally still.

Conor looked up and his eyes went dark again with terror. He pulled back from James, but as James was still holding him, he could go only so far. A long moment passed between them as Conor studied James's face. Then tentatively he reached up and touched red paint, dried on James's cheek. "Not dead?" he asked.

"No. I'm not dead. It isn't blood, Conor. It's only paint."

"The cat is dead."

"No. The cat isn't dead either. The cat only fell in the paint."

"The cat's dead."

James rose slowly to his feet, helping the boy to his. "Come here. Let's wash your kitty off, shall we? See? It's not blood. Just red paint. Here, I'll turn on the tap and put Kitty under. See? There it goes."

Tears still wet on his cheeks, Conor had begun to watch James sponge soap over the stuffed animal's fur to get the paint out.

"Where are his cats?" Conor asked softly.

"Kitty's right here."

"*His* cats," Conor said and reached a tentative finger out to touch the cuff of James's shirt. "Where are the man's cats?"

"*My* cats?"

Conor nodded slightly.

"It's safe in here," James said, "so you think I must have cats here protecting me?"

Conor looked up. "Yeah."

Before James could respond, Conor took off, circling the periphery of the room. The tangle of strings trailing behind him, paint on his skin and his clothes and in his hair, he began to push toys aside, peer into the dolls' house, rummage through the farm animals in an increasingly obsessive search for cats. Of which there didn't seem to be any in the playroom, an oversight James had been unaware of until now. Dogs, ducks and aurochs, yes, but the playroom appeared to be a cat-free zone.

In a box on the shelf was a set of cardboard-cutout farm animals that James had found at a jumble sale. They were thirty years old and he'd bought them purely for sentimental reasons, because he'd had the same set himself as a young boy. Modern children, however, had not been so entranced by such plain toys and the box had sat largely undisturbed on the play-room shelf.

Now Conor pulled off the lid and ruffled through the figures. There he found it. Among the assortment of animals was a grey-striped tabby cat in a standing position, ears erect, tail up in a friendly greeting. Around its neck some long-ago child had tied a piece of string for a leash.

"Look!" Conor cried in amazement. His small face brightened and he made direct eye contact with James. "Look! Look! A mechanical cat!"

Chapter Twenty

"Torgon's killing that baby with the cleft palate continued to haunt me," Laura said. "Even though I'd gone on to write other stories about her life in the Forest, that first one sat with me in a dark, secret way, bubbling back up to consciousness at odd moments, leaving me to mull it over.

"In the course of all this thinking, I started to understand the role ignorance plays in our actions. Torgon *wasn't* evil for killing that child. She had been doing the best she could, because she simply didn't know what else to do.

"This insight fired me up, because I realized this was true not only for Torgon's world, but here, in our world too. There were many places like Torgon's village, where lack of skills or equipment meant needless lives were lost, where people were forced to accept horrible solutions because they had no alternatives. This felt like a golden key to me, the thing I had been looking for to connect Torgon's world and my own.

"I suddenly came alive. My life at last had purpose. In direct response to Torgon's behaviour with the cleft-palate baby, I decided I would become a doctor."

Laura smiled at James in a soft, almost ironic way.

"My family was in shock," she said. "I had this reputation for being dreamy to a point of absence and suddenly I picked this hugely ambitious goal. Just as incredible to them was the fact that medicine was the kind of out-of-reach, professional job people like us didn't aspire to. 'We aren't *rich*,' Dad said with horrified emphasis, when I told him. 'That'd take *years*, Laura. We would still be paying for your education when Tiffany is ready for college.' Marilyn saw a completely different range of problems. Like, for instance, how was I ever going to get a decent husband if I spent my time competing with them? If I liked medicine so much, why not become a nurse? That was easier and cheaper, and I'd stand a better chance of marrying a doctor.

"I wasn't deterred. The decision gave validity to everything in my head. I felt suddenly as if I'd been ordained, as if I was like Torgon herself – chosen unexpectedly to follow a sacred path – and for the first time in years, I was genuinely happy. So I refused to be cowed. I worked out budgets, shopped around for scholarships and filled in reams of applications. I was accepted at my second choice, a university in Boston, almost two thousand miles from home."

"I can remember my last night at home before leaving for college. Marilyn came downstairs to my room.

"'This is going to be a big change for you,' she said quietly and sat down on my bed.

"I was clearing out my bedroom and putting everything in boxes, because they wanted to make a rec room out of it. So I was up on a chair, taking down all the magazine pictures that had been tacked on my walls.

"'I hope you'll be happy,' Marilyn said.

"'Yeah,' I replied.

"'I hope you'll get what you want out of life.'

"'Yeah, I'm sure I will,' I said with that certainty you only have in adolescence.

"I climbed down and began stacking the pictures carefully on the top of my desk. Mostly they were the ones of Brigitte Bardot that I'd collected over the years. I remember pausing as I came to the one from *And God Created Woman*. Of all of them, that one was still the most evocative of Torgon and every time I looked at it, it made me feel good.

"'I'm sorry,' Marilyn said.

"I glanced at her. 'For what?'

"'I'm sorry we couldn't make you happier.'

"Surprised, I said, 'I'm happy enough, Marilyn.'

"She let her shoulders drop.

"'I *am* happy,' I said again. 'Maybe it's a different kind of happiness than what you had in mind for me, but I still am happy. Isn't that what matters in the end?'

"From the expression on her face, I could tell she didn't agree. I felt bad then. I regretted that I couldn't have been the cheerleader, the prom queen, the debutante that she'd wanted. I wouldn't have wanted any of those things for myself, but I felt flawed for wanting something different. Moreover, I felt guilty for having got it.

"'Perhaps you'll like it better where you're going,' she said, her voice still soft. 'Perhaps you've made a good choice.'

"'I think I have.'

"'Maybe you can come back here when you want to get married and settle down.'

"I shrugged slightly. 'Yeah, maybe.'

"'You *do* want to get married, don't you, Laura?'

"I looked at her. She was glancing sideways at the stack of pictures on my desk but I was too naïve to read deeper meaning into the question. I took it at face value, pondered it and then said, 'I don't know.'

"'You do *like* boys, don't you, Laura?'

"'Yes, some of them.'

"'Do you like women?'

"'Yes, some of them.'

"She ducked her head a moment, then looked back. 'Do you *prefer* women? Is that why you haven't ever tried to get any boyfriends?'

"Comprehension dawned and my jaw dropped. 'Geez, Marilyn. Is that the only explanation you can think of for my not wanting to do things your way?'

"'Well, it's just if that's the way things are, your father and I deserve to know.'

"'That's not the way things are. But what would be the big deal if it were?'

"She shrugged slightly. 'Well, it wasn't so much that you haven't had any dates. It was that you don't seem to *want* any dates. Boys don't just happen to you. You have to make an effort with yourself. And you never have.'

"'I've had other things to do,' I said.

"A pause.

"'I just need time,' I said.

"Then sadness permeated the air again. Marilyn hung her head. 'Well, maybe going back East will be the right move for you. Maybe you'll find more of your own kind back there.'"

* * *

"Maybe I did find more of my own kind, because university was a magic time for me," Laura said. "And the magic could be summed up in one word: freedom. For the first time in my life I felt able to be who I really was without anyone hawking over me. If I wanted to study, I could study. If I wanted to write, I could write. If I wanted to plaster pictures of Brigitte Bardot all over my bulletin board, I could do that. No one minded.

"No one minded if I was a bit different either. I listened to folk music and protest songs instead of rock, and dressed in baggy shirts and jeans instead of fashion. I wasn't the dorm hippy, but I was the edgy, creative one and everyone was good with that.

"In fact, the social set-up at college really worked for me. I wasn't somebody to have friends. It wasn't so much that I didn't want them or didn't like them; just that socializing took time that I preferred to spend in other ways – writing, or even studying, because I was enjoying the academic side of college too. But it was nice having people around generally, nice being able to stop out in the sitting area of the dorm and have a cup of coffee and talk to someone. Then, when the coffee was finished, I could get up and leave without anyone thinking I was rude. I liked people having their own lives, so that they weren't so wrapped up in mine."

"So you did a lot of writing during this time?" James asked. "Was this different writing? Were you still writing about Torgon."

"Just Torgon. That's what I'm trying to say," Laura replied. "There was this enormous freedom. For the first time I could be with Torgon whenever I wanted. However much I wanted. No one censored my time. No one made me feel guilty for it. It's difficult to explain what the sensation was like. Writing made Torgon very present for me. I could hear everything in my head, almost like dictation. I was always experiencing her world at the same time as mine, laid down over my everyday life. This wasn't a conflict for me, this layering of two realms. It felt good. I remember being really happy."

Undoing the tie, Torgon let her trousers fall from her waist, then slipped the benna shirt over her head to leave only her undergarments. There were so many crawling, biting things that she was reluctant to remove all her clothes, but the white showed too plainly here midst all the green-on-green. She removed the undergarments too.

She knelt to spread the paste of water herbs over her body to mask her smell. Laying the trap carefully, she sank down prone in the tall grass and waited.

Time passed. The sun grew hot across her back, making sweat that brought flies. The strong smell of water herbs would deter the biting flies, but the lesser flies were not bothered and swarmed noisily above her.

A hare appeared but did not go near the trap. It sunned itself, lolling in the grass not twenty feet from where Torgon lay. It rose and idly washed its flanks. Torgon waited.

Whoosh! The trap went at last and she sprang like a great cat to snatch the hare from the rope before it went too tight. The creature kicked and squirmed, its jaw working wildly to produce an eerie, almost canine growl of terror.

"I have you, little one. Don't fight," she whispered and smiled at the creature. Then she bagged it, dressed quickly and loped off through the forest and back to the compound.

Taking the hunting bag into her inner cell before opening it, Torgon knew she had to work fast now or the creature would die of fright.

Everything was ready except the death oil. She hadn't dared remove the death oil from its wooden casket for fear the Seer might happen by and see it out. Removing the candle holders from the top of the ornate wooden box, Torgon lifted the lid. All the holy oils were kept in there and the mingled scent was so overpowering that Torgon always had to step back for a moment or two to let fresh air in. The Seer would know she'd been into the chest just by the smell of her room.

Which one would be best? She'd long pondered this question. Finally she chose the one in the blue bottle. It was more inclined to upset the stomach than the other death oils, but it wasn't as toxic. And it was easier to dilute.

She tipped a drop or two into a vial of spring water. Would this be strong enough? Too strong? Her hands were shaking. Pausing, she took in deep, measured breaths to slow her rapid heart. The Power would tell her. If she could relax enough to let the Power come, it would give her again those eerie visions of organs still quick with the life force that had haunted her thoughts for all these months.

Torgon knew well enough already what existed within the body. As a child hunting with her father, she'd watched the ritual removal of the internal organs from the animals killed, had partaken of the special nourishment of still warm liver and brain, had seen the heart given to the hunter to grant him the animal's bravery. But those had all been lifted lifeless from dead, defeated things. The Power showed her very different images – visions of hearts still pumping, lungs frothing with air and blood moving in a current, as if it were a river – visions of life and growth.

The hare had been her own idea and Torgon was pleased at her ingenuity, at this effort to make the visions come real. Holding a cloth soaked in the diluted death oil, she felt the fight seep slowly from the animal. It was a prolonged process and once, when she removed the cloth too soon, the hare burst back to life and leapt from her grip, although it was too drugged to do more than flop dozily around her feet. The second time she kept the cloth there longer and at last it stayed limp.

Amazed, Torgon regarded it. In her experience living hares were panicked, struggling things, but this one lay heavy and warm in her lap. For several minutes, she did no more than study it, watching the animal's side rise and fall rhythmically. She stroked the fur to feel its softness, but gingerly, for it had fleas. This in itself was worth the effort, Torgon thought, for she was gaining much just by being able to look at a living hare so closely. As the animal had already made her wiser, she offered it the gesture of veneration.

Laying the hare out on the stone floor, Torgon loosed the ceremonial dagger from its sheath at her wrist and then cautiously slipped the knife under the skin of the hare's belly. She slit it in a neat line. Easing back the skin carefully, she saw smooth muscle beneath it.

Blood was suddenly everywhere. Consternated, Torgon fingered hastily along the edge of the flesh until she came to a small gushing vein and squeezed it. Carrying the limp hare with her to the fireplace, she plunged the tip of the knife into the embers left from the morning fire. She'd often watched her father take the manhood from the young bull calves to make them quieter for the cart, and it was his hot knife that had sealed the blood. Yes, it would do so here too, she discovered. There was a sizzle and a faint smell of burnt flesh, but when Torgon gently wiped away the blood, none came to replace it.

While waiting for the knife to cool, Torgon brought over the needle and silver thread that Mogri had got for her. Then she settled down again on the stone floor. Slipping the tip of the knife through the translucent covering over the body cavity, she pulled it aside and there beneath her fingertips was the small beating heart of the hare.

This is a great wonder! *Awe momentarily overcame her. She'd meant to venerate Dwr at this moment for showing her so great a miracle, but she just stared, bewitched. Here was the heart. Here was the liver. Here was the stomach. Each part she'd perceived before only a bit of meat. Now it juddered with life.*

Gently she prodded the stomach, feeling the living warmth of the creature for herself. Lifting her fingers, she smelled the scent. It was all just as the Power had shown her in her dreams, with each part of the living body coexisting peacefully in small separate kingdoms. Laying down the knife, Torgon lowered herself, pressing her face against the cold flag floor to do full obeisance to the sacred hare.

Afterwards, Torgon carefully pressed the flaps of peritoneum back together, then the muscle and finally the skin. Taking the needle with its shimmery thread, she bent close over the body of the animal and endeavoured to stitch its skin back together.

The hare didn't live. Indeed, it never woke from the sleep of the death oil and Torgon was obliged to go back out into the forest and trap another. And neither did that one survive, so she had to go again. And again. And again. As she waited in the grass for yet one more to approach her trap, she fretted that the summer would soon pass and it'd grow too cold for hunting.

* * *

"*What unholy thing is this?*"

Startled, Torgon jerked up. She was in her innermost cell. The Seer had no right to enter without seeking her permission, but he was there nonetheless.

Panicked, Torgon leapt quickly to her feet. She tried to hide her hands. There was blood on both of them and blood on the floor. Blood, she'd long since realized, was very disinclined to stay within its kingdom. The small room stank of it.

"This is the work of the Power," she said as calmly as she could. "It has commanded that I do this."

"What? *Dwr* has commanded the letting of blood by your own hand? On holy floors? Do not add blasphemy to so many sins."

"I am not letting blood. Blood has flowed but the animal still lives. See? I can show you a great miracle: its beating heart."

His eyes grew huge with horror. "This is not *Dwr's* domain!"

"*Dwr's* domain is greater than we have even dreamt of."

"You have allowed yourself to be led into darkness! Dwr does not command your hands in this. Why would Dwr countenance the breaking of so many holy rules? Answer me that."

"Holy sir, I do not wish to be discourteous to you for you are old and should be venerated, and you have taught me much of what I know. But the truth is, I have no need to answer you for anything. I am the divine benna. So I answer not to you but Dwr alone, as Dwr answers only to the One."

"You dare *speak* to me thus?" he cried. "Divine benna? You? What know you of sacred things, except for what I've taught you? Were it not for me, you'd still be living midst the dung and mud from whence you came." He raised his staff and swung it out.

The staff had struck countless times before. Despite his age, he could swing it very hard, and Torgon had always cowered quickly, because she was embarrassed to be seen with so many bruises. Not so on this occasion. When she saw him lift the staff, she reached out to stop it. Not in anger. Indeed, Torgon found she had no feelings at all in that very moment. Her blood, instead, lay in her veins like shattered ice.

When the old man realized she meant to take the staff, fury raged through him, turning his face from pink to red to nearly purple. A terrible struggle ensued. He wasn't going to let her have it, while Torgon now realized she had to finish what she'd started. She didn't wish to hurt him. Ferocious as he was, youth and strength were on her side. It would be unjust to hurt him. Moreover, even as she realized she must take possession of the staff, she knew it was unseemly that they should fall to fighting thus, hand to hand, as if they were naught but beggars after scraps.

Unable to get a hold on the flailing stick, Torgon finally plunged past it and grabbed the old man by his robes. He jerked back. She grabbed the flesh of his neck to keep him from breaking free. Within a heartbeat she had both hands there, her thumbs pressed to his throat. At that, his anger passed abruptly into fear.

"You have sought to be my overlord too long," she said. She was only inches from his face and her voice, staccatoed by panting from the struggle, was naught more than a whisper. "Drop the stick."

The staff clattered to the floor.

Beneath her thumbs Torgon could feel the rapid flutter of his pulse. It would be easy as crushing the dry reeds at the riverside to close her grip, and in that fleeting moment, she knew he expected her to do it.

She met him eye to eye. "Know that I am made for better stuff than the killing of an aged man. It would be unseemly to take the life of someone so much weaker than myself."

When she let go, he staggered, then fell to his knees, then finally forward until he was as an animal on all fours.

"You are at the feet of the divine benna," she said quietly. "Show rightful obeisance."

The old man went down prostrate on the floor.

"Kiss the holy shoes lest you forget again who serves whom."

He did.

"Now rise."

With anguished slowness the old man struggled first to his knees and then, totteringly, to his feet. He kept his head down as he turned and began to hobble towards the door.

"Here." Torgon bent and picked up the wooden stick. "You forget to take the staff which aids you in your walking." She held it out to him.

The Seer reached for it but when his hand was on the staff, Torgon didn't release it. "First tell me one thing, old man," she said. "Is this really all there is to power between the divine benna and the holy Seer? A stick and who possesses it?"

He said nothing.

She let go of the staff. "I am sickened to my very soul to think that such a thing is true."

The eighth hare lived and Torgon saw this as an auspicious sign, for eight had been given her as her luck number on her naming day. Summer had ended by then and it was the month of the big moon, so Torgon fed the animal generously on fresh-made hay and harvest roots to make it strong again. Each night she examined its abdomen to feel the tiny ribboned scar where the skin had knit back together again.

This success made her brave and she captured one of the village dogs. The dog was easier to catch, but it felt unholier this time. Dogs were unclean creatures, forbidden in the compound, and she had to resort to guile to get it into her quarters. This gave the activity a *shameful aura and kept Torgon keenly aware of how many holy rules she was forced to break to follow where the visions led her.*

Yet after Torgon lay the sedated dog out on the stone floor of her private cell and began the now-familiar process of opening the body cavity, a sense of renewed wonder overcame her. The dog's organs were hand-sized, not minuscule like the hare's, and their strange, living smell filled the room. She sat in awe and stared. This was not evil. Torgon knew this utterly. No matter how profane what she was doing might look to others, Torgon knew she had been given insight into a truly sacred thing.

Chapter Twenty-One

"When you talk about your university years," James said, "I hear real happiness. You were enjoying the freedom to be yourself, to study what interested you, to experience Torgon whenever you wanted. You talk about enjoying the social set-up because it provided interaction without – from what I'm hearing – too much commitment. You could just dip in and out as you pleased. But what about boys?" James asked. "Did they figure during these years too?"

"Yes," Laura said. "I had my first boyfriend in my sophomore year. His name was Matt and he was a fellow pre-med student. We were both a bit socially inept." She laughed heartily. "In Matt's case, it was just brains. He was one of those people who could think better than he could do anything else. And he was absolutely passionate about medicine. He was planning to become a specialist in tropical diseases. Life with Matt meant getting excited about parasites and Lassa fever. Hormones would overcame us periodically and we'd indulge in a bit of kiss-and-cuddle, but it was so innocent. We never had sex. We never really even made out seriously. I didn't mind. After Steven, I didn't want anything to do with sex.

"The relationship was sustained by our mutual obsessions. While we didn't share each other's interests, we both knew what it was to have such an all-consuming enthusiasm for something. Consequently we spent most of our time together separately, me writing, him reading. Hardly a word would be exchanged between us for hours. He never asked me what I was doing; I never asked him. The relationship lasted about two years and happy as clams we were during that time, just being who we were."

"Medical school was when it all really came together for me," Laura said. "My undergraduate years had felt free simply because home had been such a cage, but I outgrew college quite quickly. My focus shifted and I became an increasingly serious student. Because I was doing it for Torgon, classes meant more to me than just grades. I really felt motivated to learn the stuff. So it got annoying when other people were farting around, getting drunk, making noise in the middle of the night. I'm an eight-hour-a-night girl. Without it I can't concentrate. So if people were making noise and I didn't sleep well, it meant I couldn't focus in class but it also meant I couldn't focus on writing.

"Medical school was entirely different. Everybody was serious there. It also meant having my own place for the first time. I was twenty-two and my first apartment was dark and dinky and up five flights of stairs, but I loved it for just that reason. It was a regeneration of my attic bedroom on Kenally Street, only this time without Steven Mecks.

"Studying medicine was just so fantastic. I had chosen medicine because of that child with the cleft palate in Torgon's world, and that inspiration was burning so brightly by the time I got to med school. I was able to relate everything I studied to Torgon, to societies like hers where people died from easily preventable causes. Wonderful plans were beginning to form in the back of my mind. When I finished my degree I decided I would go abroad to work in the Third World, and this would bring to reality what I'd been overhearing in dreams all my life. It just seemed so right to do this, such a complete full circle. Torgon had given me a deep awareness of the importance of medicine and I, in turn, would bring this knowledge back to people like hers. This gave a powerful sense of meaning to my life. Torgon was no longer a silly fantasy, or worse, a form of mental illness. She was a muse, an inspiration directing me to a vocation. A calling. Isn't that what the word 'vocation' really means? And how can you be 'called' without hearing a voice?

"I don't think I was ever so happy as I was in those first two years of med school. During my classes and seminars I would consciously pull Torgon into my mind and try to see it through her eyes. How would this information look to someone who was not literate? Who had never seen an operating theatre? Who had no recourse to antibiotics? How would she evaluate it? How could she use it? When I looked at things that way, everything stood out in such clear detail. Through her eyes, everything was new and incomprehensibly fascinating. School became almost a spiritual experience for me."

* * *

James had got into the habit of opening the folder of Torgon stories as soon as Laura's session had ended and reading. In the beginning, he'd read whole stories at a time, soaking up thirty or forty atmospheric pages of life in Torgon's rigid tribal society. Of late, however, he'd been rationing them. There were only about a hundred of the dog-eared, typewritten pages left, so he tried to restrict himself to only four or five at a time.

Now he opened it where he had last left off, and began to read.

During the month of deep snow, Torgon was awakened in the night by distressed crying from the acolytes' quarters. Someone was ill.

She remained in her bed and listened. The health of the acolytes was the Seer's domain, not hers. She wasn't expressly forbidden to come into the presence of an ill person, but as she was divine, it was assumed she wouldn't wish to taint herself. Consequently, no one expected her to leave her cells.

At first she didn't. The Power was stirring, as it often did when she awoke in the night, stirring and turning, as if making itself comfortable within her body, much as she imagined an unborn child must do within its mother.

What came to her as she lay in the darkness was the image of the moon-kissed child. More than three years had passed since the baby had been put to death, but the child's shade still lingered near, something Torgon never dared mention to the Seer. And it came now, wandering into her mind as a girl of five or six, smiling, her mouth healed to naught but a crooked line. Like the line on the belly of the hare, *Torgon thought.*

Could lips and palate be sewn back together? As with the abdominal skin? Like a flint struck in darkness, the idea sparked through Torgon's mind. Was there a real possibility of repairing a moon kiss with a weapon no greater than a needle and a thread? She tried to visualize the act.

A sudden clamour outside in the corridor dissolved the vision.

One of the holy women was hurrying down the corridor, a basin of steaming water in her arms. A gaggle of acolytes came trotting after. "Holy benna, we have awakened you," she said. "I'm so sorry." She dipped her head in a brief gesture of obeisance.

"What's happening among the acolytes?"

"One has fallen ill with the retching illness."

"Take me there."

"The Seer is already with her, holy benna. Do you not think it better you should remain here? You would not wish to take the illness yourself."

The Power stirred, interfering with Torgon's view of the woman. "No," she replied. "It is Dwr's will that I go."

A murmur of surprise ran through the throng of children when Torgon entered. They knelt quickly in obeisance. Beyond them in the second row of pallets the Seer was beside a young girl clad in the night garments of a high-born child. Torgon came nearer to see that it was Loki, the warrior's daughter.

The Seer already had holy candles lit. With his fingers he dripped cleansing oils into the small flames. The oil's astringent scent mingled with the sour smell of vomit.

The girl was as pale as a ghost, her eyes dull and dark in the wan light of the holy candles. Nonetheless, she managed a flicker of a smile on seeing Torgon. "I am honoured by your presence, holy benna," she murmured, "but I am sorry, for I cannot do you obeisance."

"I'm sure it is in your heart to do it, Loki," Torgon said, and pulled over one of the low stools.

The Seer reached a hand out to prevent her from sitting. "It would be better if you are not so close. She has grown sorely ill and the candles have not burned for long."

Ignoring him, Torgon sat anyway. "How old are you now, Loki?"

"I've seen thirteen summers pass, holy benna."

Torgon reached forward and stroked back the girl's dark hair. "You are very hot. How long have you felt ill? For when I saw you at your prayers this evening, I noted nothing wrong."

"My stomach has been vaguely sore a day or two, but I have not felt ill. It only comes upon me now and gives such pain. It makes me bring my stomach up, but even afterwards there is no relief from it."

Torgon could hear the wise woman in the corridor. She wore all her jingles and rattles tied around her waist so that a cacophony of sound preceded her arrival.

The Seer bent close. "Come away now, holy one. The wise woman is here to draw the evil spirits forth."

"I wish to remain."

The wise woman approached the pallet. Her dark hair was oiled and scented and bound up in numerous tiny braids. Her face was painted brightly with many colours to warn the evil spirits of her previous successes. Bending over Loki she spread her hands wide, the fingers splayed, and began the ritual movements necessary to locate where in the child's body the evil spirits dwelled. As she found each place, she set a small iron amulet over it. When all nine were placed, she untied a huge red rattle and began to shake it rhythmically. She closed her eyes and crooned for the birds of night to come and fetch away the spirits.

Torgon watched her intently. There was no holiness in the wise woman. She drew her powers from the dead and it was well known that wise women had no souls.

"Divine benna, come away now," the Seer whispered. *"It is not seemly that you should sit so close to her when she is at her magic. Besides, I wish to talk to you."*

Rising reluctantly, Torgon withdrew to the altar room with the Seer. *"Yes? What would you say?"*

"Your time would be better spent in prayer at the altar. I have felt the child's belly and fear there is naught the wise woman can do for her. It is in my mind that she has swallowed a plum stone."

"What? Surely not."

"Aye," he said. *"For it always comes as this — a pain here where the stone catches, a fever, death — I have seen it several times before. Her pain is so sudden and so acute that I fear even now the evil spirits have broken free of the plum stone to rule her body."* His expression grew sad. *"It shall be a sorrow to her father, for he has always been greatly fond of her. As of this winter, his wife has given him his sixth son, but she remains his only daughter."*

"Is it certain she will die?" Torgon asked.

"Aye, when the plum stone becomes trapped, it rots and that attracts the evil spirits. The wise woman will try to draw them forth but I've never seen her master these. They lie deep within the body and can resist her charms."

Torgon looked pensive.

"Come. We shall pray together at the altar for the safe passage of her soul."

"No," she said.

The Seer looked puzzled.

"No. I don't think it's as you say," Torgon murmured. *"For why would she have swallowed a plum stone now, when winter is so deep? We are well past the time of plums."*

"A stone will sometimes be missed when the plums are being dried. Or perhaps she swallowed it in summer and it was slow to rot. The weather, as you know, has been very cold this year."

"This offends my reason," Torgon replied. *"For as I think more upon it, it's in my mind that Loki does not like the taste of plums. Why then would she have any cause to swallow up the stone?"*

The Seer shook his head. *"I do not know the answers, holy benna. I only know what I have learned from long experience and this serves me well. So we must leave the wise woman to her rattles. The time has come for you and me to pray."*

"No. Dwr bids me stay beside the girl." And she left the altar room.

Moving through the small crowd gathered around the young girl's pallet, Torgon knelt beside Loki. *"The Seer fears you have been eating wild plums."*

Grown tearful with the pain, Loki struggled to keep her composure. *"No. No, holy benna, I have touched no wild plums."*

"I know the storeroom is a great temptation. And wild plums, especially when they're dried, are very sweet. It is in my heart to understand how much a child loves sweetness. I wouldn't be angry with you, Loki, if you were to tell me now you did not resist."

"But I ate no wild plums at any time. I don't like them."

Torgon nodded. *"Very well. Then may I lay my hands upon you?"*

The Power swelled abruptly as Torgon's fingers touched the young girl's skin. Her eyes went blind to the grey stone walls, flickering in the candlelight. What rose instead was the image of Loki lying on a white surface, her abdomen open like the abdomen of the dog. Each part in its own kingdom, *the Power whispered.*

The girl shrieked in pain when Torgon pressed into the lower left of her body and the noise wrenched Torgon sharply from the trance. Momentarily disoriented, she shook her head to clear it.

"Stop! It hurts too much!" Loki's hands were on her wrist. "Please, oh holy benna, stop!"

The Seer pushed through the group. "Holy benna, this is unseemly. Come away. The evil spirits will taint you. Turn your mind from this. It isn't your domain."

The Power fingered back into Torgon's mind, making it difficult to concentrate on what the Seer said. The body of the dog. Each to its own kingdom. Walk among the kingdoms. Heal a moon kiss with no greater weapon than a needle and a thread, *the Power whispered.*

The iron amulets had fallen from Loki's body during Torgon's exploration, so the wise woman leaned down and picked them up again. Replacing them on Loki's abdomen, she raised a long string of bells and clashed them noisily.

Torgon couldn't make sense of anything when her attention was pulled in so many directions. She pressed her hands to the sides of her head and turned in irritation. "Silence!" The wise woman didn't hear her and clanged her bells again. "Silence!" Torgon shouted.

Everything then fell abruptly still, save the Power, thrumming in her head. The acolytes froze, wide-eyed. The Seer's mouth fell open. The wise woman clapped the noisemakers tight against her generous bosom.

"Get out," Torgon said to the wise woman. "Such noise may drive off evil spirits but it is offending Dwr as well."

The wise woman lowered her bells. Her painted face rendered the nuances of her expressions unreadable, but her eyes rolled white like a frightened calf's. There was a long, uncertain moment, as she looked from the Seer to Torgon and back again, but then she nodded and backed away from the bed.

"This is not of Loki's making," Torgon said. "It is not a plum stone. Dwr speaks to me even now as I stand among you and says *to me that one kingdom in her body is rising up to wage war against its peaceful neighbours. They have not the means to stop it; their warriors have already been defeated, but this kingdom must be overthrown. The child will die if its warriors are allowed to leave its borders."*

"What difference does it make," the Seer asked, "to call this a warlike kingdom and not a poisoned plum stone? If the other kingdoms have already lost their warriors, nothing can be done."

"Dwr bids I take up weapons and fight on their behalf."

Pouring the heavily scented death oil into a soft cloth, Torgon leaned close to the child. "Don't be frightened," she said gently. "Where I am sending you this night I have journeyed many times myself when in search of spirits. It is not a bad place, but only as a dreamless sleep, because Dwr allows you no memory of it when you waken." She then pressed the cloth over the girl's face. Moments passed and the movement seeped from Loki's body. When Torgon lifted the cloth away, the girl lay limp, her breathing shallow.

"Does she walk now among the dead?" one of the children asked.

"Aye," Torgon said. She raised her head and searched the crowd of acolytes. "Morra? You are eldest. You be my arms bearer. I need fire, that I may pass through the kingdom of blood. I need a good whetstone, that I may keep my weapons very sharp. And I need a fine, metal needle. You'll find one in my inner cell, lying on the window ledge. And last of all, I need thread. A long piece, and, I think, for a child's body it must be of gold. Look among Loki's things. She is of the high-born caste and will have fine clothes. One surely will give up its gold for her."

From her wrist Torgon removed the small knife and felt its blade for sharpness. She lay the point against the girl's abdomen and midst a shocked murmur from the group around her, she cut first through the skin and then the muscle. She pulled back the peritoneum to expose the girl's organs. As she did so, steam rose from them into the cold winter air. Fearing this might be the evil spirits escaping from the child's body, the group leaped back. A holy woman gasped and swooned. The wise woman began a soft keening sound. The Seer knelt, as did the acolytes around him.

"Aye, this is a holy sight," Torgon said. "It is right that you should venerate Dwr at this time. Such sacred things may never be shown you again."

She prodded slowly through the exposed organs, searching for something akin to what the Power's visions had shown her. Curious acolytes could not keep themselves at prayer and one by one rose up on their knees to peek at what she was doing.

"This is good, is it not?" Torgon asked a young boy leaning close. "See what a perfect little world it is, kept in its own universe, secret from us? Here is the kingdom of the liver, which is power-ful and has many smaller kingdoms which do homage to it." She gently pushed aside a section of the liver to expose the bile gland. "See? And here, this is the stomach and here too, all these coils, they are allied to the kingdom of the stomach. It is a large kingdom, but it and its allies are peaceable and do not interest other kingdoms much, except for that of blood. The kingdom of blood is interested in everybody's business! Always wanting to know what happens, it goes to all the other kingdoms and, foolishly, will even try to come to us." She smiled at the boy and at the others pressing closer. "See how it is all just like our own world? And somewhere in here there is a kingdom like that of the Deer People. And as with the

Deer People, this kingdom too will lay waste to all around it, if it is not first destroyed."

Midst the tangle of intestines, Torgon came across a reddened protrusion. The Power stirred with such intensity that she had little doubt she'd found what she was looking for, but even without the aid of the Power, Torgon would have recognized it as angrily infected. Taking a bit of thread meant for closing the wound, Torgon tied the protrusion off from the rest of the gut. Then with a deep breath to steady her hand, she cut it free.

Torgon examined the remainder of the exposed organs but found nothing else, so she brought the sides of the incision back together and sutured it closed.

"It's over," she murmured and took a cloth to wipe her dagger clean. Even in the chill of the winter's night, perspiration had formed across her brow and she lifted her arm to wipe away. With the motion, a terrible dizziness overtook her. She swayed on the stool.

Alarmed, one of the holy women hurried forward to steady her. "Are you all right, holy benna?"

"Aye, but I am greatly weary. I must rest. But you, all of you, go forth and spend the remainder of the night in prayer. Loki has had to go among the dead and you must pray that Dwr sees fit to guide her back again. You must also pray that the wise woman's powers have kept other evil spirits far away, such that none could enter the kingdoms of Loki's body in my shadow. And you must pray for me, that Dwr takes pleasure in what I've done."

Loki awoke from the death oils, but a fever overtook her and it was many days before they knew if she would live or die. Torgon spent most of the time fasting, praying, and kneeling beside the girl's *pallet, passing her hands above the incision again and again, willing it to heal.*

On the eighth day, the fever broke and Loki looked up, weak and pale, but clearheaded. Over the next few weeks the incision continued to redden occasionally and spew up bits of thread used in the stitches, but the wise woman came each day to apply a fresh poultice, and at last the redness passed altogether and all that was left was a wrinkled scar, like a sword wound.

Before the moon came again, Loki was able to stand and walk short distances, and it was clear that she would heal. Her father, in appreciation of the miracle, had a sword made from pure gold to lay upon the altar in the compound.

A tremendous celebration was held then, a feast for all the village, even though it was the fourth month of winter and the growing season was still a long way off. Dwr had worked a great healing miracle through his divine embodiment. It was only befitting they should respond with great rejoicing.

Torgon was brought forth in holy robes, the sacred circlet on her head, the golden sword in her hand. She was given the title "anaka", which meant "fierce healer", for she had gone as the anaka warriors had gone against the Deer People, and like them, had slain the war-makers. A holy fire was lit and a stag and a hind were sacrificed to Dwr. The village feasted three days and three nights and the holy fire burned throughout.

When the celebrations were over, Torgon withdrew to the high holy place above the forest. It was here that the Power had first come to her, so it was here she returned for contemplation. She'd brought with her the eighth hare, the first one to survive her efforts at entering the kingdoms of the body. She'd kept it alive in the compound with the idea of sacrificing it to Dwr on the high holy place when the appropriate moment came. Now, however, Torgon realized this would not be the right thing to do. Killing it in return for its sacred knowledge seemed unfitting. Torgon considered letting the creature go free to return to its own kind, for she sensed that would honour Dwr. But this idea too she dismissed. Dwr might be honoured by the act, but not the hare. After the sheltered life of warmth and easy food provided in the compound, if she turned it loose now in the freezing snow, it would most likely die before it found its own kingdom. Putting a hand over the creature, she felt for its living warmth through her clothing. What she would do is cease eating the flesh of hares, even in the lean month when hunted meat was often all there was. That would be her oblation. From this moment forth, hares would become a sacred animal to her, in the way of the eagle and the great cat.

Chapter Twenty-Two

"My adviser was this very crusty old doctor named Betjeman," Laura said. "An excellent teacher but we were all scared to death of him, because he was very demanding. He never accepted less than your best. Never gave you an inch. But he was also very good at nurturing talent.

"He stopped me after seminar one night and asked me what my plans for the future were and whether I intended to specialize. I said I was interested in general surgery, which wasn't an area at that time that a lot of women were in. He nodded approvingly and said, 'That's a good career choice. I've been watching how you approach your work and it's with a whole different insight to most of your fellow students. You're impressive, Deighton. I have no doubt that if surgery is your interest, you'd be capable of rising right to the top of the field.'

"It made me so proud to have him say that that I dared to tell him I had a dream. I remember saying that I knew it sounded corny, but I didn't really want a 'career'. I wanted to go abroad, in the Peace Corps or one of the medical charities, go somewhere where there wasn't enough medical know-ledge, where there wasn't the trained staff to carry out basic care. I explained that I wasn't learning this knowledge for myself. I wanted to carry it to others. I wanted to pass it on.

"I loved my studies, but there was a downside. Spending all day in classes and at the hospital and all night writing didn't leave me time for anything else. Certainly not a social life. Although moving to the apartment had given me the kind of freedom and solitude I craved, I hadn't appreciated that it would also completely cut me off from people. I didn't mind too much because I never felt lonely, but I think I knew I was missing out. That's probably what made me so susceptible to Alec."

There was a pause. Laura looked down at her hands and examined her fingernails a moment.

"Alec was a radiologist at the hospital where I was doing practical work. Tall, very skinny and with a badly receding chin. Not handsome at all," she said. "Not the kind of guy I was naturally attracted to. I expect he would have remained invisible to me except for a slapstick episode in the hospital cafeteria one day. I had just gotten my lunch and was carrying it to a table when I managed to trip over my untied shoelace and threw my spaghetti all over him. There was loud clap-ping and people shouting, 'Well done, Deighton!' I was morti-fied, but Alec couldn't have been sweeter about it.

"Anyway, it started from there. He offered to buy me a doughnut to show me there were no hard feelings, and then, as happens with these things, one thing led to another.

"Alec and I started dating and a relationship began to grow. My first real relationship. Not the parallel play Matt and I had engaged in during college. Alec and I started to share ourselves openly because we genuinely wanted to know more about each other.

"It was with Alec that I finally dared to have sex again," Laura said. "I thought maybe the time had come to try and change my attitude towards sex, because I knew I couldn't avoid it forever. I didn't tell him the full details of Steven, but he guessed because he'd had a bit of sexual abuse in his own past. So I trusted he would understand and be sensitive. And he was.

"I still had no pleasure associated with sex. Only pain and loathing. I wish I could say Alec's sensitivity fixed it all. Poor Alec. He did try. He was so gentle with me, but he just wasn't very good at it. I don't think he'd had much more experience of sex than I had. The most important thing in his mind was to make me come. So he wouldn't quit until I had had a 'good time' too, as he put it. He would rub and twiddle and tweak endlessly, even after he'd come himself. I didn't even realize what he was trying to do the first time and so the sex lasted about three hours. I just wanted to scream at him." She laughed ruefully. "After that, I just faked it straightaway to get it over with.

"Every time we tried, my mind sat like a vulture on the bedstead, watching me, as if it were outside my body. All I could think about was what a power play sex is, how, when I made him orgasm, he would surrender himself up to it and to me in the process. I'd watch Alec roll over afterwards and go blithely off to sleep and I would lie there awake for hours, thinking about the issue of power and who had it, realizing I would probably never orgasm during sex because I didn't intend on ever letting someone else have control of me like that. I realized this was Steven's legacy, but it was one thing to understand why it was there, and a completely different thing to be able to get rid of it.

"During one of these post-coital thinking periods when I was mulling over the possibility that sex wasn't ever going to be a way I could truly share myself with Alec, I started to wonder if there was some other means of achieving that level of intimacy. I genuinely did want to experience closeness with someone. That's when I realized that there *was* one thing that was that intimate: Torgon."

"This was a hard decision. How could I share Torgon? Here I am, a twenty-three-year-old med student, and I still have an imaginary companion. Would Alec think I was nuts? Would he be repulsed and never want to see me again? Or be afraid of me, because I was hearing voices? Then I thought, there'd never really be any way to share myself deeply with another person without sharing Torgon too.

"It took me about six weeks to screw up the courage. It was late autumn. The rain was beating hard against the windows. We had a huge fire roaring in the fireplace. Elgar was playing on the stereo and we were drinking steaming mugs of mulled wine. I wasn't drunk precisely, but the wine had smoothed away all my rougher edges. I hadn't been able to bring myself to actually talk about Torgon, but I offered Alec a couple of stories and let him read them while I lay snuggled against him and watched the fire.

"'*Wow*!' Alec said when he'd finished. He sounded amazed 'You're *really* a good writer! This is brilliant, Laura. You make this place and these people jump right off the page. This woman *lives*. I read it and she's just there, in front of me.'

"'Really? You think so?' I said, profoundly flattered.

"'It's amazing. How did you think all of this up?' he asked.

"The wine had taken its toll by then. I told him the whole story, right from the start, all about how Torgon had come to me, everything about the Forest and her complex society with its rigid social hierarchy, religion and laws.

"Alec was spellbound. The more I talked, the more eager he became. He asked me lots of questions about how I'd interpreted the experience. Had I thought of it in terms of my own life? What had I learned from it? Had it made me a better person? That kind of thing.

"I'd had quite a lot to drink by then, and it was getting really late, so my tongue was going without my brain in gear. I told him about how I had become a doctor for Torgon, to acquire knowledge I knew she needed, because in some strange way it made me feel like I was giving it to her.

"Alec's expression was starry-eyed with awe. He said, 'You are just so lucky.'

"I agreed, because I knew I was.

"Then he said, 'Do you think if I asked her something, she'd talk to me?'

"I said, '*Huh?*'

"'Would she talk to *me?*' he repeated with slow, precise diction, as if I had a hearing disability. 'On one of those occasions when you have her coming through.'

"'Talk to you? How ever could she talk to you? Alec, she's in my imagination.'

"'Don't you realize this is trance channelling?'

"I thought he'd said 'trans-channelling' and was madly trying to puzzle out the direction the conversation was taking by decoding the Latin prefix.

"'I have some friends you've simply got to meet, Laura. When they hear about Torgon, it's just going to blow them away.'

"'Friends?' I said with alarm. 'Alec, listen, don't tell anybody else about this. This is *private*, for goodness sake. You don't understand. It took me ages just to screw up the courage to tell you.'

"'No, it's *you* who doesn't understand, Laura. Torgon is real. She's coming through to you from a higher plane of enlightenment and giving you all this insight and self-knowledge. That's how you've gotten to such a brilliant place so easily. And you don't even realize what's happening to you. That's what's so mind-bending about all of this. You must have the most incredible gift for channelling! Once you open yourself up, you're going to be another … well, I don't know … probably like another Siddhartha. So believe me, I know people who are *so* going to want to meet you.'

"I knew Alec dabbled in New Age stuff. What I'd first experienced as a wonderful openness to his feelings was, I later discovered, one of Alec's ways of coping with a rather fragile personality. But never in a million years would I have guessed that he'd assume Torgon was a real person. What I'd wanted from the evening was simply to share my colourful, complex imagination. What Alec wanted was a medium.

Laura paused. She looked down at her hands folded in her lap.

"You know how life has these turning points?" she murmured softly. "Those 'sliding door' moments where you realize if you had made one single choice differently, it would have meant a whole different life …?"

Again a pause. It lingered.

"That was one of them. In that moment, I saw Alec for what he was. A loser, talking bullshit. Even so … I just ignored it. I let him talk me into going to meet these 'friends'. In fact, I have to admit, it didn't take a lot of persuasion."

Intrigued, James looked over at her. Laura had slid down into the enveloping closeness of the chair. Her arms were protectively across her body, which made James think she felt in danger.

"Why do you suppose that was?" he asked. "You believe completely that Torgon is just part of your imagination. You're almost mocking what Alec believed. Yet it was easy to be talked into seeing his friends?"

"That's the question I always come back to," she said softly. "Why didn't I just say no?"

Silence drifted in and James allowed it to settle because it was more a thinking silence than a silence of reticence.

"The truth, I guess, is that I wanted so badly to feel special," she said at last. "I wanted to be that wonderful, magical person Alec believed I was. A part of me did think it was wrong – deceptive – but, still, it seemed harmless. And okay to do because the initiative was coming from him, not me. Like how it happens with Father Christmas when you're a kid. How you know he's not real, but it doesn't hurt to pretend. And other people – important people to you, like your parents – want it that way too. So it creates a kind of conspiracy, this sense that if you all believe something together that makes everybody happy, somehow that cancels out the fact that it's a lie."

"On the surface Alec's group of friends were much like me. They were all young, middle class, well-educated. But whereas I'd turned inward to cope with the problems in my life, they had all turned outward to seek answers. Their weekly discussions covered a whole patchwork of things – New Age stuff, Eastern philosophy, imagined religions like druidism, alien intervention, visitation from angels.

"Alec had told them about me before I got there, so when I did come, it wasn't at all like walking into a crowd of strangers. They greeted me very warmly and ... well, reverently. They'd shake my hand, holding it a moment, and gaze into my eyes as if they were meeting a celebrity.

"Everyone seemed to go along with Alec's theory that Torgon was some external spirit from a higher realm who had chosen to come and personally guide me towards my own enlightenment. They found it amusing when Alec told them how persistent Torgon had had to be in leading me to them and how even now I was reluctantly 'being dragged kicking and screaming into the Light', as he put it. Torgon took on such a wise and charming personality in the way Alec presented her. I remember feeling all warm and fuzzy, knowing she 'belonged' to me. It was nice too, in its way, to imagine that Torgon actually did think about me occasionally, not just the other way around.

"When we broke for refreshments, a young woman came up to me and asked me how it all started, how it had felt when I'd first experienced Torgon. A man appeared beside her and he asked me if I'd actually seen Torgon with my eyes. Pretty soon other people came. I sat down on the arm of an easy chair and before I realized it, everyone in the group had clustered around my feet.

"I'm not someone who speaks easily in public. Even now. But that night was different. I found it unexpectedly effortless to talk to them. They weren't like the Loony Tunes I'd expected them to be. They were sincere and open and just wanted to know what my experiences had felt like. No analysis. No judgement. No denigration for having this impossible thing in my head. They just wanted to understand what it had been like for me, my emotions, my insights. Any worry I'd had about being deceptive passed away over the course of that conversation, because what I was telling them was the truth. These *were* my feelings and my observations. I'd spent my whole life trying to hide Torgon. For the first time people responded to me as if I had something of value. I felt good. I felt relief."

"I went back to the Tuesday night group the next week. In fact, I started going regularly with Alec. It had genuinely never occurred to me that I was lonely. I'd never thought I was. I'd believed I was really happy with my life of writing and studying. The truth is, however, I'd really, really wanted friends. I had just never dared let myself think about how much, so the Tuesday night group opened a whole new world up for me." Laura laughed in a self-deprecating way. "Except, of course, the truth was that none of these people actually wanted *me*. They wanted Torgon.

"At first, I found it weird how everyone would talk about Torgon as if she were a person there in the room with us – it was like reinventing Dena's and my childhood game – but after a while, I managed to quell the vague feeling that I was somehow demeaning the real Torgon. That was a silly idea. Torgon was nothing more than a creation of my own imagination, so how could I demean her? Right?

"So …" Laura hesitated. She looked over at James, made momentary eye contact, looked away and gave an embarrassed smile. "So, that's how I started channelling."

"Meaning?" James asked.

"Meaning that pretty soon I was saying stuff like 'Torgon tells me such and such.'"

"So Torgon transitioned from an imaginary experience to a public figure?"

Laura gave a self-conscious nod. "I wish I could say I felt bad about it or that it caused me to think lots of deep, philosophical thoughts about the consequences of deception, but I put a different slant on it. I didn't see myself as taking advantage of them. They were all vulnerable people in one way or another and I genuinely wanted to help them. Coping with life seemed to come a lot more naturally to me than to anyone else there. All I really did was make common-sense suggestions. But if it had just been me saying this stuff, no one would have paid any attention. If I said Torgon thought they should try something, however, people always took the suggestions seriously. And the suggestions *did* help. I really was doing something positive."

"So you felt that using Torgon in this way was beneficial to others? Were any other factors influencing your decision to do this, do you think?" James asked.

Laura grimaced. "Yes. I enjoyed being liked. Being special." She grew tearful.

"That brings up strong feelings?" James asked gently.

"It's hard to convey how important that felt," she said softly. "It sounds like such a selfish reason for doing something so deceptive … But it was like being back with Pamela in fourth grade. Only I got to *be* Pamela this time around. That felt so good."

"It's understandable."

"Once I started, though, I couldn't stop. I couldn't just decide the next week I didn't want to talk about Torgon. So it was only a matter of weeks before the Tuesday night group metamorphosed into my group – '*Laura's* group' – people actually called it that. New people started coming just to see me. I *loved* it. I kept thinking: 'What difference does it make if I say the advice comes from Torgon?' *I* was Torgon, so it wasn't as if I were taking credit for something that wasn't mine. And I *was* helping people. I wasn't even charging them any money. That felt noble … sort of …

"My relationship with Alec got weird, though. He was totally caught up in the whole spirit-guide thing. He was obsessed with Torgon to the point of talking about her continually as though she was actually with us, and adopting all the reverential terminology and postures that the people in Torgon's world used towards her. Honestly, he came across as a lunatic. We broke up, finally, much to the relief of both us, I suspect, because what he really wanted was Torgon and not me. This way he could just be one of the group and talk only to her."

"What about the 'real' Torgon?" James asked. "Were you still experiencing the original Torgon while Torgon-the-spirit-guide was coming into being?"

Laura leaned back into the chair and for a long moment was pensive. "I can see now that the Torgon who had sustained me for so long was starting to recede at about that point," she said. "Only very subtly. I could only see it in retrospect. But as I became more and more involved with the Tuesday night group, the genuine Torgon did become less vivid."

"Then there was a new turn of events. About two months after I'd started with the Tuesday night group, a member called Robin, an artist, asked me to lunch at her place the following Saturday. She told me all about her own spirit guide, some character with a horsy-sounding name like 'Dobbin'. She wanted my advice on making his messages more coherent, because from what she was telling me, they sounded like they mostly came off a Magic 8 ball.

"Then out of the blue, she said, 'Has Alec arranged for you to meet the Prophet?'

"Alec had never said anything to me about any prophets. When I said no, she replied enigmatically, 'I've no doubt you'll get the call soon.'

"Up to that point, I had never heard of this person, but you know how it is once you become aware of something. Suddenly everyone is mentioning him.

"His name was Fergus McIndoe but no one ever called him by his name. He was just 'the Prophet'. The story went that in his early twenties, he'd dropped out of university and gone off to 'find himself' in India. There, with all the mystics and yogis and whatnot, he learned to 'open his consciousness' and channel an assortment of higher beings, who, as they were pure energy and past the need for physical bodies, came to him only aurally. So he referred to them as 'the Voices'. When he returned to the Boston area, he established himself as a very successful psychic and had since devoted his life to passing on the Voices' wisdom.

"I was fascinated to meet him. Knowing that my own 'abilities' were gentle fakery, I was highly curious about his. I was equally interested to find out if he'd be able to detect what I was doing. Would we call each other's bluff? Or was there a kind of Magic Circle for psychics like there is for magicians, where you never told how tricks were done?

"But this guy wasn't simply someone making a few bucks off the gullible. He had also predicted a great human conflict in which only the most highly evolved beings would survive. The Voices, naturally, knew who the select would be, and they had decreed that the Prophet had been chosen to be the new spiritual leader in North America who would provide guidance to people through the dark time. Eventually he would lead them to create a new world, known as the New Atlantis."

Laura laughed good-naturedly. "I know it sounds ridiculous. But you know how these cults can start. All you need is one charismatic nutter preaching the end is nigh, and there you are.

"Anyway, it didn't bother me at all that the Prophet had these weird, grandiose ideas. If anything, it made him seem exotic and enigmatic, more like someone from Torgon's world than our own. I very much wanted to meet him. I also knew that eventually I would need his endorsement if I was to continue using my own 'powers' with the group.

"Despite Robin's prediction, however, the Prophet never made any effort to contact me. According to people in the Tuesday night group, he tended to just drop in on them unannounced occasionally and that was no doubt what would happen, but I had been going for almost three months by that point and he had still never shown up. Nor did he make himself known to me in any other way. There wasn't the slightest indication that he was even aware of my existence.

"In the end I decided that if the mountain wouldn't come to Mohammed, then Mohammed was just going to have to go to the mountain. After a bit of investigation, I discovered the Prophet used a private room at an exclusive health club near the city centre to give psychic readings. So I called for an appointment. There was a three-week waiting list. Moreover, what he charged for a fifteen-minute reading would have bought my groceries for two weeks.

"I didn't want anyone in the Tuesday night group to know what I was planning to do, certainly not Alec, and I didn't want to give the Prophet any advantage, so I made the booking in Tiffany's name instead of my own. Then I waited, curious. And curiously excited.

When I got to the health club, I remember being greeted very courteously by this young woman at the front desk. I can even recall what she was wearing – this blue and white outfit that made her look like a stewardess. She led me through the area where all the weight equipment was and then opened a door to a staircase. 'That way,' she said and pointed downward while remaining on the landing herself. I remember feeling unexpectedly nervous and wishing she'd come with me.

"At the foot of the stairs there was a very large room with a low ceiling and stucco-textured walls. The floor was covered with a deep shag pile carpet in the most startling St Patrick's Day green. The health club was built on a slope, so despite the fact that I had entered at street-level upstairs and come downstairs, this room was at ground level in the back. Early evening sunlight was slanting in through floor-to-ceiling windows on that side and it gave the carpet a vibrant aliveness, as if it were real grass, but at the same time, it made the rest of the room feel squashed because of the low ceiling. The entire room was completely empty except for the far corner, distant from the windows. There the Prophet sat behind a flimsy-looking table. The only other piece of furniture was a chair opposite him for the client.

"He remained seated behind the table and I was keenly aware of how much more easily he was able to size me up as I crossed the vast space than I was him. I tried to stride confidently. He watched me closely. I watched him watching me.

"As I came up to the table, he rose to his feet and reached out to shake my hand. With a name like Fergus I'd been expecting a tall, ruddy-haired Celt, some kind of William Wallace or Rob Roy. In fact, he was no taller than I was and looked Latino to me. Loose black curls fell down over his collar and two or three days' growth of stubble gave rebellious virility to his features. He wore cream-coloured safari-type clothes, the kind with all the pockets, and this, along with his stylish shaggy hair and dark looks, gave him the aura of Che Guevara. A very handsome Che Guevara, I might add. All the information I'd had about the Prophet, and no one had mentioned he was drop-dead gorgeous, but he was. It broke my concentration.

"The allure was in his eyes. They were dark and deep and had this magnetic vitality to them that enabled him to effortlessly fix you to the spot. Very gently. You only ever realized afterwards that he had sapped your will.

"'Hello,' he said in a soft, honeyed voice. He shook my hand firmly. Then he sat down and gestured that I do likewise. Folding his arms on the table, he leaned forward towards me. 'So, how can I help you?'"

Laura smiled. "I was struck dumb. It's not too much of an exaggeration to say it was love at first sight. All I could focus on were those melting brown eyes, so dark they looked black in that low light. No mystery here why so many women were parting with serious money to have fifteen minutes of his undivided attention. Two weeks of groceries meant nothing in comparison.

"He was unperturbed with my silence. He just said again with almost hypnotic slowness, 'How can I help you?'

"I said, 'I just wanted to see you.'

"He nodded gently and smiled. 'Very good. And why is that? There's something you'd like to discuss.' This last wasn't a question. He was still studying my face intently. I grew aware of the sustained eye contact and found it hard to keep up. I lowered my head.

"'You have a problem you'd like some help with?' he asked sweetly. He smiled but kept up the unflinching gaze.

"I found it impossible to look at him. I couldn't get my thoughts to organize, which was a weird sensation. They were there, but I couldn't pull them together into coherence. All I could really think about was how handsome he was, how masculine, and, oddly, how good he smelled. It wasn't a scent. Not like aftershave or anything. Just him. Just this warm male odour.

"He stretched his palms, upward, out across the table. 'Here, give me your hands.'

"I held them out. Taking them in his, the Prophet held them in his open palms and regarded them before slowly closing his fingers over them. His skin was startlingly hot. 'You're going to be famous,' he said, still looking down at his hands, holding mine. 'You're going to be very famous indeed.'

"This broke the spell, because I laughed out loud. 'What a great psychic chat-up line', I was thinking.

"The Prophet looked up in surprise. 'I'm mistaken?' He seemed slightly taken aback. 'I can't be. I read it very strongly. Are you famous already, then?'

"'Hardly.'

"'Ah, but you will be.' He had regained his confidence. 'I sense many people knowing who you are. Communication figures very strongly. TV, perhaps? Because I sense you communicating with millions.'

"Withdrawing my hands, I sat back and smiled. 'I bet you tell all the girls that.'

"It was his turn to laugh then, and he did, heartily. 'Ah, a sceptic.' He laughed again. 'I love your kind.' Then abruptly, mid-laugh, he stopped. His gaze grew intent. He searched my face.

"This time I kept eye contact. Torgon came into my mind. *There are small necessities one must learn, the Seer had said, that others might recognize you are holy. Never look away first. The lowering of eyes is for those lesser than yourself.*

"'You are not who you say you are,' the Prophet said in a quiet voice.

"I held his gaze.

"His eyes narrowed, as if trying to see me from a great distance. 'Who are you?'

"His gaze grew so intense that I started feeling uncomfortable in an odd sort of way. In the muted light of that corner of the room, his eyes appeared absolutely black.

"'Who *are* you?' he asked again, his voice barely audible. 'I sense the presence of another. Shimmering around you. Enveloping you in its light. Becoming you ... becoming separate ... becoming you.'

"Instantly, I thought, '*He's seeing Torgon*', and the weirdest sensation went through me, like a shake of ice shards falling inside my body. I physically shuddered. 'I'm Laura,' I whispered.

"When I said that, the Prophet bounced forward in surprise and his chair banged against the table, shattering the eerie moment.

"'*You're* Laura?' he asked with undisguised surprise, his honeyed voice gone into hoarse astonishment. '*You're* Laura? Oh my God, really? Alec's friend?'

"'Yes.'

"Falling back into his chair, he let his shoulders sag in an expression of utter disbelief. 'Why didn't I know?' he cried out. 'Shit! And I've been waiting for you for so long. *Shit*. God. I'm so overwhelmed.'

"I was feeling overwhelmed myself but with something darker. How could he have detected Torgon? What was he doing? The preceding few minutes had been so intense and so weird that I couldn't take this sudden lightness in.

He smiled broadly. 'I've been waiting for you.'

"'How do you mean?' I asked.

"'I *knew* you were the one. They told me it would be you. They said, when I called you, you'd come.'

"'Who are they?'

"'The Voices.'

Confused, I just stared at him.

"'I brought you here, Laura. I called you. You may think you came of your own accord, but I called you, with my mind. And you came because you heard me.'

I just sat there. Because what could I say? I didn't know. I didn't even know what to say to myself at that moment. I stumbled to my feet and said, 'I have to go.' Lifting up my handbag, I began to take out payment for the session.

"'Oh no, no, no,' he said, waving off the money. 'You keep that. I'd never take money from you.' He grinned knowingly.

"Still overwhelmed, I shook his hand, then turned and started towards the door.

"'Oh, and Laura?' he said after me.

"I paused and turned to look at him.

"'You *will* be famous.'"

Chapter Twenty-Three

When the session was over and Laura had left, James went over to the filing cabinet and pulled out the bottom drawer. It was easy to see how the lure of attention and real-life friends had proved too much for this lonely, isolated girl and Torgon-the-imaginary-companion began to fade into the shadows of Torgon-the-spirit-guide.

James was curious, however, about the "real" Torgon. Laura had still been writing about her, even while channelling the fake Torgon. He paged through the thick file of stories, each carefully dated, to see which ones corresponded with the year Laura was twenty-three.

"Four turns of the moon and I haven't talked to you a single time," Mogri said.

Leaning forward, bracing her elbows on her knees, Torgon covered her face with her hands. "I'm sorry, but it has been going ill for me."

"Aye, I can tell. Has there been winter sickness among you at the compound?"

"No, it is the old man. He has fallen into a deathly sleep. His spirit left his body to dwell among the dead some weeks ago, but his body has refused to follow. He must be cleaned and fed like a suckling babe, but there is no reward for it. He never wakes."

"Surely you don't do these things," Mogri said. "What of the holy women?"

"They do much of it, but all his holy tasks fall to me. I must now be the Seer and the benna both. And I feel Dwr would have me spend some time in the old man's presence, so I bring his food to him."

"Remember Old Grandfather?" Mogri said. "So it was the same with him. He similarly fell into a deathly sleep and his body followed soon enough of its own accord. Comfort yourself meanwhile with thoughts of Ansel, for now his coming isn't far."

Mogri looked over and grinned. "And he is so blessed with manly looks, Torgon. You are a lucky one! Fill your time now with dreams of how he'll touch you. I know I would, that's for sure!"

At this, Torgon smiled slightly. Crossing her arms over her knees, she rested her head on them.

"Look how tired you look," Mogri said and reached a hand out to stroke her sister's hair back.

"Do you think it's tiredness? Or am I simply looking old?" Torgon asked. "This gives me worry. I've passed twenty-nine summers, Mogri. I am no longer young. Look. Lines have come across my forehead." She leaned over to show Mogri. "I've wasted all my youth on his aged father. I fear now that Ansel will not wish me for his holy mate. He is handsome and might not want someone whose looks don't equal his."

"I wouldn't worry. You're comely yet, and from what I've heard, Ansel beds happily with any who are willing. And even a few who aren't."

"I've heard the same, but that's just the rutting fever, Mogri. I speak of the holy union. Once it's made, it can't be broken. He won't be bedding any others then."

"He's waited a longer time than you to marry. By his age, he won't want youth from you. He'll only want a mother for his unborn children." She smiled again. "Just think of his lovely curls and beard. And of the many pretty children he will give you. His kind breeds well. No doubt his manroot is as handsome as his face."

Lowering her head, Torgon nodded.

"Poor love. Listen, shall I cheer you with my news?"

"Aye. Aye, of course. I'm sorry I hadn't asked. So tell me what is happening at home?"

Mogri said, "My prospects aren't as grand as yours. I'll never bed a holy-born, but I've done well enough for me. I carry Tadem's child."

Torgon lifted her head abruptly. "I don't believe this. What? My *little sister*? Oh, now I do feel old, Mogri. I'll have grey hairs next." Torgon cuffed her sister's shoulder playfully. "So when's the wedding planned?"

"In the month of flowers. Tadem's family wouldn't have me until they knew I'd quicken. Now the baby comes in summer, so the wedding feast is set."

Smiling, Torgon leaned forward to hug her sister. "I'm so glad for you. It cheers me very much knowing you are happy."

"Things may well change for you too," Mogri said. "There's two months until the marriage. Perhaps it will be Ansel who comes to perform our rites. Who knows? Perhaps we both will carry babes."

* * *

In the month of the first sowing, Torgon came to feed the Seer. The night was bright with a full moon, so she didn't bother with a candle. She entered the darkness of his private cell and in the wan moonlight saw him lying on his bed, his mouth gone slack in death.

Relief flooded her with tears. She wiped them back with her fingertips. "What? You think I cry for you? No, old man. You taught me better manners than that. I cry for joy. I cry for me ..." Reaching out, she gently stroked his cooling hand and, through the moonlight, the tears on her fingers left glistening trails across his aged skin.

The acolytes were sent home for the mourning period and the pyre women came in and washed the Seer's body. After that, it was Torgon alone in the compound. Kneeling beside the body laid out on the stone flags in the altar room, she poured the death oils and anointed him, then said the prayers of intercession, that he might journey safely and find peace among the dead.

Torgon had never met his son Ansel face to face. As a low-born woman, she could not speak to him or even look him in the face in those years before her calling. Matters now, however, were very different. Their roles had been reversed. Holy-born though he might be, hers was the divine calling. He'd be the novice in the compound, although Torgon knew he'd never be the homesick innocent she had been. Destined from birth to take the holy robes, he'd been raised in the compound, receiving a special education apart from the other acolytes, and initiated into the ways of holiness even before his manhood rites. Moreover, Ansel was no longer green with youth. His father had lived such a span of years that Ansel had passed the best part of his manhood among the warrior band and, some would say, had had to wait too long to take up the position due him.

The investiture was held on the sixteenth day of the month of the first sowing, when winter had passed away and the world was just greening up with spring. It was a hard month for lavish feasting, for the storage huts were empty and the crops were yet all seed. Two half-grown bull calves were roasted for the feast and Torgon sacrificed a twelve-point stag in Ansel's honour.

When the ceremony was at its height, she brought the holy robes to him and laid the golden circlet on his head. It was their first time face to face and there should have been a modest dropping of his eyes at the sight of the divine anaka benna. But not so. As she came before him, he looked her fully in the face and smiled, his expression both casual and intimate, as if they'd been secret lovers all along. Torgon's cheeks burned red for fear the elders saw his look and thought it might be true. And yet … She met his gaze. It would unseemly if she did not. In the end, she couldn't help but smile too.

Chapter Twenty-Four

"When I came out of the hospital after my seminar the following afternoon," Laura said during her next session, "there was the Prophet, leaning against my car. I was startled to see him, to say the least. He laughed and said jokingly 'You doubted my ability?'

"If anything, he looked more handsome there in the waning light of a winter's afternoon. He knew how to dress well. He had on casual clothes – a sheepskin coat, a hand-knitted sweater and a very long scarf – but they were expensive and fashionable. His loose curls fell roguishly over his collar and his cheeks were reddened by the cold.

"I don't think I'd even been in love before that night. I had genuinely liked Alec and had expected love to develop from it, but it didn't happen. To be honest, I was secretly afraid Steven might have ruined me permanently and I wasn't capable of falling in love. Then I met Fergus and everything changed.

"What was so incredible, however, was that he felt exactly the same way about me. There he was, standing against my car in the hospital car park less than twenty-four hours after our first meeting. He opened his arms and embraced me in a heartwarming hug and I felt like I was coming home. I pressed my face into his coat and breathed in his marvellous smell, like woodland and sea at the same time, and it felt so undeniably right to be hugged by him. We kissed then, for the first time. Or perhaps it wasn't the first. Who knows?

"The second kiss was with a passion I'd never experienced. It was almost as if he was going to devour me. I'd never been kissed anything like that before, but far from being startled by it, I was desperate for it not to stop. My body responded with such unexpected intensity that if he'd asked me to strip and make love to him right there in the hospital car park, I'm sure I would have considered it. The only thing I could think was: '*This is it. Mr Right. Prince Charming. The fairy tales really are all true.*'

"'Come with me,' he said when we broke apart. 'Let's go eat.'

Of course, I went without question. We got into his car and he headed off towards the city centre. All the way he chattered. Fergus was bursting with vitality. This was his most enchanting quality: he was always just so temptingly alive. It was almost a kind of electricity, fizzing and crackling around him. There was none of the eeriness nor profundity of the night before. He talked to me as if we were good friends, as if I had simply been away somewhere on a long journey and had now at last returned. When I called him 'Prophet', he chastized me good-naturedly, saying, 'What's with this false reverence of yours? It's not as if *you* were one of the acolytes.' Even with the unexpected use of the word 'acolyte' my mind did not stray from giving him my full attention.

"We went to a small, rustic Italian restaurant – like something out of a lost corner of Sicily with red gingham tablecloths, candlelight, a Verdi aria playing softly and the room redolent with the scent of fresh-baked bread and olive oil.

"I loved this scooped-up-and-embraced sensation of belonging to him, but it was still overwhelming. I had only met this man the day before. At one point, I sat back and blinked in surprise at what I was doing.

"Fergus was such a master at reading emotions. His expression melted into sympathy. 'Oh, poor darling,' he whispered. 'You don't remember any of this, do you?'

"'Remember what?' I asked.

"He reached out both his hands and put one either side of my face. Then he leaned forward across the table until we were sitting almost forehead to forehead. 'Close your eyes,' he murmured. His breath touched my skin as he spoke.

"Pressing his fingertips more firmly against my temples, he whispered, 'We've been evolving upwards together all these eons, you and I. Inextricably connected through countless lifetimes. Blackness. Let your thoughts go. Give your mind over to blackness.'

"With my eidetic ability to visualize, the moment he said the words, it was as if black velvet dropped across my thoughts.

"'Accept the visions the Voices give you,' he whispered so softly as to be more a breath than a sound. His head was touching mine. To others in the restaurant we must have appeared as if we were praying. 'Remember, remember, remember.' His voice was hypnotic. 'You will still possess some shadow of memory, for we've been together so long, you and I. Since Egypt. Since Atlantis. Since time before the stars.'

"Stars and planets spun across the velvet blackness of my mind as he spoke. Helixes formed, like the DNA models I'd seen in the lab at the university. A flash of gold appeared and then the masks of Egyptian sarcophagi.

"'We'd almost reached the light, you and I,' he murmured. 'I would have joined the Beings of Light. I would have been among the Voices now. But I lost you. I came into awareness and you were gone …' His voice cracked with sudden emotion. 'I *had* to come back for you. To find you. I couldn't leave you here alone.' He lowered his hands.

"When I opened my eyes, I saw his face was awash with tears. He smiled beatifically through them. 'And now, at last, I've found you.'

"What could I say? I was astonished to find myself at the centre of such a florid, yet achingly romantic story. It was so beautiful. While part of me found it weird, a much more powerful part of me wanted it *and* him. I wanted to touch him, to kiss him, to make love to him. I wanted that more than anything else at just that moment. More than being a doctor. More than Torgon or the Forest. Way more than common sense. So, as out-of-this-world as his ideas were, I felt something in them. I felt maybe this moment *had* been destined since time before the stars.

"The next evening it was out to dinner again. Fergus couldn't pick me up until after eleven because he had appointments to do readings at the health club through until ten o'clock.

"All day I'd been thinking about him obsessively. Any desire I'd had to test him or to show him up as a fake had vanished entirely, as did any desire to deceive him about myself. I decided that I was going to be fully truthful with him about Torgon from the onset. I was going to describe Torgon exactly as she was – the *real* Torgon – and not the hokey thing she'd turned into for the Tuesday night group.

"Fergus was very interested in my relationship with her. How had I first got in contact with Torgon? How had I maintained the contact? What information had I got from her? How did I use it in my everyday life? When had I first felt compelled to share the information with others? What goals had she set for me? What world goals had she offered?

"*World goals?* The conversation had been getting out of hand well before we got to world goals. I was trying to be very honest with him, to explain to him that Torgon wasn't really a spirit guide, but he kept asking questions to the point that it was clear he just wasn't hearing me when I said I was giving people my own advice and simply presenting it as Torgon's. But world goals? Even in my most extravagant imaginings, world goals had never been involved.

"'With as great a gift as you have,' Fergus said, 'you must start thinking this way. It's wrong to keep it to yourself when you are meant to do good with it.'

"I protested and tried to explain that 'using my gift' to help unhappy people at the Tuesday night group was doing quite enough good.

"'No, no, no,' he said and lovingly touched my face. 'We have much greater things to do, you and I.'

"We talked for several hours that night. We were still sitting at the table in the restaurant at one in the morning and the proprietor was making obvious noises with his keys. When I realized what time it was, I became concerned because my alarm was due to go off in only four-and-a-half hours. I mentioned to Fergus that I'd better go and he said '*No,*' in this anguished tone and pleaded with me to stay longer. Flattered as I felt by his insistence, I was too tired and needed to go home. When I objected, however, Fergus became not quite so loving. He said dismissively that I was only tired because I let my body rule my mind, although he did relent and take me home.

"Needless to say, my practicum at the hospital the next day was a session in hell and I sat through Betjeman's afternoon seminar with all the animation of a starfish in formaldehyde. When it was finished and I was preparing to leave, Betjeman stopped me.

"'Stay a moment, Deighton,' he said.

"I was thinking, 'Oh God, not now, not today.' Whatever he had to tell me, I was too tired to care.

"He closed the door to the seminar room and turned to me. 'Are you having problems?' he asked.

"'No sir,' I said. 'I'm just a bit tired today, sir. I stayed up too late last night and realize now I shouldn't have.'

"'I mean more broadly, Deighton. Some of the shine seems to have gone off your work over these past few months. Is there something wrong?'

"My heart began to sink. My work *had* slipped. With all the excitement of the Tuesday night meetings and getting together with people to talk about Torgon's advice, I couldn't do the amount of studying I'd done before. As I'd never had any kind of social life before this, I didn't think I was expecting too much in wanting to enjoy it a little bit. I didn't think I was being excessive. Things would no doubt settle down again, and I'd be able to get back to my studies and catch up on what I'd let slide.

"'Are you still thinking about going abroad when you're through?' he asked.

"'I guess,' I said. I still intended to follow the jungle doctor idea through, but I wasn't in quite the same hurry to get at it as I had been the previous year.

"'I'm asking,' Betjeman said, 'because a colleague of mine down at Johns Hopkins told me there'll be an opening in their surgical programme under Dr Patel by the time you're ready for your internship, and as I'm sure you know, Patel is the best. I prefer seeing people rise on merit, so it isn't my policy to give personal recommendations, but your talents are so special, Deighton, that if you were interested, I'd put your name forward.'

"He paused to regard me. 'You'll still have to be damned ambitious to get it. Even if I recommend you, there'll still be a lot of other people out there who'll want it too and many of them will be just as good as you are.' He smiled. 'But I'd wager none of them is better.'

"'Thank you, sir,' I said.

"'But you must get yourself back into gear again.'

"'Yes, sir.'

"He looked me over carefully. 'I hope you appreciate that you've been given a very rare chance in life, Deighton: both a dream and the talent to fulfil it. Don't waste it, all right? Even the best chances are worthless, if you lack the passion.'

"I came out of the seminar room chastened. Betjeman was right. I had lost sight of my long-term goals. I made a pact with myself then and there that I'd go home, get a good night's sleep and then start hitting the books again.

"To my astonishment, Fergus was waiting for me again in the hospital car park. He embraced me warmly; we kissed and my good intentions vanished like mist.

* * *

"Nothing was by halves with Fergus, and nothing really mattered to him except the spiritual world and his Voices. There was no way to have a conversation with him over football or the plot of a new movie. These things didn't exist in his world. And he didn't know the meaning of 'down time'. I've never come across someone with quite as much energy. He was so alive as to be almost incandescent. It emanated from him, like a force, and it made everything else around him seem a little bigger, a little brighter, a little better just for being in his presence. It affected me too. When I was with him I felt more alive and focused myself. By comparison, everything began to feel dull and grey when we were apart.

"That night he took me back to his house, an elegant old townhouse, opulent with dark oak floors, twelve-inch wide woodwork and antique furniture. Persian carpets and large tapestry cushions were everywhere, giving the rooms the lush aura of a scene from the Arabian Nights.

"'Would you like tea?' he asked, taking me into the kitchen with him.

"When I said yes, he turned to this huge basket on the draining board of the sink. It was full of freshly-cut mint, so much that he must have been growing it himself. He took out whole sprigs, put them into two tall, bevel-sided tumblers and filled the glasses with boiling water from the tea kettle. The room came alive with the most wonderful fresh odour.

"I'd never had mint tea before, had never seen tea made from anything but tea bags and the first thing to spring to my mind was the tea Torgon drank, made from what were called 'water herbs' in her world. I'd always taken 'water herbs' to be a kind of mint. This sudden fusion of Torgon's world with

Fergus's made the evening feel good and right. I forgot immediately how tired I was. Or that I should be studying.

"He took me into a small room lined with books. There was an exquisite little fireplace at one end with a cast iron inset and delicate tiles featuring lilies. A modern black metal desk that seemed quite out of keeping with the rest of the decor was at the other end of the room. On the corner of the desk sat a large crystal ball on a stand, such a beautiful thing that I couldn't resist touching it.

"'Here, come sit down with me,' Fergus said and took a seat midst the cushions on the floor facing the fireplace. The fire had already been laid, so he leaned forward and put a match to it. It sprung to life with a whoosh of yellow flame and engulfed the kindling.

"Before I knew it, his hands were in my hair and his mouth closed hungrily over mine. The scent of burning pine in the fireplace mingled with the watery freshness of our still-undrunk tea and that formed the fabric of my memory of that night, that scent of mint and fire.

"He drew me closer and closer. I felt his fingers at the buttons of his shirt and my hand came up too, frantically undoing my own. My breasts became taut and the feel of my nipples against his hot, hot skin, against the teasing hairs of his chest sent shudders through me of a kind I'd never experienced before.

"He cradled me, crushed me with his lips and sought out the deepest places in me with his tongue. In one fervent coupling, Fergus erased Matt's schoolboy fumbling, Alec's ineptitude and even Steven's bleak violence.

"In the aftermath, we lay wrapped in each others' arms in companionable warmth. I felt very much in love with him at that moment. In the back of my mind was also the awareness of how I'd never thought this moment of love would come for me. It made me cherish Fergus even more. Already I knew I could never live without him.

"The next day followed a similar pattern: hard work and miserable tiredness at the hospital and in seminar, then exhilaration at seeing Fergus waiting for me, food, love and talking into the early hours.

"As we lay languorously in the aftermath of love, I explained how Torgon had arisen from my childhood imagination and, as a consequence, wasn't the same as his Voices. 'She can't come "through me",' I said, 'because she *is* me.'

"'Of course she will come through, Laura,' Fergus said gently.

"'No, it's a different experience for me. Not direct, like you have. There's an aspect of Torgon that isn't me, but I think that's what creativity is – bringing into being something unique and alive in its own right, something that both is and isn't oneself – but it still comes from within me.'

"'You just aren't sufficiently evolved yet, Laura. You'll bring her through in time. You'll hear her voice. I'm here to help you now.' He caressed the hair back from my face. 'This time I won't ascend without you.'

"'But that's the thing, Fergus. I *don't* hear her. Torgon doesn't speak to me. She never has. She can't. She's locked away in a separate universe that's totally inside my head.'

"'Don't you suppose that's all *we* are? What God imagined? That we are simply the universe that is totally inside His head? What are prayers, if not talking to God?'

"'I don't know. But that's not what I'm trying to say. This is really hard for me to admit to you, Fergus, but I have to. I'm already in love with you and I want this to be a totally honest relationship. What I'm doing with the Tuesday night group … that never was Torgon. Ever. The people in the group, they're nice people, but they're grasping for any straws they can find because they are so confused and desperate to alleviate their misery. But to be perfectly honest, Fergus, they don't need help from celestial beings. Someone with common sense and an objective point of view, someone who *cares* about them is all that's required. And so that's what I've done. Since they think it's someone who's really special, like a spirit guide, who cares about them, they're willing to try. All this time I've been telling myself that I'm not doing anything wrong, even though it isn't strictly honest, because sometimes I think the end does justify the means. But I don't want *you* to think Torgon was doing all this. Fact is, Torgon doesn't even know they exist.'

"Fergus wrapped his arms more tightly around me and kissed my hair. 'Of course it's only you. There's absolutely nothing wrong with that. When I'm at the health club, ninety-nine percent of the people I see are lowers. They aren't in any way evolved. So they come to me wanting to know stuff like whether or not they should fuck the chauffeur. Or invest in some dodgy-sounding property deal. Or marry some jerk just because he's got a yacht and a summer home on Martha's Vineyard. These people don't want enlightenment. They want money, a good lay and three-inch fingernails that don't break. For them, there is no more to existence than that. So I bulge my eyes, sway a bit to give them a good show, tell them whatever it is I know they want to hear and leave it at that.

This makes them happy. Their money makes me happy. And that's the end of it. Is that wrong? Do I feel guilty? Am I a fraud? No. Because they're unevolved, Laura. They can see no further than the pains and pleasures of this life, so they live as if there is nothing more there, like two-year-olds, living in the present because they have no concept of next week. Such people would not be able to cope with what the Voices are really communicating. This is why the Voices choose to come to people like you and me.'

"He smiled gently. 'You'll grow accustomed to this paradox. If people are not evolved, if this isn't their lifetime for enlightenment, nothing you do will bring them to the Light. Each person has to make that journey for themselves. So you do what you can to ease their suffering and leave it at that. That's not wrong. That's not deception. That's compassion.'

"For several moments I lay, listening to the beating of his heart. Finally, I said, 'I wish I had your certainty.'

Chapter Twenty-Five

J ames paged through the folder of stories to where he had
last left Torgon, smiling seductively as she anointed Ansel
as the new Seer.

*When Ansel came for the first time into the compound as the Seer,
Torgon stayed distant so that her interest in him would not appear
unseemly, but curiosity kept her watching discreetly from the open
window of her cell.*

*He was handsome. His build was tall and manly, the taut
muscles of his shoulders surging beneath his deerskin shirt as he
carried in his things. His eyes were as brown as the ancient wood
used in carving amulets, and his hair was rich and rusted with just
the slightest touch of grey, like fallen leaves in autumn, their tips
crystalline with frost. In curls about his ears, his hair blended with
his ruddy-coloured beard, groomed carefully in the warrior style.
It was apparent from everything about him that he was holy-born.
Every move had elegance, as in the manner of a man accustomed
to his power.*

He immediately set about clearing his father's cells. The doors were left hanging wide open as he did so, as if they were not holy rooms at all, and he chucked the old man's things out unceremoniously onto the stone flags in the corridor. The acolytes and holy women were still absent, so perhaps it did not matter. Torgon watched in silence for several minutes. Then she retired to her duties.

As evening approached, Torgon laid out bread and chunks of ripened cheese on the table and gave the benediction.

Entering the dining area, Ansel surveyed the table. "Have we no better than this?"

"It is holy food. It has been blessed."

"Aye, blessed perhaps, but it is cold. Where's something hot? And where's the meat?"

"It is not my role to prepare the meals," Torgon replied.

"Why? Do you not know how? Did you not learn to make yourself marriageable?"

"I am the divine benna, lest you forget. It is not my role to prepare the food."

Ansel gave an unconcerned shrug. "Do you not know how?"

"Yes, of course I know how."

"Then you should do it. This is not a fit meal for a warrior."

"You are not a warrior here."

"No," he replied, "but my stomach doesn't know that."

"If you wish something different, you shall have to prepare it for yourself," Torgon said simply. "For I have other duties."

Ansel looked over, then unexpectedly he laughed. "Oh aye," he said. "I can see I will enjoy myself in such spirited company."

*　　*　　*

After the meal, Torgon retreated to her cells. She'd meant to spent the evening in meditation, but the long weeks of the old man's decline had brought a bone-aching weariness to dog her. She lay down on her bed without even removing her clothes and within moments was asleep.

"What form of laziness is this to be abed at such an early hour? Did my father encourage slothfulness?"

Startled, Torgon shot up from the bed. Ansel stood in the doorway of her inner cell. He was clad not in the holy vestments of a Seer, but in the leather girdle and deerskin undertrousers warriors wore. His broad chest was bare.

"Did your father teach you rudeness? These are my private cells and I need not open them to you. So go now. I have not sent for you."

He grinned cheerfully. "You are very quick with answers. I see you've been given the title 'anaka' rightly, for you are a proper little warrior. My father did well in choosing you."

"I am Dwr's choice, not your father's. Now go."

He didn't move a muscle. "I've come to claim my rights with you."

Torgon moved away from him. "You have no rights with me."

"I am the Seer. You are the benna."

"Aye, but we have not yet observed holy laws. We've made no offerings to Dwr. We haven't gone together to the high holy place. And the acolytes are still absent, so you have yet to receive the holy cup."

"Those are naught but silly customs, Torgon. We are alone here, you and I. There's no need for such foolishness between the two of us."

"Your father was negligent in taking his stick to you. You seem to feel you are above the holy laws."

Ansel raised an eyebrow. "Who are you to lecture me on holy laws? You meet your sister secretly when you know full well it is forbidden for you to see her. I know you do that. I'm not the old man my father was. I keep track of where my women are."

"I am not your woman. I am the divine benna and you should be mindful of that. So, go. I refuse to bed you at this time, for I will have Dwr's blessings on what I do."

Instead, he began to unbuckle his girdle. "Is it that you do not like the ways of men? Surely not. It would be a pity in one as beautiful as you. No. I think it's only inexperience. It's been naught but old grandfathers and callow lads who've bedded you 'til now." He let the girdle drop to reveal his bulging undertrousers. "But see how great stands this warrior's sword? Come. It's time you knew a real man."

"This is unholy, Ansel. We have not had Dwr's blessing and I will not bed you. I refuse. We have not followed holy law."

"Would you be shut of holy law!" he said, his voice betraying anger. "Holiness! It's all you talk about. Do you not realize you are the benna solely because my father chose you?"

"I am the benna because Dwr *chose me. Your father was only the vessel of his choosing."*

"You think that's so? Dwr and all these holy laws? You don't believe them, do you?" he said, his voice incredulous. "Holiness is naught but cradlesongs for workers and nothing more. Just as the goose boys sing to their flocks to keep them soothed."

Torgon's eyes went wide.

"Of all people, you should know the truth in this. What chance is there that my father would have been given visions of a worker's child? If visions were a real thing, would not the benna be a decent woman and well bred? One suited to the role of holy office? But

there's nothing out there in the heavens except darkness. And you were naught but my father's choice. Or better put, the choice was mine."

"Blasphemer!"

Ansel shrugged indifferently. "Don't take it hard. You've been given a priceless chance to leave the worker caste behind and found a new line for your blood who will be high and holy-born. What sweeter thing could I bestow as a betrothal gift?

"When Father came to me and said, 'We must decide between us who you will have when it is your time to wear the holy robes.' I said I wasn't choosy. 'All that matters to me,' I said, 'is that she is fair of face, for I shall have to live in close quarters with her and care not to start each new day looking at an ugly woman.' We considered the matter and he said to me, 'What of Argot, whose father is a benita warrior? She is of excellent blood and also quiet and well-mannered. Thus your mother was, and this is a blessing in a woman.' But I said, 'No, Argot is not comely enough for me.' So he replied, 'What of Marit? Her grandfather carries the royal blood of the Bear People in his veins.' And I said, 'No, I had already lain with Marit and find her breasts too small. They will not feed the strong sons I will get from my woman.' So finally I said, 'Who I desire is Torgon, the carter's daughter, for to my mind she is more comely than any other. She has wide hips for bearing the strong sons befitting of a warrior. And good breasts, for I have seen her swimming with her sister.' My father was irate. He said, 'A worker's *daughter? Here? Living in the holy compound? She will be vulgar and temperamental and like as not have fleas.'"*

"Fleas?" *Torgon cried. "My kind are as clean as you are, holy-born. Cleaner! For I have had years of smelling your father's stinking undertrousers."*

Ansel laughed heartily. "Aye, well, I told him I didn't mind about the fleas. My dogs have fleas, and a warrior must often sleep among his dogs."

"You are a truly wicked man. Go. Now. I command it."

"Yes, well, I too grow weary of so much talk."

"Talk is all you'll have of me. Your father was old, his breath was rank and he bedded me with the clumsiness of a turtle, but at least he was a holy man. I see now that despite your pretty skin, you'll never equal him. Don't think I'll bed with you. Go. Leave this place tonight and return to living with your dogs."

"No more talk, I've said." He took a step in her direction. Torgon stepped back, but he was quicker. With a hunter's practised speed, he shot a hand out and grabbed her hair. In one deft move, he pulled her to him.

"I like you much," he said, drawing her against his body. He kept his hold on her hair, pulling it just enough to hurt. "I would rather you came to me of your own free will, since this is our first bedding, but it is of little consequence to me if you don't." He smiled, showing a row of even, white teeth. "You are, if anything, more comely when you're angry, and I have a mind to get a child on you this very night, that your angered spirit might make a mighty warrior of him." And with that, Ansel pressed his mouth forcefully over hers.

Torgon struggled no longer. There was no point to it. She would only be hurt and to what good? So, when Ansel pushed her towards the bed, she went.

This pleased him. He grinned with boyish delight. Loosing the straps that held his small warrior's dagger, he lay it on the table beside the bed. Then he undid the tie of his undertrousers. It occurred to Torgon as she watched his smiling face that he did genuinely want her. This saddened her, for she too had long dreamt of this moment. But not like this.

He wasn't rough. He didn't lord his victory over her. Indeed, Torgon doubted he even realized there'd been a victory. He was so accustomed to the warrior's way of taking what he wanted that resistance was of little consequence to him. Now he was all smiles and tender touches, as if nothing had gone before.

Ansel was well-practised at this manly art. He smiled and touched her face, running his thumbs along the ridges of her cheekbones. He took undisguised pleasure in the roundness of her breasts, cupping them individually and admiring them, then pressing his mouth to the nipples, as if he were a suckling babe. Running his hands down either side of her torso, he felt the muscles, smiled and felt again. "You are strong and lean as a great cat," he said delightedly, as if her worker's body were preferable to the rounded softness of a high-born woman. Indeed, he actually said, "I could not ask for anyone more beautiful than you." Then he spread her legs and admired further what he had won.

Torgon did not resist. Before she'd been called to the holy life, she wouldn't have been able to cope with this. She'd have fought or cried or, at the very least, had muscles too tight for coupling, but ten years of being a benna had taught her much about control. He explored her body unhindered. She lay quietly and waited.

His manroot was swollen huge with his desire and Ansel paused to show it off to her. He would have her touch it and taste it and experience it with all her body but she simply lay.

"Aye, well," he said, "it is seemly that you're overcome. You'll not have seen so great a sword before." He grinned. "But with your lively spirit, I've no doubt that soon you'll want to help me wield it." And with that, he thrust it in so forcefully that Torgon feared it would reach through her to her heart.

When at last the seed was sown, Ansel fell sated on the bed beside her. "There," he whispered and kissed her hair. "You know now a real man has done you."

Torgon remained silent.

He looked over. "Tonight we shall sleep together here. The acolytes are still absent, so it matters not who lies in which bed. The time comes soon enough for holy rules, so for tonight I want to lie beside you." He reached a hand over and touched her breasts again. "I've had to wait overlong for the mother of my sons. Thirty-eight summers have passed by me already and I should have sons as tall as men by now, but I've never wanted bastard children. Before this night I've ploughed but never seeded."

Torgon sighed.

"And now I've bedded you, I know it has been worthy of the wait. My choice was right, for I can tell I love you well already. In time perhaps you will come to love me too."

"Do you treat all things you love as you have treated me?" she asked.

"It is a warrior's way. You will grow used to it," he replied gently.

"But it is not the way of a holy man and that is your rightful destiny."

"Let us not talk now of holiness. Here. Put your arm here, that I may lay my head against your breast and listen to your heart. The time is come for sleep. I'm tired." With that he smiled and kissed her one last time.

He slept. The candle at the bedside burned low, its small light flickering faintly in the darkness. Torgon regarded him. He was so much handsomer than Meilor, who'd been short and inclined to swarthiness. Ansel's limbs were long and sinewy, the skin drawn taut over mighty muscles. His hair showed ruddy brown by candlelight, glinting like the fur of the great running stag.

Torgon drew in a long breath and let it slowly out. She would have liked the relief of tears just then to wash clean the bitter disappointment that she felt, to ease the grief for a future she knew now was stillborn, but no tears came. She lay in dry-eyed melancholy there beside him.

Had Ansel come for her before her calling and taken her then to be a warrior's wife, she probably would have grown to love him. Young and green and knowing naught of holiness, she would have tolerated rough ways for such a favoured marriage. Why, if he'd wanted her so long, could he not have just taken her from her father's hearth? Now it was too late. She was already wedded to a greater goal.

"It's more than cradlesongs," she murmured. "I truly have the Power. Your father knew that by the end. Why did he not tell you?"

Ansel stirred, readjusted himself and settled again.

"For I can't have you as you are. Your soul is long gone into darkness and I've not the means with which to call it back again. For Dwr's sake I shall need do what must be done."

"Why are you speaking?" Ansel muttered sleepily. "Put out the candle. The night is fairly gone."

"For your holy feasting I sacrificed a red deer in thanksgiving, a stag of many points," she said. "And I am thinking now it is the colour of your hair."

He smiled drowsily. "Torgon, this is not the time for lovers' talk. My strength is spent. Put out the candle."

"I speak, that the stag might know it was not I, but Dwr who commanded my holy hand in the taking of his life."

"You are inclined to speak when silence would be better. Shhh," Ansel said and put a finger to her lips. Then again he closed his eyes.

So silence came.

Torgon lay, listening for his breath to draw out deeply into slumber again. When it had, she leaned over and lifted from the table his small warrior's dagger. "Dwr now commands my hand again. Go among your own kind, Deer Man, for you no longer bear a holy soul." And with one skilled movement, she slit his throat.

The blood flowed, bubbling up like water from a spring. Torgon watched his face. Pink to momentary purple it went, then white and then the ash-grey colour of death.

It was a quick way to die. She knew, for she had used it many times with the stags and bulls at sacrifice, the malformed babes, and those whose souls had fled before them into darkness. Torgon looked at Ansel, lying motionless midst a sea of bedding made sodden scarlet with his blood.

"What have I done?"

Panic flooded through her. Everything was wet and red and stank of blood. All control left Torgon in that moment. She began to cry with fright. Rising from the bed, she attempted to lay Ansel's body straight, but he was such a big man and so heavy. Each movement pushed up more blood from the wound to ooze thickly red onto the bedclothes. She struggled until terror finally overcame her. Then she fled.

Chapter Twenty-Six

Entering the playroom with a quick, decisive step, the toy cat cradled in his arms, Conor didn't actually smile at James but there was the feeling of a smile in his expression. Pressing the cat against the sleeve of James's suit jacket, Conor said, "The cat knows," in a friendly voice, as if it were a greeting.

"I see a boy who looks happy today."

"Yeah. Today is Tuesday. The boy comes here. The man's cat is here? Where's the mechanical cat?"

"See if you can find him."

Conor went to the shelves and searched out the box of cardboard cut-out farm animals. Bringing it back to the table, he pulled off the box top. "Here it is!" he said cheerfully. He extended the little string leash and smiled.

Pulling out the chair opposite, Conor sat down in a confident manner. He fitted the little cardboard half-moon onto the bottom of the cardboard cut-out and then set it on the table between them. Then suddenly Conor was up from the table. He went over to one of the baskets on the shelf and took out a ball of modelling clay. Bringing it back, he pinched off a small bit, stuck it to the end of the string around the cat's neck and then pressed it to the table top. An expression of glee crossed his features. "Plug it in!"

"Yes, that's what you've done, isn't it?" James replied. "You've made a plug for it. You plugged it in."

"Yeah." Conor looked pleased.

Pulling his stuffed cat from under his arm and setting it on the table too, Conor looked over. "There's the boy's cat. Standing on the table. Standing by the mechanical cat."

James smiled. "Yes, there they are. Two cats."

"Cats can see ghosts."

"You believe cats can see ghosts," James reflected.

"Many ghosts. Many ghosts to be seen. Many cats to see them."

James watched Conor align the two cats carefully side by side.

"'Come here today.' That's what the cat said. 'Wake up, Conor. Time to go to Rapid City. Time to see the man. Today is the man's day. Today we see the mechanical cat. Today we go where there are no ghosts.'"

"Are there ghosts at your house?" James asked.

"Are there ghosts at your house?" Conor echoed. He raised a hand and flapped it in a gesture James now understood to be an expression of anxiety. Then Conor recovered himself by picking up his toy cat. He pressed the stuffed animal's nose to his own. "Lots of ghosts. Whispering, whispering. The cat can see ghosts. The cat says, 'The ghosts are here. The man under the rug is here.' The cat can see. The cat knows."

Clutching the toy cat against his chest, Conor bent down to better examine the cardboard cat. He inspected it carefully, then reached a finger out and touched the string hanging down from around its neck. "Here are the cat's wires. Plug it in. Make him strong."

"Like the mechanical boy?"

"Yeah." Conor stretched out the string leash and pressed it to the table top. "Electricity. Zap-zap. Mechanical things are made of metal. They don't die. They can last forever." He touched the faded colours. "This cat has very good metal. It looks like fur."

Unexpectedly Conor swooped the cardboard cat up in the air, as if it were a toy airplane. "Look, the man's cat can fly. Machines fly." He looked over at James.

A pause.

"Ghosts fly," he said and his voice trembled slightly.

"Many things fly," James said. "Birds fly. Mosquitoes fly."

"Angels fly," Conor said. "At Christmas time many angels fly."

"Yes, it is almost Christmas time, isn't it? We see lots of pictures of angels now, don't we?"

"People don't fly," Conor replied. "Only angel-people. Only ghost-people." Rising to his feet, he glanced nervously around the room as if he were doing a dangerous thing. Then he swooped the cat in a tentative figure eight. "But the mechanical cat can fly."

"Yes, you are making him zoom through the air."

"Machines are strong. They can fly a long way." A more energetic swooping followed. Up, down, around. These were the most uninhibited movements James had seen Conor make. Whoosh, the mechanical cat sailed past James's nose. Zip, it whizzed over the notebook.

Then Conor said, "I am going to run?" His tone was a mixture of question and statement, almost as if he were asking permission to do this normal thing.

He did run. The first steps were very tentative, up on tiptoe, then more boldly. All the time the cardboard cat was held high, dipping and swooping through the air ahead of him. "The cat can fly," he said over and over.

Conor sailed around the room until he was breathless and only then did he stop. Holding the cardboard cat up before his face, he caressed the paper features. "The boy can do what he wants in here. The mechanical cat says, 'Boy, do it. You're safe. No ghosts in here!'"

From the moment the next session started Conor knew exactly what he wanted to do. Getting the cardboard cat from the box, he began to fly it through the air. At first the movements were hesitant, just between James and himself, but then he stood up and moved more overtly. Soon Conor was running, the cardboard cat held high above his head.

On one occasion as he approached the table, he stopped abruptly. There was a brief glance to James and then unexpectedly Conor jumped up on the chair opposite. "The cat can fly," he said with an almost defiant tone to his voice.

"Yes, the cat is flying," James mirrored.

Conor lifted up one foot as if to step on the tabletop then hesitated. "I'm going to get on the table," he said but didn't do it.

"Today you feel like standing on the table."

"The mechanical cat says yes. The boy can get on the table." There was a moment's further hesitation and Conor softly set his foot on the table. He paused, as if waiting for James's remonstration, then triumphantly stepped up with the other foot. "The mechanical cat is strong! The boy can do what he wants!"

With that he took a flying leap off the table and ran away.

This bit of derring-do gave Conor more confidence. He came running around again, clambered up onto the table and once again jumped off.

"You are strong," James said as Conor's shoes passed in front of his pen.

"Yeah!" Conor called and leaped down to the floor. The cardboard cat was held high above him like a parachute. "Up and down, up and down. The mechanical cat can fly!"

Suddenly he halted and looked over. "That's a song," he said and smiled. "Did you hear it? That was a song."

The comment surprised James. He raised his eyebrows.

"Listen. I'll sing it:

Up and down, up and down

The cat can fly.

It will never die.

Metal fur.

It will never die.

Lots of wires.

It will never cry."

He spoke a high, thin, crystalline sing-song.

"That's quite amazing," James said. "I like your song."

Conor skipped gaily around the room, his movements free and fluid.

"The cat he knows,

His eyes, they glows.

The cat can fly and never die."

Bending over his notebook, James scribbled quickly to record the precise words.

Conor noticed this. He paused. "You're writing what I say again."

James nodded. "Yes. It's a beautiful song. I want to remember it."

"Then you must write this: 'The Song of the Mechanical Cat'. Write that at the top because that's its title."

"All right."

"Now, underneath it you must write 'By Conor McLachlan'."

James did so.

Conor came around to James's side of the table and bent down to see the notebook. "The Song of the Mechanical Cat, by Conor McLachlan," he read. "That means it's my song. I am the author. I created it."

"Yes," James replied.

"Will you keep my song? In your notebook?"

"Yes," James said.

"Everything the boy says, the man will write down. In his true book. Everything the boy says. All the true things. It'll be our book."

Conor smiled and held up the cardboard cat. "Today you will write: 'The boy heard the mechanical cat's song. He heard it out of nothing and made it something. The boy sang the song all day long.'"

And so the session went with Conor singing freely, his conversation bright and natural, his movements those of any normal, happy boy.

James always gave a warning to the children about the approach of the session end. So, as usual, when only five minutes of the session were left, James said, "It's almost time to go. When the big hand reaches the ten, that's the end."

"No. Today I don't want to go."

"You've been having a very good time today and don't feel like going," James interpreted. "You'd like to stay longer."

"Today I'll stay longer," Conor replied. "I'll do finger-paints."

"You wish you had more time," James said. "Unfortunately, every visit is the same amount of time. When the clock reaches ten minutes to, it's time to stop."

"But not today. Today I made a song."

"Unfortunately, even today."

"But I don't *want* to stop. I'm not finished yet."

"You'll be here again on Thursday. Then you can continue."

"No!" Conor cried in an anguished tone. Then defiantly, "The mechanical cat says 'No!'" He held the cat out in front of him like a crucifix. "The mechanical cat says, 'Don't listen to that man!'" Conor ran off across the room. Clambering over the bookshelf, he hid behind it.

The clock ticked away the last minutes.

Rising from the table, James crossed to the playroom door and opened it.

Alarmed, Conor stood up and peered over the bookshelf.

Dulcie was standing in the hallway outside the room, Laura behind her. "There's your mum," James said. "It's time to go now."

Conor screamed. Scrambling over the bookshelf, he ran towards James. "No!"

"Here, let's put the mechanical cat back in the box with his friends," James said.

"No!" Conor pressed the cardboard cat tight against his chest, shrieked, ran around the table and then out through the open door. He burst past Dulcie before she could catch him but Laura managed to grab hold of the shoulder of his shirt.

Conor screamed so loudly that James's ears reverberated.

"What's he got?" Laura asked. "Conor, what's in your hand? What is it? Here, give it to me. You can't take things out of the playroom, honey. Let Dr Innes have it back." It took all three of them to prize Conor's fingers open enough to remove the cardboard cat.

He howled.

Over the din, James said to Laura, "Would you like to take him into my office? I have another client coming into the playroom, but if you want a few moments to calm him down, Dulcie can go with you."

Laura shook her head.

"Are you sure?" James asked.

"*No*," she replied through gritted teeth, "but, please, just notice what he's like." James saw tears in her eyes. "Notice, so that you'll quit taking Alan's side on this. Because he *isn't* getting better. I'm living in hell at home. He's like this *all* the time with me. I honestly don't think I can take it much longer. I mean that. I can't."

Then the tearful mother and sobbing son departed.

Chapter Twenty-Seven

James felt that Conor's behaviour at the end of his session was a positive sign indicating that Conor was confident enough to express anger when his wishes were thwarted.

Laura's behaviour, on the other hand, troubled James. He and she had shared so many positive sessions together, establishing what had felt to James like a good rapport, and yet she was still so quick to perceive him as taking Alan's side.

This led directly into what had been James's other long-time concern about Laura: why did she never bring Conor up? Why did she never enquire about his progress or openly talk about her issues with him at home? Aside from the very early days when they were establishing intake information for Conor, Laura had never even spoken her son's name in therapy. Indeed, the way she'd thus far structured the therapy sessions by giving this careful chronology of her life's unfolding story, she'd made it fairly difficult even for James to bring Conor up.

This created a conundrum for James. An important aspect of his therapeutic philosophy involved giving the client complete control. James did strongly believe in the value of this. With a sense of control, with the ability to decide when and how things would be revealed, clients came to trust James and James's environment enough to explore the fears and secrets that had paralysed their lives. But how long did one stay with that? This had been where everything had come undone in New York. Taking the passive role of listening, reflecting and waiting patiently, James had been too slow to save Adam.

When Laura arrived for her next session, she looked distinctly nervous. Appearing at the door of his office, her hands pushed deep into the pockets of an oversized cardigan, she wrapped them tight around herself as if she were cold.

James smiled kindly. "Come on in." He gestured to the conversation centre.

She crossed to sit down in the big overstuffed chair. The "womb chair", as Lars liked to call it. James exchanged a few pleasantries with Laura, mainly about the impending holiday season.

Then Laura said, "I'm sorry about that scene with Conor."

"No problem," James replied. "Do you want to talk about it?"

"Not really," she said and didn't meet his eyes.

James let the silence flow in around them.

"I really don't," she said.

"That's all right," James replied. "In here you decide."

"It's Fergus I need to talk about."

James nodded.

She began quietly, her voice slowly growing in confidence as she relaxed back into storytelling.

"If Fergus had any uncanny gift, it was his talent for turning up wherever I happened to be in spite of my complex schedule and the size of the city. Occasionally, even when I was out shopping, I'd return to my car in the car park to find him standing beside it. He said he did it by focusing on my life force and because he loved me so much. He couldn't bear to be away from me. However much time we spent together, Fergus always wanted more.

"I didn't find this attention overwhelming in the beginning. I was in love with him and wanted to be with him every moment I could. Besides, being his girlfriend was such a buzz – a lot of people really did take this 'prophet' business seriously and they looked up to him. They admired him and they envied me, being so close to him. I liked that.

"It felt like a dream, being the centre of Fergus's life. He made no disguise of how much he wanted me and how much he wanted to please me. For example, my birthday is in June – well past the lilac season in Boston – so he drove all the way up to Maine to find lilacs still in bloom in the cooler elevations and bring a huge bouquet for me because he knew they were my favourite flower. No one had ever done such a thoughtful thing for me. I loved feeling so wanted.

"It wasn't unconditional love, though. Fergus was always turning up with books on philosophy and religion and even quantum physics – two, three, four at a time – saying, 'Read this and we'll set up a time to talk about the ideas.' There was no question that I would not only read the books and digest their ideas but also discuss them with him in considerable detail. It was almost as if I were taking second degree alongside medicine.

"He was very keen to improve me. He was appalled that I ate 'dead flesh' and insisted the only way to purify myself for my role as his consort in the New World was to become vegetarian. He was mystified by my inclination to be incoherent with tiredness when he wanted to see me late at night. To him my exhaustion indicated a lack of discipline as far as my body was concerned. It showed weakness or perhaps even a wilful choice of the physical realm over the spiritual. And then there were my 'worldly connections', as Fergus termed them. This included my CD collection, my enjoyment of going to the movies, and most definitely the time I put into studying. He was the only person I'd ever met who was dismissive of medicine as a discipline. He could not see the value of traditional education, which he regarded as rigid and 'establishment', aimed solely at perpetuating the status quo. But worse, he even saw the time I spent writing about Torgon as 'worldly' and thus, an activity I needed to let go of.

"'I *have* to write the Torgon stories,' I'd protested. She was, after all, what had got me where I was.

"Fergus was adamant. Writing about Torgon, he insisted, only stifled my evolution as a pure channel. Torgon should only come through me directly.

"We talked about Torgon constantly. This Torgon, like the one I trotted out for the Tuesday night group, had long ceased to be related to the real one. Fergus translated and reshaped her continuously in order to help me to understand her for what she really was: not a figment of my imagination, not a character from my writing, but a Being of Light, who had come to me through my play as a child because this was all I was capable of holding in my mind at that age. Now, however, it was important that I allowed Torgon to return to her natural form and to accept her mission for me.

"Fergus explained in great detail how she was passing wisdom through me to help bring about this new world of peace and universal love. I needed to accept this and purify myself with an appropriate diet, meditation, and the right kind of company in order that I might better open myself to this beautiful expression of universal love.

"I did say at one point that Torgon had never seemed to me to be a particularly shining example of universal love. Her life was altogether as frail and human as mine, and her society was downright brutal. Fergus ignored this. All he was concerned with was that I opened myself up for direct communication with her.

"I desperately wanted to believe what Fergus was telling me. I loved him and wanted to live to up to his dreams and I wanted life to be the way he said. I longed to be the genuine psychic Fergus believed I was capable of being. I wanted to channel a true Being of Light who really had chosen me alone from the billions of people on earth. I just so yearned to be what everybody already thought I was."

When the session was over, James wemt in search of this "real" Torgon. There were only a few stories left, none of them very long. Sitting down in the "womb chair", he put his feet up on the coffee table and started reading.

Coming down the steep path from the high holy place to look for the food offering, Torgon saw a figure standing in the shadows at the forest's edge.

"Who's there?"

The figure didn't move.

Torgon slipped down between the last of the large rocks. She paused a moment, her heartbeat in her throat. At last she ventured closer. "Mogri! It's you! How my heart cheers to see you."

"I wish I could say the same."

Mogri stepped out of the shade of the trees. "Here. I've brought your food that you may eat while keeping your communion with the gods." Angrily she chucked the basket out onto the grass.

"Mogri?"

"No, take it. Mam has sent it especially for you. For you must always have the best. So take it, Torgon. Eat."

"I can't. Not here. I must return to sacred ground to eat."

"Aye, that sounds like you. Very well. Keep your holiness intact." Mogri turned away.

"Mogri? What goes so ill with you? What's happened?"

Mogri burst into tears. "Tadem's dead."

"What?"

"Aye, Torgon. Three days ago. Working in his father's smithy, he took a cut across his hand. Just here. Just a tiny cut, a graze. But evil spirits entered and he's died a writhing death."

"So fast? Did not the wise woman come to put a poultice on?" Torgon asked.

"It never should have mattered. But there are so many evil spirits now. The wise woman came but the spirits had already grown deathly strong and she couldn't call them out."

"Oh, this brings much sorrow to my heart." Torgon reached out. "Here, take the comfort of my arms and I shall weep with you."

"What good will that do me now?" Mogri said and pulled away. "Where were you three nights ago? That's when I needed you. *We prayed all night in the holy temple and lit candles that your spirit might see and tell you to return, but you did not come.*"

"*Oh, Mogri, I'm so sorry.*"

"*That night of Ansel's death, when I counselled you to tell the elders that the two of you had simply been in disagreement and the knife came accidentally between you, you said no. You said, 'I will tell it as it is, that he showed himself to be unfit for sacred duty and Dwr commanded me to end his life.' You said, 'To do less than tell the truth would make me what he said I was. It is in my heart to show that I am more.' And* this *is more? Hiding on the high holy place so Ansel's brothers can not touch you, while we in the village suffer with no holy guidance?*"

Torgon turned away. She slumped, discouraged, against a tree. "*So, what would you have me do? Say, yes, I ran fear? All right. I ran away, afraid. And for that weakness I'm very sorry, but I'm divine only in so much as I am human. I feared being parted from my life before I had a chance at other courses. So, I withdrew here to let Dwr tell me what he would have me do.*"

"*And what would he have* me *do, Torgon?*" *Mogri replied bitterly.* "*I was never Tadem's wife, for there was no Seer there to marry us and I now carry an eight-months' babe inside me. What man will want me now, when I'm so soon to yield a crop he didn't sow?*" *Bringing up a hand, Mogri wiped back her tears.* "*What should I do? Leave the babe to die to make myself more marriage-able? Or stay forever a daughter in my father's house?*"

"*I am* sorry, *Mogri. I've never meant that my burdens should fall on you.*"

"*Perhaps not, but they have and you've never stopped to lift them up again.*"

"*Mogri, please. Do forgive me. I'm truly sorry.*"

"Yes, I know you are." A second sigh. Mogri wiped back the tears. "I know too it's not your fault alone. But life does seem much unfair to me. And my heart is sorely sick with it."

Torgon approached her.

"At the very least, won't you come back among us?" Mogri asked. "Can't you make strong your heart and fight the fear? It's quiet now. The elders will give you fair hearing for what you've done."

"Shall I tell you truly why I bide here yet?" Torgon asked and her shoulders drooped. "The Power's waned. I know not why, but fear I lose my holiness. I've stayed here, awaiting its return, for I am naught without it."

"They say in the village that you are already dead, that Dwr's relieved your body of your spirit in fair payment for the holy Seer's death. If you stay away much longer, the Power will most definitely pass into another's hands and you'll never get it back. So, won't you please make yourself strong enough to return again and prove the rumour-mongers wrong?"

Chapter Twenty-Eight

As much as James longed to have Becky and Mikey at Christmas, it was important to him that Christmas be a time of good memories for the children, not of fighting parents. His own parents now passed away, his brother living on the other side of the country, James knew he couldn't provide a traditional Christmas with all the trimmings like Sandy's family celebrated. So, in the end, he and Sandy both agreed that Becky and Mikey would spend Christmas with her and then travel to South Dakota for New Year's Eve.

James had worked hard to create new traditions for this holiday. The kids were still too young for staying up late, so they had settled on celebrating New Year's Eve by having a "picnic" in front of the fireplace in the living room. James let them roast hotdogs and marshmallows over the dancing flames. They finished off by throwing handfuls of specially treated pine cones into the fire afterwards to make the flames turn different colours.

Their other tradition was to go shopping on the 31st to buy each child a new outfit to wear on New Year's Day and a new toy to play with. The latter James realized was an indulgence so soon after the glut of presents the kids had received at Christmas, but the pleasure they had shopping together always outweighed his better judgement.

Coming in through the glass double-doors of Toys 'R' Us, James stomped the snow off his boots and then pulled a shopping cart out of the rack. Mikey jumped on the end to ride. Becky skipped alongside.

"You know what thing gives me the best feeling in the world?" she said cheerfully.

"What's that?" James asked.

"When we come in through the door at Toys 'R' Us and I see you get a shopping cart instead of just walk on in!" She beamed.

"Yes, you know we're going to buy stuff then, don't you?" James said with a smile.

"Yeah, I *love* coming here with you," she replied and locked her arms around his right wrist as he pushed the cart.

A trip to Toys 'R' Us with Becky had always involved a long, slow meander down the Barbie aisle. Often it was just to browse. Indeed James could make a good outing for Becky by doing nothing more than coming to Toys 'R' Us to admire the fancy Barbies in their special glassed in case, all way too expensive to buy as toys. Equally fun for Becky was browsing through the endless assortment of tiny accessories for a doll who seemed to perennially waver between being a vet or a Playboy Bunny.

"Look," said James. "That's a new kind of Barbie horse, isn't it?"

"Yeah," Becky said.

"Wow, that's good," James said. "I like that black colour. And see, it's the kind that goes with the carriage."

"Yeah," Becky said. She had moved down the aisle

"Would you like that?" James asked.

"What I'd like is a Bratz doll. They're in a different aisle. The one I'm dying for has got really long, blonde hair and these cool black boots. Let's go look at those."

"When did this happen?" James asked, catching up with her. "Last I heard, you couldn't stop going on about that Barbie carriage Uncle Joey got you."

"I don't like it any more," she said.

"Any reason?" James asked.

Becky reached for a Bratz doll and took it down from the shelf to look at it. "Well, 'cause Uncle Joey got it for me, for one thing. I hate Uncle Joey."

Surprised, James regarded her. "Why's that?"

"I hate him being around all the time. I wish he'd go away."

"Yes," Mikey piped up from the end of the shopping cart, "but he isn't going to. He and Mum are maybe gonna get married."

"I *hate* him," Becky muttered. "I only want you," she said and put her arms around James.

The New Year's Eve picnic in front of the fireplace was a great success. Glutted on hot dogs and corn-on-the-cob, their mouths haloed in chocolate and sticky crumbs from S'mores made with marshmallows toasted on the fire, the children snuggled up on either side of James to watch Disney's *Sleeping Beauty*. Mikey fell asleep only about a half an hour in, but Becky saw it through, cuddling up close, wrapping James's arm tight around her.

When the film was over, James carried Mikey into the bedroom, gently undressed him and tucked him in. Becky slid under the covers in her bed.

"Nighty-night, sweetheart," James said and bent to kiss her.

"Daddy? Can I ask you something?"

"What's that, lovey?"

"Can me and Mikey come to live with you?"

He smoothed back the hair from Becky's forehead. "Is something not working out for you at home?"

"I don't want to live with Uncle Joey. I don't like him."

"Why's that?"

Becky shrugged. "I just don't. I don't want him moving in with us. I want to come live with you."

"I'd love to have you live with me, sweetheart. But your mum and I would have to talk about it, because that's a big decision. Besides, you've got all your friends back there. And Grandma and Grandpa. And the cousins."

"I know. I wouldn't mind. I've got Morgana here. Her and me have been writing e-mails and really, we're pretty good friends already, even if she's littler than me. And if Mikey and me lived here, we could have a dog. I really, really, really want a dog, Daddy. That's what I want so bad for my birthday. So, please?"

"It's a big decision. But I'll think about it, all right?"

"Daddy?"

Sleepily James rolled over. "What is it, Becky? What's wrong?"

"I can't sleep." Her small form was indistinct in the deep night-time darkness of James's bedroom. "Can I get in bed with you?"

James lifted up the covers. Becky crawled in and snuggled into the curve of his body.

"Brrr, you're cold," James said. "Did that wake you up? Maybe we need to get another blanket for your bed."

"No, I just can't sleep."

He stroked her head. "Why's that?"

"I'm worried about tomorrow."

"What? About going home."

James could feel her nodding against him. "I don't want to leave you. I want to be with you."

A sudden, terrible thought occurred to him. Perhaps there was a much darker reason for Becky's behaviour.

"Becks," he said urgently, "what's happening at home?"

"Nothing."

"No, it's something, Becks. I can tell."

"Couldn't you come back to New York?"

"To keep you safe?"

"No, to be my daddy. Because I don't want Uncle Joey."

"What's Uncle Joey doing, sweetheart? It's okay to tell me."

"Nothing."

"But you said you hated him. If he's hurting you, if he's doing something, Becky, I need to know. You can tell me."

"He isn't doing anything, Daddy," Becky murmured, snuggling close. "The reason I hate him is just because he isn't you."

Children in therapy typically experience small regressions during breaks and holidays, but when Conor arrived for his first session in January, he bounced in enthusiastically and went immediately to the shelves to pick out the box of cardboard animals and brought it to the table.

"Here is the man's cat." He set it on the table between them and pushed the little glob of clay against the tabletop to "plug it in".

"Here is the boy's cat." He set his stuffed toy alongside, then briefly glanced up at James.

"Yes, there are our two cats," James reflected back.

"I can't have that cat," Conor murmured. "The mechanical cat stays here."

James picked up his pen and opened the notebook.

"Is my song still there?" Conor asked, pointing to the notebook. "My cat song?"

"Yes."

"Read it. Let me hear it."

James flipped back through the pages until he came to the notes from the last session in December. He read out the words to the song.

When James had finished, Conor gave no response. He just stood there.

At last he turned from the table and walked away, leaving his stuffed toy cat on the table.

"I don't know what I want to do today," he said. He meandered over to the windows, then back again to the shelves. Taking one hand from his pocket, he poked a finger at the plastic road sheet, folded up on the first shelf.

Then he went to the dolls' house. Kneeling down, he opened the back of it to expose the rooms. He reached in and took out the dolls, first the man, then the woman, the boy, the girl and the baby. "There are no animals in here," he said. "They have no cats."

He set the boy doll in the uppermost bedroom. "Go to bed. Stay in bed. Don't get out. You're always out."

There were stairs going down through the middle of the house, dividing it into two equal sides. Conor tried to balance the woman doll on the stairs but it would not stand. "I could get clay," he said. "I could put it on her feet to make her stand up."

"Yes, that would work. You've thought of another good use for the clay," James replied.

"Look, the bad boy has got out of bed. 'Get back in bed!' she said. The mother said that. 'I can't stand you like this! Stop your crying. I must take care of the baby.' Conor moved the mother doll down the stairs and put the baby in her arms.

Taking the girl doll, he placed her in the other uppermost bedroom on the opposite side of the staircase. "Here's where the girl sleeps. She's good. She doesn't get out of bed. But look. Here is the bad boy and he's getting out of bed again." He put the boy doll on the floor of the bedroom and then moved the mother doll back up the stairs.

"Oh, You're a bad boy. You are a bad, bad boy. Why don't you do as I say? I have other things to do. I can't worry about you. Why can't you be good?" Conor picked up the girl doll. "She's a good girl. Better than the boy."

"You think the girl is better than the boy?" James asked.

"Yeah. She doesn't go away to school. She stays in her bed. And now, see, she's here. She says, 'How come you don't stay in bed?' The bad boy says, 'I am a machine. Don't talk to me. Machines don't talk.' The good girl leaves. See? She goes down the stairs to where Mummy and Daddy are. That's okay. Because she doesn't see any ghosts."

"Are there ghosts in this house?" James asked.

"Yeah," Conor replied. Then he rose. "Where are the rugs?"

James raised a querying eyebrow.

"Over here." Conor crossed to the table and picked up the box of tissues. He yanked one out and went back to the dolls' house. He lay it on the floor of one of the rooms on the ground floor. "There's a ghost under the rug. In the downstairs room. The bad boy knows. The cat knows. The cat says ... The bad boy ..."

Suddenly the play had become too powerful. Conor leaped to his feet and backed away from the dolls' house. James could hear his breathing grow shallower. The skin along his jawline began to mottle as he stood, mesmerized by the toy figures, and James half-expected him to scream. He didn't. Turning, he ran to clutch up his cat. Pressing it to his chest, clinging to it, he stood a few moments, panting. Briefly he glanced at James, meeting his eyes. Then he looked down at the table, at the small cardboard cat standing there.

"Zap, zap," he whispered. Reaching down, he loosened the clay plug on the string and picked the cat up. He walked back to the dolls' house. Kneeling, he very carefully stood the cat in the middle of the dolls' house kitchen. He pressed the clay plug onto its printed linoleum floor.

Sitting back, Conor studied his work. Kitty was still tight against his chest. "Zap, zap. Metal cat. Metal fur. Mechanical cat." His voice was almost inaudible.

Silence.

"Zap, zap."

Conor reached in and took the boy doll from the upstairs bedroom and put him down beside the cardboard cat in the kitchen. "There's a ghost here. Under the rug. Nobody can see it. The man can't see it. The mummy can't see it. The baby can't see it. The good girl can't see it. But the boy can. And so can the mechanical cat."

Chapter Twenty-Nine

James gestured towards the conversation centre as Laura came in. "You were telling me about Fergus when we left off before the holidays. Why don't we go back to where we were? So what happened next?"

"In order to be with Fergus, I stayed in Boston over that summer and worked at the hospital, rather than go back to South Dakota as I had in previous summers. During September, I was invited to accompany Dr Betjeman to a medical conference in Miami where he was giving a presentation.

"Fergus was uncomfortable with this separation. It was the first time we'd been apart since we'd been seeing each other and he voiced strong reservations. There wasn't much to be done about it, however. He couldn't come to Florida with me and I didn't want to miss this opportunity; so despite his vociferous protests, I went.

"The experience didn't turn out to be quite as fun as I'd thought it would be. I felt adrift in the world of ordinary people, which seemed so bland without Fergus. I was short of money and unable to do much except sit in the conference hall and listen to medical researchers droning on. My heart just wasn't in it. So once Dr Betjeman gave his presentation, I decided to return to Boston two days earlier than planned and surprise Fergus.

"It was about 9 pm when I got home, so I was startled to hear the doorbell ring soon after.

"'Who's there?' I asked cautiously, as my old-fashioned door didn't have a peephole.

"'May I come in?' said a familiar voice.

"'Fergus!' I cried in surprise and opened the door.

"'Welcome back. Here. I've brought you a present,' he said. To my utter surprise, he held out a bottle of burgundy.

"'Thank you,' I said and took it from him.

"He leaned forward to kiss me and I could smell he had already been drinking. 'I hope it's a kind you like. I'm not very good at this sort of thing. But as you grew up on South Dakota beef, I reasoned you must be a red wine drinker.' He laughed.

"I felt unsettled. While I had come home especially for him, I had expected to be the one doing the surprising. It was unnerving to find him at my door so quickly. Moreover, I wasn't accustomed to his drinking, or drinking with him. It all seemed out-of-character from a man who had so often made me feel a full night's sleep was self-indulgent.

"'Well, aren't you going to invite me in?' he asked and took the wine from my hands. He slipped on by and went into the kitchen. 'Where do you keep your corkscrew?'

"I followed him in and fished around in a kitchen drawer. 'How did you know I was back?' I asked.

"'How could I not know you were back, Laura?' he replied simply. Reaching into the cupboard, he took down wine glasses.

"Leading the way into the living room, he flopped into an armchair. 'God, I've missed you.'

"I looked at him. Familiarity had stolen some of the intensity from his dark eyes and made him less startlingly handsome to me. I tried to look at him as a stranger would, to see what one would see who did not know him.

"'I have been so depressed since you left,' he said. He drained the wine from his glass and reached for the bottle to refill it.

"We drank in silence for several moments. The wine bottle was soon empty. It had tasted very good to me, as it clearly had to Fergus as well, and I was toying with the idea of going to see what I had in the house. Would Fergus want me to suggest another bottle? It still seemed peculiar to drink so casually with him.

"'I'm going to get us something more,' I said and rose. I went into the hallway, because once Fergus had begun reforming my dietary habits, I'd moved what little wine I owned to the floor of the hall closet so that he wouldn't know I still had it. My wine cellar now consisted of four bottles in a wooden rack pushed beneath the winter bedding. Most had been laid down before Fergus had come into my life, and as my income had never extended to any seriously good wine, the majority was probably now vinegar. Opening the door fully, I knelt down and started to pull them out. I hadn't bothered to put the hall light on. The hallway itself was minuscule and there was enough light cast from the kitchen to read the labels.

"Fergus materialized in the gloom behind me. Putting his hand on my shoulder, he leaned over to look at the bottles. As always, the heat of his touch caught my attention.

"'There isn't much good in here, I'm afraid. All cheap stuff,' I said.

"He knelt behind me. Leaning forward over my left shoulder to read the labels, or so I thought, he instead gently slipped a hand into my blouse and cupped my breast. I paused but didn't pull away. Fergus continued to fondle my breast, his fingertips massaging the nipple into erectness. He pressed his body tightly to my back and I could feel his penis hard against my spine.

"'Fergus, not right now,' I said. 'It was a lot of travelling today. I'm really very tired.'

"He began undoing the buttons of my blouse.

"'Fergus, please. I don't want to.'

"'Yes, you do,' he said."

"Once he had his arms around me, I forgot my protests. We made love right there on the floor in the half-light provided by the kitchen doorway, the bottles of merlot and burgundy rolling around us, clinking softly against each other. A little fierce-looking in the gloom of the hallway with his thick, unruly hair and his dark, dark eyes, Fergus pressed me to the carpet and mounted me with such forcefulness that it would have been frightening, had I not anticipated it. He was a dynamic lover, and my body responded as if foreordained. With no time to prepare for it, I climaxed very quickly. My body was wracked with it, more consumed than satisfied, as wave after wave of sensation overtook me with no interlude to recover. Indeed, there was such an uninhibited ferocity to Fergus's love-making that I was left doubting whether or not love actually came into it. It was in its way more like a battle between us.

"Finally Fergus climaxed himself and as he did, he kissed me. It was a hungry, devouring kiss, as invasive as his penis, or perhaps more so, because I hadn't been antici-pating it. With his coming, however, some of his energy seemed to dissipate. He kissed me further, still deeply but less forcefully. Finally, he relaxed onto the carpet beside me.

"We lay together on the floor for several minutes and did not speak. As so often happens, it was the tiny things that began to make an impression on my consciousness first – the feel of the shaggy carpet on my back, the faint, faint smell of carpet shampoo, the irritated skin of my elbows, rubbed sore from friction.

"'This is how it should be between us,' Fergus murmured in a soft, satisfied way. 'Just like it always was.'

"'Mmm?'

"'Don't you remember?'

"I looked over to make out his features in the darkness. 'Remember what?'

"'Atlantis.'

"'*Atlantis?*'

"'Yes, don't you remember? When you were queen and I was your lover. Your secret lover. Remember how I came to you at night? How I came in my little boat and moored it up alongside that stone wall? Surely you must remember that. Cast your mind back.'

"'Fergus, come on. You don't have to bring all this into it. What we have between us is great all by itself. You don't need to turn it into something else.'

"'No, Laura, close your eyes. Look back. Free your soul and look back to that stone wall. Can't you see it? Those huge, square blocks the masons made, how they built that great wall running from the palace down to the water? And the wooden pier? Our secret pier. It's night. Remember? Remember how you would always wait midst the trees for me? The moon was shining on the dark water and I was pushing my little boat up. Fly free with your soul, my queen. Don't you see it? Don't you see me coming to you? Dying for you, there on the pier?'

"The thing was, I *could* see it, the whole scene unfolding rapidly in my mind with such eidetic clarity that I saw the moon-cast shadows, the ripples on the black water, the blood on the stones of the wall. With my acute ability to visualize, all he needed to do was construct the merest mood and I, lying in the darkness, dropped into an entire world instantly.

"'You do see it, don't you?' Fergus said confidently.

"'I've created a picture in my mind, yes. But with my kind of imagination, Fergus, I can create anything. You know that. I can picture the dark side of the moon, if that's what I go after.'

"'But *is* it a picture? Or is it reality? What proof is there that you're not really seeing the dark side of the moon? That what you're seeing isn't real?'

"'Because I'm making it up,' I said.

"'Laura, Laura, *Laura*, whatever will we do with you?' he moaned softly. 'Where do you get this resistance that so ill becomes you?'

"'It isn't resistance. I only said, why do I have to believe? Isn't it enough that it's there in my mind? Why does it have to be real?'

"'Clear these continual doubts out of your mind. They lower you.' He leaned over to kiss me.

"'But why can't you accept things for what they are, Fergus? Why does everything have to be more than it seems? Why must you grab at even the most tenuous ideas in an effort to connect everything to everything else?'

"'Because everything *is* connected.'

"'*Is* it? Does it have to be? And does it matter, if it isn't? I mean, I'd be happy if there were other lives, if I'd been a queen in Atlantis and we'd been lovers, but I'm still happy even if we weren't. We made good love, Fergus. Why does it only have value in your eyes, if we were once lovers in Atlantis?'

"'Because otherwise nothing would make sense, Laura. If nothing was connected, there'd be no meaning to what we do. What would be the point of anything? Why exist at all?'

"I had no answer to that. But as I lay in the darkness the scene from Atlantis came into my mind again. The wall, built of dressed grey stone, was to my left. A cobbled boat sloped into the water between the wall and the small wooden pier. The water itself was not a lake, but a river of huge, Nile-like proportions, moving sluggishly in the right-hand direction. His little boat, moored to the pier, bobbed in the dark water. It was crudely made and easily sunk.

"Not only could I see this scene, but the story formed quickly around it – how my husband, the king, had discovered my unfaithfulness and sent the guards; how my lover's death sparked rebellion among the commoners and brought about the downfall of the kingdom; how I ran, panicked, through the darkness, the branches of the shoreline bushes flicking my face as I struggled to escape my own inevitable fate.

"I lay, seeing the faces, hearing the voices, and wondering: Why does my mind do this to me?"

Chapter Thirty

"After finishing his readings at the health club, Fergus often stopped by my apartment. He had his own key by that point, so he would just let himself in. I was normally studying at my desk in the bedroom.

"'God, you take this shit so seriously,' he muttered one night, shifting a pharmacopoeia aside so he could sit down on my bed.

"'I need to.'

"'*I* need to unwind. Let's go to Jay's Place for a while.'

"'I'd love to, Fergus, but I can't. It's my turn to present the patient case tomorrow, so I need to be prepared.'

"'Do it later.'

"'If we go out, I won't have a "later". I need to get some sleep as well. I'm exhausted.'

"'Have you been meditating?'

"'Yes, I've been meditating. But I still need sleep.'

"'Yes, but *have* you been doing the meditation? The way I showed you? Because if you're doing it the way I showed you, Laura, you shouldn't need so much sleep. The body requires no more than four hours' sleep to regenerate. Anything past that is wasteful.'

"'*I* need more than four hours, I'm afraid,' I said. I sighed. '*And* I still need to get this finished.'

"He paused to look at me, his expression displeased. 'I wish you weren't so resistant.'

"'Look, I'm sorry,' I said. 'It's not that I don't want to go out, but that I can't. I *have* to complete this.'

"Fergus regarded me intently. When he couldn't get me to cooperate, he smiled in a sad sort of way that thinly disguised disapproval under sympathy. 'Here, I'll make us a cup of tea,' he finally said.

"Picking up the dirty mug from my desk, he glanced offhandedly into it, then blanched. '*Coffee?*' Said with astonishment befitting the discovery that I'd been knocking back mugs full of whiskey.

"'Yes, coffee,' I said.

"With completely unexpected force, he threw the coffee cup. It hit the edge of the bookshelf and fell to the floor, shattering. '*Why* do you do this to me?' he asked angrily. 'Why do you resist every effort I make with you?'

"'I'm sorry. I'm just tired.'

"'You're *not* meditating,' he said fiercely and loomed over me.

"'Fergus, I *am* meditating, but I don't have enough hours in my day. I'm trying to do your stuff. I'm trying to do my stuff. And I'm shattered.' Tears came to my eyes.

"'No wonder Torgon refuses to come through you directly,' Fergus muttered blackly. 'You don't even try to meet her halfway.'

"Huffily he disappeared into the kitchen, while I got up to clear away the pieces of broken mug.

"When he returned, he was carrying cups of herbal tea. No matter what the label said, every tea Fergus brought tasted the same to me. Their herb-and-flower smell had become inextricably connected in my mind with Fergus's presence.

"He pushed the books out of his way and flopped down on my bed. 'What I actually came to talk to you about is this course on channelling I want you to go on. It's in San Francisco. I know the leader personally and he's top of the league. It's a private course, only for those who have already achieved a certain level of enlightenment, and I think it'd be ideal for you. There'll be a lot of other people like yourself who've already made good contact with their guides but aren't fully at home with channelling. Gavin, this guy who runs it, channels professionally. He's, like, done it for all these movie stars and business people. Really famous people. And he's rich as shit.'

"'I can't go on a course, Fergus It's right at the end of the term. I could never get the time off.'

"'We're only talking two weeks. Two weeks, Laura, and you'd have the benefits for a lifetime. I've already talked to Gavin about you. He's confident that once Raif – that's his guide – once Raif talks to you, it'll make all the difference. This guy isn't Mickey Mouse, Laura. If anyone can help you bring Torgon through clearly, it'll be Gavin.'

"I remember sitting there, listening to him and feeling depression settle over me. I wanted to please him. I loved him so much that I longed to be everything he wanted me to be, but how could I do it? There simply wasn't enough time to do all the things he wanted me to do and my studies as well, and he became so impatient with me when I didn't manage it. As for the issue of Torgon … it had been one thing creating an alter ego for myself out of Torgon to use with the Tuesday night group, but what Fergus was trying to 'bring through' was something very much grander and I just didn't have it. There *was* no 'real' Torgon for Gavin and Raif to find. Nothing for me to channel unless I faked absolutely everything. But Fergus refused to hear me when I tried to explain this. He kept insisting it was all my fault that Torgon wasn't real to me, that if I just did what he said, if I meditated more, lived a purer, more worthy life, studied the things he gave me, just *listened* to him, then Torgon *would* come to me as a true Voice.

"I tried to explain that it just wasn't possible to go on this course he'd arranged for me. I didn't want to make him angry, because I'd already discovered a very tigerish temper lurking in his love for me. He could roar up in such a fierce way that there wasn't much distance between passion and violence in his behaviour. I knew it was all my fault, but as much as I wanted to please him, I simply couldn't do it. I said, 'Betjeman's fed up to the back teeth with me as it is. He's called me in twice now to read me the riot act because my work's slipped. Once upon a time I was a straight-A student so I've had to promise him I'd focus on my work. And I have to. I've got a microbiology course this term that I'm really struggling to pass. I need it to get this degree, so I *have* to study.'

"'Betjeman? Why is it always Betjeman?' Fergus replied angrily.

"I sighed.

"Fergus gave me a very penetrating look, his dark eyes moving slowly across my face. Then suddenly he leaped to his feet to tower menacingly over me. 'Are you fucking Betjeman? Is that why you're so caught up in what he wants?'

"'*No*! God, no, Fergus. Why would you ever think that? He's just my adviser.'

"'I don't believe you.'

"'Fergus, don't be insane. He's like a million years old. I'd never even consider him in that way. You're the one I love.'

"'Well, if that's so, then prove it to me.' His voice was quiet. 'You choose.'

"'What do you mean?'

"'Him or me. Tell Betjeman to stick it up his asshole and come with me to California. Or choose him and I'm done with you.'

"Astonished, I looked up at him. 'Come off it, Fergus.'

"He kept his dark eyes on my face.

"'I'm not hearing this,' I said and shook my head. 'I'm not hearing what you just said.' I opened a text book and bent over it.

"'I knew you were going to betray me,' he replied. 'Just as you did before. Just as you've always done.'

"I didn't respond. I kept my head down, my eyes on the text of the open book and pretended to read, but my mind was elsewhere, a million light years away, darting through parallel universes, other dimensions, the darker reaches of the imagination.

"'And I'll tell you something else,' Fergus said. 'That first night in the health club when you said you were studying medicine, my heart sank. The Voices had already told me this was not where your life was going, even when I didn't realize yet who you were. That very first night in the health club. I looked at you and I already knew you were on the wrong path.'

"I raised my head. Bracing my forearms on the desk, I leaned towards him. 'You keep telling me to tune into what Torgon wants, to what wisdom she has to offer me. The truth is, the only time I have ever genuinely done that was in regards to pursuing medicine. They have no doctors in Torgon's world. No books. No science. And precious little knowledge on how to keep people from dying of the simplest maladies. Just an old woman covered in paint and goat oil who shakes rattles at the injustice of it all. So, I thought, *I* can learn it for her. *I* can go out and *I* can make a difference with my learning. Torgon inspired me. That's the one single choice I've ever truly made because of Torgon. So how can you tell me now it isn't my path?'

"'Because the Voices have said otherwise. They have told me however hard you work, you will never spend a day as a doctor.'"

"I think I could have blanked out that bleak prediction, but then came exams, the end of term, the Christmas break, and, with the start of the new term, my grades. I'd been dreading them because I knew I had been spending far too much time with Fergus and not enough studying, but on opening the envelope, I was forced to acknowledge things were much worse than I'd thought. I had failed the microbiology course.

"I sat at the kitchen table and stared at the paper containing my grades. My blood turned to ice. What was going to happen if Dad and Marilyn found out? My parents had no inkling of my academic decline. Indeed, my family knew very little about my current life at all, because it had been ages since I had been home. I'd avoided contact, because how in heaven's name would I explain Fergus? All these years Marilyn had so wanted me to have a boyfriend and now that I genuinely had one, what could I say about him? That he earned his living as a psychic? That he was planning to become the Sun King after the apocalypse?

"How had all this happened? How in eighteen months had I gone from being the shining star in Betjeman's heavens to failing a critical course I needed to graduate? Sitting there at the kitchen table on that dull January morning, I attempted to recreate that sense of awesome yet innocent joy I'd felt when I'd pulled Torgon into my mind during classes or lab work, and tried to see what I was learning from her perspective. I couldn't feel it now. I couldn't even remember how it felt.

"Classes these days were a pain, something that got in the way of what Fergus wanted me to do or interfered with my work at the Tuesday night group. Over the previous six months I'd started charging for the channelling advice on Tuesday night – just a little bit, just a small fee to help out with expenses, because I was hardly what you would call rich. Besides, Fergus had said I should. It gave the whole thing a more professional aura, he said. And no one objected. In fact, I now had more people coming to see me at the Tuesday night meetings than ever before. It made the commitment greater, however, as I had to make extra time to see the extra people.

"I stared at the letter and realized that somewhere along the line I'd turned into someone I didn't know.

"Picking up the telephone, I dialled.

"Tiffany answered. She said, 'Laura? Is that you?'

"'Yeah, it's me.'

"'You sound funny. Do you have a cold?'

"'Something like that,' I replied and wiped the tears out of my eyes.

"'Are you calling to talk to Mum and Dad? Because if you are, you've missed them. They just went to the store to get groceries. Cody's at hockey practice.'

"'That's all right. I was just calling to hear familiar voices. You'll do.'

"'Geez, Laura, that sounds like a really bad cold. Did you catch it at the hospital?'

"'Guess you could say that.'

"Then silence. Tiffany was chewing gum. The smacking sound carried better across the continent than her voice.

"'What's been happening there?' I asked.

"'Not much. Dad's been taking me and Cody up skiing most Sundays. That's about it. I'm getting pretty good. You ought to see me.'

"'Yeah, I wish I could.'

"'How come you didn't come home at Christmas, Laura? I missed you. It's been forever since you've been home.'

"'I was busy.'

"'At the hospital?' Tiffany asked.

"'Just busy.'

"'Mum says you have to work really long hours to be a doctor.'

"'Yeah, something like that.'

"'I was thinking I might be a vet,' Tiffany said, 'but I'm kind of changing my mind. I wouldn't want to work all the time and never get to see my family.'

"'Yeah, well, probably animals aren't as bad as people.'

"'Are you crying, Laura? You sound like you're crying.'

"'No. It's just a really bad runny nose. Listen, Tiff, I was thinking ... do you want to come visit me sometime? You know, like maybe during your spring break?'

"'Wow!' Tiffany screamed into the phone. 'Really? *Really*, Laura? That'd be brilliant! I'd *love* to.' A pause. 'Would you ask Mum and Dad today? Call back later? When they get home from the supermarket and ask them? 'Cause I'd just love to!'

"Beyond me came the sound of the key in the door lock. Fergus walked into my apartment.

"'Listen, Tiff, I've got to go. There's someone at the door. Bye-bye.' I hung up quickly.

"'Who was that?' Fergus asked.

"'My little sister.'

"'What are you talking to her for?' His voice sounded vaguely suspicious.

"'Because she *is* my little sister.'

"'Did she phone you?'

"'Does it matter?'

"'She's a kid, isn't she?'

"'Yeah, she's twelve.'

"'So what did you want to talk to her for?'

"'Because she's part of my family, Fergus.'

"He peered closely at me. 'You've been crying.'

"'No, I haven't.'

"'What's the matter?'

"'Nothing. Really.'

"He studied me more intently, his dark eyes holding my gaze.

"'Okay, so I was,' I said. 'But I'm fine now.'

"'Why were you crying?'

"I shrugged. The paper containing my grades was lying open on the table. I didn't want to call his attention to it by flipping it over but I didn't want him to catch sight of the university logo either.

"'You haven't been meditating,' he said.

"'I *have* been meditating.'

"'How about those yoga exercises? Are you doing them?' he asked.

"'Some of them.'

"'But not all of them.' He frowned. 'This is the whole problem, Laura. You are not committed. I don't want you to spend time talking to your family. We're reaching an important period here and you're starting to bring up a lot of difficult emotions from your past lives. They won't understand what you're going through, so talking to them is only going to draw this stage out for you.'

"I could feel the tears rising again, so I turned away and went to the window.

"'Laura, relax. I can sense your tension from here. Calm down. You don't *want* to feel this way, do you?'

"'No.'

"'So take a deep, slow breath. The way I've taught you.'

"'I did.

"His voice softened. 'Come here. Come over here and sit on the floor with me. I'll massage your shoulders.' He opened his arms.

"At the sight of that loving gesture, I couldn't keep from crying any longer. 'Everything's falling apart,' I said. 'I don't know which way to turn.'

"'To me,' he said so tenderly, pulling me in against him. 'Not to some kid sister. Not to Betjeman. Not to any of them. They can't help you. Only I can do that, my queen. Because no one else loves you like I do.' His voice went honey sweet. 'Don't go to them. Only *I* know. Only I can help. Only I love you.'

"I wept.

"'So, relax now, my sweetheart. Relax. Feel your muscles. Here. They're like iron, aren't they? Let's do some of the exercises. I'll do them with you. Rotate your neck. Like this. Follow me. It'll release the tension. Now lift your shoulders up.'

"I was crying so hard. I couldn't stop.

"Leaning forward, Fergus placed his hands on either side of my face. 'Here, give it to me,' he whispered. 'Give me your pain. Let me share your burden.'

"Fergus's hands were very hot. They felt good against my skin, as he held my face and watched my contorted grimaces. Through them flowed the enormity of his love for me. Really. I could feel it. It surrounded me and absorbed my distress. Even in the depth of my despair I grew aware that no one, ever, had loved me with the strength that Fergus did.

"'Come to me,' he said and pulled me close into his arms again. He kissed my forehead, my wet cheeks, my hair and held me close as a baby in the womb. 'You're safe,' he murmured. 'I have you. We're together again and nothing ever, ever will part us. I promise you that. I promise with my life that I'll protect you forever.'"

Chapter Thirty-One

"I want a cowboy hat," Conor announced when he came into the playroom. He crossed over to the dressing-up basket. Selecting the cowboy hat, he clapped it on his head. "He's my son," he said to no one in particular. "I don't want him to go away."

Conor looked over at James. "Daddy's strong. He lifts me up. Hands under my arms. 'Up, up.' he says. And I go up. Daddy laughs. I felt his breath."

"You're enjoying the things your father does," James reflected.

"Yeah." Conor crossed over to the table. "My mother isn't strong. She doesn't wear a cowboy hat. She said, 'He needs to go away.' But Daddy said, 'No, I don't want that.'"

James smiled.

"I wasn't here last time," Conor said.

"No, you didn't come."

"I was sick in the night – I threw up. Three times. Messy on the floor. My mother said, 'He needs to go away.' My mother cried. Tears running down her cheeks," Conor said and pulled a finger over his cheek. "Daddy said, 'He can stay with me. If he is sick on the floor I'll clean it up.' But I wasn't sick again. I was well then."

He turned. "Where's the mechanical cat today?" He went to the shelf and picked up the box. "Here you are. Where's your stand? I'll put it on your stand so you can stand up and see." Coming back to the table, he set the cardboard cat down and pushed it over towards James's notebook. "Here. The mechanical cat will read what you write today." Then he took off, trotting around the room in a sort of half-skip.

"You seem happy today," James ventured.

"Today's the day I come here. Today's the day I spend with the mechanical cat." He swooped down on the table and picked up the cardboard cat. Excitement overtook him and his body went momentarily rigid. "Read me the poem."

James paged back through the notebook to find Conor's mechanical cat song. He read it aloud.

Still tense with excitement, Conor fluttered his fingers at the small cardboard form. "You're strong. You're brave. No ghosts. You know there aren't any ghosts here. You tell me, 'Boy, You're safe with me! I can see all the ghosts but there are no ghosts to see. Boy, you can do anything in here. You can be yourself.'"

"The mechanical cat makes you feel safe and strong," James remarked.

"I don't need my wires. Did you see? I have no wires on today." Conor pulled out his shirt to show that the usual coil of string and foil was absent.

"You've decided to be an ordinary boy today."

"Yeah. My strong father says, 'You don't need these. Leave them at home.' I don't need them. Nothing happens. The mechanical cat says, 'You don't need them. You're strong too.'"

Setting the cardboard cat down on the table, Conor veered off towards the easel. "Today I'll paint. Finger-paint. Coleman School Supplies Blue. I'll do blue. I haven't done blue."

James rose to help him get the materials ready. Once the newspapers were down on the table top and the damp paper was laid out, Conor came over to where James was sitting. He put his stuffed cat into James's lap. "No accidents this time!" He laughed.

Conor tackled the painting with enthusiasm. He seemed to have less interest in actually painting than in dumping paint on the paper, because he kept adding to what he had. Around and around he sloshed it, lifting the excess paint up and letting it drop back onto the paper.

"Now yellow? Coleman School Supplies Yellow?" he asked, raising his head to look at James.

"Yes, you may add yellow as well, if that's what you want to do."

"Yes! That's what the boy wants to do. And in here, if the boy wants, the boy does!" he said with relish. A glob of yellow paint joined the blue. The two colours together formed a rather ghastly green.

"This paper is wearing out. It has a hole," Conor said.

"So it has."

"I'll put it over there. I'll take a new piece."

"Can you put water on it yourself?" James asked.

"Yes, I can do it!"

James smiled at the child's budding confidence.

While Conor was carrying the paint-soaked paper over to the counter beside the sink, the wet weight in the middle proved too much. The paper broke and the excess paint spilled onto the floor. Conor jumped back in surprise but he didn't lose control. Indeed, unexpectedly, he laughed.

"Look! Sick! The painting says, 'Too much in my stomach. Throw up on the floor!'"

"Yes, it does rather look like that."

"Who will clean it up?"

"Shall I help you?" James asked.

Conor regarded the splatter of paint pensively. "She says, 'He needs to go away. He's too much for me.' She's crying. Tears running all down her cheeks." A pause. "Sorry, Mummy," he murmured in the tiniest voice. "The boy wants to say that, but his stomach feels sick. He wants to say, 'Be strong. Don't cry. Don't let tears come down your cheeks. The ghost man will come. He will drink your tears.'"

James had risen from his seat to come and help, but he paused, not wanting to disturb Conor's thoughts. Conor looked over. He reached his arms out for the stuffed cat.

Bringing the cat to him, James then went to get paper towels to clean up the paint. Conor helped to soak up the dirty water on the carpet with a paper towel. His mood was more subdued, but he still didn't lose control. In fact, he went ahead and dampened another sheet of paper to continue finger-painting.

Back at the table, Conor laid the new paper out. He picked up the blue jar of paint but then hesitated just before it actually poured from the jar. He set it down again. Locating the lid, he screwed it back on and returned the blue paint to its place. He did the same with the yellow. Taking the red finger-paint from the shelf, he brought it over to the table, took off the lid and scooped out a large amount.

Laying his hand flat in the paint, Conor moved it around with an almost rhythmic slowness. Lifting it, he looked at his red fingers. Then he put both hands in and moved them around. Again, he brought them up and looked at them carefully.

"Is it paint?" he asked softly. "Is it paint? Is that it?"

Back into the paint he went, around and around, again he lifted his hands up. "Hasn't Mummy been messy with her paints? Mummy, what a mess. You've used up my whole jar."

He continued to spread the paint around, his mood slowly changing as the activity drew him deeper into it. The buoyancy was gone. His concentration grew more and more intense as he studied the motion of his hands.

A pause in the activity.

Conor lifted up one hand and very carefully laid it on the bare skin of his forearm to leave a clear print of his palm and fingers. "Maybe it's blood." He glanced up quickly at James, his expression worried.

"No, it isn't blood," James said quietly. "It's only red paint."

"Only red paint. The man says only red paint. Strong cats live here. Only red paint."

He put his hand back into the paint and pushed it around. He paused again and from it grew a deep silence. His brow furrowed in concentration as he scrutinized the handprint on his forearm.

James sat in silence, watching the boy. What role had blood played in the events that had traumatized Conor?

Abruptly, Conor looked up with an expression of undiluted horror. Lifting his dripping red hands from the paper, he screamed.

Jerked from his thoughts, James rose quickly. "What's happened? What's wrong?"

Rigid with fear, Conor just screamed.

"Shall I help you wash it off? Here, come back to the sink," James said and put a hand on the boy's shoulder to guide him. Conor held the paint-streaked arm out stiff in front of him. "It's just red paint," James reassured again.

Turning on the faucet, James cupped up water in his hand and ran it over Conor's skin. The finger-paint began to dissolve, turning the water sloshing down the plughole a pale red. James was standing directly behind the boy, his body keeping Conor close enough to the sink to allow the paint to be washed off, and he felt the easing of rigid muscles.

Taking paper towels, James dried Conor's arm. "That was a little too much all at once, wasn't it?"

"A little too much for today," Conor murmured. He turned. "Where's Daddy?"

James knelt and put his arms around the boy. "You're feeling frightened, and you would like your dad here with you."

Conor nodded.

"He'll be here soon. When the hand on the clock reaches ten, he will be waiting for you in the other room and it'll be time to go home then."

"Read me the poem."

James didn't need to read it. He knew it off by heart.

Conor let out a long, relieved sigh at the sound of the familiar words. "The mechanical cat is strong," he murmured. "We're safe. The mechanical cat can never die."

* * *

When Alan arrived, James left Conor with Dulcie for a few minutes and invited him into the office for a quick chat.

"Actually, if you hadn't asked me, I was going to ask you," Alan said, following him in. "Because I've got to say, he's become a different boy in the last few weeks."

James smiled. "Yes, he's been showing some good progress in here."

"He still talks in circles most of the time, but, you know, the two of us are actually starting to have conversations," Alan said. "He can make his wants known now, if you keep him calm."

"I think your involvement has been critical to his success," James said. "I'm seeing important signs of bonding with you. Today, for example, when he became upset in the session, he asked for you, not just his cat. That's a huge step forward."

Alan smiled with pleasure. "I'm trying to live up to being that guy he thinks I am." Then a more wistful expression. "It makes me feel bad when I think back on when things started going wrong for him. I feel like we let him down."

"Please don't judge yourself with hindsight," James said. "Normally people do try their best. Especially with kids. If we make mistakes it's usually because we really couldn't see any other way to do things at the time. How is Laura getting on with him?"

Alan shook his head glumly. "Not well. They've got a whole different dynamic going between them. Conor still won't talk for her, you know. He's talking quite a lot with me, but with Laura he's as incoherent as ever. As crazy as ever. That makes it very difficult to convince her he's making any kind of significant progress."

"Why do you suppose that is?" James asked.

Alan was pensive. "I don't know. There's just all this tension between them. He's uptight. She's uptight. They feed into each other. Anyway, I've agreed to take Conor more. I've still got hope that Laura and I are eventually going to be able to resolve things between us. I don't want to push her into moving out of the house. So I've put a second bed in the cabin so he can be my bunk buddy. He seems very happy with it."

"One thing I wanted to ask you more about," James said, "and that's about the miscarriage of Morgana's twin. Conor seems to have some serious fears regarding blood. Could he have witnessed her miscarriage?"

Alan considered for a moment. "He was at home with her when it happened, but I don't know. His problems had begun before that. His clinginess started well before Laura could even have been pregnant, because I remember it coinciding with just about the time I got the TB diagnosis on my cattle and that was more than a year before Morgana was born. But … because Conor had become so clingy and never wanted Laura out of his sight, I suppose it's possible he did witness blood."

"Did you ever talk to him at all about it?" James asked.

"No. He wasn't even three. It's not the sort of thing you talk over with a child that age, is it?"

"I'm just thinking that if he witnessed the blood or Laura's distress …" James said. "Especially as he was clearly a very bright, perceptive little boy. Because I think Morgana was saying Conor could actually read by two, yes?"

"Not read properly. He knew his letters. Maybe could read a couple words, but that's all."

"Nonetheless, that's still very advanced. So he's a very, very bright boy. But with a two-year-old's experience of life, it would have been hard for him to interpret what was happening."

Alan gave a faint shrug. "I dunno. I'm not aware of him witnessing anything and if so, Laura never said."

"Okay," James said.

There was a small pause.

"One other thing I wanted to ask," James added. "I'd like to do a couple of sessions with Conor and Morgana together. Would that be all right?"

"Yes, that's fine," Alan said. "I'll arrange for it."

Chapter Thirty-Two

"Tiffany arrived in Boston the final Saturday in March," Laura said. "Fifteen months had passed since I'd last been home, so I was surprised by how much she'd grown. She'd always had Marilyn's body type, but what had been willowy on Marilyn was lanky on Tiffany. She was twelve now and nearly as tall as I was.

"We enjoyed a splendid first day together. I took her to the shopping mall near my apartment and Tiffany was awed by the size and number of stores. I threw off all Fergus's teachings about healthy food and treated us to drinks at the Orange Julius stand and doughnuts and caramel corn. We spent ages in the pet store watching the puppies and the tropical fish and pondering who would want a tarantula for a pet. Tiff said she might, but she'd rather have a chameleon. Or a grass snake. In the toy store we fondled the stuffed animals and admired the expensive, imported dolls. In the bookstore, we browsed languidly.

"I didn't want to go home. I was worried Fergus would be there, waiting, because I knew he'd stop our fun. So, instead

I took Tiffany to a pizza place for dinner and afterwards we went to the drive-in to see *Star Wars*. We'd both seen it already, but we both loved it. I bought us a gigantic container of popcorn and quart-sized drinks, cranked back the car seats, and we sat through both the early and late showing. Tiffany was dazed with tiredness by the time we returned to my apartment.

"I lay on the bed, watching her as she unpacked items from her suitcase. In the normal course of things, she always wore her long hair pulled back in a ponytail, but as she changed into her nightgown, she pulled her T-shirt off and the band holding her ponytail came off too. Her hair tumbled down over her shoulders. Like her mother, Tiff's hair was black, but unlike her mother, she'd never bothered to curl it, so it was utterly straight. Seeing her there in the soft light of the bedside lamp as she removed the last of her clothes, her dark hair falling forward, I was abruptly drawn into Torgon's world. I was thinking how Torgon must have looked like this at twelve and for the first time in months the shadowy world of the Forest laid itself down almost instantly over the world of my bedroom like a fallen transparency.

"We were both still in bed the next morning when I heard the snick of the front door lock. Hurriedly I clambered over Tiffany still asleep on the floor in her sleeping bag and grabbed my robe, because I knew who it was: Fergus.

"'What's this?' he asked, lifting the empty popcorn container out of the kitchen garbage. 'There are animal products in this. What else did you eat? Sugar? Animal fat? I can't believe you're doing this.' Angrily he smashed the empty container between his hands and threw it back into the bin.

"Tiffany appeared in the doorway of the bedroom.

"Fergus looked at her, his eyes going dark, like a frightened cat's.

"'Hi,' she said tentatively and looked from him to me and back again. She smiled timidly.

"'Fergus, this is my sister Tiffany. And this is my friend Fergus, honey. Fergus and I are, well, sort of together.'

"'Oh?' Tiffany said with surprise. 'Are you coming to Salem too?'

"'Salem?' Fergus said sharply. 'You can't go anywhere today, Laura. You and I need to work. You're channelling on Tuesday night.'

"Tiffany looked confused.

"'I promised Tiff I'd take her up to the Salem museums. She's only here for five days.'

"Fergus dug deep into the pocket of his trousers and pulled out a money clip. Peeling off a five dollar bill, he held it out to Tiffany. 'Here. Go get lost for a couple of hours.'

"'*Fergus*,' I said in dismay.

"He turned back to me. 'Two hours, okay? That's all I ask. We'll work on your channelling for two hours and then you and she can have the rest of the day off.'

"Reluctantly I nodded. 'Okay.'

"Tiffany, who was still in her pajamas, looked at the five dollars in her hand and then up at me, her expression perplexed.

"'Would you mind, Tiff? I've got some stuff I need to do before we can go out.'

"'But what am I supposed to do with this?' she asked, confused. 'I haven't even had breakfast.'

"'Yeah, well, that's the point of it,' Fergus replied. 'Take it and go have breakfast.'

"'There's a doughnut place just two blocks down the street. You like doughnuts, don't you? Just think. You can pig out to your heart's content.' I grinned. 'And here. I'll give you another five dollars. You go down there and have breakfast and then by the time you're done, the stores'll be open and you can look around.'

"'By myself?' Tiffany asked in a bewildered voice.

"'Just for a couple of hours, Tiff. You're big enough to do that on your own, aren't you? Just think, you can tell your mum when you get home. That'll freak her,' I said and grinned evilly.

"With a confused sigh, she turned and went back into the bedroom to change. I followed her in and closed the door. 'Look, I'm really, really sorry about this, Tiff. I didn't know Fergus was going to come over. But be a good egg, would you? For me? Just go out and amuse yourself for two hours. Then we'll go to Salem just like we planned.'

"'Yeah, like we *planned*,' she said. 'How come you've got to stop now and do whatever he says just because he's here?'

"'Because that's less trouble in the long run.'"

"Fergus refused to leave Tiffany and me alone. While he wanted to work on my channelling, this wasn't a realistic option with Tiffany around. Since he couldn't do that, Fergus decided to accompany us on the outings we'd planned together.

"Tuesday came, which was Tiffany's last full day in Boston before going home. I would have preferred to skip the Tuesday night group, if I could have, but Fergus wouldn't consider it. I was uncomfortable leaving Tiffany alone in my apartment at night, so I ended up having to bring her along too.

"That was a mistake. I felt inhibited with Tiffany there, afraid, I think, of what she would go home and say to my parents. I couldn't get into the right mood to do the sorts of things I usually did, so I took a back seat that night and let Fergus take over. Nonetheless, it was still exciting because one of the other women in the group began speaking in a strange language right in the middle of the meeting. Fergus immediately identified it as a Being of Light coming through.

"When she stopped speaking, Fergus told her it was paramount that she begin cleansing her mind by practising stringent meditation techniques. He then made her lie down prone on the floor while he pressed his fingers to her temples. He said he sensed the nearness of many spirits, not all of them good, but for the most part they were Voices. The woman seemed delighted with all this attention.

"At home afterwards, Tiffany and I prepared for bed. She didn't talk much. Indeed, she'd been virtually silent all evening, which I took to be tiredness because we'd been really on the go, trying to fit everything in.

"'You can sleep on the plane home,' I said, as I flopped down on my bed. 'It'll make the trip go faster.'

"Tiffany nodded and picked up her pajamas. Laying them on the bed, she pulled the band out of her ponytail and shook loose her hair before beginning to unbutton her shirt.

"I had found myself living for this brief moment every evening when Tiffany loosened her dark, straight hair and evoked that brief, flickering vision of Torgon. I would experience then a faint echo of the enthralling sensation I'd always got even as a child when accessing the Forest.

"When she was changed, Tiffany leaned over and gave me a toothpaste-scented kiss before settling into her sleeping bag.

Not quite ready for bed myself, I wished her good night and then got up and went into the living room.

"Lying on the coffee table was one of the notebooks Fergus had been using to transcribe what I was saying in my channelling sessions for the Tuesday night group. I leaned forward and picked it up.

"'*Torgon says: The tapestry of your own existence operates as an impediment, highly detrimental, to the facts of inner unity, where physical being, individually, obstructs the collective realization of a multidimensional actualization*,' I read.

"An odd, vaguely repulsed feeling came over me. There was no meaning in that sentence. I couldn't remember now if the person I had been channelling for thought it made sense, but looking at it now, I realized it said nothing. Just words in the right grammatical order, as bereft of meaning as if the phrases had been randomly generated by a computer.

"I thought then of Torgon – the *real* Torgon – the one who shimmered into existence as Tiffany pulled the band from her hair. That Torgon was so far distant from this shambolic sentence that it was almost obscene to have ascribed it to her. How long it had been since I had gone properly into the Forest like I'd used to? Months, I realized and I had been so busy with Fergus that I hadn't even noticed.

"Was I still able to go? It wasn't something I could just 'call up', like I did with the bogus Torgon. I had never actually stopped to consider what exactly I'd done for all those years in order to 'go to the Forest'. It had just been there when I'd wanted it. I'd done it intuitively. Now it wasn't there. Except for that brief moment in the evenings with Tiffany's loosened hair, there was nothing. Even that was just a resonance, the way a crystal glass will pick up a distant note.

"Leaning back into the cushions of the sofa, I closed my eyes and tried to bring the Forest to life. The last story I'd written had been of Torgon fleeing to the high holy place after killing Ansel. I thought about the events, but I was just remembering them. I wasn't there.

"Maybe I needed to relax more, I thought. Using the meditation techniques Fergus had so carefully taught me, I worked at calming my mind. In some distant part of me I could still sense what had been happening in her world while I was caught up in mine.

"A new Seer had been called – Caslan, Ansel's youngest sister. Torgon had met with the elders of the village council and had managed to convince them that killing Ansel had been a holy act, done at Dwr's command. This was not sufficient, however, for Ansel's three younger brothers – the holy brothers – who were also warriors. Being proud and high-born, they felt humiliated by the way he died: naked, asleep and killed by his own knife at the hand of a low-caste woman. Loki's father, who was leader of the *benita* band, had come to Torgon's defence and that had set the warriors arguing among themselves, some siding with the holy brothers, some with the *benita* band. Civil war loomed.

"I opened my eyes and stared up at the ceiling of my living room. What had happened to us? What had happened to both Torgon and myself? Our futures had been so promising. How had it all gone so wrong?

"It was after midnight when I finally went in to bed. I crept as silently as possible around Tiffany in her sleeping bag, pulled back my covers and lay down.

"'Laurie?' came the soft, small voice in the darkness.

"'I'm sorry. Did I wake you up? I thought I was being quiet.'

"'No, I haven't gone to sleep yet,' Tiffany said.

"'Not yet? You've been in here for hours. Is something wrong? Are you feeling okay?'

"'Yeah, I'm fine.'

"'Probably just the excitement of the big trip tomorrow then,' I said. 'I always find it hard to sleep before a journey.'

"'No, it's not that.' A pause, 'Can I ask you something, Laurie?'

"'Yeah, sure. Shoot.'

"'Promise me first you won't get mad.'

"'Well, try me.'

"'Do you really love that guy? That Fergus?'

"'Yes.'

"'I mean, *really* love him?'

"'I can hear what you're thinking from your voice, Tiff, and I want to say, you haven't seen his best side. He's not so good with kids, but the truth is, he can be really, really loving.'

"'That's not what I'm thinking, Laurie. I don't know how to say this so it doesn't sound wrong, but the truth is, I think he's nuts.'

"'He's not, Tiffany.'

"'I can't figure out what's happening here,' she said softly. 'I can't understand why you're hanging around with people like him and those folks at that meeting tonight. They're all nuts.'

"'That's not for you to judge, is it?' I said defensively. 'Who are you to know about any of this? You're just a mouthy kid from South Dakota.'

"I heard her expel a frustrated breath.

"'I don't want to get in a big argument at this time of night, Tiff, so I'm not going to,' I said. 'It's none of your business. You're not old enough to understand my friends.'

"The atmosphere felt sour then. Wearily, I pulled the covers up and turned over to face the wall. Several minutes of silence followed.

"'Laurie?'

"'Now what?'

"'I don't want to argue either, but just tell me one thing first, okay?'

"'All these questions *are* arguing.'

"'Please? Then I promise I'll leave you alone.'

"'Okay, *one* thing.'

"'Tell me that really, deep down, you don't believe any of this rubbish.'"

Chapter Thirty-Three

"The following Tuesday, I had a shift in the emergency ward at the university hospital," Laura said. "A little girl about seven had been hit by a car and was brought in with very serious head injuries. She was still alive, but unconscious, and we were absolutely frantic because no one knew who she was. Despite our efforts, we couldn't find her family in time. She died, nameless and alone, except for me, cradling her poor broken head in my hands.

"Because of this, I was late to the Tuesday night group. Fergus was already there. Sitting next to him where I normally sat was this young woman who came only occasionally to the group. Her name was Philippa, although she was known as Pippa, and most of us just called her Pip. She looked like a Pip – small and gamin-like with dark red, cropped hair.

"A discussion was underway about increasing 'prosperity potential'. Someone said how he was now connecting with higher energies during meditation and this was allowing him to let go of old, negative programming. He said he'd hooked into a lot of subconscious programming that wasn't affirming his prosperity potential, but now since he'd raised his vibrations and connected with the infinite wisdom of the Beings of Light, he was sure his new business venture would succeed.

"Pip suddenly said, well, *her* spirit guide had been in contact with Torgon last week and Torgon had given information to her guide on how to help Pip centre her life in a way that would encourage wealth.

"I couldn't believe what I'd just heard. I was sorely tempted to call Pip's bluff because that was just not something Torgon would do, neither the real one nor even my channelled construct of her, but I hesitated. If I did challenge Pip without explaining how I knew for certain she was making it up, people would just think it was sour grapes on my part. If I admitted how I did know Pip's claim was false, my own falsehoods would be revealed.

"We were all sitting in a circle on the floor and, as I was considering this matter, I was looking from Pip around to the other members of the group. Suddenly I caught sight of my shoes. There was blood on one of them. Only two tiny drops, but I knew immediately it had to be the blood of the young girl I had been treating in the ER.

"The sight of those drops of blood hit me as if someone had thrown a hammer at a plate-glass window. My mind just shattered. Glancing around the circle at all those well-fed, well-dressed, well-educated people, so gormless and gullible, I suddenly lost it. I thought, *What the HELL am I doing here? What kind of monster have I turned into?* And as I did, a terrifying panic overwhelmed me. I couldn't stay a moment longer. I jumped up and ran out of the room.

"Fergus jumped up after me and came running out too. 'What's wrong?'

"I'd already begun to cry. I yelled at him to go away. Trying to grab me, he said, 'Shhh, relax, Laura. Breath deeply now. Take a deep breath.'

"Fighting him off, I ran to my car. I was crying so hard by that point I could hardly see the road while driving home. Once inside my apartment, I pulled off my shoe and rushed into the kitchen in an attempt to wash the blood off, but as I reached the sink nausea overcame me. I threw up all over the dirty dishes that were piled in there.

"About half an hour later there was a snick and the familiar sound of Fergus pulling his key from the door. 'Laura?' he called out, 'Are you here?'

"He appeared in my bedroom doorway. 'How are you?' he asked, his voice concerned. Coming over, he sat on the edge of the bed. Behind him came Pip. Pip turned the overhead light on and then sat down on the bed beside Fergus.

"'Are you feeling better?' Fergus asked. 'You were looking very pale. I noticed that when you came in.'

"Pip said, 'I channelled tonight. Just like you've been doing. Too bad you missed it.'

"I just went berserk. I shrieked at her to get out of there and leave me alone.

"Fergus rose up and spread his arms out wide towards Pip, as if he were herding geese. He said. 'Go on home.' I remember hearing Pip asking, 'But aren't you coming?'

"'Why the hell did you bring her here?' I sobbed when Fergus returned. 'This isn't Grand Central Station. Why don't you think of me sometimes?'

"'Laura, all I do think about is you,' he said gently and reached out to smooth back my hair. I'd been afraid he'd be angry at my outburst, but he was just the opposite. His expression was so loving and his eyes as soft and deep as the darkness. 'Without you, there is no sun, no moon, no world for me,' he whispered. 'The universe is empty. I am only alive, knowing you're alive.'

"Slipping off his shoes, Fergus pulled back the covers and climbed into the bed with me. He enveloped me in an astonishingly tender embrace, pressing me so close against him I could hardly move. He covered my face with gentle kisses. Reaching my cheekbones, he touched his tongue to my tears and tasted them. He smiled. 'The sorrows of this world are too harsh for you. You are a true sensitive.'

"'No, I'm not', I sobbed. 'I've sold my soul. I am absolutely nothing.'

"When I woke in the morning, it was as if I were rousing from a drunken sleep, waking in the aftermath of heavy partying, when everything that had seemed so wonderful in an alcoholic haze now looked shoddy and insubstantial, when waking was not a refreshing experience, but one of pain and disappointment.

"Wearily, I got out of bed and got ready to go to the hospital, but the sensation affected everything I did. That afternoon, I just walked out. It was late in the day, 4:30 or so, and I was due at a seminar, but I just grabbed my coat and left.

"It was spring by then, cool and clear. The air was faintly scented with something floral – hyacinths, I think – that wove itself in around the traffic fumes. I walked, not thinking.

"I needed to talk to Fergus. He'd be at the health club by this time, but wouldn't have started his sessions yet. If I went over now, I could say what had to be said to him and then leave without there being enough time for him to drag a retraction out of me.

"I let myself in at the side door of the health club and went down the stairs. The light was on, spilling out into the stairwell, illuminating the emerald-green carpet. The room was empty, but the door was open to the small room behind, the private room where Fergus kept his things. I came to the doorway. I could hear he was in there, so I entered. There he was with Pip. On the floor. Fucking her from behind, like a bull on a cow. He sensed my presence and looked up

"'*Laura*,' came the horrified gasp, but I didn't wait for more. I turned and fled.

"Within twenty minutes of my arriving home, Fergus was there. He didn't even knock. He just came barging in.

"'Get *out*!' I screamed.

"'Laura, it isn't what it looked like.'

"'It damned well *was* what it looked like, Fergus!' I was in tears before I could finish the sentence.

"'Laura, calm down, so I can talk to you. I'll explain.'

"'There's nothing to explain, Fergus. I saw you.'

"'It's nothing with Pip. Pip isn't evolved. She's a lower. She's got no Voices. She's just faking it for attention, that's all.'

"'So you just tell yourself the woman's a lower, and then it doesn't count if you fuck her?'

"'No, try to understand.'

"'I'm done understanding, Fergus. I'm done with all of this. I'm done with channelling. I'm done with the Tuesday night group. And I'm done with you. So go. Leave. Now.'

"Fergus hesitated, which was the first time I'd ever seen a glint of uncertainty in his expression. A wretched anger overtook me. I picked up the channelling notebook from the coffee table and threw it at him, because it was the only thing of his I could lay my hands on. '*Go*!'

"He paused a moment longer, his expression sad. Then he opened the door and went out. I retrieved the channelling notebook from the floor and threw it again, feeling only minimal relief at the thud of paper and cardboard against the door.

"Picking up the phone, I started dialling directory enquiries. I asked for the number of the airlines. Six hours later I was on a plane for South Dakota."

"For all their insensitivity during my adolescence, Marilyn and my dad both made a sincere effort to welcome me back into the bosom of my family without too many questions or comments.

"Depression overtook me. I retreated into the basement and lay in bed for entire days without regard for anything, not the courses I'd left behind, not Dr Betjeman, not Fergus.

"I had expected Fergus to barrage me with phone calls but the days passed into weeks and there was no contact. Not once. From the moment I left Boston, I didn't hear from him again.

"This silence generated an unpleasant mix of sorrow and anxiety in me. I felt confused and lonely, as if I literally didn't know how to think or act without Fergus there to tell me what to do.

"In the end it was Tiffany who encouraged me to come up out of my cave in the basement. School was finished for the summer, so she came down to sit on my bed in the morning and talk to me. She started joining me for the morning cartoons, and, much to her mother's dismay, sharing my addiction for raspberry jam on toast. Between the two of us we would go through half a loaf of bread each morning.

"One morning, she said, 'I know how to make blueberry muffins. If I make them for us tomorrow, we could take them out on the patio and eat them at the picnic table.'

"'Tiff, I don't want to go out on the patio at eight o'clock in the morning.'

"'Would you like pancakes better? I can make them too. And it's nice outside at eight o'clock in the morning. It's not hot yet.'

"I emerged from the basement in mid-June, feeling like a bear coming out of hibernation. I schlumpfed out in my night gown and slippers and Tiffany did cartwheels on the lawn."

"Tiffany remained my unlikely guardian angel. She watched over my every move back towards normality, gently helping me along in a way I would never have accepted from an adult.

"'I think you should cut your hair, Laura,' she said one day, holding part of my hair out from my head. 'It looked better when you had it shorter.'

"I didn't answer.

"'*I* can cut it!' she said brightly.

"'Oh no, you can't. I'm not letting you anywhere near me with scissors.'

"'Just let me try.'

"'*No*, Tiffany. I don't want a twelve-year-old to cut my hair.'

"'Then, how about Mum? Mum could do it. She could cut the straggly bits off. You'd look nicer.'

"'Fergus wouldn't think so.'

"'Fergus isn't here.'

* * *

"One evening in late June, Tiffany said, 'Let's go somewhere.'

"'Like where?' I asked. I hadn't set foot off the property in the six weeks since I'd returned to South Dakota. Not even to the supermarket.

"Tiffany shrugged nonchalantly. She was desperate to see a horror movie she wasn't old enough for, so I expected her to ask me to take her to that. Instead, she said, 'How about the Badlands?'

"'The *Badlands*?' I replied in surprise. 'That's an hour's drive away and it's already after seven. It'll be practically dark when we get there.'

"'Yeah, I know,' she said, still smiling. 'I like it when it's evening in the Badlands. In the daytime it's too hot.' She rose up. 'Come on. Let's ask.'

"It was an unexpected destination. I'd been genuinely frightened of the Badlands as a child. I'd gone only once with the Meckses. I was very little and had found the eerie landscape profoundly unsettling. During the journey home, I got car sick, which was something that almost never happened to me. Ma took me up into the front seat with her and Pa. They were casually discussing a patch of land near Rapid City, saying how it looked like it was eroding into badlands and Pa said how the Badlands had been growing since the Dust Bowl days of the Depression. The conversation made me cry. I remember lying on the front seat with my head in Ma's lap and feeling hideously nauseated, while the Badlands loomed up in my child's mind as a diabolical threat, trying to spread lifelessness everywhere. I was in my teens before I fully understood how slowly geological changes take place and that I didn't need to watch warily for them to attack. Even so I'd never felt fully comfortable there. Consequently, it seemed like a strange place to choose for coming back to life.

"By the time Tiffany and I had spanned the fifty-some miles between Rapid City and the borders of the national park, the sun had dropped almost to the horizon. We weren't going to manage much viewing unless we wanted to do it in the darkness, so once we were inside the park, I stopped at the first overlook I came to.

"'Hey, yeah, this is good!' Tiffany cried enthusiastically. There were a few other hardy souls risking a walk down the path to the overlook in the fading light. Tiffany bounded off.

"This was my first time away from home in several weeks, so I opened the car door slowly, stood up and stretched. Cautiously, I looked around. An unseen bird called. The slightest sliver of a waning moon hung in the eastern sky.

"Bursting with energy, Tiffany ran all the way down to the lowest point of the outlook, then back up the steps to me, still beside the car, then down an unofficial path worn through the prairie grass. I lingered behind the low wall in the car park and assessed the just-visible tops of the nearest outcroppings. Finally I walked down slowly to the first vantage point.

"I'd been to the Badlands so seldom that I'd forgotten what a bizarre place it was with its eroded soil, bare and ghostly white, reaching up towards the sky like the crumbling marble spires of some vast, unremembered city. The sun had slipped below the distant undulations of the Black Hills to bring on the lingering twilight of midsummer. The crescent moon grew bright and sharp, a pagan sickle for huntresses and offerings of mistletoe. The same bird called again, a long, shrill note.

"Tiffany was already down again at the lower outlook and I walked down to join her. The ground below the guard rail sloped off steeply, dropping several hundred feet to the floor of the basin.

"Everyone else had gone, leaving Tiffany and me in the haunted silence. I leaned my forearms on the metal railing and regarded the surreal formations stretching off as far into the dusky distance as I could see. I didn't feel the fear of it that I had as a child, but I still felt overawed. It was a numinous place, particularly in the moonlight.

"'Come on,' Tiffany said and slipped through the guard rails.

"'*Tiffany*!' I shrieked. 'For God sake, don't go down there. Jesus! You're going to kill yourself.'

"'No, I'm not. I've been down here before. Me and Cody both. There's a path. Come on.'

"There looked to be no path to me, just a sheer drop off into an alien landscape.

"'Come on, Laura. I want to show you something.'

"Leaving all common sense behind, I crawled between the guard rails and followed her down into a white gully of frighteningly crumbly soil. Down we went steeply and I didn't dare think how we'd ever get back up again. 'Jesus, Tiffany, stop! Jesus Christ, this is for mountain sheep, not people. Your mum is going to murder me, if she ever finds out I let you do this.'

"'Don't worry,' she replied, sitting down in order to slide further down into the deeper gully below us. 'Both me and Cody have been down here millions of times. There's a picnic ground just a little further down the road and Mum and Dad always stop there 'cause it's got shade. Me and Cody have done a lot of exploring around here. I know where I'm going.'

"And she did, for suddenly we came out onto a narrow ledge that harboured three ponderosa pines and a scruff of grass over the white soil. We were about two hundred feet below the viewpoint, although still dizzyingly high above the floor of the basin. On all sides of us the pale landscape stretched upwards in slender spires, like skeletal fingers grappling at the sky.

"'How ever are we going to get back up from here?' I murmured.

"'Laura, shut up, would you? If I thought you were going to be such a grown-up about this, I wouldn't have brought you,' Tiffany said. 'With all your jabbering you're going to ruin what I'm trying to show you.'

"I fell silent.

"Coming to the brink of the ledge, we both gazed out over the landscape. Twilight was fading into night, but the white soil was almost luminous by starlight. The sickled moon hung low, the rest of its shadowed orb faintly visible against the darkness. Tiffany touched my arm and pointed to the gaunt hillside opposite us on our left. There, about level with us, was a doe working her way along the precipitous slope. Behind her soon came twin fawns. A light-coloured owl called, flying down past the pines and into the abyss below.

"'To the Sioux Indians, this was a holy place,' Tiffany said, her voice soft. 'I think maybe they were right.' She looked over at me. 'It's not a church or anything, but you can still feel it, can't you? I can. I can feel there's something here that there isn't in most places.'

"*Like the high holy place*, I was thinking, this secret place with its white soil, its vast overlook, its innate sacredness. I glanced at Tiffany, absorbed in her own thoughts again. Clad in cut-offs and a mucky T-shirt, her knees scuffed with the white soil, her sneakers worn through at the toes, she made an unlikely spirit guide; but I recognized her now for what she was.

"Torgon stirred. Not the Torgon who had been coming to me in Boston. The real Torgon. In the old, familiar way. I didn't see her right away, I only felt her, but she began roiling inside me, breaking the surface occasionally, like spawning salmon do when returning to the too-small streams of their birth."

Chapter Thirty-Four

"*O*h, show her to me. Let me hold her. Here." *Torgon reached out her arms.*

Carefully, Mogri unwrapped the baby.

"She's strong. You've done well by her, Mogri.

"I plan to call her Jofa when her naming day arrives."

Torgon caressed the baby. "Oh, look at you, you little darling. How beautiful you are."

"I wish she seemed as beautiful when the owls are out," Mogri said and sat down. "She still doesn't know the night from day and leaves me feeling very weary."

"Well, you sit and rest and I shall hold her." Torgon cuddled the baby close. "You can meanwhile tell me how everything goes at home."

"I'm leaving the fields to learn the loom with Mam."

"You? The loom? Mogri, you've always loathed the loom."

"Aye, but with a babe, what can I do? It's indoor work, it's warm and dry and won't require I carry her on my back all day."

"Ah."

Mogri reached over to stroke the baby's temple gently. "If only Tadem could have lived. I look at her and think, what will become of us? What world is this I've brought her to? No father. No brothers or sisters." She looked over at Torgon. "I was going to take her life from her when she came from the womb. I'd made up my mind it was the best solution … but when I saw her, I hadn't the heart to do it … yet I fear that letting her live will be the greater cruelty."

"Well, she won't grow up alone."

"How so?"

"There will be another growing with her. I wasn't going to tell you this, not yet, but if it gives your heart some peace …"

Mogri's brow furrowed.

"Ansel made good his word with me. He said that night he'd bed me for a child and so it seems he has. She'll have a cousin before the spring comes back again."

Mogri's eyes went wide. "Torgon, is it true?"

"Aye. I've been troubled by my stomach for many weeks and this had made me suspect as much. Now the faces of the moon have come and gone three times and I've still given forth no monthly blood."

"Oh, holy Dwr." Mogri searched her sister's face. "I want to think this is good news, but is it, Torgon?"

Torgon shook her head. "I don't know … what it means and what will happen, I'm hesitant to think."

"And where might you be coming from?" He stepped out suddenly from behind the tree, as Torgon worked her way down through the forest.

It was Galen, eldest of Ansel's brothers.

"What brings you here?" Torgon asked. "This is holy ground and not for common passage."

"I spoke first, anaka benna, so mine's the stronger question. Where have you been that finds you skulking back along such a tangled forest path?"

"Be gone with you, Galen. Go on." Torgon moved to push past him.

With unexpected speed he drew his sword and barred the way. "Do not speak so dismissively with me. Do you forget that I am holy too? Pause, divine one, and honour me with conversation."

Torgon glared at him.

"Or perhaps should I mention to you first how easily I find this blade will run a worker through? It's sharp. Feel it, if you doubt my word. And there are too many of the worker kind. Did we not wonder at last council how we'd manage to feed them all? Especially babies. The worker kind keep breeding. But my sword is quick with babes. Perhaps you wish that I should show you how."

"Among my kind, we learn that only cowards hurt those weaker than themselves. It is not the work of noble men."

Turning the blade of the sword flat, Galen reached out to place the tip of it under Torgon's chin. He gently raised it making Torgon raise her head as well so that he could study her face. "Aye," he said, "Ansel was right in his taste for you. You have a comely aspect. But I like not your eyes. They are too pale. They give a spirit look to you."

Torgon said nothing.

"He spoke well of your breasts too." Turning the sword deftly again, Galen jabbed the point against her abdomen. With one quick flick, he brought it up and rent the white cloth of her shirt. The sword tip nicked her skin causing crimson beads of blood to rise. "Show me your breasts, that I might judge the matter for myself."

Torgon did not move.

Galen jabbed the point of the sword against her skin again. "Show me."

"Be gone. Go back among the dogs, who are your kind."

Galen poked the sword against her chest enough to force her into stepping back. "You're naught but tits and cunt of worker kind, the sort a warrior pays but pennies for. Naught but a trifle my father chose to placate Ansel's rutting."

"Base men are always victims of their lust. It doesn't matter how your father made the choice. In the act, Dwr's will was done."

"You think far too highly of yourself."

"No. It's just I think too low of you. Now move your sword and go your way."

"No, holy benna, I would have us talk."

Torgon regarded him.

"I would, for one thing, have us speak about my brother, whose bones lay midst the ashes of his funeral pyre. There's been no golden summer's day for him."

"What's done is done. The elders sat in council and made their judgement. You know that well, for you were there, so nothing more remains for saying."

"There was no honour in my brother's death. You know that well, anaka benna. Even you were so ashamed of what you did, you ran."

"I took retreat that I might seek Dwr's counsel on how to heal the evil that your brother wrought."

"So, holy one who talks with gods, what counsel did you get? More ways to use a warrior's knife?"

"You've all sent your souls before you into darkness and care not to call them back again. For this, Dwr says the end is come for holy born."

His face reddened. "Woman! *What is the matter with you? Were you born lacking all forms of common sense? This sword sits within a minute of your life and we are deep here in the forest where none would know who'd done the deed, yet still you preach at me. Put you so little value on your life? Show me rightful respect or I will simply run you through.*"

"*I know you will. For Dwr told me that as well.*"

He looked astonished.

She smiled. "*But not today. The time's not right to kill me now. For if you do, you will kill your brother's unborn child as well.*"

Chapter Thirty-Five

"This isn't the moon," Conor muttered, flapping his fingers in front of his face. "We didn't go to the moon."

"Come on in, Conor," James said, holding the playroom door open.

"I don't know why he talks like that," Morgana muttered. She pushed past him and went over to the table.

"Kiss?" Alan called to her.

Morgana ran back and bounced up on tiptoes to give her father a kiss. Conor, oblivious, just stood clutching his cat. Alan brushed his lips across the boy's pale hair. "See you later, kids."

"See you, Daddy."

Then the door was closed.

"How come you wanted us both here?" Morgana asked. "How come me and Conor didn't get to come at our own times, like usual?"

"Because sometimes I like to see brothers and sisters play together," James replied.

"Him and me, we don't play together," she said. "He doesn't know how."

"We didn't go to the moon," Conor murmured.

Morgana wandered off across the room. "What're we supposed to do in here today? Am I supposed to do something with him?"

"You decide," James replied.

"Conor? You want to do something with me?" Morgana called to him.

No response.

"He *won't* play with me," she said to James, her tone rather weary. "I could've told you that. He never does."

"Well, that's all right."

"Guess I'll make Lego," she said and brought the large plastic container over to the table. "I'll make a house."

Conor remained immobile by the door.

"I'd like to build a castle. Have you seen them? Them Lego castles? You have to buy a special kit. But they're really hard to do. My dad says I can't have one, 'cause I'm not big enough to put it together and I'd just lose the parts. But I'd really like a castle to play with."

"What would you like to do with it?" James asked.

"I dunno. Just play. Fairy tales, I guess. You know, like Rapunzel and stuff." She picked up some bricks.

James raised his head and looked over at Conor, still standing by the door. For a brief moment he caught Conor's eye before the boy quickly looked away.

"Would you like to join us?" James asked. He rose from the table and went over.

Standing stiffly, the stuffed cat pressed to his chest, Conor stared straight ahead, his eyes vacant.

James knelt to the boy's height. "With your body and your face, I see you saying, 'Go away and leave me alone.'"

A faint expression of surprise crossed Conor's features at James's accurate interpretation and he looked at him. "Yeah," he said softly.

"Things are different today and I can tell this doesn't make you happy."

"This is the boy's room."

Morgana swivelled around in her chair in astonishment. "He talks sense to you!"

"Perhaps you could show Morgana what you like to do in here," James suggested.

"No."

"Would you like to come to the table and join us?"

"No."

"Will you talk to me, Conor?" Morgana asked, getting out of her seat and coming over. "What kind of things can you say?"

His expression hostile, Conor looked at his sister.

"Can you really talk just like everybody else? Come on, Conor. Do it for me."

No response.

"You want to come play Lego with me?"

James went back to the table and sat down. "I want Conor to feel welcome to join us. I'd like you to be part of us over here, Conor, but you don't have to, if you don't want to. In here, you decide."

He marched over. "I *have* decided. I've decided I don't want her here. This is the boy's room."

"Did you forget that Morgana was coming along today?" James asked

"I want to do my book today."

"What book's that, Conor?" Morgana asked. "Does he mean stories?" She rose up brightly. "I'd like to hear a story too."

Conor turned on her. "It isn't your story. It's not for you."

Deflated, Morgana sat back down in her chair.

"You can't play with this," Conor stated and approached the dolls' house.

"I didn't say I wanted to play with it," Morgana muttered.

"You don't feel like sharing the dolls' house," James reflected back.

"When I am here, I decide and I have decided that."

"What if I decide I want to play with it?" Morgana asked, her tone not belligerent, just curious. She looked over at James. "What happens if I decide I want to but he decides I can't? How's it work in here then?"

"You would wonder that," James replied with a grin. "And if it happens, then we'll try to talk it through until we have a solution."

Morgana shrugged. "It's okay. He can have it."

Alarm suddenly crossed Conor's features and he moved swiftly to the bookshelves behind Morgana. "She can't have this," he said and snatched up the box containing the mechanical cat.

"Why? What is it?" Morgana asked.

Conor pressed the box tightly against his chest. "It's mine. You can't have it."

"No, I didn't say I wanted it, Conor. What is it?"

"It's the mechanical cat," Conor replied a little less gruffly.

"A mechanical cat? Really? What does it do?"

"It's the mechanical cat," he repeated.

"Let me see it. Please? I really like things like that. Please, Conor?"

He clutched the box tighter to his chest.

She turned, her expression an appeal for James's intervention. "Can't I see it?"

James smiled but didn't reply.

"I do like things like that," she said rather sulkily. "I seen this mechanical dog once. It had a ball in its mouth and when you wound it up, its tail wagged and it moved around and shook the ball." She looked back at Conor. "What does your cat do?"

"It sees ghosts."

"Oh, great." Morgana let out a pained sigh. "You're going to start crazy talk again."

Silence.

"This girl at school, her name's Britney, and she's got a brother who's nine like Conor," Morgana said to James. "He can build really good Lego. He got a Lego rocket ship for Christmas and he brought it to school to show, after he'd built it. If Conor was like him, he might have been able to make me that castle I want. 'Cause my dad won't. He says it takes too much fiddling. But Conor might have done it for me, 'cause he's nine."

At the other end of the table, Conor sat down. He still had the box of cardboard animals pressed against his chest, but he loosened his grip a little.

Morgana resumed her play with the Lego bricks.

The next several minutes passed in complete silence.

Furtively, Conor watched Morgana's activity. When she didn't look up from what she was doing, he quietly lay the box of cardboard animals on the table. Checking briefly to see what Morgana was up to, he then let his hand creep under the lid of the box and he carefully extracted the cardboard cat. Slipping it quickly into his lap, he held it there, looking at it, tenderly caressing the faded print of its fur. Still holding it in his lap below the table level, he fitted the cat into the stand. Another furtive glance at Morgana. Then Conor stood the cat on the table. There was still a tiny wad of clay adhering to the end of the string leash, so Conor pressed it to the table top.

"There," he said.

Morgana looked up.

"Here's the mechanical cat."

Her eyebrows knitted together. "How's it mechanical? What's it do?"

Conor seemed perplexed by this question. "It's the mechanical cat," he replied in a tone of voice that indicated he felt this was self-evident.

"But what's it do?" Morgana insisted. "Where's the mechanical bit? Because it should move or something and it just looks like cardboard to me."

"It has electricity. Zap-zap." Conor fingered the string around the cardboard cat's neck. "It sees the man."

"What man? Him? Dr Innes?"

"The man under the rug."

Morgana rolled her eyes. "Here we go again." She looked at James. "How come Conor talks nonsense, if he actually knows how to talk proper?"

"You know what I'm thinking?" James said, "I'm thinking it mustn't feel very nice to hear other people in the same room talk about you like you aren't there. What do you think?"

"My mum and dad do that all the time."

"And how do you feel?" James asked.

Morgana shrugged. "I dunno. Once I heard them talking about me being naughty. That's why my mum and dad are getting divorced."

James looked over at her. "You think your mum and dad are getting divorced because you've been naughty?"

Morgana nodded. "Yeah, they said so. My dad told my mum he was getting divorced because I lied about Caitlin's party." Tears sprung to her eyes.

"Come here," James said, reaching an arm out. "Come stand right here beside me while I tell you something."

Morgana set her Lego down and came around the table to him.

"That isn't true," James said gently. "Your parents aren't getting a divorce because of you, Morgana. They have grown-up problems that they haven't been able to solve and that's why they're divorcing. I know for a fact that both of them love you very much and you didn't do anything to cause the divorce."

"No sir. 'Cause I did lie. I wanted the marking pens for the Lion King, so I pretended they were for Caitlin. My daddy got really mad and spanked me. And I heard him say to Mum he's going to get a divorce from her because I lied. I *heard* him say it," she said tearfully.

"That's a very big worry for a little girl. I'm glad you've told me," James said, "because then I can help you understand that even though that's what *feels* like happened, even though it *sounded* like that's what your dad meant, it isn't. I've talked to both your mum and your dad and I know all about Caitlin's birthday party. I also know that they both love you very, very much and they'd both feel terribly unhappy to know that you thought you were responsible for the divorce. If your dad did say that, it was only because he was feeling angry at the time and said something he didn't mean. That happens, even with grown-ups sometimes."

A small silence followed. Seeking comfort, Morgana nuzzled into the fabric of James's suit jacket.

Conor had watched this exchange, but now he rose to wander around the room. Coming to where the large white plastic sheet with the roads drawn on it was folded up on the shelf, he took it out and laid it out upside down on the floor. There was a basket of small plastic figures on the shelf nearby. Conor started taking them out, one by one, and endeavoured to stand them up, but the road sheet hadn't been laid out smoothly enough and most fell over. Finally he began just piling the figures on top of each other.

Still clinging to James, Morgana noticed Conor's activity. For several moments she watched silently and then she pulled away and crossed tentatively over to see what was going on.

"What are you making?" she asked.

Conor didn't respond.

"Why don't you turn it right side up, so it looks like a highway?"

No response.

"You could make a ranch. With those animals."

Still no answer.

Morgana reached down and picked up a horse, lying on its side. "Here. Stand this up."

"No," Conor said firmly and pushed her hand away.

Rebuffed, Morgana backed off, but she didn't leave.

"Can I play too?" she asked finally.

He didn't answer.

"Can I have some of the animals?"

No response.

"No fair, 'cause you got them all." She turned to appeal to James.

James smiled. "See if you two can work it out."

Initially Conor didn't appear to be paying attention. He continued piling things from the basket onto the plastic sheet in a rather ritualistic manner. Then unexpectedly, he held out a small plastic figure of a woman to Morgana.

"Can I have more? Can I have some animals?"

Conor grabbed a handful from the basket and dropped them on her end of the sheet. "Where's the mechanical cat?" he said suddenly, looking at James. He jumped up, went to the table to get it and brought it over. Carefully, he stood it up halfway along the sheet.

"Oh, there's your cat again," Morgana said. "What do you call him? Does he have a name?"

"The cat says here's the boy's side. Don't come here. Don't use this side."

Several minutes passed in silence. Morgana fashioned a small world at her end of the sheet. Folding it back to expose part of the road, she brought over toy cars from the shelves and parked them along the side. The few animals Conor had shared she set up in a row.

Conor watched her furtively. On his side there was nothing more than a heap of plastic figures. He gathered them together in a steeper pile, but then paused again to watch what Morgana was doing. He picked up the mechanical cat and laid it on top of the pile of animals. He laid it first on its side, then tried to make it stand amid the plastic legs and tails. With some effort, he achieved this.

"I'm going to make a ranch for my animals," Morgana declared. "But I wish we had some trees. To make it look pretty, like down at the creek."

"Trees and flowers," Conor said. Unexpectedly he reached a hand out and gripped Morgana's arm. "Where the Lego is." He pulled her up from where she was sitting. "Trees and flowers. In there. See?" He leaned down and rooted through the big bin holding Lego. He lifted up one of the small green Lego trees. "See?"

"Hey, good! Yeah, that'll work, Conor."

He bent down and pulled tree after tree up out of the bin. The little Lego flowers appeared too. Morgana returned to building her ranch, but Conor continued to bring up all the trees and the flowers. When he couldn't find anymore, he paused over them. Lining them up on the side of the bookcase, he counted them. "Twenty-five trees. Thirteen flowers. Thirteen red flowers. Eight blue flowers. Eleven yellow flowers." He came over to Morgana. "Twenty-five trees plus six trees. Thirty-one trees. Six trees here for your ranch. Twenty-five trees on the shelf."

"Yeah, okay, Conor, I got the idea. Now let me play."

"Twenty-five trees. The boy has twenty-five trees on the shelf."

James watched, fascinated by Conor's efforts at conversation. He obviously wanted to communicate with Morgana and there was a poignancy in his clinging to the one topic she had praised.

He returned to the shelf and picked up as many trees as he could carry in his hands. He brought them to his side of the road sheet. "Here are eleven trees. The boy has eleven trees." He let them tumble through his fingers onto the pile of animals.

One plastic tree hit the cardboard cat and knocked it off the pile. Hurriedly, Conor picked it up. "It isn't hurt," he said to

James. Crossing the room, he held it up close to James's face. "The mechanical cat isn't hurt. A tree fell on it and knocked it off, but it's okay. The mechanical cat can't die."

James smiled.

"It's safe in here. The mechanical cat is safe." These were almost questions, the way Conor inflected them.

"Yes, you're safe in here," James said.

"Not on the moon," Conor replied.

He went back to the road sheet and carefully put the mechanical cat once again between his half and Morgana's half. "In terria," he murmured.

Carefully, Conor picked out three trees. He stood them up together on top of the sheet. "They are like this," he said. "Three trees on the moon."

Morgana looked up. "I don't think the moon's got any trees, Conor. I think I heard that once."

"Three trees on the moon."

"The moon doesn't have any trees growing there, does it, Dr Innes? Conor's got it wrong."

"*I* saw. *I* know," Conor said. "You weren't there. You didn't go to the moon."

"You've never gone to the moon either," Morgana remarked.

"With the man under the rug. In a rocket ship. Three trees on the moon," Conor said. James saw his fingers beginning to flutter at his side.

"Conor, you got to be an astronaut to go to the moon. Kids can't go."

"The ghost man was on the moon."

Morgana looked over at James beseechingly. "I don't like it when he talks about ghosts."

Conor reached out and picked up the mechanical cat. He pressed it to his face, to his lips and over his eyes. "The mechanical cat is here," he murmured. "He says, 'You're safe here, boy. You're safe here, girl. I'll never die. I'll watch out for you forever.'"

Chapter Thirty-Six

"I returned to Boston revitalized and ready to start again," Laura said at the start of her next session. "Over the summer I'd come to terms with the fact that I'd never be that jungle surgeon. I saw it for what it actually was – one of those idealistic dreams you have in adolescence. All I wanted by that point was simply to complete my medical degree and start my internship.

"I'd had no contact with Fergus while I was in South Dakota and in my mind it was over. However, the day after I returned to Boston, the doorbell rang. I knew instinctively it was him.

"I opened the door. For a moment we just stood, looking at each other. Then he flung open his arms and enveloped me in a huge hug.

"'Oh God, oh God, oh God,' he murmured into my hair and hugged me so tightly to him I was muffled into his chest. 'I've missed you so much.'

"I asked him in.

"In the living room Fergus flopped heavily into the big armchair by the window. 'I've been in a depression all summer,' he said. 'I didn't appreciate how crucial your life force is to mine. With you gone I have hardly been able to face anyone.'

"Fergus leaned back into the chair and closed his eyes a moment. He looked beautiful like that, his features relaxed, his dark curls bathed in the glow of the floor lamp, like a care-worn, street-corner Christ.

"'It's sleep,' he murmured. 'I can't sleep. Weeks now and I can't sleep.'

"A pause.

"'I was wrong,' he said. 'I should have met you on more equal terms. You were right to leave me. I see that now. I see that you didn't have any alternative and I'm sorry. I'm so, so sorry.'

"I nodded. 'Thank you for saying that.'

"'It's been so hard, Laura. I've been dying without you.'

"'Torgon's returned to me,' I said.

"His brow furrowed.

"'I'm writing again. I won't stop it this time. I need to write.'

"'Torgon never left you.'

"'That Torgon never existed, Fergus. What I was chan-nelling – *pretending* to channel – was just me. I've finished with that now and I refuse to do it again.'

"Fergus's expression was enigmatic.

"'I only did it then because I longed to be that person you wanted me to be. Sometimes, when we want something so much, we make it real, even to ourselves. But that doesn't make it true. Real and true are different things.'

"'You are *so* gifted,' Fergus said, his eyes bright with wonder.

"I shook my head. 'No. I am so messed up. That's what became clear to me over the summer. Somewhere along the way, I got lost. I left the path my life was on, and I've screwed up as a result. So I need to say "stop" to a lot of stuff I was doing. I won't go back to channelling. And I won't be going back to the Tuesday night group.'

"'Yes, I understand that.' Fergus leaned back in the chair again and a deep, weary silence formed. He really did look tired. I suddenly felt very sorry for him. Reaching my hand out, I took his.

"He smiled faintly, closing his fingers over mine. 'I'm so sick of this world, Laura,' he murmured. 'So fucking sick and tired of it all.'

"Leaning over, I kissed the hand I held. 'I'm sorry you're feeling low.'

"'There's so much shit in this world.'

"'Yes, but there're good bits too.' I kissed his fingers and smiled. 'Yes?'

"He leaned forward and embraced me. Within moments we were lost in one another's arms and all the bad parts of the last two years vanished midst the kisses. I wasn't used to being the strong one in our relationship but I liked it. I liked the warm tenderness I felt for him, the sense I could take care of all his sorrow.

"He nuzzled his face through my hair but then stopped, pulling back to look at me. 'Why did you cut your hair?'

"'I just wanted a change,' I said.

"'But you knew I liked it the way it was. Why did you take that away from me?'

"'Take it away from you? Don't be silly. I did it because I felt like it. It looks nicer.'

"He studied my face carefully, smiling more fully as he did so. Lifting up one hand, he traced my features with his fingers very, very gently. 'You are my queen, my beautiful one. We'll be together forever now, won't we?'

"I smiled back.

"'You won't leave me again, will you?'

"'I'll try not to.'

"'You won't. Will you? We'll be together forever. For all time.'

"I smiled.

"'I'd die for you,' he said quietly. 'Like I did before. Like I've always done before. I've always died for you, my queen. Every lifetime. I thought I would again this time when you left me.' Only the faintest smile touched his lips. His dark eyes were fathomless. 'Would you die for me? Would you make the sacrifice for me that I've made so many times for you?'"

"In November I was doing my practical work in the university hospital's neonatal unit when a baby boy was airlifted in from another county. He had been born with no kidneys. In the normal course of things, babies like that die within a very short time. The parents, however, had had a hard time conceiving. They felt he was their only chance at having a child, and they were just so desperate not to lose him. As a consequence, the doctors decided to try a transplant. This treatment was still highly experimental at the time. Although the procedure had been tried previously, it had never been successful. Indeed, kidney transplants in general did not work well with young infants. The doctors had agreed, however, to try keeping the baby alive long enough to find a suitable donor.

"The little boy was so seriously ill that he required continuous medical supervision, which was how I and two fellow medical students came into the picture. Working eight-hour shifts each, it was our task to remain with the baby continuously to aid the nursing staff in providing the necessary level of care in the pre- and post-transplant period.

"I was pleased to be part of it. It was exciting to have an opportunity to see medical research in action and to interact with the doctors on the transplant team, many of whom were as gods to us students and usually just as inaccessible. For me personally, it was also an opportunity to redeem myself in Betjeman's eyes. He'd gone the extra mile for me by allowing me back into the program after my 'breakdown', as he called it.

"I didn't talk much about this new responsibility with Fergus. Our separation over the summer had taken its toll on him in an odd, inexplicable way. On the one hand, he always wanted to be with me and could easily become distraught when we were apart. On the other hand, however, he was more impatient and more irritable with me than before. He kept getting crazy ideas about my being unfaithful. It became easier just not to tell him too much about anything he couldn't be part of. I still felt confident of keeping everything in balance, though.

"When the first shift came, I was quickly caught up in the excitement of it all. It was cutting-edge stuff and when the child arrived, there was an almost palpable tension at the hospital. This still hadn't left me by the time I came out to meet Fergus at eleven.

"To my surprise, he wasn't there when I came out. He was supposed to meet me, so I wasn't happy, as I had to take several buses to get back to my apartment and it was very late when I arrived home.

"I opened the door to the dark hallway. Immediately I heard Fergus speaking in a soft, slightly dreamy voice.

"'My Voices tell me about you,' he said. 'My Voices say that this isn't a Being of Light. They're worried, Laura. And so am I.'

"'*Jesus*, Fergus, you scared the life out of me. What are you doing here anyway? You were supposed to pick me up.'

"'You're being seduced by Darkness. You are relinquishing the Light to return to the Darkness.'

"'*Fergus* …?' I came around to stand in front of where he was sitting. I looked at him carefully. He didn't seem drunk. I couldn't smell anything on him. He did use recreational drugs occasionally, but the few times I'd witnessed him using them, they hadn't done much more than make him sleepy.

"Then he said in a more intense voice, 'I've really done my best, Laura. I know I pushed you way too hard. I know I put you into a position of receiving more energy from the Voices than you could sustain, so I've really tried to be understanding. I've tried to meet you at your level. But there's just no point carrying on, if you're not going to channel again. I've had to come down to your level to meet you, and I've been willing to do that in order to lift you up, but you need to understand it's not my level. I'm simply here to help you. Now you're sinking below my reach again. You're *choosing* to fall. And I'm shitting myself, seeing everything I've worked so hard for in this lifetime slipping away from me. Realizing it's going to be another lifetime and more searching and …' He put his head in his hands melodramatically. 'I can't see an end to it.'

"I was confused. 'Are you breaking up with me?' I whispered.

"'These actions of your lower self … I can accept I have to pander to them, if we're ever going to move you upward, but don't think I'm going to wallow in them. I've been here thinking this over and I can't go on like this.'

"I was beginning to feel extremely uneasy. 'How long have you been sitting here?' I asked suspiciously. 'Haven't you been at work?'

"'You *disgust* me when you act like this,' he replied. 'We're not equals, you know. You don't actually deserve me yet.'

"'Fergus, I'm not sure what's going on, but I'm not comfortable with it.' Something just wasn't right in the way he was acting. 'I think you should go. Now. I mean it.'

"He continued to sit, completely motionless.

"I really didn't know what to do. Finally I said, 'Okay, if you want to sit there, sit. I'm going to go have a bath and go to bed.' I turned and left him. Walking down the hallway to the bathroom, I shut the door firmly behind me and locked it.

"'Laura?' I could hear him coming into the hallway.

"'It's late. You need to go home,' I said through the locked door. I turned the water in the tub on.

"'Let me in.'

"'No, it's too late. I want to go to bed. Goodnight, Fergus.'

"'Let me in, Laura,' he said more forcefully.

"'*No*, Fergus. Go home now.'

"'Let me *in*!' he demanded in an irate voice. When I didn't respond, wham! He kicked the door. Hard.

"Terrified, I looked around the bathroom for something to jam against the door. There was nothing.

"Fergus grabbed the door knob and rattled it roughly. 'Let me in.' There was less anger in his voice this time.

"Still frightened, I didn't answer.

"'Laura? Laura?' A panicky note came into his voice. 'Please don't leave me.'

"'I've not left you. I'm right here. But go away now, okay? Go home and get some sleep. Phone me tomorrow.'

"'I'm sorry for what I said. I don't know what happened. I didn't mean it. Please forgive me.'

"I didn't answer.

"'*Laura?*' he cried in a truly heart-rending manner.

"It sounded like he was crying. Confused and concerned, I cracked the bathroom door open. Fergus was on his knees.

"'Oh, my queen, please don't leave me,' he begged and reached out to grab me around the legs.

"I bent down to hug him. 'Fergus, what's the matter with you tonight? Here, stand up.'

"He rose and wrapped his arms around me so tightly that I could feel his beating heart. 'Oh God, I need you so much,' he whispered. 'I need you. I can't live without you. How can you frighten me like this?'

"'*Me?* How can I be frightening? It's *you* who's doing *my* head in. You've scared me witless tonight. Whatever's brought this on?'

"'I'm sorry. Please forgive me.' He was so pathetic.

"'Yes, of course I forgive you.'

"'Tell me you love me,' he pleaded.

"'I love you, Fergus. Of course, I love you.'

"'I won't lose you. Not again. I won't let it happen,' he said. 'I'll fight. With all my heart and strength, I'll struggle to bring you back into the Light with me. I'll die before I let you slip away again.'

    "'Shhh, let's not talk about all that right now, okay?' I whispered. 'Because I love you and that's what matters, isn't it?'

    "'As much as you did in Atlantis?' he asked.

    "I nodded. 'Yeah, sure. As much as then.'

    "He kissed me tenderly. 'As much as in Atlantis, my queen, when you sacrificed it all for me?'"

Chapter Thirty-Seven

When Morgana came into the playroom that afternoon, she said nothing, not even hello. Instead she went straight to the huge window and climbed up on the window ledge. Spreading her arms out wide, Morgana pressed her face and chest against the glass.

James wasn't concerned because Morgana was entirely safe. There was no way to open the windows and they were double-glazed, toughened glass. He said nothing so as not to impede whatever feelings she wished to express.

"It's windy outside today," she said, her voice soft.

"Yes," James said. "It's coming in off the plains, so it's cold."

"I'm like a bird up here," Morgana said, her arms still outstretched against the window. "There's the plains out there and I'll sail on the wind."

"You're feeling like a bird today," James reflected.

"No," she said, her back to him, her face against the glass. "These big windows just make me think that. I always wanted to do this. Ever since I came in here."

"I see."

"And the wind made me think about doing it today."

"Why's that?" James asked.

"Because the wind carries your dreams. That's what my mum tells me. She says that's what the Sioux believe. That dreams come to you on the wind."

When Morgana said that, James immediately thought of Laura's first book about the Wind Dreamer, the young man caught between the real world and his world of "voices".

"Sometimes in my dreams I fly," Morgana said. "Not in a plane or anything. Really fly. I just put my arms like this and off I go."

"Yes, those are wonderful dreams, aren't they?" James replied.

"Do you get that dream too?" Morgana asked and for the first time she turned around, although she remained standing on the window ledge.

James smiled. "Yes, sometimes."

"I'd like to fly," she said pensively. "I always hope that maybe on a windy day it will happen." She hopped down from the ledge to the floor, "But I don't think it ever will."

Morgana moved off across the room to the shelves. Walking slowly beside them, she trailed the fingers of one hand along the wood of the middle shelf. "I had a bad dream last night," she said. She picked up a baby doll.

"Would you like to tell me about it?" James asked.

Morgana brought the doll back to the table. "No," she said. "It was too scary."

"It was a nightmare?"

"Yes. I dream it all the time. Then I wake up crying. Sometimes my mum has to come in and cuddle me."

"Are you sure you wouldn't like to talk about it?"

"No. I never tell anyone about it. Not even my mum."

"I see."

"That's 'cause she might get mad. I mean, when it's daytime and I'm okay, I know she probably wouldn't, 'cause it's just a dream and I'm not doing anything for real, but when I first wake up I'm never very sure."

"I understand," James said. "But that must be hard, keeping such a scary thing to yourself."

"Mostly I try not to think about it, because it can scare me even when I'm awake."

"It does sound very frightening," James replied. "Perhaps if you shared it with me, I could think of something to help."

Morgana bent closer to the doll and James felt the silence deepen. "I wish we hadn't talked about that dream. I'm feeling scared now. My mum says, 'Just don't pay attention to it.' But it's in my head and it's hard not to pay attention to what's in your head."

"You know I wouldn't get mad," James reassured her. "I never get mad at children who come to the playroom, because I understand that sometimes strong feelings make us do things we shouldn't. To get problems sorted out, it's important that children can show their feelings in here."

Morgana raised her eyes to him without raising her head. There was a long pensive moment and then she looked back at the doll. She rocked it tenderly.

"The dream's about me and my horse. I got a horse called Shaggy that Daddy got me last year. He's got brown fur and that's why we call him that. In the dream, him and me are out riding. We are going down on the road. On the highway. Actually, I'm not riding Shaggy. I'm walking him; I have him by the reins."

"I see," James said.

"I'm not supposed to be down on the road. It's too far away and it's dangerous. But in the dream I am. And this car comes up behind me. I can't see who's in it. I think it's a man. And he's driving real slow. I start to get scared."

"What do you think is going to happen?" James asked.

"I don't know. That's why it's hard to talk about, because I don't know what's going to happen, but it makes me feel really scared. I want to turn around and look at him to see who it is, but for some reason, I can't do it. I just know he's there. Anyway, he drives real, real slow. I'm scared he's going to stop. I think he's going to do something."

Morgana stopped. Her eyes were fixed on the doll. She cuddled it close against her. "There's something else in the dream too. It sort of happens before. I never actually dream the before part, but I always know it happened. And what it is, is that I've gone into my mum's study. See, me and Conor, we're not supposed to go in there by ourselves because Mum doesn't want us messing up her stuff."

Morgana paused to caress the doll's hair. "She's got this itty, bitty little cat statue in there. Made of stone, I think. It's only this big." She measured out about two inches with her fingers. "It's grey-coloured and it's sitting down on its bottom, you know, like cats do. And my mum keeps it set up on the tower part of her computer. She showed it to me once. She let me hold it. But she said if she wasn't in the room, I mustn't ever, ever touch it."

"The cat statue sounds very special to your mum," James reflected.

"She thinks maybe I'll lose it or something, if I play with it. Or maybe drop it. See, it costed a lot of money because it came from Egypt. That's a place they talk about in the Bible and it's a long, long way away from here. And this little cat's as old as the Bible. My mum says. She told me the person who made this little stone cat statue lived in Bible times and when he was done carving it, he put it in the coffin of a king."

James raised his eyebrows. "Wow. That's amazing."

"A coffin is where you put a dead body. The king's dead body, before he gets buried," Morgana said. "And then it goes in his grave. And that's where this little cat statue was until an arkologist dug it up. And then this friend of my mum's gave it to her. And she put it on her computer. And she told me never, never to touch it without her knowing about it, because it's really valuable."

"I can understand now why it's so special to your mum," James said.

Morgana leaned down and tended to the doll a moment.

"So how does this little cat statue figure in your nightmare?" James asked.

"Well, because in the dream when I'm walking along the road with Shaggy and this car starts driving along real slow behind me, I get scared and want to go find my mum. But then I put my hand in my pocket and the cat statue is there." A quick, rather guilty glance to James followed. "I don't know how it got there but I know I must have gone in her study and tooken it. In the dream I don't *remember* taking it, but I know she's going to be really, really mad at me when she finds out. First I think maybe I should throw the cat statue away and then my mum won't know I have it. But then I know it's so valuable and she loves it so much and, really, I don't want to throw it away. But I don't know what to do. So, I get really scared that the man's going to get me, but I'm scared that if I call out for help, people will find out I have the cat statue. I'm scared I'm going to be in so much trouble and I didn't even know I'd tooken it."

"Yes, it sounds very scary," James said.

"The dream's a little different each time. Sometimes it's not always the same car. It was a white car last night. Once it was a red car. And one time I remember it being a white station wagon. But there's always this driver guy who makes me feel scared and I can't turn around and see who he is. And every time I want to get help, I put my hand in my pocket and find out I got the cat statue in there."

"What do you think the driver might do?"

"Kidnap me. Take me away from my mum and my dad and they wouldn't know where I was."

"And what feels the most frightening about finding you have the cat statue with you?" James asked.

"Because it's such a surprise that the cat's in there and I don't remember taking it, but the minute I find it in there, I know I must have tooken it and everyone's going to think I did it on purpose."

"And that makes you feel afraid?"

"I feel scared, 'cause …" She paused, her forehead wrinkling in concentration. "Because … I'm running away. That's how come I'm on the road with Shaggy, but I only remember this when I feel the cat. I want to go back so the kidnap guy doesn't get me, but I'm running away 'cause I stole my mother's cat."

"That sounds like a very complicated dream. All sorts of things seem to happen that you hadn't intended. You feel like you caused them, but, in fact, you didn't. They just occurred."

"Yeah, that's right."

"So what happens next?" James asked.

"I wake up."

"It doesn't go any further? The car just drives behind you? The cat statue is in your pocket?"

"That's right. I never have any more of the dream than that, but I get that dream a lot. I'm always crying when I wake up and I feel so scared. Last night I went in Conor's room."

"Was Conor awake?"

Morgana nodded. "I think I woke him up by crying, 'cause he had his eyes open when I came in but he wasn't sitting up 'adjusting'. He had the covers up like this around his neck and he was just watching me come in. I said, 'I'm scared. I had a bad dream. Can I get in bed with you?'"

Morgana paused. "Conor used to have all this stupid stuff around his bed, like metal junk, but lately it's been pretty normal. His bed's like anybody's. So now sometimes I get in with him. And that's what I did last night. 'Cause I didn't want to call for my mum, in case it wasn't a dream. That's what always worries me when I first wake up. That maybe it's real and I'm going to find I did steal the cat."

"I see. So what did Conor do?"

"He said, 'Don't be scared. I got the mechanical cat.'"

"I said, 'Where'?"

"He said, 'Inside me.'"

"I said, 'What'd you do, Conor? Swallow the one at Dr Innes's playroom? Because it sounded weird the way he said it.'" Morgana laughed, her eyes twinkling. "That'd be funny, huh? If Conor ate your mechanical cat. You know, that cardboard cat you got."

James grinned.

"But he said, no, but he could hear it singing. When I got in bed with him, he told me the song. It isn't a song really, because it doesn't have any music, but he said it to me. I felt better."

"So you let Conor take care of you last night?" James asked.

She nodded. "He said, 'I'm not scared of what you dream. I got strong cats.' I said to him, 'You're strong all by yourself, Conor.' And he said, 'So are you.'"

Chapter Thirty-Eight

"Working with the transplant baby wasn't what I'd expected," Laura said. "He was adorable, with blue eyes and a smattering of ginger hair. A good size for a baby – over eight pounds – but he wasn't healthy. He never cried. That was what made the biggest impression on me. This baby just laid there, staring at me.

"I did things like help administer the drugs that kept him in condition to allow dialysis, kept him connected to his machinery and kept tabs on the necessary drips. I also fed him, changed him, cleaned the equipment. Afterwards, I'd sit in a chair beside the incubator and watch over him until it was time to do it all again.

"Doubts began to plague me. Sitting there, watching him for eight hours at a time, I found it impossible to ignore what we were doing to him. Just to keep him alive long enough to try the transplant meant we had to subject him to extremely invasive medical procedures, and realistically there was only a very small chance of success. As I sat next to the incubator, I could sense his pain. The drugs used to paralyse his muscles kept him quiet.

"I kept thinking, what I was doing there? Why did I want to be a part of this? We were *hurting* this boy. Knowingly. We were pretending to help him, but the truth was, we were doing it for us. Keeping him alive to learn more about transplants. One of the specialists even dared articulate that. It was for the 'greater good', he said. We justified letting this child suffer.

"In the long hours of vigil beside the incubator I found myself mulling over Torgon and her society. If this baby had been born a Forest child, he probably would have died before his three-day feeding and that would have been the end of it. If not, Torgon would have taken him to the high holy place and put the knife across his throat.

"When I'd first learned that they did this to babies in her society, I'd been horrified. It went so deeply against the grain of everything I'd been taught in my own culture. Yet now as I sat beside this baby connected to all his expensive, invasive equipment, it occurred to me how much more complicated the issue actually was than it had first seemed. Was what we were doing to this baby any more defensible than what Torgon would do?

"The case overwhelmed me. I couldn't leave it at work. Everything else in my life at that time began to pale because everything else seemed trivial in comparison to the issues surrounding this baby.

"I tried to explain to Fergus what was going on, why it was affecting me so strongly. It was life and death I was dealing with. If I couldn't make my peace with what was happening, I wasn't going to be able to go forward very well with my career. However, he just didn't seem to understand.

"We were in my apartment one afternoon, in the bedroom, intertwined lazily on the bed, and my mind was back on the transplant baby. I said idly that I thought Torgon would be appalled by my involvement in this situation.

"Fergus snapped alert. 'Is Torgon telling you it isn't acceptable?'

"'No, what I meant was that, to us, it's about the advancement of science, so we think it's right. But that's not the only perspective. Right and wrong aren't absolute. Torgon would be appalled that we are letting the baby suffer, because in her culture we're dishonouring the child's soul. The right thing would have been to kill it straightaway.'

"Fergus stared at me. 'You're saying Torgon's telling you to kill the baby?'

"'No, of course not,' I said irritably. 'Torgon isn't telling me anything. I'm simply starting to realize that, well, maybe we're not in such a good position to judge how others do things. Maybe what we justify in the name of science is no better than what she justifies in the name of religion.'

"Fergus was watching me carefully. 'What does Torgon tell you to do? Does she tell you to kill the baby?'

"'Aren't you listening to me at all? She's telling me *nothing*, Fergus. She never has. These are *my* insights.'

"'Relax,' he said in his warm, honeyed way and drew me close to him. 'Close your eyes and float, my queen. Let's go from this earthly plane.'

"I closed my eyes. I took in a deep breath, held it, let it slowly out and felt myself relax. Inside my head was blackness, like the night sky without stars.

"'Does she tell you to kill the baby?' Fergus whispered softly.

"My eyes popped open. I'd assumed he was relaxing me because I was tense. This had always been a core of our relationship – my fording out into the hard world of science and everyday life, and Fergus's drawing me in again and helping me relax. The minute he said that, however, I knew he was on a different tack. 'Torgon is *not* telling me anything. I'm not channelling her. I told you I don't do that.'

"His eyes flickered dangerously. 'You can't tantalize me like this,' he said. 'You tell me Torgon thinks you should kill the baby, and then you drop it. You're always teasing me like that. I know you have her in your head. Please share her with me.'

"'Torgon is most definitely *not* telling me to kill this baby. Got that? It's disgusting.'

"Fergus nodded. 'All right. But she is telling you things, isn't she? You can't keep it from me, Laura. The Voices know you're channelling. They're never wrong.'

"'If that's what they're telling you, then I'm afraid they are wrong.'

"He had a particularly beguiling expression on his face, like a little boy pleading for a cookie. I leaned forward. 'I'm not keeping anything from you, Fergus. Honest. Here, let's just forget it. Give me a kiss.'

"Fergus pulled back sharply. 'You can't give up. You can't just say you'll no longer be a vessel, if you've been chosen. The Voices demand you share Torgon's wisdom.'

"I looked at him and sighed. '*Fergus* …'

"Suddenly he lifted his palms to either side of his forehead, as if he had a dreadful headache.

"An uneasy feeling flitted over me. 'Are you all right?'

"'They're growing so impatient with me.' He stared at me with a strange desperation. 'You must let me speak to Torgon.'

"'I can't.'

"'*Try!*'

"'Fergus, I *can't*. She isn't real.'

"He still had his hands to either side of his head. Lowering his head, he rocked forward on the bed. 'Please. Please don't let that be true.'

"Opening my arms, I went to pull him against my breast. 'Here. Come here to me.'

"Rather than accepting my comfort, he exploded. 'Take your hands off me!' he screamed.

"I jumped back in surprise.

"'All you want to do is fuck, you little bitch.'

"'Fergus, that's not what I was …'

"'You are *not* my queen! You are the Queen of Darkness.'

"'*Fergus!*'

"'Torgon's *evil*. She is not a Being of Light. She is the voice of the Queen of Darkness.' His face was going a horrible mottled colour.

"'What's happening to you? Calm down now. Come on. You're frightening me, Fergus.'

"'Then *channel* her. Bring her here now. Prove she is what you say she is. Bring her to me.'

"'I *can't*. Because I was *faking* it! I've told you that a hundred million times now. I've *told* you. I was *never* channelling anything. Torgon is just something I made up, nothing more than an imaginary companion from my childhood. *Please*, you've got to understand that.' I was growing tearful.

"He grabbed me. 'You just want to fuck. That's all you ever wanted from me. Base lust.'

"'Fergus, no! Don't!'"

"Grasping the front of my blouse so hard the buttons popped, he pulled me down on the bed. 'I tried to raise you up,' he said. 'I tried to bring you to the Light.'

"'Stop!' I cried, so frightened now.

"But he wouldn't. With ferocity, he wrestled me under him and forced me hard against the bed. I struggled. I pushed and pushed. He thrust his penis into me with such force that it could have been a stake through the heart.

"'You are the Queen of Darkness! You refuse to be lifted to the Light.'

"I was sobbing. 'Please, please stop, Fergus. You're hurting me. Please. *Please*.'

"When he came, he pulled his penis out to let the semen spew across my face. 'Here. Eat it, you dirty, filthy cunt.'"

"I sat on the side of the bath. It had a hand-held shower attachment and I kept washing and washing. He'd left hours earlier and it was about 3:30 in the morning by then, but I couldn't stop. There was nothing cut, nothing bleeding, nothing to show what had happened but I felt like I had worms crawling out of me.

"Just then the front door rattled abruptly. Sheer terror shot through me.

"The key turned in the lock. The handle turned. The front door went open, then hit the extent of the chain lock, clanging loudly.

"'Laura?' came Fergus's voice. It was no longer fierce but querulous at the unexpected chain.

"I opened the door to the bathroom slightly but remained in the shadows, too scared even to breathe.

"'Laura? Where are you? Let me in.'

"'Go away,' I said softly.

"'I'm sorry, Laura. I'm so sorry. I'm really, really sorry. I've come back to tell you that. I don't know what happened. I didn't mean to do that.'

"'I don't want to talk about it. I don't want to see you again. Just go away.'

"'Oh Laura, *no*,' he said plaintively. 'Please forgive me. I didn't mean it. Please forgive me. It won't ever happen again. Please let me in.'

"I remained standing in the darkness of the hallway, the towel clutched to my bare skin. 'No. Go away.'

"'Laura, please? Say you forgive me.' I could hear tears in his voice.

"He had his hand through the small opening afforded by the chain and was grasping up and down at empty air. From the height of his hand, I realized he was on his knees. 'Please, please forgive me,' he was pleading. He started to sob.

"I began to cry myself.

"'My queen, *please* don't do this to me.'

"Then things changed. When I wouldn't answer and wouldn't let him in, his tears began to turn to rage. He rattled the door loudly and yelled. 'Let me in!'

"Frightened, I went back to the bathroom and locked that door.

"'You bitch!' he shouted. 'Let me in!'

"Understandably, this woke my neighbours. I heard doors to other apartments opening and someone telling him to shut up. They threatened to call the police. I prayed they would.

"He shouted, wept and pleaded for an hour or so longer. Then, at long last, came silence.

"Still locked in the bathroom, I listened. Listened so hard my ears hurt. I didn't have a watch on. I had no idea what time it was. I just kept listening. Was he still outside my door? Had he left? Was he down by my car, waiting there? I grew nauseated with fear. I vomited and still did not feel any relief.

"When I finally dared to let myself out of the bathroom, it was seven thirty in the morning. Around me were all the familiar sounds of the apartment building coming to life. I went into the bedroom, past the rumpled bedding, past my torn blouse lying on the floor, and got out a pair of clean jeans and a sweatshirt. I went then to the kitchen and opened the window because it looked out on the car park where my car was. Nothing seemed out of the ordinary down there. Gathering my courage, I went to the door of my apartment and opened it to the full extent of the chain. Seeing nothing, I took it off the chain and put my head out. Vanessa, the girl who lived down the hall, was coming out.

"'You okay?' she asked. 'I mean, your boyfriend was pretty out of it last night, wasn't he? Was he drunk?'

"I nodded. She locked her door and left. I went back inside. Getting my car keys and my purse, I closed the door to the apartment, went down the hall, down the back stairs and let myself out into the car park. I peered carefully into the back seat of the car before unlocking it. Once in, I locked it back up, started the ignition and pulled out of my parking space. A November dawn, pale and heavily overcast, made headlights a necessity. Pulling out of the car park and onto the road that led to the freeway, I headed west. And so it was that I left Boston and Fergus and my medical career behind and I never returned."

Chapter Thirty-Nine

When Laura had gone, James pulled the pages of the final story from the folder and began to read.

"I wish to go now to the high holy place and make communion with all-seeing Dwr. You will need to carry these things," Torgon said, giving the food bags to Loki, "for what I carry is heavy enough for me."

Loki lifted up the bundles and secured them over her shoulders.

The winter's afternoon was waning by the time they reached the small hut.

"Look at the straw!" Loki cried in surprise, as she entered. "There's piles and piles of it! Are animals allowed to stay here when it's not in use for cleansing rites?"

"No."

"I didn't imagine this would be such a pleasant place by day, for 'isolation hut' sounds so cold and dark to me. But there's dry wood here and the fireplace is clean. Shall I start the fire and make us food? Or do you wish to undertake your journey to the high holy place tonight?"

Torgon had begun removing her heavy outer garments when the first hard contraction came. Clenching her teeth, she arched her back against it.

Loki froze, her eyes going wide and dark. Laying down her things, she came quickly over. "My mother says one shouldn't stiffen against the pain, for it will then go worse with you." *She reached out to pull off the last of Torgon's outer clothes.*

Torgon sank down into the straw as the contraction passed.

All the girl's carefree cheerfulness had vanished. "Oh anaka benna, what shall we do?" *she asked, her voice dismayed.* "I wish now we'd never embarked on such a journey, for it's brought the baby on."

"No. The journey didn't bring the baby on. It was already coming when I left. The straw you see here is what my sister brought when she prepared the hut for me. And you are here to give me aid. I trust with all your brothers, you've had generous experience of your mother's birthings."

"Me?" *Loki cried and pressed her hands against her cheeks.* "Oh great Dwr, me? To birth a holy child? You and me alone? Here in the forest?"

"Birthing's easy among worker women, Loki. It's common to make them stay in the fields until the birth and then be back again at work before the day is done. I'm sure you've heard your parents say how workers do it no differently than cows."

"Anaka benna, it is not the time to chide me for my caste."

A pause.

Torgon lowered her head. "Aye. Well said."

A long silence fell across the hut.

"I should have told you what I intended here and let the choice be yours." *Torgon looked at the girl.* "If you do not now wish to stay, so be it. I understand. I will not command it of you and I will not hold the decision ill against you."

"I wasn't meaning I would leave you," Loki said. "Of course, I wouldn't leave you, holy benna. It's just that I fear my aid will be a paltry gift. It would be much wiser to have the aid of those more accomplished than myself."

"You will do for me. If I or the babe dies tonight, it will only hasten what will happen anyway."

The child was born in the darkest hour of the night. It came easily, sliding wet and steaming into the cold, candlelit darkness of the hut. Loki lifted the baby up to show Torgon. "A boy," she said and smiled. "A big, strong boy, anaka benna. And look at all his hair! He is shaggy as a calf."

The cord was cut and Torgon had him in her arms. She fingered over him, touching his cheeks, his tiny hands, his plump genitals. He whimpered and squirmed against her warm skin, searching for her nipple.

"Here, holy benna, put this cloak around you. The labour's over now and you will soon grow chilly, for the room is very cold."

Torgon didn't hear what else Loki said. For the moment there was nothing in the universe other than the babe.

Loki knelt down beside her. "What would you have me do now? Go with a secret message to the holy Seer that you have been delivered of a son?"

"No."

The girl's brow furrowed."

"No. I will stay here with the child until he's had his three-day feeding. During that time it will be between you and me alone that he is come."

* * *

"*Anaka benna! Anaka benna! Awaken, please!*" Loki cried.

Deep in exhausted sleep, Torgon roused only slowly.

"*Wake up!*" Loki jostled Torgon roughly.

The sudden motion startled the baby and he gave out a cry. Torgon raised her head. Day had come. The hut was filled with sunlight made brighter by the snow.

"I see warriors. They are far off, but they are coming in this direction," Loki cried.

Torgon drew the baby close. "Did you recognize them? Were they of your father's band? Or cariuna warriors? Or anakas? Could you tell?"

"They are warriors of our people, but they were not of my father's band. From a distance it was hard to make out the colour of their cloaks."

Torgon drew in a sharp breath. "If they find me unprotected, they will kill me now and take the babe." She glanced around the room. "You must hide me."

"Hide you, anaka benna?" Loki cried in alarm. "Could not you get to the high holy place in time?"

"I bleed heavily with the birthing. Their dogs would scent me easily and move faster than I could do. No, you must hide me. Quickly. And then keep them and their dogs outside."

Torgon rose up with the baby and crossed the small room. "Here. I will lie over here and keep him at my breast so he won't cry. You must pile the straw over us. The soiled straw first, so it is not obvious there is blood. Then the clean straw. Quickly, Loki. Do as I say."

There were seven or eight of them, with two of the holy brothers – Maglan and Galen – among them. Opening the door of the hut, Loki came out into the dappled sunshine that filtered through the leafless trees.

"*Ah, Marek's daughter,*" *Maglan said. The other warriors came up to stand in a semi-circle around Loki. Their dogs shifted restlessly about them.*

"*What finds you here?*" *Galen asked.*

"*I have accompanied the anaka benna. She wished to go to the high holy place to commune with Dwr in preparation for the holy birth, but the Seer felt it unwise she go alone so deep in winter. So, the Seer has bid me come here to the hut to keep a fire and provide food, should the divine benna need it.*"

"*I hear you are of unusual piety,*" *Galen replied.* "*Do you find this then a joyful task?*"

"*Oh no,*" *Loki replied quickly.* "*It is only that I am eldest now among the acolytes, and so the chore falls to me. Fact is, it's cold and lonely here, for the anaka benna seldom comes, and when she does, she keeps a vow of silence. She is preoccupied with thoughts of Dwr and of the coming birth.*"

"*I see,*" *Galen said.*

"*She is close then to the birth?*" *Maglan asked.*

"*Aye. Another week or two, the Seer said.*"

The dogs kept moving. In and out among the men, around Loki, around the foundations of the hut. The warriors made no effort to control them.

Loki endeavoured not to watch the dogs, but it was hard to ignore them since they were so active. In turn, she was aware of Galen watching her. He scrutinized her face closely.

"*It is in my mind that you feel fear,*" *he said.* "*Your skin gives away your nervousness with blotches.*"

"*It is the cold,*" *Loki replied.*

"*I think not. I saw you at the door. You did not wait to greet us, as a warrior's daughter should.*"

"*Your father has been too lax with you,*" *Galen said scornfully.* "*You lose control of your emotions.*"

"*I am* sorely *afraid, holy sir. I'm afraid of you, if you must know the truth. For when I saw you at a distance, I did not know who you might be. And I am here all alone and unprotected. You frighten me with all your swords and threats.*"

"*Put your sword away, Galen. She's but a girl and understandably afraid.*"

"*Your father is of the warrior kind, so you need have no fear of us,*" *Galen replied.* "*We wouldn't think to do you harm.*"

Loki took in a deep breath and nodded. "*I am sorry to have acted in such a foolish fashion, but at first sight I knew not who you were and I am of the age when girls must be most careful of these things. My chastity is all I have, so I put much value on it.*"

For the first time, Galen smiled. "*Yes, it's clear you'll soon take your rites of womanhood. I find it pleasing to discover you are prudent with your worth.*" *He resheathed his sword.*

Loki managed a weak smile back.

He tipped his head and looked Loki up and down. "*Six brothers to defend you and you are your father's only daughter. You will command a lordly price.*" *He continued smiling.* "*Perhaps I shall consider you for a son of mine. Your blood is good and your piety no doubt has made you biddable. Too bad you have not a more comely face.*"

"*My heart makes up for that,*" *Loki replied.*

"*Aye, I'm sure it does.*" *Then he turned to the others.* "*Call up the dogs, that we may go. The stag runs far ahead.*"

Loki waited until the warriors had disappeared from sight and even then she remained at the doorway of the hut until the forest all around had fallen silent as the snow. Finally going in, she barred the door behind her before crossing over to the straw heaped in the far corner.

"Anaka benna?" she whispered and began to pull the straw back. "Are you all right?"

From midst the soiled straw Torgon struggled into a sitting position. The baby, pressed against her skin inside her shirt, was sleeping peacefully.

Seeing them safe, Loki burst into tears. "I'm sorry. I'm so sorry, but I cannot help but cry. They made me so afraid."

"You did very well," Torgon replied. She leaned forward to pull the girl against her. "Here, take the comfort of my arms for I do not find your tears unseemly. You showed great resourcefulness in dealing with the holy brothers. You were very, very brave."

"I didn't feel brave at all. I felt only very, very frightened."

"Aye," Torgon said and smiled, "but that, sad to say, is how true bravery feels."

Chapter Forty

*O*n the third day, Torgon stood in the doorway of the hut. Dawn had coloured the sky a pigeon-feather grey, but through the leafless trees she could see threads of red marking where the sun would rise. Coming back inside, she closed the door and in the dim gloom lifted the baby up.

"This morning I shall go to the high holy place and present the child to Dwr," she said to Loki. "He needs a name and we can not wait for a naming day."

"What have you chosen for him?"

"I shall call him Luhr, after the great cat, that Dwr may grant him the great cat's strength and valour."

"What will the Seer say? It's not a holy name."

"No. But it is a name of power and he will need that more." She looked over at the girl. "While I am gone, will you make your way to my sister? Go discreetly and to her alone and not to my parents. When you have safety to speak privately, tell her the babe was born this day and none yet knows. Tell her I wish to see her and that she should bring her daughter Jofa with her, so my son may meet others of his blood. Tell her also to bring food. Say we *have not enough here and I dare not send you to the compound, so we need food for at least three days."*

Loki's expression grew perplexed. "There's not much truth in what I'm being sent to say."

"Aye, I know, but say to my sister only what I've told you. Don't add anything else yourself."

The snow began to fall even before Torgon reached the top of the escarpment. She'd come many times before in winter, but never burdened with a baby meant to live. Tying the child close within her clothes, she used both hands to clamber up over the icy rocks.

She was well supplied with holy tools, as they had been the only things she could bring from the compound without risking the Seer's suspicion. Now Torgon laid the deerskin bag down and opened it. The naming oils were all there, the holy knife, the sacred clay. Item by item, she laid out the things that she would need.

As she worked, the snow fell in large, soft flakes, a beautiful snowfall. She paused, watching it drift down, and marvelled at its beauty.

As she undressed him, he cried at the cold and made water, as all new babies seemed to do when suddenly unclothed. Taking up the sacred clay, Torgon painted holy marks across his face, down the length of his body and over his penis. So sad that this was done alone, she thought, and the thought intruded over the state of holy trance she should have been maintaining. So sad, on this, the most joyous celebration of his life, that the holy child was not surrounded by the loving circle of friends and family who should have attended on his naming day.

Torgon uncorked the naming oils, anointed his forehead, his chest, his genitals, and touched it to his lips. Then she lifted the naked baby up, high above her head in offering to Dwr. I give you this child: Luhr, the Great Cat.

Concerned for the welfare of the baby after exposing him to such intense cold, Torgon bound him close against the bare skin of her chest and warded off the bitter wind by removing her shirt and doubling it over his body before putting her outer clothes back on. When she reached the hut at dusk, she was herself miserable with cold.

Loki had long since returned. The small fire was burning cheerfully and a pot of broth made from dried deer meat was steaming over it. She helped Torgon to remove her outer garments and took the baby. Gratefully dishing up a bowl of broth, Torgon sat down cross-legged before the fire.

The door rattled.

A look of terror went between the two of them. Loki quickly put the sleeping baby down in a far corner in the straw.

"It is only I," Mogri called. "Let me in."

Loki unbarred the door.

A whoosh of snow came in with her. "There's no danger of being followed on a night like this," Mogri said and shook her garments. "My tracks were covered before they could grow cold."

Her own baby was tucked deeply into the folds of her clothes. On her back was a sheaf basket. "I've brought you bread and cheese. There wasn't much else for taking." She dropped the sheaf basket to the floor. One eyebrow quirked upwards as she regarded Torgon at the fire. "You're looking well, sister, but I say, you take a relaxed pose for a woman newly come from childbed. Was it such an easy birth as that?"

"I bore him three days past."

"*Oh* Torgon," *Mogri cried with disappointment.* "And you have lied to me?" *Then sudden concern.* "What's going on here, you two? Where is your babe? Is he all right?"

"Aye, he's fine." *Torgon went to lift the baby from his nest of straw.*

Mogri opened her arms to take him. "Oh, look at him, he's big!" *she cried.* "Well done, Torgon!" *Sitting down, she lay the baby on her lap and examined him more closely.* "So much hair. But will it go red? It's quite dark now, but look. I think it has a ruddy tone. Does he have your eyes? Open up, sleepyhead, so I can see you properly."

"I don't think he does," *Torgon replied.*

"Well, it's hard to tell in one so young. All babies' eyes are dark." *Mogri pulled back his wadding.* "You've done well, though, to have a boy. The Seer will be pleased with you. And so too her holy brothers. Perhaps at last this will bring peace among you all."

Torgon wiped her eyes.

"Aye, I see now you're right about three days. You're crying, poor love," *Mogri reached a hand out to push her sister's hair back.* "But it means more milk. More tears, more milk." *A pause.* "But what was your idea in coming here alone? When you bade me make the hut ready for you, I assumed that others would come with you. Is this how the holy do it? Not wise, I think. You should have the company of other women at a time like this. Perhaps it works for the high and holy born, so spiritless are they, but it won't suit a woman of our kind, shut away like this."

"It is not that."

"Why do you fight your tears so, Torgon? Your body would have you shed them. You have workers' blood and are not meant to show a lifeless face."

"*Mogri,* please. *Don't go on at me about such simple things. I have matters of a graver nature I must say to you tonight.*"

Mogri regarded her.

Leaning forward, Torgon took the baby from Mogri's arms and pressed him to her.

"*What Ansel said to me that night is true. There is no longer any holiness among his kind.*

"*My spilling Ansel's blood is not why they hate me. Were I naught but his wife and had knifed him in a lover's tiff, there would have been an awful scene, a public flogging in the square no doubt, because I am a worker and a woman, but as I was his choice and bore his first-born son, it would have ended there. The holy brothers would have accepted a crime of passion, for it's a human failing, and this they understand. It is what is not human about me which disquiets them. When that wicked man who sired them sent me forth to call the Power down, I did. And it is this they find unbearable in me, for they know my holiness is real.*

"*Because of this, they will not let me live. They can not let me live. Because I am proof the Power exists; that there truly is something greater than ourselves we can call down. But more than that, the Power cares not for caste or class or gender. Or even piety, but simply for the ability to listen openly and the strength of will to follow.*"

Mogri said, "*There's no doubt the holy brothers wish to take revenge on you for Ansel's, but they will not kill you. The council ruled firmly in your favour and the holy brothers would never go against the elders. They know it'd bring us into civil war. And kill the divine anaka benna? Torgon, they wouldn't dare.*"

"*They would. They will. And in their heart they already have.*"

Mogri sat back.

"*And they shall succeed for I'm no longer holy.*"

"*What do you mean?*"

Torgon lowered her head. She had the baby to her breast and she regarded him. "*Since Ansel's death my Power's waned. I fear now my holiness is broken too.*"

"*Oh, Torgon, surely not.*"

"*It's so, Mogri. I don't know why. Sometimes I can still feel the Power there inside me, but now, unlike times gone by, it very seldom speaks to me. I do not wish to be like Ansel and his kind, using my own voice when the sound of Dwr's voice grows dim . . .*"

Silence.

Torgon looked down again at the baby. He slept, his mouth gone slack against her breast. Gently she lifted a finger and wiped away the milk that dribbled from his lips. "*My fear is for the babe,*" *she said softly,* "*for yes, I think you're right. When I am killed, there will be civil war.*" *She stroked the baby's head.* "*His parentage means he will be neither holy born nor worker kind and yet he will be both. Both sides will harbour those who'll think his death judicious. And babies die so easily . . .*"

Torgon raised her head. "*Loki? Would you bring my bag of holy tools?*"

The girl rose and fetched them, carrying the bag to Torgon. With her free hand, Torgon opened it and spilled the contents out onto the floor. Among the bottles of oil and ointments, she took a smaller bag. "*Here, Mogri, undo it for me, for I can't manage with one hand.*"

Mogri knelt and picked the knot undone. Pulling the leather thong out she emptied the bag onto the floor. Her eyes grew huge with surprise.

"*Aye, it's gold,*" *Torgon said.*

"*Where has it come from?*" *Mogri asked in a hushed voice.* "*I've never seen so much.*"

"I've been melting down my holy ornaments, for it is unlikely I shall have much need of them again."

Apprehensively, Mogri looked across to her. "I see this has been well-planned ... I am worried now."

"And now I am going to plead with you on the life of my newborn son ..."

"Oh Torgon, no —"

"Take my son and set forth tomorrow morning at first light. Go to the kingdom of the Cat People. When the king was here last, he showed himself to be a man of wisdom and great piety. He honoured Dwr, even though Dwr does not walk among his gods, and he saw to it that his warriors all did likewise, so he is also a king of strength and power. Tell him that it now goes very ill with me and this is the holy child. Give him the gold that I have here and beg that he protect my son."

"No, I can't!"

"Ask him to instruct Luhr in the ways of a good and noble man and to keep him safe until he comes of age to reclaim his rightful place. I think the king will do this. He was much distressed when we last met, for he and his queen have been denied the holy gift of children. He asked for my divine intervention, that they might be blessed with royal fruit. If his queen has since given birth, he will take my babe from indebtedness. If she has not, he may welcome the chance to take the baby as his own, particularly as it may also mean a future kingdom. If nothing else, leave the gold to speak, for it is not a paltry sum."

"Oh Torgon —"

"No, Mogri, please. Please do this for me. I no longer have my holy visions but I have dreams and in them I see the babe grown to be a man. A king. A divine king with Dwr's holy gift of Power. But if he stays here ... he will walk all too soon among the dead with me. I see that too."

"If it has really come to this, Torgon, wouldn't it be far better to take the babe and escape with him yourself, so that at the very least you could raise him in the ways of holiness?"

"I've spent many hours in thought on this, for, of course, it's what I'd wish to do, but in the end the answer's always no. If I went too, the Cat King might well refuse us aid. My eyes are my curse. No matter how careful I might be in my disguise, they would still give me away, and sheltering the divine *anaka benna* would surely bring our warriors to his gates. Why would the king wish to risk war over me? But one baby looks much like any other and you could pass easily for a travelling peddler woman.

"More importantly, no one yet knows the babe is born. I can go back to the compound and forestall the Seer and the holy brothers another week or two, perhaps even longer, as this is my first child and first-born children are often slow to come. It would give you time to reach the borders of the Cat People without pursuit. And even then I can tell them that the babe's a girl. Or stillborn. Or, for that matter, that I killed the babe myself lest they should take it from me."

"And they will kill you."

"Mogri, they are going to do that anyway."

Tears filled Mogri's eyes. She lowered her head.

"I fear I have even more to ask of you," Torgon murmured.

"Speak on, then. Get it over with."

"When you have reached the kingdom of the Cat People, I beg you to remain there with him. I ask this not as the holy benna, but simply as your sister, who loves you and him very much. It will be dangerous here in days to come. When it is discovered he is gone, they will guess you've helped me and your life will be taken too. So stay there and care for him as I would do. He needs a guardian. Even if the king should take him, I fear what might befall him.

*What if he is mistreated? Or he falls ill and is alone? I want him
to know the kind of love that you and I enjoyed in youth, for that
is how noble men are made. Even kind indifference, which does
not hurt the body, marks the soul and leaves a hollow space. So,
please,* please, *Mogri, remain and care for him."*

Lowering her head, Mogri nodded. "Very well."

"Holy benna?"

*The hut was totally dark. No hint of dawn distinguished the
high-set window from the walls. Turning in the straw, Torgon
tried to gain her bearings.*

"Holy benna?"

"Aye, Loki. I'm awake," *Torgon whispered into the darkness.*

There was the sound of the girl crawling through the straw. "I
cannot sleep," *she murmured.*

"No. Nor can I."

"I have been thinking all through the darkness of the night, holy
benna."

"Here, Loki, come under the covers with me. I wish not to wake
my sister. Lie here close. You're cold. Perhaps when you are warm,
you'll sleep."

"No, I think not," *she said softly, but she accepted the warmth
and pressed close.*

"I have decided, holy benna, that when they depart, I shall go
with them."

"No, Loki."

"Aye, holy benna. I have thought much about it."

"It is in my heart to do this. It will ease your sister's burden. She
can not easily carry two babies and the basket. With so much snow,
it will make her journey slow. I shall go with them. I can take the
holy child and keep him warm while she carries her own babe."

"No, Loki."

"But people will be suspicious if she has two babes. They are too far apart for twins, too close for normal bearing. Someone might accuse of her of child stealing. If so, then ill would befall them all. But if I am with her, I can say that he is mine, and they will assume I am cast out from my tribe for loss of my virginity."

"This is too great a sacrifice."

"I want to do it," Loki said.

"Aye, with your courageous heart, I know you would, but we must be practical too. You are too highly born. Mogri won't be missed, but if a warrior's daughter disappeared, there'd be an outcry and they'd search for you. It would be safer if Mogri went alone."

"I've already thought of that," Loki replied, "and I want you to tell them I have died. Say to them that while I was in the forest waiting on you, a great cat came and devoured me, and there is now naught left of me but my few clothes."

"You've been too long with me. You've learned my way with lying."

In the darkness Loki chuckled. "No, it is my own secret mind at work. Besides, it carries truth in its own way. He bears the name of the great cat, not so? And I am already devoured with love for him."

"No, Loki. You are too young to understand the sacrifice you offer. A good life lies here ahead of you. It isn't right that you should exchange it for a refugee's existence in a foreign court."

"Anaka benna, I have no desire for the life that lies here now. I would not stay to make a marriage to some high-born son, knowing as I know now that worker children starve in their huts while mine play carelessly with silver baubles. And certainly, I would not stay to watch you die. If you are gone, my life would have no *meaning here. So let me go with him so that the baby king grows up knowing he leads his people even now."*

Torgon felt through the darkness to touch the girl's face. "Very well. If you so wish it, may it be so."

They rose at dawn and broke their fast with bread and broth. The remaining food was packed into the sheaf basket, and then the extra clothing. Loki lifted it up for Mogri and fastened the straps tight. Then came the babies, Jofa into the folds of Mogri's garments, then Luhr into the folds of Loki's.

Torgon hesitated as she held the baby out. He'd just been well fed and was growing sleepy. Then with a sigh she placed him close against Loki's budding breast and began the task of binding him. She paused and caressed his dark hair, touched, as Mogri said, with just the glint of red. "Oh, Dwr keep you safe, my little one," she whispered and leaned down to kiss his face. She rested so, her lips against his skin, and Loki stood quietly, feeling the warmth of Torgon's head through the folds of clothes.

No one spoke otherwise. The three of them worked silently until all the tasks were done. Then Torgon lifted up the heavy bar across the door. Outside, the snow had ceased and lay inviolate.

"Give my love to Mam and Da, Torgon."

"Aye."

"Find your way to them. Don't leave the task to someone else. Go to them yourself and tell them what has befallen us, for while your heart cries out at losing one child, remember they are losing two. And grandchildren besides."

"Aye. I shall. I promise."

They stood, silent.

"Travel well," Torgon whispered, for the words wouldn't come out any louder. "And may Dwr keep you all."

"*And you,*" *Mogri said.* "*May Dwr keep you too. For if the future you describe is just your sensing and not visions he has sent, then perhaps it will go differently. I shall stay in the court of the Cat People and not go elsewhere so that you will know where you can find us, if you ever come to seek us out. And while I'll raise Luhr as if he were a child born of my own body, I shall teach him he is not mine and that he must stay ever watchful of the eastward road, in hopes he might someday see his true mother coming.*"

"*Here,*" *Torgon said and reached out.* "*Embrace me one last time. Let me kiss you. And you too, Loki. No. Kiss me not as the benna, for the time of bennas is past. Kiss me here, upon the face, like the sister you now are to me. And then I'll bid you both farewell.*"

James turned over the final typewritten page. He looked at it, blank on the back, dog-eared, slightly yellowed at the edges with age, and he felt a sense of loss that it all was over, that the story had ended, that Torgon was returning to die and her nobility hadn't saved her. Loss too at no longer having this shadowy mirror to hold up to Laura's life.

It occurred to him, as he regarded the unpretentious stack of pages, that this was the only place Torgon existed. All that life, that vibrancy was nothing more than a set of marks across a page that he and Laura and a handful of others had experienced. And yet he felt loss. Strange, really, if you thought about it.

Chapter Forty-One

"So that's how it ended for Fergus and me," Laura said. "I didn't finish my degree. So, Fergus was right there. I never did work a day as a doctor. Instead, I left Boston that November dawn and came back here. There was a vacancy for a paramedic in the ambulance service out on the Pine Ridge reservation, so I took that and started the long, slow job of patching my life back together again.

"The first weeks were awful. That really black depression I'd had in the spring didn't overtake me, but anxiety did instead. I was scared to death Fergus would find out where I was. The only time he ever did seem psychic to me was in his uncanny ability to find me, wherever I happened to be. It was terrifying to think that maybe somehow the Voices *could* tell him where I was, because how do you protect yourself from that? I saw him, like a ghost, hiding behind every dark corner. This gave me chronic insomnia. I'd wake every night with a pounding heart and lie there panicked in the dark. It carried over into the daytime as a kind of edginess that left me feeling nervy and irritable and unable to concentrate on anything.

"The only thing that helped was strenuous physical exercise. The reservation borders the south side of the Badlands, so in my free time I started hiking. The Badlands were a good place to do it. I felt safe in their openness, and their bleakness, especially in the winter, matched my mood. I went out in all weathers: wind, rain, even snow. Always alone. My parents were absolutely paranoid about how dangerous it was to do all this walking alone in case I fell or something. Truth is, I think I would have actually welcomed something happening, something that would take the responsibility for disaster away from me. For hours and hours I walked the basins, climbed up the gullies, scrambled over the rocks, and during the entire time my mind was absolutely vacant. Which felt so good. So healing.

"One Saturday – it must have been about three weeks after I'd returned – I had spent the whole day out hiking. The weather had been absolutely foul, and by the time I got home, my clothes were soaked, my cheeks wind-burned and my fingers and toes numb with cold. I started cooking my supper, then opened a bottle of red wine and poured myself a glass. I felt like some music, so I went into the living room and put Saint-Saëns's Requiem Mass on the stereo.

"I was sitting, relaxing in the armchair with my wine when that unusual brass intro to the 'Agnus Dei' began. I've listened to it many times before, of course, but what happened then … suddenly I was in the Forest. Seeing it with the same abrupt, eidetic clarity as I'd experienced it in my youth, in the old days before Fergus. I was there once more in a way I'd long since given up hope of experiencing again.

"Torgon was in the isolation hut. She was shutting the door. Mogri and Loki had already departed through the snow with

Torgon's newborn baby. She'd watched until they'd disappeared from sight, then she closed the door and turned back into the darkness of the hut.

"That slow, eerie part of Saint-Saëns's 'Agnus Dei' had begun …" Laura raised a hand absently, almost as if conducting the unheard music. "I could hear it, music, I mean. Even as I was in the Forest, seeing Torgon. The music was somehow part of it. Or maybe I just wasn't as fully in the Forest as I thought, because I was so aware of the music.

"In the isolation hut the loneliness was as penetrating as the 'Agnus Dei'. Torgon was picking up her few things, putting them slowly one by one into her bag in preparation for returning to the compound, and there was such a sense of total desolation. She knew she was going back to her death, and she knew she was returning utterly alone, without any support whatsoever. Without Loki. Without her sister. Without her child … and … I realized for the first time, without me."

Laura looked over. "Because, of course, *I* was the Power, wasn't I?"

James looked at her.

"I mean, you've figured that out by now, haven't you? Torgon's world was my inspiration for trying to become something more than I could be by myself, but in the same way, I was hers. She had become great by imagining my world." Laura's eyes brimmed with tears. "But then she lost her visions, because I'd abandoned her."

"That's an interesting premise," James said. "But 'abandonment' is a very strong word."

"No, it's the right word. I *chose* to leave her. I chose to turn her into something less than she was, because I wanted …"

Laura halted a moment and wiped her eyes. "Because I just wanted to be ordinary. To have what everyone else had."

"So, you're saying that you feel responsible for Torgon's fate?" James asked, intrigued by this surreal complexity.

Laura's brow furrowed. "Can you understand what I'm talking about? The difference? Between the real Torgon – this beautiful, noble creature who came to me in childhood – and the caricature I'd turned her into, which was no more than an extension of my ego?"

James nodded.

"There was Fergus with all his talk about destiny. I kept hearing that word all around me and never paid enough attention to it, never recognized I already *had* a destiny. I didn't need Fergus's version of it."

Laura let out a long, slow breath.

"In some different, better world, I would have stayed on course with what I was fated for. I would have become that brilliant doctor and gone off to some god-forsaken corner of the world to do immeasurable good. People would have looked at me and said, 'She's inspired.' Maybe even, 'She hears the voice of God.' Because there *are* indeed Voices in this world, call them what you may, and if you heed them, you *are* special."

Laura paused and in her silence James detected a faint defensiveness. "But the frank truth is," she said, "very few of us have it in us to be Mother Theresa or Martin Luther King. It's easy to think that we'd all be capable of that kind of greatness if given the chance. But that's a dream. The reality is very different. Torgon demanded everything of me from the moment I met her that night on the path the summer I was seven. She wanted my time, my attention, my social life, my education, my career. To do what she wanted of me meant I couldn't have friends. I couldn't have a family. I couldn't have anything except her. That was too much for me. To follow Torgon required a nobility from me I just didn't have.

"So … I left her there as she was, to return to the village alone, and I moved on to create a life of my own. I'd had a remarkable apprenticeship, doing all that writing on the Forest, so I've put it to good use. My books are quality literature. They bring enjoyment to a lot of people and, I like to think, some depth and insight to the issues I write about. I'm a decent person. I try hard to do the right thing whenever I can. But I'm tired of feeling that I didn't live up to what might have been. The way I see it, yes, a golden chalice was passed to me, but it wasn't meant to be mine. So I drank from it and passed it on."

"There is a story here," Conor announced, taking a large, blank piece of drawing paper. He carried it over to the table. "It looks like there is nothing on it, but really there is a story here. Do you see it?" he asked James.

"I see a piece of white paper."

Conor reached over and took one of James's pencils and then sat down. "You will see the story soon, because I'm going to draw the pictures for it. Tomorrow when you look at this paper, you will see the story's there." He bent forward and began to draw a long line across the top of the paper.

"I was thinking about this when I was in my bed this morning," he said, as he continued to draw. "I thought, the story will be on the paper tomorrow. So is it always on the paper? Is it just the way our eyes are that we can't see it because it's today and not tomorrow?"

"That's a big thought to be thinking," James said.

"I think big thoughts."

"So I've noticed."

"Tomorrow is hidden. My story here is hidden until I've done it. The world is full of hidden things." He was drawing vertical lines on the paper, dividing the space into boxes. "My mechanical cat is hidden. No one can see it, because it's in here," he said and tapped his chest.

"You know inside you there is something strong," James said.

Conor nodded. "Yeah. I hear it singing. My mother can't. She says, 'Put on your socks, Conor, it's time to go.' I say, 'The mechanical cat is singing.' She says, 'Don't be silly. We haven't got time.'" He looked up. "But the mechanical cat knows. Nothing's hidden from the mechanical cat."

James looked at him.

"The mechanical cat can see everything. He can see the story hidden on this paper. He can see tomorrow. And at our house he can see the ghost."

"This is the man under the rug?"

Conor didn't answer. He had finished dividing the paper into sections and now turned to the box in the top left-hand corner. "I'll draw a picture of the man under the rug. Then you'll know what you're looking for."

Tongue protruding between his lips, head bent close to the paper, Conor threw himself into the activity. A figure appeared, lying prone, but the drawing was hard to decipher because there were many faint, spidery lines coming out from the body in all directions.

Conor moved on to the next box and drew a picture of a man standing up. It wasn't a particularly unusual picture, just a typical child's drawing of a man with wide-open eyes and a blank expression, dressed in trousers and a plain shirt.

In the third box Conor drew another man. This time the picture was gruesome. He made blood come out of this man's mouth and out of wounds over his body. The man was still standing, but there was a knife in his side and a second knife in his neck.

"They shouldn't be in this order," Conor said thoughtfully, as he sat back to look at the drawings in their little boxes across the top of the page. "This is going to be one of those tests that doctors give you. You will see the pictures and then you must put them in order to tell a story."

Leaning back over the paper, he moved to a new box and drew a picture of a bed. He put a child of indistinct gender in it, under the covers. The child wasn't asleep. Its eyes were staring circles. Conor paused to study the picture a moment, then went back to work, lavishing much more attention to detail on this picture than he had on the others. He drew a rug on the floor and a toy truck and a little horse. He added hair to the child's head and made stripes on the blanket. Then he began to draw the body. "You and I can't see this part," he said as he worked. "It's hidden under the blanket. But the mechanical cat can. Nothing is hidden from the mechanical cat." Conor drew pyjamas on the child and beneath the pyjamas, genitals. It was a boy, lying on his side in the bed and James could tell he was urinating.

"Now here, in this one …" Conor had moved to the next square and he began to sketch a man much like in the first box, lying prone on the floor. He drew a line over the man. "That's the rug. I don't know how to draw a rug so you can tell what it is looking at it from the side. And the boy came downstairs. Very quietly. Quiet as a mouse. He did pee-pee in his bed. See up there?" He pointed to the other picture.

Conor stopped. A long, pregnant moment followed, as he regarded the series of drawings. Then he lay down the pencil and looked over at James. "This is my dream."

"You've dreamt all this?"

"Yeah. Many times. When I am asleep, I dream it. When I am awake, I dream it too. Even when I am not dreaming, it's there. But no one knows this. It's one of the hidden things."

The next pause lengthened and grew into a full silence, soft and deep

Conor finally looked up at James. "I am listening for the mechanical cat now. He can sing louder than the dream. That's what he does. *Zap-zap. Metal fur. Never cry. Never die.*"

James smiled. "He sings to make the dream go away?"

"Yeah."

Another pause.

"In here, the boy is safe."

"Yes," James said

Conor leaned over the paper again and in the next box he began to draw a picture of a child, standing beside a table. "Here is this room here. This is the man's table. See? Right here. This table." Conor patted the wood. "The boy is standing beside it. 'No ghosts here,' he says. He says that to himself."

Leaning closer to the drawing, his body going more rigid as he worked, Conor said. "And here inside the boy, *here* is the mechanical cat. Can you see it? I have drawn it, so now it's not hidden. Can you see?"

Inside the torso of the child who was standing beside table, Conor had carefully drawn a small cat. It sat upright in the manner of cats, its ears pricked forward, its eyes watching out from the picture. It had a tiny upside-down triangle for a nose and an almost wistful smile on its face.

Conor drew thin lines down through the head, the arms and the legs of the child, all connected to the cat, as if it were a feline puppeteer working its big creation.

"I need to colour this," Conor said. He rose up and reached across the table to the basket of crayons and marking pens, then coloured the cat black with a white blaze on its face, white socks and bib and a little pink nose. He coloured the eyes green and then made whiskers and very, very neat little claws just showing from the white paws. He didn't colour the boy at all.

"I want to cut this out. Where's some cardboard? I want to paste it on cardboard first to keep it good. I need cardboard," he announced and jumped up from the table. Without waiting for a response from James, he crossed over to the shelves and rummaged through the assortment of art materials. Finding a small piece of poster board, he returned. Taking up scissors, he skilfully cut out the figure of the boy. He glued the picture to the poster board, then endeavoured to cut away the excess to leave just the figure of the boy with his internal cat.

Conor was very pleased with the result. His face lit up brightly. "Look! See? Here it is. *My* mechanical cat." He leaped up and ran to the shelves to get the box of cardboard animals. Pulling out the little cardboard tabby, he fitted it into its stand as he came back to the table. "See? My cat and your cat. Here. I'll get clay, so mine can stand up too. Mine and yours! I can take this home! This one belongs to me."

"Yes, you've made your own mechanical cat now, haven't you? What a good idea you had."

"Yeah! I have done it all myself, so I can keep it." He flashed a brilliant smile at James.

Conor leaned back to admire the cats on the table, but as he did so, his eyes drifted towards the paper he'd been drawing on. "I didn't finish that," he said. He picked up the paper with its missing square. "I should have made another picture. I didn't do the whole dream." He made no effort to resume.

"Can you tell what has been left out?" James asked.

"I didn't put her on the stairs. Made a picture of the stairs." He felt around the hole where he had cut out the drawing of the boy and the cat. "She said, '*Don't* come down.'" Conor looked at the other drawings. "She said, 'You're a bad, bad boy. You must *not* get out of bed.' She wanted to play with my finger-paints. She didn't want to ask first.

"I needed to do pee-pee. I thought, 'I must get up. I need the potty. I can't get my pants down by myself.' But she was crying. She'd used my finger-paints without asking. She said in a scream, 'You bad, bad boy! You *bad*, *BAD* boy! This is for coming downstairs.' The bad boy came downstairs. So, he ran back up. Quick as could be. Quick as a fox. Quick under the covers. She is screaming. The boy is screaming too. Screaming and crying. Where's his strong daddy? He wants his daddy, but his daddy isn't there. The mechanical cat isn't there. No one is there and the boy pees in his bed."

Conor ran a finger over the picture of the boy in bed. "Yes, that's what happened. It was a very bad dream. A dream I kept having."

"It sounds very scary indeed," James said. "I can understand how you would feel so frightened."

Conor put his hands over his eyes. "I don't talk about it. Keep my mouth zipped shut," he gestured across his lips. "'Don't talk about it,' she says. 'It isn't real. It's just a dream.

It will go away, if you don't pay attention to it. You make it real with your thoughts. But thoughts aren't real.'"

He was rocking back and forth, his fingers pressed tight to his eyes.

"Who's saying this to you?" James asked.

"The mummy. She says it isn't real. You just heard them in a dream."

"What about this other picture?" James asked, pointing to the last one of the boy and the man under the rug. "What can you tell me about this?"

Conor lowered the cut-out. "This is in the dream too. They're all part of the dream. But this is the quiet part. When there is no one but the ghost man. Mummy isn't here. Daddy isn't here. The ghost man isn't running down the hall. The boy is thinking, 'This room looks different.' He is thinking, 'What is that big lump?' So he goes over and lifts up the rug to see why it's so lumpy and *there is the ghost man!* The boy gets *very* scared. He runs. Like this." Conor raced two fingers across the tabletop. "He runs very fast because he knows the ghost man is going to get up and come get him like he did before."

"The ghost man 'got' you before?" James asked, slipping in the pronoun change from 'he' to 'you' in hopes of bringing more clarity to what Conor was telling. "When was this?"

"In the hallway," Conor replied, as if this made sense.

"What happened then?"

"Mummy says, 'We will go to the moon tonight and the ghost man will come with us. We will take a rocket ship.'"

Confused, James didn't ask for more clarification.

"There is terria outside the window when the rocket ship lands," Conor said. "And three trees. One-two-three. He can count. No one has taught him how, but he can do it. He counts the trees."

Picking up the sheet of paper, Conor studied the series of pictures a moment. Then with no warning, he tore it in half. Then he tore the halves in half again. And again and again until the paper was reduced to little more than confetti.

"You didn't want to keep the pictures of that dream," James said quietly.

"No. Now it's hidden again." Fiercely, he pushed the bits of paper off the table, letting them flutter to the floor. "You want to keep your mouth shut. You never say."

Conor put his head down on the table top. "I'm very tired," he said. "I don't feel well. I don't feel like I can talk."

James nodded. "That's all right. In here, you can decide."

"'In here, you can decide.' You always say that." Conor smiled weakly at him. "In here, I have decided. The dream is gone. I have decided that."

Chapter Forty-Two

James's original psychiatric training had been strictly Freudian, and the practice in Manhattan had been almost exclusively psychoanalytic. In this cloistered world nothing was ever as it seemed, but was instead an expression of hidden or repressed desires, aversions and anxieties that the client slowly uncovered as he gained self-awareness in the presence of the benign but detached psychiatrist.

James found it hard to cast off some aspects of that decade's training. He was comfortable in the traditional psychiatric role of passive listener, allowing the client to set the pace without his active interpretation. It was natural for him just to listen, to hold himself in a non-judgemental place that did not draw active conclusions of any sort. Clients could tell that about him – that he did not presume or have a pre-set agenda for uncovering what he believed the problem was – and they responded well to it. It had often made him successful where others had failed.

In addition, James was well aware of how very florid the mind of a disturbed child could be. Children *did* imagine. Children *did* dream. Children *did* misinterpret.

James sighed. He still found it challenging to probe actively for literal meanings in the confusion of dreams, fantasies and misinterpretations that made up childhood. He was determined, however, that there would never be another Adam.

So what was he to make of Conor's conversations? James was certain there had been an event around age two to three that had impacted Conor deeply. Was it a real event? Did it involve an actual death? Was the red finger-paint blood? Were the ghost man and the man under the rug the same person? Was he a real person? Conor was a very intelligent boy, which would have made him more perceptive than adults would have given him credit for. He was also very young and sensitive. These aspects would have affected the accuracy of his interpretation of any literal events. Everything was being filtered through the limited experience of an anxious toddler.

It all could just as logically be a symbolic event. Based on his psychoanalytic training, James would interpret "the man" as Alan, as an expression of Conor's Oedipal stage in which, according to Freud, the son harbours strong hidden desires to kill his father and marry his mother. The "ghost under the rug" would then be interpreted as Conor's guilty conscience. Perhaps Alan's impregnating Laura at this point, just when Conor was being forced into separation by daycare, proved too much. Perhaps he came in on Alan and Laura having sex, a classic traumatic event in Freudian psychiatry. Perhaps he felt supplanted by Morgana, who distanced him further from his mother.

Of course, Conor's disturbance could also be a thoroughly confusing mix of the two, of literal events Conor was too young to understand and half-remembered dreams. So much of it, like the rocket ship and the trip to the moon, made no sense to James in any context, such that he remained reluctant to draw conclusions without further information.

In the end, James decided to ask Alan back in yet again and see if he could glean more from an adult perspective.

"I really appreciate your coming in," James said, as Alan settled himself into the conversation centre.

"Hey, I'm pleased to help," Alan replied heartily. He pulled off his duck-billed cap and ran a hand through his rumpled hair in an effort to smooth it down. "I can't tell you how great Conor's been doing, especially now that his homeschool teacher has started. He comes down to the cabin almost every day now after his teacher leaves. All by himself. If you'd told me in September we could get to a place where we'd actually trust him to walk safely between the house and the cabin on his own, I'd have said, 'Knock me over with a feather.'"

James smiled. "I'm very pleased with his progress myself. But listen, what I'd like to explore with you once again is that period when Conor's problems started. The more verbal Conor becomes, the more confused I seem to get. Clearly events affected him when he was two or three, but I'm having a devil of a time piecing together what exactly may have happened," James said.

"Yeah, I can imagine," Alan said.

"Sometimes the events that impact a child can seem quite minor to adults. Because children are very egocentric at this age, they sometimes put a different spin on things and believe they've caused an event that was in reality entirely unrelated to them. Occasionally the event hasn't even happened at all. The child has a false memory, either given to him accidentally by someone around him, who's talking about something, or

created from a dream or a TV program or something similar."

James paused. "So this is where I'm at right now. To help
Conor fully, I need to identify more clearly what was affecting him then, but this is a challenge because at the moment he
can't tell me."

Alan considered this a while. "I think I've pretty much told
you everything," he said finally. "I mean, it *was* a very disruptive time. The financial troubles and nearly losing the farm. The
unexpected pregnancy. Conor being diagnosed as autistic ..."

"That's too far along the timeline," James replied. "Conor
isn't autistic. I'm absolutely certain of that now and I know
other professionals would agree. He withdrew. He stopped
talking and began all this magical thinking about cats and
mechanical things in response to the traumatizing event or
events, so it would have to have happened before he was diagnosed. He was diagnosed at four and up until he was two, you
remember him as developing normally. So I think the event
had to have happened in that period in between."

Again, Alan was pensive. Slowly, he shook his head.

"Do you remember anything with blood?" James asked.
"Any unusual amount of blood? Any blood where it shouldn't
be? Anything where Laura would be involved?"

Alan lifted one eyebrow. "That's kind of a scary question."
A pause. "The only thing I can think of is the miscarriage."

James nodded. "Anything else you remember? What about
anything going on with Laura?"

"The truth is, I really feel bad that I left her alone so much,"
Alan said. "I can appreciate now how it must have contributed
to all of this. Not only because I wasn't able to stay on top of
what was going on at home, but because Laura was vulnera-

ble there by herself. She did tell me that at the time. But I was so worried about losing the ranch that I just didn't see I had any choice but to keep trying to find extra work to stay afloat."

"Yes, I can understand," James said sympathetically.

"The only other thing I can think of during that time was that fan. The obsessed guy who was bothering Laura. I never actually saw him, but if Conor did – well, I suppose that could have been pretty scary for him …"

"Can you remember this guy's name?" James asked.

A small silence filtered in as Alan sat, lost in memory. James could hear sleet hitting again the large picture windows in the playroom

Finally Alan shook his head. "No. I'm afraid not."

"Could it have been Fergus somebody? Does that ring any bells?"

Alan again shook his head. "No, I don't think so. Why? Was there a Fergus that I should have known about?"

James shrugged. "It was just a guess. Somebody Laura had mentioned from her time in Boston."

"Boston?"

"Yes," James replied. "When she was getting her medical degree."

Alan's features drew down in an expression of bewilderment. "Boston? She didn't get her medical degree in Boston. She got it at the University of Minnesota in Minneapolis."

"*What*?"

"To my knowledge," Alan said, "Laura's never even been to Boston."

After Alan had left, James stood in stunned silence before the office window. Hands in his pockets, he stared out eastward across the vast expanse of plains. The sense of shock kept his mind absolutely blank for several minutes.

How could Boston not be real?

Maybe Alan was wrong. Maybe a mistake had been made. But then James realized that Laura had to have lied to someone. If not him, then Alan. A sense of betrayal began to sink in.

Like Scheherazade charming the king, so too had Laura used the power of storytelling, gently getting the upper hand with her long, gentle, softly spoken monologues. James had simply been following his "in here you decide" creed. He'd never wanted to interrupt her with many questions. Indeed, somewhere along the line questions had largely ceased forming for him. He had *wanted* her to continue uninterrupted.

The real spell, however, had not been cast by Laura, but by Torgon. James might have been able to stay on even keel if Laura's monologues had been all there was. Even as the line between personal history and story blurred with Laura's tales of an altered reality, that still remained within the scope of an ordinary therapy session. What had changed it all was the arrival of the Torgon stories.

With those, Laura's imagination was no longer confined to two hours a week at the clinic. It went home with James. Ate with him. Went to bed with him. And when he read, his mind became one with Laura's and together they created a new reality. James had started the stories as nothing more than a means of better understanding Laura, but as he became more and more caught up in what happened next to Torgon, he ceased to be an objective bystander. He became, instead, a participant in Laura's imagination, and from that joining had sprung a Torgon – and, indeed, a Laura – of his own creation.

Chapter Forty-Three

"I know it's been my practice in here to let you decide how the sessions go," James said as Laura settled into her usual chair in the conversation centre. "But sometimes it's necessary for me, as the professional, to step in and put things back in balance. That's my role in this and it's the difference between a therapeutic relationship and just an ordinary, everyday relationship."

A flicker of alarm crossed Laura's features.

"So there are a few things we need to clear up."

"Don't scare me, okay?" she said, a worried note in her voice.

"I'm scaring you?" James said.

"Yes." A pause. She looked down at her hands in her lap. "Because I've come to really trust you. I've been very honest in here and talked about things that have been so hard for me to acknowledge to anyone."

"You've trusted me?" James said with irony. "You've been honest?'

"Yes."

"Such as when you told me about Boston, for instance?" he asked.

Laura's gaze snapped up to his face. There wasn't the shock of being found out that James had expected to see there. Just a momentary flicker of surprise, followed almost immediately by an expression of deeper weariness, like a fox run to ground.

"Boston was not true, Laura. You were never at school in Boston."

"*Boston* wasn't true, as in the physical *location* isn't true. No. It was not Boston. But what I told you is true. Every single experience I told you about really happened."

"But it wasn't in Boston?" he asked.

"No," she said heavily, "it was not in Boston."

James looked at her.

"The name of the city had no importance," she said. "We weren't discussing vacation destinations. Or good restaurants or whatever."

"The problem is, you didn't just say 'back East' or something else equally vague," James replied. "You gave it concrete parameters the moment you called it Boston, and it became a lie the moment you didn't qualify that."

"I didn't think I needed to qualify it, because it wasn't important. I simply wanted to make the place easy to refer to, but I didn't want to use specifics. James, I'm not anybody. I'm relatively well known. And I've been telling you about some very personal – and embarrassing – episodes in my past. In the city where it all took place, there are still plenty of people who would only remember me as a charlatan psychic or, worse, as Fergus's New Age 'queen'."

"Okay, I can understand your wanting to protect your privacy, but can you see how not knowing about this discrepancy impacts on what's going on here, in therapy? How it then makes me question everything else you've told me?" James asked.

"But what I'm telling you *is* real. Saying 'Boston' was a detail that made no difference whatsoever to the story."

"Yes, '*story*'. I suspect we have a key word there, Laura," James said softly. "Now we have to clarify this concept of 'story' because I think it's behind quite a few of the problems that have resulted in your ending up here. When we talk about events that have really happened, it's not a story – it's a set of unalterable facts and we can't depart from them without telling people why. Boston is Boston. Paris is Paris. Tokyo is Tokyo. One doesn't mutate into another indiscriminately."

"The world is not that fixed," she said, just as quietly. If I learned anything from my experiences with Torgon, it is that all this around us that looks so concrete is, in reality, just as insubstantial as she is. Things are not more true simply because we can see them or hear them or find them on a map. Everything is just perception. We have no way of getting outside ourselves to verify if something exists. I see and feel this table, so it exists for me. It's 'real'. But an aboriginal living in the outback of Australia can not see or feel this table and has no knowledge of it, so it does not exist for him. If he has any knowledge of it at all, it's only in his imagination. So how do we know the table is *real*? I perceive the Forest. I see and feel it with my inner senses, so it exists for me. You don't perceive the Forest, so that place is unreal for you. But if I give you the stories to read, then soon you will see it and feel it with your inner senses. How do we know if that's real? We both perceive it. Boston was Boston because you perceived Boston in what I told you, Boston existed for you. But that has nothing to do with whether or not Boston really exists as a place you can experience with your five senses. If you had perceived this place as Seattle or San Francisco or Kathmandu, what I told you still would have been just as true."

"That's impressive reasoning," James replied, "but it's on a scale a little more broad than most of us use. What's important to keep in mind is that when you are talking to someone else, it's not just about your perceptions. It's about theirs too. So, what happens to me is that when I find out that your location wasn't the real location, I begin to ask myself what else in your stories might have been regarded as 'flexible reality'. I wonder, did you really meet Alec, for instance? Was the Tuesday night group real? And what about Fergus? Is he who you said he was? Or did you create Fergus in the same way you did Torgon?"

"*No*! Oh, good God, *no*." Her eyes went wide with horror. "Of course I didn't 'create' him. How the hell could I create somebody like that?"

"But isn't that what you just said? 'I perceive the Forest, so it exists.' How do I know you don't just 'perceive' Fergus and thus he exists as well?"

"*Why* would I create someone like that?" she cried. "Why would I want to think all those horrible things had happened to me? Fergus was *evil*, James, and he managed to destroy just about everything that was good about me."

"Sometimes," James said, "very strong, difficult-to-deal-with events happen in our lives and they are so overpowering that the only way we can cope with them is to put them into a separate part of our minds. It's the only way to get enough peace to carry on living.

"When we do this, these things do sometimes take on a personality of their own. They're part of us, but they have their own identity representing what we are dealing with. This isn't wrong, Laura, so I'm not chastising you in any way, and I'm not trying to make you feel bad about doing this. It's just a way of coping. Because of the abandonment, the isolation, the sexual abuse that you suffered in childhood, it is very possible Torgon is an 'alter' personality. It would be quite understandable if Fergus is an alter as well. I think considering the possibility of multiple personalities would explain much of this 'lying' you've had such trouble with through your life. And you're right – it *isn't* lying. Switching back and forth between these personalities is going to create inconsistencies you really can't help."

Tears sprung to her eyes. "You're *wrong*."

"I know this is a huge concept to take in, so I understand –"

"I'm *not* crazy. I didn't make him up. You want proof this is not all in my mind?" she cried angrily.

James looked at her.

"Because it's been right in front of your face all along, James. Just fucking *look* at Morgana."

"What do you mean?"

Laura began to cry in earnest. "Are you blind? How could she be Alan's child?"

Astonished comprehension overtook James.

"She's Fergus's daughter," Laura said between angry sobs. "I only wish I *had* made him up! I wish it had really been Boston, because maybe then I never would have met him."

She reached for a tissue. Snuffling, she mopped her eyes.

James sat in stunned silence.

"I managed to elude Fergus for about ten years," Laura said. "Which was enough time for me to think the thing with him was over. And for me to meet a decent man like Alan and settle down.

"For the first time in my life I was happy. I had a husband who loved me madly, a wonderful home in a beautiful landscape, and work I adored. And I was pregnant with my first child, which – please let me emphasize – meant so much to me. I *wanted* to have children. I grew up in a world where I never quite belonged to any of the people I lived with, so having my very own family was a dream come true. That's why Fergus crashing back into my life at that point was such a devastating event."

James listened warily. "So, Fergus was your 'demented fan' – the stalker Alan has told me about?"

Laura nodded. "Yes, I didn't want to tell Alan my whole past, so that's how I described him."

James paused thoughtfully. "I want to believe you," he said slowly. "I really, really do, Laura. But things still don't quite add up for me. You say you were pregnant with Conor when Fergus reappeared, but Alan says the fan was stalking you around the time Conor was two. And Morgana didn't come along until Conor was three."

"I dealt with Fergus on my own for a very long time," Laura said. "I was desperate for Alan not to know about him. I finally had a normal life. I wanted to leave my past behind. What would Alan think of me, if he found out I'd spent years making money off gullible souls as a fake psychic? Or if he knew this insane guy had been my lover and that I'd stayed in such an abusive relationship for so long? I just wanted to keep it hidden, which wasn't all that hard, because Alan was not around that consistently. He went off for a day or two each week buying and selling cattle, and even when he was home, I had most of the daylight hours on my own because he was out on the range. One of the reasons Alan and I work out so well is that we're both independent people. We both do well with solitude. It was an ideal life for a writer, but, of course, it worked in Fergus's favour too.

"Fergus had this way of just materializing without warning. In the old days, I'd believed this was evidence of his psychic ability, that he had a paranormal ability to sense where people were. By this point, however, I knew there was nothing mystical about it. It was just the result of his obsession with me. He was stalking me, plain and simple. I could be anywhere – at the house, at the supermarket, at my antenatal appointment – and I'd come outside to find him waiting by my car. He always said he only wanted a chance to talk to me, but he didn't. The truth was, he wanted me to go away with him. He thought I would just walk out on this life I'd built in the meantime and return to … what? Being his 'queen'? Fergus behaved as if all the years in between hadn't happened, as if we'd never been apart. When I told him no, that I was never going to leave Alan, that I wanted him out of my life for good, he would get seriously angry with me.

"I had quite a hard birth with Conor. I haemorrhaged, so I was kept in the hospital a few extra days. I had a private room and Conor was with me. One evening – it was well after visiting hours, because Alan had long since gone home – Fergus appeared in my room. I was bed-bound with a drip in my arm and a drainage tube, so I couldn't move easily. He breezed in and the first thing he did was pick up my buzzer for ringing the nurse. He set it on the side dresser out of my reach. Then he went over to the bassinet and peered into it.

"I told him at once to leave the baby alone, but he reached in and picked Conor up. Fergus didn't cuddle him against his body the way you usually do with a baby. Instead, he held Conor out like this" – Laura demonstrated, holding her hands out away from her body, as if she were clasping a basketball. "He said, 'This should have been our son. Try as you might, you can't escape your destiny, my queen.' And with that, he dropped Conor. Just opened his fingers and let him fall. And walked out.'

Laura's face drained white with the memory. "I screamed," she said. "I lurched forward to get out of the bed, to pick him up. I dislodged the tubing. I was screaming and crying when they all came rushing in …" She looked over and tears were in her eyes. "But you know what? They thought *I'd* dropped Conor. I kept trying to explain it had been Fergus, but no one had seen him. I don't know *how* they missed him, but they did. They thought I'd done it. They wouldn't believe me."

James regarded her and thought, *Can I?*

Laura wiped her eyes and sat back. "Suddenly it felt like I was back in my attic at the lake house with my kitten Felix and Steven Mecks telling me he could do anything he wanted. Only this time it was my baby. I knew in Fergus's warped mind, he saw my destiny as his and it was unthinkable that I should have another man's child. He would kill Conor, I was sure of it. Conor was never going to be safe."

"I'm not necessarily doubting you here, but a man has just come in and seriously assaulted your newborn son and you believe there's a good chance he's going to kill the baby. Why didn't you call the police?" James asked.

"And say what exactly? Nobody believed he was real. They thought it was post-partum psychosis. They gave me Haldol to stop the hallucinations.

"Fergus disappeared for a while after that incident. This was typical of his pattern. He'd be around for several weeks, then vanish for months at a time. My guess is that he was being hospitalized. I was certain by then that he was seriously mentally ill, because he just wasn't operating in the real world. His thinking was less and less clear every time I saw him, and it had to have been getting him into trouble in other ways. So I just kept praying each time he went away that it would be permanent.

"Conor was nineteen months old when Fergus next showed up. I was in Spearfish up off Interstate 90. I'd stopped at the big supermarket there to get groceries before going back to the ranch, and as I was coming out with my stuff, there he was, sitting in the driver's seat of the car parked next to mine. I hadn't realized who it was at first because I was preoccupied with getting Conor into his car seat, but when I finished and closed the car door, I turned and saw him. I nearly jumped out of my skin. My *God*. Honestly, the way Fergus could turn up, it was like something out of a horror film.

"Anyway, he rolled down the window and, calm as could be, he said – with no preamble whatsoever – 'A lion, when he meets his mate, will kill all the cubs that are not his.' I thought, *It's now. He's going to do it*. I rushed around to get into the driver's side of my vehicle but before I could unlock and relock, he just slipped into the front passenger's seat, and there we were, side by side in my car, like any couple, looking ordinary to people passing by.

"My overwhelming sense was that he was going to kill us. I was madly trying to think of what to do.

"He said, 'We're bound together, Laura. Don't keep fighting it. There can be no other love but our love.' Then he turned to look over his shoulder into the back seat where Conor was. Conor started to cry.

"I knew I had to act fast. So I did the only thing I could think of. I hit him. Just with my fist. It was all I had. But hard as I could on the side of his head by his temple. It stunned him. He stopped abruptly and blinked in surprise. Then he turned to look at me, and in his eyes was a look of pure hate. I thought, 'Oh my God, we're done for.'

"I think he would have done something then and there, except that the person whose car was parked opposite mine just happened to return to it at that moment. Instead of just getting in and driving off, he sat down in the driver's seat and then opened a packet of Ritz crackers and started eating them." Laura shook her head faintly. "Weird to think your life could depend on such a small, random act by a stranger.

"So Fergus just sat there, waiting and staring at me with those eyes. At last he said, 'You can never escape your destiny, my queen.' Very softly, like it was a caress. Then he got out of my car and into his and left."

"But you *still* hadn't told Alan about any of this?" James asked.

"No."

"That does seem an extraordinary thing to keep from him, Laura. Fergus is threatening his son's life and you fail to share this with him?"

"I was trapped," she said, her voice plaintive. "It felt like Fergus could still destroy my life without doing a thing."

"Okay, but by not telling Alan about such an important thing, you give the impression of trying to control everyone's life. Or else that you are simply ruthlessly censoring out whatever doesn't suit you. I get the sense that you enjoy the freedom of not being confined to normal notions of what's real and what's not. With your kind of thinking, if Alan doesn't know his son has been threatened – doesn't perceive that – then it doesn't exist for him, does it? You can treat it as if it didn't happen."

Laura was looking down at her hands. She didn't answer.

"You may have managed to keep Alan in his place," James said, "but what about Conor?"

"Conor?"

"If these events are real, then he experienced them all alongside you."

"He was just a baby, though. Far too young to have been aware of any of it."

"When was the last time you saw Fergus?" James asked.

There was a long pause before she finally said, "The night Morgana was conceived."

"Would you tell me what went on that night?" James asked.

She hesitated, then sighed heavily.

James waited quietly

"That night," she mumbled. "That night, that night, how do I talk about it?"

Silence.

"I knew the situation had got serious. I took out a restraining order, so that I could get the police there, if I needed them, because I knew we were in real danger. That's when Alan found out, so we did talk about it then. I couldn't go into the detail. I just couldn't bear Alan thinking of me like I was in those years with Fergus. 'Demented fan' pretty much said what was going on. Once Alan realized that he had an unhealthy interest in Conor and me … he was so protective. It nearly broke my heart knowing I was the one who had put our family in that danger.

"Fergus then vanished for about three or four months. Alan believed we'd chased him off and I only hoped we had. But then I was coming back to the ranch one afternoon, there was a car parked in a pull-out to a picnic grounds, near where our road meets the highway. No one was in the car, but in the rear window the words 'My queen' had been written in the dust. It sounds like such a small thing … words written in dust on a back window … but it was like an arrow through my heart.

"Alan was at a cattle auction in Denver, so I was alone on the ranch for about three days, and I was sure somehow Fergus knew this. That was the scariest part about him, that he always *knew* what was going on in my life.

"It was almost a parody of that occasion back when I was in medical school, that night when he'd brought wine to my apartment to welcome me back from the conference, because on this occasion too, he came right up to the front door, wine in hand, and acted as if I were expecting him and would be glad to see him.

"Conor was already in bed, so it was just me, alone. Fifteen miles from anywhere. My instinct was to slam the door in his face and lock it, but I thought that would upset him. I was scared to do that. Instead, I decided to play it cool. I let him in. I let him open the bottle of wine. I let him waffle on about how he was getting all these visions about the 'new world', not just voices anymore but actual visions that he wanted to share with me. Back in the old days I would have thought this sounded very important and mystical, but by that point, quite frankly, he only sounded deranged. I let him talk and drank wine with him and all the while I was madly calculating how best to trigger the security system without his being aware of it.

"When he went upstairs to use the bathroom, I thought here was my chance. I lifted the phone to dial 911 and that's when I realized he'd cut the line.

"I was so terrified, James. Fergus had to have cut the line before he came to the door, so clearly he had been intending to do something all along. I was desperate to escape, but Conor was upstairs in bed.

"When he came back into the room, I could tell what he intended to do. He pushed me to the ground.

"The rest was just ... Well, I think raping me was the whole point of everything. He wanted that kind of power over me, needed it – the humiliation, the degradation – so I didn't struggle. I thought *I'm not going to be able to save Conor, if I get myself killed*.

"And when it was over ... He got up. But he didn't just walk away. He pulled out his cock and he pissed on me. Then he kicked me. Hard. Here, in the small of my back. As if I were nothing but a dog. Then the door slammed and he was gone."

There was a long pause. Deep silence settled in around them. James looked at her, but he didn't speak.

"That was the end of it," Laura said softly. "The real end. He left me lying there in a pool of piss and I never saw him again. Somehow I knew I wouldn't. That was the real conclusion of our relationship."

"And Morgana's conception?"

Laura nodded.

"Does Alan know the truth about her parentage?"

Laura bowed her head. "I don't know," she said wearily. "I can't imagine he doesn't see it. But then again, I'm always seeing more than other people see."

"Was there any chance Conor witnessed any of this between you and Fergus on this last night?" James asked.

"No. He was upstairs in bed asleep."

"Any idea where Fergus is now?"

"In Hell, I hope."

Chapter Forty-Four

"A picnic?" Becky said sceptically. She pressed her face against the living room window and peered up at the sky. "People usually don't go on picnics in the winter, Daddy."

"It isn't winter. Technically, it's spring."

"I don't think so," Mikey said. "Stuff's supposed to grow in the spring. Everything I see is dead."

"Why do you want to go on a picnic anyway?" Becky asked. "Let's just go to the mall."

"And then afterwards we can watch *Spiderman*!" Mikey cried and leaped off the edge of the chair in imitation of his hero.

"Because there's more to life than shopping and watching DVDs. You can do that in New York. Let's do something special together that we can only do in South Dakota."

"Like what?" asked Becky, her tone still sceptical.

"What about the Badlands? You've never been out there."

"Badlands? What's that? Is it a beach?" Becky asked.

"Badlands! Badlands! That's where they got lots of crooks!" Mikey screeched. He pushed Becky off the couch.

"Stop it! Daddy, make him stop. He's being a pain. Give him time out. That's what Mum does."

"Mikey, settle down."

"He's so stupid," Becky muttered. "He thinks he's so smart, but really he's stupid."

"You need exercise, don't you, young man?" James said, lifting Mikey way up in the air above his head. "That's half your problem. So we're going to run your steam off. Come on. Get your shoes on. Let's get this picnic under way."

Admittedly, it wasn't really a day for a picnic. Thin high cloud made the sunlight wan and the sky milky. A distinctly cool breeze fluttered the roadside buffalo grass as James followed the interstate east across the high plains.

He wasn't quite sure why he'd been drawn to the idea of going out to the Badlands. He'd only been once since arriving in South Dakota. It'd been July and so searingly hot that he hadn't even bothered to get out of the car. He just drove on through the park.

James knew his wanting to go there now had something to do with Laura, with his confused wavering between belief and betrayal, as if something in the alien landscape that had so nurtured her might speak to him too. Mikey had won the coin-flip for the prize of sitting in the front seat on the trip out, but this privilege seemed wasted on him. He had brought two small toy planes along and spent most of the journey engrossed in circling them noisily in the space in front of him. Becky sat in the back and sulked.

"I ought to get to sit up front. I'm older," she muttered.

James ignored her protests and Mikey's loud flying noises.

"I always get to sit up front at home. Mum lets me."

"I'm sure not every time," James replied.

"He's just zooming his stupid planes around and he could do that in the back."

This was true enough but James didn't say that.

"It's not fair. We never do anything I want. Mikey always gets to pick."

"Mikey didn't pick. He won it fair and square."

"Well, I didn't want to come on this picnic. Why couldn't we just stay home?"

"Because you can 'stay home' at home," James replied. "You've just flown 2000 miles to do something different."

"Then I ought to have got to choose where we're going," she muttered. "*I* wanted to have a picnic at the beach."

"Becky, we're in the middle of the continent. There is no beach. You'll like the Badlands. They're just like a beach, only hilly. And with no water."

Glum silence.

Oblivious, Mikey crash-landed one of his planes on the dashboard, making accompanying explosive noises.

"Mikey, don't do that. This is Uncle Lars's car and he won't want scratches."

"I'm going to be a pilot when I grow up," Mikey replied.

"Not if you fly your planes like that, you won't. Why don't you look out the window for a while?"

"At what?" he asked, peering out at the passing prairie.

"Look for pronghorn antelope. When Daddy first came out here from New York, that was the most exciting part of the journey. I had been driving and driving and driving all the way from New York City and I was *so* tired. I thought, 'I'm never going to get to Rapid City. I'm never going to see this new place.' And then I looked out the window and there was a whole herd of pronghorn antelope in a field near the road. There must have been about twenty of them and I thought, 'I'm here! I'm really in the West.'"

"Why did you want to be in West?" Mikey asked.

"When a person says 'the West' they mean the wide open spaces. Where there are real cowboys. Where the Native Americans used to hunt buffalo."

"Why did you want to be where cowboys are?"

"Because he didn't want to be in New York anymore," Becky piped up. "Daddy didn't want to live with us."

"No, Becky, that's not true. My moving was a grown-up decision between Mum and me. I didn't want to leave you and Mikey."

"Are you a cowboy now, Daddy?" Mikey asked.

"Mum says you ran away. When her and Uncle Joey are talking, that's what she always says. 'James ran away from his responsibilities.'"

"Did you run away to be a cowboy, Daddy?" Mikey asked.

"No, I did not run away to be a cowboy, Mikey. I didn't run away at all."

"Uncle Joey says —"

"Becky, let's call a moratorium on what Uncle Joey says, okay? Know what 'moratorium' means? It's a nice way of saying it's time to shut up about Uncle Joey's opinions. And Mum's too, for that matter. Because we're here now, and you're with me and we're going to have a wonderful time."

Mikey looked over. "Did you run away to hunt buffalo, Daddy?"

* * *

The eerie thing to James was how, in this broad, flat expanse of grassland, the Badlands could stay hidden so long. Even after they'd passed through the national park entrance, the monotonous sweep of plains continued unbroken right up to the first viewpoint. Then, within the distance of a man's arm span, the world suddenly sank away, transformed into a jagged panorama of spires and shadows that stretched as vastly towards the horizon as the grassland had before.

"Wow," Becky murmured, impressed. She leaned against the viewpoint railing. "It must be like a million feet down to the bottom."

"Pretty far," James replied.

"I'm sure I wouldn't want to fall down there."

"No. Me neither," James said.

Mikey was more interested in the steps leading from the car park down to the lower viewing area. He kept running up and down them, fast as he could.

"Are we going to have our picnic here?" Becky asked.

"Yup. That sign says there's some picnic tables just a little further along. Then you guys can have a good run-around."

"You know," Becky said, "this place *is* sort of like the beach with all this dirt. Sort of like Long Island, only without any ocean."

"Don't kid me," James replied. "Long Island doesn't have any beaches that look this good!"

It felt as if they were the only people to visit the park. No cars drove by. No one else showed up to look at the view. Other than the chatter of a few hardy birds, it was startlingly silent.

The sky had remained overcast but the wind had died down, so it grew pleasantly warm for March. The kids shed their coats and scrambled noisily up and down the grassless pinnacles beside the picnic area while James set out the food. Then they tucked into cold chicken and potato salad before the kids ran off to play again.

Mikey appeared back at the picnic table. "I got to go to the bathroom, Dad."

"There are toilets right over there. See? Get Becky to take you; she probably needs to go too. Becky?"

The two children trotted off while James put things away, pausing to pick all the candy wrappers out of Lars's Jeep. They couldn't have been gone for more than five minutes before he heard Becky yelling. Her expression panicky, she came running back down the path.

"Daddy! Daddy! Come quick!"

James dashed over. "What's wrong?"

"You got to come help Mikey. He's got stuck."

"Stuck? Where? How did that happen?"

"Well, I don't know. I was going to the bathroom." She grabbed James's hand to pull him faster. "But when I came out he'd gone down this path on the other side of the toilet building and now he can't get back up again."

When James reached the toilets, he saw no path anywhere near.

"No, over here. This way. Down there."

Below the viewpoint railing the ground fell away into a bizarre wonderland of spires and gullies all formed from the same pale, crumbly, unstable soil. Although it might have been nothing more than the eroded course of winter run-off, a path of sorts appeared to begin near the drainage ditch along side the guard rail. It dropped almost straight down the slope and then snaked out of sight around a massive columnar pinnacle. About thirty feet down Mikey was on all fours, clinging to a leafless bit of brush.

"Oh holy *Jesus*, Becky, how did he get down there? Why weren't you watching him? That's what I sent you along for."

"I was going to the bathroom, Dad. I couldn't watch him and do that at the same time."

"Mikey? Mikey, are you all right?" James could tell he was crying. "Just stay there. Don't try to move. Daddy will get you."

But how? James glanced around him. There was not another soul anywhere. He had seen absolutely no one since driving away from the park ranger in the booth at the entrance to the park. He pulled out his mobile phone. No signal.

James gazed across the vast panorama. The floor of the basin was literally hundreds of feet below.

Tentatively, he slipped through the guard railing. The path was very steep and the soil alarmingly loose. Heights had never been his thing and he had no delusions about being a wilderness man, so the thumping racket his heart made in his ears was a definite hindrance. Inch by inch, James managed to lower himself down to where his son was clinging.

"You're okay, buddy. Just hold on. Don't move."

Mikey was sobbing.

Reaching an arm out, James gripped the fabric of Mikey's sweatshirt and pulled him up. "Got you. There we are. All safe. Daddy's got you."

"I haven't got my shoe," Mikey cried.

"What?"

"We were playing and Becky threw it down there. See? And I can't get it." He pointed down the gully.

James steadied himself on the path. "Mikey, you should *never* have tried to get it by yourself."

Mikey sobbed anew.

Craning to look down the steep-sided gorge, James saw Mikey's other shoe lying far down in the dust. His knees went to jelly. "We're just going to leave your shoe there, Mikey. We've actually got other problems to worry about. Daddy's a little concerned about how crumbly the soil is. I'm not sure we can get back up the way we just came down without slipping."

Mikey cried harder.

"Listen, sport, we're having an adventure here, aren't we? Think what you can tell your friends when you get home. Yes? Exciting, huh? So here's what we're going to do. You stay right here and keep holding onto this bit of bush. Let Daddy get by you. I'm just going to look around this sticky-out bit of rock and see where the path goes, because maybe we can get back up easier on the other side. Don't move. Okay?"

Mikey nodded fervently

James edged his way along until he cleared the knobby pinnacle. From there, the path broadened slightly. He slipped around a second corner.

Startled, he halted abruptly.

Ahead of him, the path dead-ended on a ledge of rock perhaps five feet wide. Beneath the ledge, the wind-ravaged land dropped away precipitously to the basin floor hundreds of feet below. The opposite end of the ledge met the upward spiral of an adjacent pinnacle of soil. At that juncture, three ponderosa pines grew, their green, bushy-needled lushness an unexpected contrast to the desolate hillside.

Three trees on the moon.

Chapter Forty-Five

"*Another* picnic?" Becky said in amazement as James loaded them into the car.

"What about having Morgana along?" James said and started the engine. "You were exchanging emails last night. Wouldn't it be nice to see her?"

"You want to have another picnic *tonight*?" Becky asked suspiciously.

"I'll phone Morgana's mum and ask," James said.

"Why do you want a picnic at night?" Mikey asked.

"No, not at night. Just in the evening. At dusk. We could make a fire in one of the campfire pits and roast marshmallows. That would be fun."

"When am I going to get new shoes?" Mikey asked. "'Cause I can't go around with just one."

"Daddy, I'm not sure I want to do this," Becky said. "One picnic is enough in a day. I don't think I want a picnic for dinner too."

"We're going to invite Morgana's brother too. You haven't met him. He's quite a big boy. He's going to be ten soon. We'll invite both of them along."

Becky touched his arm. "Daddy, are you listening to me? I said I'm not sure I want to."

James looked over. "Well, I'm sorry, Becky, because we're going to do it. I know we've already done a lot of things today that I've wanted to do, and you've been very good about it and I'm proud of you, but hang in there with me a little longer, okay? I want to do this one more thing."

"Why, Daddy?" she asked.

"I just do. And tomorrow we'll do anything you guys want, all right?" James grinned at her.

"Can we watch *Spiderman* again?" Mikey cried out from the back seat. "'Cause that's what I want to do!"

"Yeah, cowboy, anything you want," James replied.

From the tone of Laura's voice, it was obvious she was as bewildered by this evening picnic idea as Becky was. "And Conor?" she asked quizzically. "You want Conor to come as well?"

James had always been a stickler for honesty because it was such a basic component of trust and trust was so essential to his work. Consequently, he'd always assumed he'd be the sort of person who would fail miserably at deception, if only because he'd had so little practice. But he found it surprisingly easy to sound as if this were the most natural thing to be doing on the South Dakota plains in March. A cookout, he explained: hot dogs on sticks, fire-roasted potatoes, marshmallows. And the more the merrier, so, of course, he wanted Conor to join them. James kept a studied levity in his voice, hoping that after all the minor breaches of professionalism their relationship had enjoyed, Laura wouldn't think too carefully about this one.

* * *

James had never been out to the McLachlan ranch before. After the wastes of the Badlands, the rich, forested reaches of the Black Hills were a stark contrast. The ranch buildings lay in a secluded valley of open grassland protected by a ponderosa forest. The road to the house wended its way through a series of wooden-fenced corrals and neatly kept barns.

When the Jeep pulled up, Morgana came running out of the front door. "Hi! Hi!" she cried. Laura appeared in the doorway, herding Conor gently in front of her.

"Guess what!" Becky said to Morgana, as she leaped out of the car. "This is going to be our *second* picnic today. We had a picnic lunch too."

"See my new shoes?" Mikey piped up.

Conor clutched his toy cat closely against his chest.

"Why don't you get in the car," James said, extending a friendly hand to him. "You can sit up front with me." He opened the passenger door to the Jeep.

"You're being very brave to take this whole crowd on an outing," Laura said in a gently mocking voice.

"We're going to the Badlands," Becky chimed in.

"Come on, Becky. We haven't got much time. Get in the car," James said.

Laura frowned. "The Badlands? That's a long way. There are some excellent campgrounds very nearby, James. I can give you a map."

"Daddy *likes* the Badlands," Becky said. "Don't you, Daddy? Because, you know what? We've already been out there once today, and Daddy likes it so much there he wants to go again."

Laura's brow furrowed more deeply.

James grinned sheepishly. "Yes, silly Daddy, eh? But it's very beautiful in the evening. So come *on*, Becky, get in the car."

"Yeah, look at my new shoes!" Mikey said cheerfully and lifted a foot up. "Becky threw one of my other ones down the hillside at the Badlands and Daddy couldn't reach it, so he had to buy me new ones. These got flashers on the bottom."

"Becky, Mikey, get *in* the car. *Now*."

Laura caught James's eye. He looked away, leaning in to check the kids' seatbelts. Then he bid a cheery goodbye, climbed into the driver's seat, started the engine and left.

"Things are going to be a little different than we'd planned," James said, as they approached the interstate turn-off for the Badlands. "By the time we go to the supermarket and get stuff for a cookout, there won't be enough time to make a fire and cook it before it gets too dark."

"But you *said* …" Mikey cried.

"I know and I'm sorry. I made a mistake about how much time driving to Morgana's house would take. So instead, we're going to stop at the Dairy Queen and get hamburgers."

There was a moment's silence in the back and then Becky leaned forward until James could feel her breath on his neck. "Daddy?" she whispered.

"Yes, sweetheart?"

"Can you tell me yet what's going on?"

Conor appeared much less normal at the Dairy Queen than he did in the playroom. He wouldn't speak at all and he wouldn't make eye contact. He only ate his hamburger after pulling it entirely apart and separating the food into little piles. He then consumed each item individually, starting with the patty of meat, then the ketchup-covered pickles, then the bun. When not occupied with eating, he faintly flapped the fingers of his right hand over his food. Kitty remained tightly clutched to Conor's chest throughout the meal.

They were soon all in the car again, speeding out over the prairie towards the Badlands. The Black Hills, far distant, stood silhouetted against the western horizon by the dying colours of the day. The moon, a few days past full, peered out of the east like a heavy-lidded eye.

"Where are we going anyway?" Mikey queried.

"To the picnic area where we were at lunch," James said.

"How come back there?" Becky asked.

"I want to show Conor something. That's why we're coming out here. Because Conor's been telling me about a place and I think no one believed him. We all thought it was just something in his dreams. But at lunchtime when I was helping Mikey get back up the path, I think I saw the place Conor's been talking about. So I wanted him to see it."

"Why?" Becky asked.

"Because if people keep telling you that the things you experience aren't real, it can make your life very scary and unsettled."

"What are me and Mikey and Morgana supposed do while you're showing him this place?" Becky asked.

"You can just play in the viewpoint area. We won't be there very long."

"We're supposed to play in the dark?" Mikey asked incredulously.

"Your Uncle Jack and I used to do that all the time when we were little," James replied. "We played hide and seek and kick the can and lots of other great games outside after dark."

"I don't think kids play like that anymore," Becky said doubtfully.

They passed through the entrance to the park and approached the first viewpoint. The Badlands themselves weren't yet fully visible because of the way erosion had formed them from the level of the plains, but the moonlight was beginning to illuminate changes in the landscape.

Conor sat abruptly upright. He leaned close to the windshield and peered out. "Where's this?" he murmured and turned to look at James.

James pulled into the car park at the first viewpoint and let the children out. Conor gazed in amazement at the bizarre splendour unfolding as they walked down the steps to the overlook. Pressing his stuffed cat tight to his chest, he turned, looked at James and then looked back at the landscape.

"I wanted you to see this place," James said gently to him. "When I was here earlier and saw it, I thought, 'This is what Conor is telling me about.' I thought you should come and see it too."

Bewilderment suffused Conor's expression. "There's the moon," he said softly and pointed up at the pale, uneven orb bright in the dusky sky. He turned back to the jagged landscape. "But here's the moon too. Terria. This is terria. Everywhere is terria. Or is it?"

"Does Conor think this is the moon?" Morgana asked.

"Probably the moon does look like this," Becky said.

"Where are the trees?" Conor asked.

"There's lots of trees down there, Conor," Becky said and pointed into the abyss below them. "If you kind of stretch yourself out over the rail, you can see lots of trees at the bottom."

Leaning far over the guardrail, Conor stared into the dusk of the deep basin.

"Why did you want to show Conor this, Daddy?" Becky asked.

"I know," Morgana replied. "'Cause this is where the man under the rug lives, isn't it? Huh, Dr Innes? This is the place Conor always talks about."

Before James could answer, Conor nodded. "Yes," he said.

James heard the car engine from a long way off. At first it hardly penetrated the antediluvian silence that lay over the vast landscape. It was just a faint drone, like a fly trapped beyond a window pane.

Then Becky said, "Someone else is coming to see this place at night."

"Hey! That's *our* truck," Morgana shouted.

James's blood ran cold.

Before the car had even pulled into the car park, Morgana was charging up the steps from the viewpoint with Becky and Mikey in hot pursuit.

"Becky! Kids! *Stop*! Come back here." Grabbing Conor's hand, James bolted up the steps two at a time to catch the children. James could see Laura at the wheel of the truck and two rifles in the gun rack on the rear window of the pick-up cab. "Kids, get in my car. *Now*. All of you." He pushed Becky in the direction of the Jeep. "I mean it. Get in and lock the doors until I say."

"No, it's just my mum," Morgana replied.

"Yes, I know it is. But do as I say. All right? Just for now. Conor, you too. Get into the car, lock the doors and stay there until I tell you."

"Why?" Becky cried

"*Do it*."

Laura turned the engine off but left the headlights on. For several moments she remained in the cab and didn't get out. James, trapped in the glare of the headlights, stood staring at the guns silhouetted in the rear window of the cab.

Finally the truck door opened and Laura descended onto the asphalt. "What the hell is going on?" she asked, her voice tense. "What are you doing out here with these kids?"

She didn't have anything in her hands from what he could tell but she wasn't moving away from the open door of the truck, so James put himself between Laura and the children in his Jeep.

"Laura, I *know*," he said as quietly as he could manage.

"Know what?"

"About Fergus. It *is* Fergus, isn't it?"

"I don't have a fucking clue what you're talking about."

"The man under the rug. The ghost man."

"Don't get crazy on me, James."

"I'm not."

"Morgana?" she called out. "Can you hear me, sweetie? Get out of the car. Get Conor and come here. It's time to go home."

Behind him, James heard a door of the Jeep open and then a second door.

"Morgana, don't move. Kids? Everyone. Just stay there a moment," James said. "Get back in the car."

A numbing calm overtook him. It made all his senses more acute. He could hear birds – owls maybe? – calling far distant across the darkness. He could smell the sharp, cold, sage-brush-scented evening air mingled with the lingering odour of petrol fumes from the pickup's engine. He was aware of his feet growing cold. Everything felt detached and unreal.

Around them a most terrible silence grew. Although he couldn't see them because his back was still to the Jeep, James could sense the children were out of the car, but no one moved and the moment felt eternal.

Then abruptly a shriek from one of the children. "*Conor*!"

James whirled around to see Conor disappear over the guard rail and down the steep embankment.

Becky screamed.

Laura tore past James and around the Jeep to the railing.

Morgana flapped her hands in fright. "It was his cardboard thing," she wailed, "that cat he keeps in his pocket. He took it out and it came out of his hands and –"

His mechanical cat. The small drawing that Conor had made in the playroom drifted gracefully on an updraft from the chasm below.

Beyond the guard rail Conor had slipped almost immediately on the soft, crumbly soil and then slid about fifty feet down the steep side of the ravine before catching himself on the slope. He remained there, spreadeagled, crying in fright.

Laura vaulted the rail in a single, smooth motion and began sliding down the unstable soil.

"*Laura*! Wait! We need to get help."

"I know these hills," she shouted up. "I've been up and down them a million times."

Before Laura could reach Conor, however, his grip gave way. He slid and then tumbled, disappearing over the edge of the outcrop below the viewpoint. To James's horror, Laura started to slip too and before he could react, she too had disappeared down the steep gully.

"*Mummy!*" Morgana started screaming.

James had seen the rope coiled up with Lars's other hunting equipment in the back of the Jeep. It was just ordinary nylon rope meant for tying deer to the vehicle, but it was rope.

With trembling hands he fastened it around one of the posts holding the guard railing. He tugged at it several times to make sure it was secure and then climbed through. Knotting it every few feet so he'd have something to grip, he said to the children, "Okay, you three, you stay right here. I mean it. Don't move from right here. Becky, you're the oldest. You take care of Morgana and Mikey for me, all right? No fooling around. You're the grown-up now."

Cautiously he lowered himself down the steep slope. Clearing the jagged ledge of soil abutting the viewpoint area, James could just make out Laura below him in the wan, moonlit darkness. She was about a hundred feet further down into the ravine, but still far above the floor of the basin.

"Laura?" he called.

She moved. Despite the moonlight, it was too dark for him to be able to tell if she was injured or not.

"Are you all right?"

"Conor's hurt," she called up. "Can you get to us?"

James lowered himself to the full extent of the rope but it wasn't nearly long enough. He remained at least seventy feet above them on the crumbly soil, his weight held by the rope. He'd long since gone from fear into a kind of numbness that left his mind detached and his limbs not feeling wholly like his own, so he hung there over the ledge and contemplated how to get the rest of the way down. In the end, he just opened his hands and let go.

There was an eerie loneliness to being caught without support on the steep hillside. He could no longer hear the children above, and all around him was the alien landscape, illuminated only by hazy moonlight. James grappled at the crumbling white soil. To his surprise, he didn't fall when he let go of the rope but remained just where he was.

Immediately, this felt worse because he realized he would actually have to launch himself to get down to where Laura was. He took a long, deep breath, which made him aware he had not been breathing properly for ages. Taking in a second deep breath, he expelled it slowly.

To his surprise, what came to his mind was Torgon. For a fleeting moment Laura's descriptions of the high holy place in the Forest, of Torgon standing at the edge of the white cliff and looking out over her world filled James's mind brightly, and he had a momentary sense of being somewhere else. It helped. Briefly distracted, he felt calmer. Gently he pushed against the loose soil and let himself slide downwards.

Laura's fall had been stopped by a flat ledge and with careful effort James was able to reach her with nothing worse than scrapes on his knees. Laura hadn't been as lucky. She had removed her shoe and sock from one foot and was using the sock to bind her other foot.

"I've done something to my ankle," she said. Her voice was hoarse with annoyance.

"Where's Conor?"

"There."

James peered over the edge of the outcropping to see Conor directly below them. "Is he hurt? Conor? Can you hear me?"

The boy looked up but he didn't respond.

"Do you have a belt or something?" Laura asked. "Something I can hang onto so I can let myself down over this ledge?"

"No, Laura, don't. You're injured already."

"If I can get him, I can lift him up to you."

"And what if you can't? Then you're both trapped there. Instead, we need to get you back up and then go for help."

"And leave him here? No. This is my son." She looked at James. "And it's my fault he's down there on that ledge. Because yes. The man under the rug was Fergus."

A brief moment of surreal awareness flooded James. She was a murderess. She had killed a man. He'd expected everything to change with that confirmation. It didn't. He didn't hate her. He didn't fear her. He didn't perceive her as evil. All he felt was sadness.

Laura had bits of debris from the fall in her hair. Gently James reached across and pulled a broken stalk of prairie grass out. He flung it away and it fluttered downwards into the basin.

"On that last night, when Alan was gone and I was alone, he raped me. But when it happened, I knew it wasn't going to stop there. Sooner or later, he was going to kill my child. Maybe me.

"I knew where Alan's hunting knife was. So I thought, *Fergus, I've passed up greater destinies than yours. I'm not going to let it come to this* … So I did what Torgon did."

"Then Conor appeared at the top of the stairs and suddenly what I'd just done became very real. I felt utter panic. I screamed at him to go back to bed, to get out of there so he wouldn't see. All I could think to do was wrap Fergus's body up in the rug by the fireplace. I got it out to the truck, but I had to take Conor with me. I couldn't leave him in the house alone. The only place I could think to go was here, to the Badlands. I'd come to know this land so well when I was working on the Pine Ridge reservation. I knew no one can see into the bottom of most of these ravines."

"And you thought none of this would affect Conor?"

"He was hardly two. I hoped it would be nothing but a bad dream to him."

There was silence. Confusion flooded over James, as he considered her plight alone on the isolated ranch, fending off Fergus, trying to protect her small son set against the years of trauma in the aftermath of murder.

"Give me your belt," she said, her voice soft. "I'm going down."

James hesitated.

"I mean it. Whether you help me or not, I'm going to get him."

James took off his belt. "All right."

Laura leaned over the ledge. "Are you ready, Conor? Mummy's coming for you now."

Chapter Forty-Six

The roar of helicopter blades sliced through the chilly stillness. Spotlights parted the darkness and within moments the steep slope was swarming with rescuers. Lifted carefully onto a stretcher, Conor was winched up into the helicopter hovering above. James watched the paramedics examine Laura's injuries and prepare her to be moved. Then finally they came up the slope to him and he was helped into a safety harness too and lifted from the hillside.

The viewpoint and its adjacent car park were alive with activity when James alighted from the helicopter. Conor and Laura had been whisked away to the hospital in Rapid City, but he hadn't been injured in the incident. He brushed off the attentions of the paramedics to reach the three children.

"It was me and Morgana who called them!" Becky said excitedly. "Morgana's folks got a radio thing in their truck and, guess what? I turned the truck on all by myself so we could use it!"

"When we get home, I want to phone Mum," Mikey said, "and I'm going to tell her we had an adventure and you rode in a helicopter! And you're a hero, aren't you, Daddy? 'Cause you saved that little boy and his mum. Just like Spiderman! I can tell everyone you're a hero!"

"I don't feel like much of a hero, buddy."

"We *did* have an adventure," Becky said. "And we can tell Mum that me and Morgana called the helicopter guys all by ourselves."

"Yes, and I'm very, very proud of you. All three of you were very responsible."

"Well, not Mikey," Becky said. "Know what he did? He peed over the side of the rail. I told him not to. I told him to go into the bathroom like he was supposed to, but he did it anyway."

"Guess how far this boy in my class can pee, Dad," Mikey said.

"Come on, you two." Reaching Lars's Jeep, James opened the door. "In you go. Let's get back to town. You too, Morgana. You come with us. Your dad's going to meet us at the hospital."

Turning the Jeep out of the car park, James stepped on the accelerator. The car park – brightly lit with emergency lighting – faded in the rearview mirror. They plunged into the brittle moonlit March darkness.

Mikey fell asleep even before James had passed the park entrance. Becky was soon flopped over the top of him asleep by the time they reached the interstate. Only Morgana, sitting in the front passenger seat beside James, remained awake.

She had her elbow braced on the door armrest, her cheek in her hand, and she stared out into the darkness. James glanced furtively at her, trying to reconstruct from her dark features what Fergus must have looked like.

"That was a lot of excitement," he said at last. "I'll bet you're tired."

She nodded.

"It's all right to go to sleep, if you want. It'll take us a while to get back to town."

"I'm not sleepy."

The darkness sped past.

James looked over again. She seemed so tiny strapped into the seat.

"What happened tonight was very scary, wasn't it?" he said. "Is it still on your mind?"

"Yes."

"Do you want to talk about it?"

"I thought my mum was going to die."

"Yes, it was awful, wasn't it? Luckily, though, everything's turned out all right. Conor's going to need to stay in the hospital overnight, I think, because he's had a bump to his head, but he'll be okay. And your mum isn't really very badly hurt at all. She'll probably be able to go home when we get to the hospital."

A soft silence followed, plumped up with the sound of deep, peaceful breathing from the back seat.

Morgana turned her head away from James to look out of the window again. "What scared me most was thinking about the Lion King," she said. "His mother died. He was just a baby when it happened, so he doesn't even remember what she looks like. I always feel so frightened when he talks about that, because I wouldn't want it ever to happen to me. But tonight I thought it was going to."

"So, you're still playing with the Lion King?"

She nodded. "Yeah."

Silence.

"Listen, Morgana, I'm very, very sorry I told your parents about him. I broke your trust and that was wrong of me." James said. "And I've felt bad that you thought you couldn't talk to me about him anymore."

"That's okay," she replied softly.

"No, it isn't okay. It was something that should have stayed between us because you made it really clear that you were telling me in confidence. I was wrong to tell without your permission."

She shrugged. "No, it's okay. When I told the Lion King about what you'd done, he said it didn't matter. The same thing's happened to him. His auntie doesn't want him to play with me either. She told him she would give him a spanking, if she found out he was still seeing me."

"Why does his aunt not want him to play with you?" James asked.

"She doesn't believe him. She doesn't think I'm real."

James looked over questioningly.

Morgana turned and smiled. "Isn't that silly? The Lion King said to me that when he told his auntie that he had seen me down by the creek, she said, 'Don't you dare *ever* speak to me of visions, Luhr! You sound just like your mother.'"